D1124203

THE ROSE REVIVED

ALSO BY KATIE FFORDE

Living Dangerously

THE ROSE REVIVED

Katie Fforde

MICHAEL JOSEPH

LONDON

MICHAEL JOSEPH LTD

Published by the Penguin Group
27 Wrights Lane, London W8 5TZ
Viking Penguin Inc., 375 Hudson Street, New York, New York 10014, USA
Penguin Books Australia Ltd, Ringwood, Victoria, Australia
Penguin Books Canada Ltd, 10 Alcorn Avenue, Toronto, Ontario, Canada M4V 3B2
Penguin Books (NZ) Ltd, 182–190 Wairau Road, Auckland 10, New Zealand

Penguin Books Ltd, Registered Offices: Harmondsworth, Middlesex, England

First published 1995

Filmset by Datix International Limited, Bungay, Suffolk
Printed in England by Clays Ltd, St Ives plc
Set in 10.75/13 pt Monophoto Plantin Light

A CIP catalogue record for this book is available from the British Library

ISBN 0 7181 3782 5

The moral right of the author has been asserted

To D.S.F., as ever

ACKNOWLEDGEMENTS

To Sara Clee, actor, Lyn Coleman, artist, and everyone else who helped me with my research either knowingly or unknowingly. To Sarah Molloy for her continued support, and especially to my editor, Richenda Todd, who took my horrid, furry-edged manuscript and, cheerfully and uncomplainingly, turned it into a book. Also to my family for finally realizing that I don't sit at home all day watching the afternoon soaps.

CHAPTER ONE

May's Doc Martens tripped over the step and brought her into a small room which smelt of stale cigarette smoke. Five women, all apparently bored out of their minds, looked up at her and then looked away.

'Hi!' said May. 'Is this right for Quality Cleaners?'

One of the women nodded. She had two-tone hair and obviously knew her way round a vacuum cleaner. 'There's a pile of application forms over there. You have to fill one in.'

'Blimey,' said May, picking one up. 'It's long.'

'Yeah,' said the woman. 'You have to push it under the door when you've finished.'

'Oh. How unusual.' May didn't carry a handbag, but she patted her pockets hopefully. 'Um, has anyone got a pen I could borrow?'

No one moved for a moment, then one of the women, who was about the same age as May, put down her book. May recognized it as one on the Booker Prize shortlist. 'I have. Here.' The girl rummaged in an ancient shoulder-bag and produced a fountain pen.

May regarded her more closely. What sort of cleaner – or potential cleaner – read proper books and wrote with a fountain pen? She was berating herself for stereotyping cleaners when she noticed a new-looking holdall under the girl's chair, as well as a soft-topped suitcase and a small vanity case. Another time, May would have been intrigued as to why anyone would bring luggage to an interview, but for now she was too concerned with filling in the form for idle speculation. She smiled at the girl and took the pen.

'Thanks.'

May's block capitals were inclined to let her down on forms, but she made a special effort with this one. She needed the job so badly. Well-paid, unskilled jobs were as rare as rubies – and to May, infinitely more precious.

When at last she'd devised answers for almost all of the many questions, she returned the pen. She gave her an I'm-friendly-please-talk-to-me kind of smile, but the girl's lips just flickered and she went back to her book. The chance of conversation gone, May settled back to inspect the competition.

There was the woman who had shown her the forms, older than May, possibly too old to fulfil the ad's 'young and enthusiastic' criterion. There was a mother with a toddler on her lap, who was undoubtedly young, but whose dark circles under her eyes and totally worn-out expression seemed to make her lacking in the enthusiasm department.

There was the girl who'd lent her the pen. She was young, obviously intelligent, but, in her navy-blue suit, little pearl earrings and black velvet headband, looked far too ladylike to be applying for a job as a cleaner.

Still, I hardly look the part myself, thought May, for the first time giving her own clothes a critical appraisal. She had put on her best pair of dungarees, the ones with only a tiny splatter of blue paint on them, and her jumper was clean, if a bit baggy at the sleeves. Her Doc Martens, worn with scarlet socks were quite shiny.

She sighed regretfully. She didn't have any of her smarter, more conventional clothes on her boat, and had rushed to the interview almost as soon as she had spotted the advertisement. It had been on one of the sheets of newspaper she was about to light the stove with, and although May was not superstitious, it had seemed as if fate was offering her a helping hand. She had leapt on to the Tube before all the 'opportunities to be part of a team' were taken. But even in the right clothes she felt she had little chance of convincing this 'new branch of an established business' that she could get a grip of that stubborn limescale.

No, if the advertiser had any sense, he'd employ the remaining two women who had competent expressions and the sort of clothes which fitted naturally under nylon overalls. You could tell, just by looking at them, that they could dismantle a rebellious cistern and have it working before you could say 'Harpic'.

May curled her feet under her chair and looked about for some distraction. She picked out all the paint which was lodged under her nails and examined her fingers. There was something about living on a boat which made hands permanently dirty, so if anyone wanted to shake May's she curled her fingers so they wouldn't notice the grime.

If only she'd brought something to read. The woman with the baby had joined it in a nap – she probably needed it more than the baby did. The girl in the navy-blue suit was still reading; the others stared blankly into space. Inevitably, in spite of her best efforts to think only pleasant thoughts, her brain replayed the dreadful record of the last twenty-four hours.

It had started with Mike, the new owner of the boatyard, calling on her. 'I've been checking the books. You – or rather *The Rose Revived* – owe over a year's mooring fees. It comes to three and a half thousand pounds.'

May had collapsed on to the stove, but it was too hot for sitting on, so she had to get up again.

'I want at least five hundred up front and the rest paid within three months. I need the space, May. I can't moor a seventy-foot narrowboat for nothing. It's pay up or sell up.'

'I haven't got that sort of money! This is my home you're talking about!' she had squeaked. 'It's not some disposable asset!'

All her protests had been in vain. Mike hadn't bought the boatyard for charitable reasons. He told her that she'd get more if she sold her boat privately than if he was forced to call in the bailiffs, but that was no consolation. No wonder May had lost her rag when she went to work at the Union Flag that evening. Usually, however sexist, racist, or grammatically incorrect the customers' remarks were, she managed to keep her mutterings for when she was under the counter refilling the shelves with mixers.

But last night, when her world was in shards about her, she tipped a pint of mild over the head of a particularly obnoxious punter. She wasn't surprised, or even especially sorry, when the head barman ordered her to leave just as soon as she mopped up the mess.

Well, at least I've had some recent cleaning experience, thought May with an optimism born of desperation.

May pressed her arms into her churning stomach. Could you actually die from boredom and anxiety, she wondered. In a moment I'm going to be thoroughly un-English and start up a conversation.

Just then, the inner door opened and a tall, incredibly glamorous young woman came out.

''Ow d'you get on then?' asked one of the women May classed as professional cleaners.

The girl collapsed into a chair. 'God knows! He stared at my legs so long, I thought I must have a ladder in my tights or something!' She stretched them anxiously in front of her, examining the black Lycra for flaws.

''Ardly surprising, the amount of them you've got on show!' said one of the other women. 'He needs cleaners, not bleedin' Tiller Girls.'

'I know! I know! This is quite the wrong outfit,' said the owner of the legs. 'But I came on impulse. The money seemed so good.'

In a tomato-red jacket and little black skirt – probably 'designer', May thought – she added much-needed decoration to the drabness of the room. Her dark hair was short, cut exquisitely, so it framed her heart-shaped face, making her eyes huge and doe-like.

The woman who'd been asleep woke up and hitched her still-sleeping toddler further on to her lap. 'He's a leg man, is he? 'E should have put that on the form. I might as well go now. I thought the money was too good to be true.'

'Oh no! He really does want cleaners! He asked me to wait.'

'You don't look like a cleaner, if you don't mind my saying,' said May, chewing her lip, aware of her own sartorial shortcomings.

'We don't all 'ave wrinkles in our stockin's like Nora Batty,' said the mother. 'But I don't reckon there's any point my staying. If he wants night work, I can't do it. And for that money he probably does.'

'Night work?' asked May, suddenly panic-stricken. 'What do you mean?'

'Office cleaning, at night or very early in the morning,' said another woman impatiently. 'Haven't you done this sort of work before?'

'No,' said May.

'Are you working now?'

'No,' she said again.

Yesterday she had had a job, albeit a horrid, badly paid one, a narrowboat which was also her home, a mooring which she had thought of as secure and an easygoing lifestyle. She had already lost the job, and if her 'youth and enthusiasm' weren't enough to get her another, she might lose everything else too.

'Nor am I,' sighed the glamorous one. 'But then, I'm an actress. I'm used to it.'

'Don't they call that "resting"?' asked May.

'No one who's actually experienced it would. When you're not schlepping around to one unsuitable interview after another, you're having voice lessons, or dance lessons, or any other sort of lesson which might put you ahead of the others. And if you're not doing that, you're ringing your agent who sends you for more unsuitable parts just to get you off her back. Eventually you'd be grateful for a non-speaking role as a cucumber sandwich. Restful is the last thing it is. I thought cleaning might be an easier way of earning a living.'

Several of the women regarded the actress as if she were one lipstick short of a make-up kit.

'You don't need to do the splits to clean a toilet, that's for sure,' said the woman who had spoken first.

Everybody laughed, including the actress. 'Shame,' she said. 'I can see it now, "Sally Bliss, princess of the privies". I do a wicked lambada.'

The feeling in the room softened towards her. No one had expected such a glamorous creature to be able to laugh at herself.

'Well, I was pushing my luck applying,' said one of the

5

efficient-looking women. 'The ad did say "young". And if 'e's asked Miss Lovely-Legs to stay, I reckon he wants more than cleaning. I'll stick to the job I've got.' She gathered up her belongings. 'Piss-poor wages, but at least I know they only want me to wash the floors.'

After she had gone, silence fell again, as oppressive as the air and heavily laced with anxiety.

Sally twisted a ring round and round on her finger. 'Do you think that's true? I mean, I know I'm an actress and all that, but I draw the line at being a topless waitress or something.'

''E's offering good money,' said the woman with the child. 'But if he wanted topless waitresses, 'e'd 'ave asked for 'em. There was enough questions on that form.'

'True,' said Sally. 'But why, when none of my work experience was at all relevant, did he even want me to hang around to be interviewed, let alone ask me to stay?'

'Well dear, I reckon you should watch yourself.' She picked up her child's dummy which had fallen to the floor. 'Me, I've got three other kids, varicose veins and no energy.' She started to gather up her things. 'If he wants to interview me, 'e can write a letter. 'Ere, Dustin, 'ave yer dummy.'

Another woman got to her feet. 'I'll give you a hand. I don't think there's much point in my staying, neither.'

'Am I next?' said the last professional-looking one. And, as no one else volunteered, she got up and knocked on the door.

The girl who was reading put her book down, looked at her watch, sighed, and picked up her book again.

May was about to go mad from boredom. She turned to the actress. 'Hello, I'm May.'

'I'm Sally, Sally Bliss.'

'You look a bit fed up, if you don't mind me saying so.'

Sally sighed and pulled a face. 'This is the second interview I've had today. Piers, that's my boyfriend, was madly keen on me going to the first, for a play about Chernobyl that I was totally wrong for. He doesn't know about this one. Still, I daren't go home without some sort of gainful employment, or he might throw me out.' She laughed to show that she was joking, but obviously wasn't.

6

Sally couldn't afford to be thrown out just now. When she'd saved enough for the three months rent required as a deposit, she could find a flat of her own. Then she would have the huge satisfaction of leaving Piers, and he'd have to find someone else to polish his ego. But until then she was stuck with her role as biddable girlfriend. Which, she admitted, flexing her toes inside her shoes, was a part she was typecast for. Sometimes she feared it was the only role she would ever fully master.

May wasn't sure how to react to Sally's problems with Piers, so she said, 'What sort of things did he ask you? The interviewer, I mean.'

The girl who was reading looked up.

'Well, nothing much about cleaning. He asked about me, really. He didn't seem to mind that I'm an actress. Said he was looking for go-ahead sort of girls.'

'Girls!' said May. 'That's not very PC, is it?'

'Welcome to the real world!' said the professional-looking woman as she came out of the interview room.

'Did you get the job?' Sally asked her.

'Nah. He more or less told me straight that I was too old. Experience counts for nothing with the likes of him.' Justifiably indignant, she left the room.

'Excuse me,' said May to Sally. 'Are you sure he didn't – you know . . .?'

The girl in the corner lowered her book again.

'I swear! Honestly! You'll find out for yourself in a minute.'

The girl with the book got up. 'Do you mind if I open the door? I need some air. I feel a bit sick.'

'No, go ahead. It's frightfully stuffy in here,' said Sally.

'You do look a bit pale,' said May.

'I'm all right – fine, really. It's just that I always feel sick when I'm nervous. I need this job so badly.'

'So do I,' said May. 'If I don't get it, I'll lose my home. Well, my boat – but I live on it, so it comes to the same thing.'

'You live on a boat?' said Sally. 'That sounds very –' wary of giving offence, she sought for the right word '–romantic?'

May laughed ironically. 'I don't know about that. Though I suppose that was what I thought when I first saw it.'

'Oh?'

May realized, having started, she'd better finish her story. 'I bought it from a boyfriend and apparently he hadn't paid for the mooring in ages. I've only just found out. That's why I'm here. I've got about three months to raise the money.'

'At least we're not competing with each other,' said Sally. 'In my business it's awful when you're up for the same job as a friend who probably needs the money just as badly as you do. At least the ad said he needed a team.'

'A team of what?' said May, flippant with nerves. 'Performing poodles? I know nothing about cleaning. I haven't a hope of getting this job. Perhaps I should go now, rather than wait to be turned down.'

'You might not be turned down,' said the girl with the book.

'I hope I'm not. The only other job I saw advertised was for a traffic warden. Desperate I may be, but I don't think I could hack that.'

Sally considered. 'I don't know. The hat is quite attractive. And you could meet all sorts of celebrities and they might offer you a part in a West End show, just because of your beautiful eyes.'

May's eyes narrowed with scepticism. 'Oh, right . . .'

The girl with the book was fidgeting in her seat.

'You go next,' said May, thinking she looked so nervous she might very well throw up if she wasn't put out of her misery soon.

'Oh no. I've already been. I'm just waiting to hear. It's your turn.'

'Oh Christ! Is it?' Tripping slightly in her big boots, she got to her feet and went into the office.

Just visible behind a pall of smoke was a man in a suit. He had the build and slick good looks of a nightclub bouncer and looked nauseatingly prosperous. He had shadowed, penetrating eyes which, May feared, could differentiate between a woman who could clean and one who couldn't instantly

8

and accurately. Some women, May acknowledged, would find him attractive.

He indicated that May should sit down and she noticed that he had a ruby ring on his little finger – a reassuring sign that he knew how to make money.

'Now, my dear,' he began. 'You are?'

'May Sargent.'

He extracted May's form from among the others on his desk. He scanned it briefly before looking back at May.

'I'd like to know a little bit more about your background before I tell you about the business I'm setting up. I see you live on a boat.'

'Er – yes.'

'With your parents?'

'No.'

'And where do your parents live?'

May's outspoken manner and feminist principles had lost her a job only yesterday. 'In Hertfordshire,' she said meekly.

'See a lot of them?'

'Umm – well, not as much as they'd like.'

He looked again at May's form. 'So you live on your own, on this boat?'

'Yes.'

He nodded. 'So tell me, May, why did you apply for this job?'

'I need the money.' Though honesty wasn't always the best policy, May hadn't had a chance to think up a better reply.

'Wouldn't your parents lend you money if you needed it?'

Why did people keep thinking her parents were the World Bank? Mike had suggested she asked them for money. 'I've left home. And I can keep myself.'

'Can you? You've done quite a lot of courses, haven't you?'

This was more familiar. Her failure to find a career being examined by critical eyes. Guilt and frustration made May defensive. 'Only three.'

'But you're not working in any of these areas now?' His ruby ring hit the paper dismissively.

9

'No ... My parents ...' She couldn't say her parents forced her into doing them. Her parents wouldn't force her into doing anything, but it was to please them that she'd considered being a tour guide, a dental nurse and a hotel manager. 'My parents felt they were a good idea.'

The man regarded May with unnerving intensity. Eventually, he spoke. 'Well, May, although you look scruffy you talk nicely, very nicely, in fact.'

May gulped.

'And you've got a good general education, and as I'll provide a uniform, your clothes needn't be a problem.'

'Oh, good.'

'You've read the advert, so you'll know that this is a new venture for me. I'm planning to extend my range of businesses to include a cleaning service for the more upmarket client. It's going to be called Quality Cleaners. Which is why I'm looking for young ladies.'

May smothered her wince with an insincere smile.

'My clients need something more than just the old fashioned Mrs Mop. They may need flower arranging, a spot of catering, waiting at table, things like that. Things which I think you can offer.'

'I can't do any of those things!' Then, seeing doubt flicker across the man's face, and with it her chances of a job, she hastily added, 'but I'm sure I could learn.'

'I'm certain you're really a very accomplished young lady if you put your mind to it.' His smile sent shivers of unease up May's spine. 'So, tell me, my dear, if I offered you a job, would you take it?'

'As a cleaner?'

'Of course. I wouldn't ask you to do anything you didn't feel capable of.'

'And you wouldn't need me to work at night, or anything like that?' After the conversation in the waiting-room, May thought she ought to make sure.

The bonhomie melted away. 'There may be a little work after office hours, but nothing out of the ordinary, and nothing that ain't kosher. I've always kept on the right side of the law. I asked for cleaners, I want cleaners.'

'Right,' said May humbly. 'Of course.'

'So, do you want the job, or don't you?'

May cleared her throat. 'Are you offering it to me?'

He shook his head. 'I'm asking if you want it?'

'Yes. Yes, I do. Very much.'

Accepting this as a submission, the man smiled. 'Very well. If there's anyone else waiting, send them in. Otherwise please wait.'

May crept away, wondering if the job as a traffic warden was such a bad idea after all.

CHAPTER TWO

'Well girls, you'll be glad to hear that I can offer you all positions with Quality Cleaners.' The girls, who had virtually given up hope of ever finding out if they had jobs or not, looked up. 'I've made out contracts for you all.' He handed them all wodges of green self-carbonated paper.

Harriet, the girl who had been reading, glanced at hers. There seemed to be approximately seven pages of small print. A closer look showed that it was full of typing errors. The smell of it made her feel sicker than ever.

'If you'd like to read through them first,' their new employer was saying. 'It'll take a while. But –' he smiled in a mirthless, knowing way. '– I'm sure as sensible young ladies, you don't want to sign anything you haven't read.'

I can't face it, thought May. I just can't. It's probably just full of stuff about pension contributions anyway, and I'm not planning to stay that long.

I know I ought to read it, thought Harriet. But it'll make my head ache. It can't really be committing me to anything very dreadful, can it?

'You could of course decide that I'm trustworthy, offering you good jobs on good terms . . .'

'I'll trust you,' said Sally, who never read her contracts and wasn't going to start now. That was what her agent was for. 'Give me a pen.'

'We're probably mad,' muttered May, taking the pen Sally handed to her.

'I am, certainly,' said Harriet, so quietly, nobody heard.

'That man is such a slimeball!' said May, clutching a piece of paper with the address of their first assignment on it. It was for the following day.

They stood on the steps of the building around Harriet's

luggage having signed their contracts and received a brief pep-talk from their employer – 'Call-me-Keith' Slater – along the lines of, I-am-a-successful-businessman-and-you-too-can-be-rich-and-powerful.

'If we're going to work together we'd better get to know each other,' May went on, turning to Harriet. 'My name's May Sargent.'

'Harriet Devonshire.'

'You know mine,' broke in Sally. 'And if I don't find a loo soon, I won't be answerable.'

'Let's find a café – with a loo – have a cup of coffee, and recover. We can arrange where to meet tomorrow,' said May.

'Good idea,' said Sally. 'There's somewhere just round the corner. Follow me, but hurry!'

She had led them away from the corner of Shepherd Market where Quality Cleaners occupied the attic of a very smart address, to where the area lowered its standards sufficiently to admit a greasy-spoon café.

They collected their cups of coffee from the counter and sat down at the only table which didn't need clearing.

'Sorry girls,' said Sally, when she was back from the ladies'. 'It's gone downmarket since I was last here.'

'But it's very cheap,' said May. 'And I, for one, can't afford to be choosy. Talking of which, why did Keith choose us, instead of all those professional-cleaner types. I mean, I hardly look like a Quality Cleaner.'

'You will do when you've got your fuchsia-pink jumpsuit on,' said Sally, sipping her coffee, which she took black.

'Not to mention the baseball cap, the firm's name embroidered tastefully in gold,' said Harriet, who seemed unused to mixing with women of her own age, and was trying hard to adopt the casual, friendly manner of the other two.

May made a face. 'Yuk! He didn't mention having to wear jumpsuits and baseball hats! He just said it didn't matter my looking scruffy as he'd provide the clothes. But still,' she persisted. 'He didn't ask me a single question about how to clean venetian blinds, or any of that stuff.'

'Nor me,' said Sally. 'I was all ready to recite a creme cleanser ad I was in once. He didn't give me the chance.'

'And I'm a hopeless cleaner,' May went on. 'I just don't seem to notice dirt, or so my mother always says. I told him I couldn't do flower arranging, or anything like that.'

Sally was horrified. 'Flower arranging? I just stick them in a vase and wait for them to die.'

Harriet smiled shyly. 'Well, I'm a brilliant flower arranger, and cleaner. I've been doing it since I was twelve. I'd be happy to pass on any tips.'

'It's not so much tips I need,' said May, 'as a whole foundation course. He must be mad, taking me on, when he had a whole roomful of experienced professionals.'

'We're young and enthusiastic,' said Sally, quoting from the advertisement.

'And we all speak the Queen's English,' said Harriet.

'What?' said May, horrified.

'Really?' said Sally.

Harriet realigned the sugar, ketchup bottle and vinegar into an orderly clump. 'Didn't he tell you he's aiming for the titled market? He gave me the impression that if a client didn't have an entry in Debrett, he wouldn't send them a cleaner. He wants us because we're "ladies".'

May shuddered. 'I really hate being called that, it makes me feel like a public convenience.'

Sally made a face. 'You mean three years of drama school learning to project to the back row of the stalls has given me the perfect voice to be a Quality Cleaner?'

Harriet stirred her coffee. 'It seems so.'

'I've never heard anything so overtly snobbish in all my life,' said May. 'If I didn't need the money, I wouldn't have anything to do with it. It's against my principles.'

'I can't afford principles,' said Sally. 'I'd be quite happy to be a kept woman, but my boyfriend says it's wrong to keep pets in London flats.' An edge of anxiety added to the brightness of her smile.

'But he can't found his new business on the likes of us, just because of the way we speak!' said May, still outraged. 'I mean, I daresay most of the clients will be out when we're there anyway. As far as they're concerned we could be dropping aitches like fag-ash all over the place.'

'He did ask if I smoked,' said Harriet.

'He was probably just going to offer you a cigar,' said May.

'Well, whatever the reason he took me on, I'm just so pleased to find work so soon after coming to London – even a job like this,' said Harriet.

'What sort of work did you do before?' asked May.

'Housekeeping, I suppose.' The avid curiosity on the faces of May and Sally obliged her to elaborate. 'I lived with my grandparents. I kept house for them.' She lowered her eyes as if hiding something.

May and Sally exchanged glances. 'So what did you do, May?' asked Sally, tactful enough not to persist. 'Before you hit skid row?'

May shrugged. 'I've never had a career as such, just a series of jobs in between a series of courses. Until yesterday, I worked in a pub. And in the summer I painted canal-ware – you know, roses and castles on wooden spoons – and sold it to gift shops.'

'I still think living on a boat must be romantic,' said Sally.

May exhaled sharply. 'I suppose I thought so yesterday. Today, I just think it's hellish expensive and fraught with anxieties.' She played with her teaspoon, suddenly thoughtful.

Harriet wiped her thumb along the edge of her cup, in case she had left lipstick on it, even though she wasn't wearing any. 'I don't suppose either of you know where the YWCA is? Or whether I could walk there from here?'

'I haven't a clue. Sorry,' said Sally.

'Why do you want to know?' asked May. 'If it's not a rude question.'

'I need somewhere to stay – just until I can sort out some permanent lodgings.'

'I would offer to let you stay with me,' said Sally. 'But my boyfriend's terribly protective of his privacy.' She didn't add that Piers surrounded himself only with the influential and the glamorous. He would condemn Harriet as a waste of space and May as a harridan who didn't shave her legs, and was therefore quite unfit for civilized company. 'He's quite famous, you see.'

'What for?' demanded May. 'What's his name?'

'Piers Fox.'

Harriet and May exchanged blank stares.

'Never heard of him,' May said cheerfully.

'Nor have I, although of course, coming from the country . . .'

Sally sighed. 'Actually, I'd never heard of him either, before I met him. He's a journalist and quite well thought of.'

'Oh.'

Separately, the other two tried to think of something pertinent to say about journalists, and separately, they failed.

May again took refuge in a change of subject. 'You could always come and stay with me,' she said to Harriet. 'At least until you've found your feet.'

'It's very kind, but I couldn't possibly impose.'

'Nonsense! You can't go and stay at some hostel when you're new to London. I'd be more than happy to introduce you to life on the canals. Unless the whole idea gives you the heebie-jeebies.'

'It would be wonderful,' said Harriet, who couldn't afford heebie-jeebies any more than Sally could afford principles. 'If you're sure. But I would insist on paying my way.'

'I wouldn't want you to pay.'

'But if you need money badly enough to work as a cleaner,' said Harriet quiet but firm, 'you need every penny you can get. I won't come otherwise.'

May sighed. 'You're right, of course. It just seems so wrong to take money from my friends.'

Harriet blushed. 'I'd have to pay someone for board and lodging. It might as well be you.'

May became more cheerful. 'And if Mike at the boatyard sees I've got someone living with me, he might feel more hopeful about getting his money. I'll let you pay the same as the YWCA – if you know what that is.'

'I'll find out,' said Harriet firmly.

'Let's go then. Let me show you your new home,' said May. 'Come with us, Sally?'

Sally was tempted. She looked at the gold watch which Piers had once hidden in a fortune cookie. As always, it reminded her of the good times, long gone. She shook her head. 'I've got to get back in time to cook something for supper.'

'It's only four-ish,' said Harriet, sympathetic to the tyranny of meals, but more accustomed to coping with it. 'There's loads of time.'

Sally shrugged. All her gestures were expansive, dramatic, expressive. 'I suppose so. But I'm such a ghastly cook and Piers is terribly gourmet.'

'Do come,' said May. 'We really need to make some sort of plan for tomorrow, and I'm sure Harriet can tell you a recipe you can run up in five minutes.'

'I can, actually,' said Harriet.

Once Sally would have cooked Piers's supper because she loved him. Duty on its own wasn't a good enough motive. 'Oh all right then, why not. But I mustn't forget to get the recipe.'

May beamed. 'Good-oh. Can I carry that bag for you, Harriet?' Not waiting for Harriet to reply, she picked it up and led the way out of the café.

May walked with fast, purposeful strides. Even Sally, in two-inch heels and carrying Harriet's vanity case, covered the pavement with surprising speed, efficiently weaving in and out of oncoming pedestrians. Harriet, in black-patent courts and with a suitcase to cope with, followed more sedately, more accustomed to wearing sturdy brogues or wellington boots. She had a blister on her heel.

'You'll soon get used to the Underground,' May shouted across the aisle to Harriet, when they were finally on the Tube to Paddington. 'It just takes practice!'

Harriet smiled weakly, convinced she would never get over the feeling that it was the London Underground which controlled her movements, and not her.

'Have you any idea where this place we're doing tomorrow is, Sally?' yelled May above the train's racket.

'Not a clue,' replied Sally cheerfully. 'But you can guarantee it's not in an area we'd any of us visit voluntarily.'

'Let's face it, we're none of us really here voluntarily,' said May.

'I am,' said Harriet, almost unaware she had spoken aloud. 'I've run away from home.'

The wind rushing past the train was deafening, but unfortunately for Harriet, May was adept at lip-reading. 'What?' May bawled. 'Did you say you'd run away?'

Harriet winced and nodded, wondering how on earth the words had escaped her. 'I'll tell you later.' She studied a scuff mark on the toe of her shoe, pondering on the vastness of the step she had taken when she'd left the safety of a comfortable, rural home for the chaos of London.

May led them out of the station, past a slip-road full of taxis, a surprisingly tasteful floral clock, over a bridge, and then into a car park.

'Where are you taking us!' said Sally.

'Trust me,' said May with a chuckle. 'Here, over this fence, then through that gap.'

Harriet, convinced that at any moment she would be attacked by the trained guard dogs which advertised their existence from small plaques along the fence, squashed herself and her luggage between a wall and the boards which surrounded a building site.

The canal, which up until then had only appeared in brief, black glimpses, opened out into a basin. Three rickety pontoons, loosely attached, reached out from the bank, a cluster of vessels clinging precariously to each of them.

'That's my boat, there.' May pointed to where a high, black hulk covered in ripped tarpaulins and slimy polythene lay like some revolting, bloodsucking river creature.

'Oh, my God,' breathed Sally.

'Can you see it?' went on May, unaware of her companions' consternation. 'It's *The Rose Revived*.'

Harriet's country heart sank. What had she let herself in for? The thought of staying in a hostel, which had seemed so desolate when it was her only option, suddenly seemed infinitely preferable to sleeping in the belly of a giant slug.

'It's breasted up against that black one, *Shadowfax*.' May went on glibly.

Harriet and Sally both located *The Rose Revived* at the same time and released a simultaneous sigh of relief. May's boat was mostly hidden by *Shadowfax*, but even with a very restricted view, they could see it was as different from it as could be, given that the two craft shared the same basic dimensions.

'We have to cross the lock,' said May. 'Be careful.' Showing an alarming lack of care herself, she clattered across, bags tucked under her arm.

The other two followed gingerly to where May was waiting for them.

'Come on. We have to climb over *Shadowfax* – if you can in that tight skirt,' she said to Sally. 'Give me your suitcase, Harriet. Oh, there's Mike.' May turned towards the buildings. 'Hi Mike!' she yelled. 'I've got a lodger and a job! I'll come and tell you about it later!'

Mike shouted something unintelligible back and waited to see Sally get on the boat.

Sally, having reached the end of the pontoon, placed a high-heeled foot on the gunnel of *Shadowfax* and swung herself easily aboard. Not for nothing had her limber, high-kicking legs earned her a part in a West End show.

'It's so *narrow*!' she exclaimed when she had stepped neatly across to *The Rose Revived*, and, to the severe disappointment of Mike and a jogger on the towpath opposite, had adjusted her skirt. 'Can I go in?'

May unlocked the door, and bending her head, Sally went through. 'Oh May! You are lucky!'

Harriet, not wishing to leave her belongings unattended in this alien territory, waited anxiously on the bank until May returned. May heaved up her bags and coaxed Harriet to follow them.

Once safely in the small well-deck, Harriet took a good look at her temporary home. Like *Shadowfax*, *The Rose Revived* had a black hull, but its cabin sides were bright blue, with white handrails. Several large windows broke up the superstructure, framed by white-painted shutters.

Harriet leaned over the side. The name of the boat was painted on each side of the bow, in large, fancy letters of the style used on old-fashioned grocers' vans, with a coloured roundel at each end. It looked clean and well-cared for, and an encouraging column of smoke curled from the black, brass-banded chimney.

Harriet's much-tried spirits rose. Life had not led her to expect much of it, but this was promising.

'Do come in!' called Sally through the door. 'It's super!'

Harriet negotiated herself and her baggage through the double doors and stepped down into the saloon. Her spirits rose a notch higher. The warmth, the glowing varnished pine, the shiny black stove, were instantly welcoming. To her eyes, even the dust, the overflowing wastepaper basket, the clothes hung over the stove to dry, had a seductive charm which warmed her heart as much as her body.

The house Harriet had left that morning was immaculate. Dust was never allowed to settle on the beeswaxed antique furniture or the Meissen figurines. The tapestry cushions, lovingly embroidered by her grandmother, were not for sitting on but for plumping up. The formal arrangements of shop-bought flowers her grandmother favoured were always disposed of before they dared to drop their petals.

The Rose Revived was uncritical. It allowed people to shed their clothes, to muddy its somewhat grimy carpet, to leave books open face down on the tops of bookcases. Harriet smiled.

It was extremely narrow – seventy feet of length and less than seven of width gave it the dimensions of a narrow railway carriage. But it was anything but claustrophobic. The walls were clad in pine tongue-and-groove boards, varnished to a warm gold. There were more than enough windows to let in the sunshine and the straw-coloured linen curtains added to the sunny effect.

'My room's through there,' said May, waving a hand. 'Beyond the kitchen. You'd have to sleep here, in the saloon.'

There was a banquette about six feet long, which Harriet realized was her bed. A table was fixed to the wall opposite the stove, and was obviously part of a longer table, sections of which hung flush against the wall. Prints of birds were nailed to the bulkheads. A piece of driftwood stood in one corner, happily gathering dust.

'It's lovely.' Harriet sank down on to the cushion-filled banquette and eased off her shoes. 'Really lovely. Are you sure about letting me stay?'

Warmed by her new friends' appreciation, May smiled expansively. 'Of course. For as long as you like. But you can see why I applied for the job? If I don't pay something off towards those mooring arrears, I'll have to sell *The Rose*.'

'Oh, May,' said Sally.

May bit her lip as she realized how near she was to crying. Hunger, anxiety and fatigue had conspired to sap her usual energetic optimism. 'But never mind,' she went on brightly. 'As I told Mike, I've got a job and a lodger. Now, who's for some baked beans on toast? I'm *starving*.'

'Oh, not for me!' said Sally. 'I'm dieting.'

May turned her attention from her own problems to inspect Sally's greyhound figure. 'Why?'

'You don't need to,' said Harriet.

'Oh, I know. I'm all right now. But if I don't watch it like a hawk, I balloon up to nine stone. Ghastly.'

'How tall are you?' asked May.

'Five-seven. But as an actress you have to be slim. Besides, Piers . . .' Sally, feeling suddenly disloyal, left her sentence unfinished.

'I'll get those beans on the go,' said May after a moment, and retreated to the galley.

May not only loved her boat, she was inordinately proud of it. With help from her parents – darling, precious, but oh so worried about their only daughter – she had bought out the man she had shared it with for a while, and had been its sole owner for three months. But having already had help to buy the boat, May had instantly rejected Mike's suggestion that she ask her parents for the mooring fees. She had caused them enough anxiety one way and another. This battle she would tackle on her own.

'How did you get into boats in the first place, May?' Sally asked.

May punctured the tin of beans and sighed. 'I suppose you could say it was a man. I was walking along the Oxford Canal towpath with an old school friend. It was autumn and the leaves were just turning. Anyway, this narrow boat was chugging along and this man was throwing a rope round a bollard. There was a small plastic cruiser in the way, and he did it so well. We got talking, and it went on from there.' She started turning the handle of the tin-opener. 'Looking back, I can see it was the lifestyle more than the man that I fell in love with. He met someone else, and my parents helped me to buy him out.'

'Weren't you heartbroken?' asked Sally sympathetically.

May shook her head. 'Nope. He was beginning to seriously get up my nose. He never did anything. When this girl came along, all pre-Raphaelite hair and flowing Indian dresses, I was only too glad to see the back of him.' She unhooked the tin-opener and fished out the lid of the can. 'My parents were so relieved!'

Harriet could well believe this. 'Have you done much to the boat since it's belonged to you?'

'Oh yes. The inside was more or less bare. I put in the table and the side-bed, and made cupboards under those steps. I sanded down the bulkheads, varnished them, and generally made it more homely.'

'You are clever,' said Sally.

'I had help. The bloke on *Shadowfax* is an ace carpenter and joiner, he showed me how to do everything. Difficult to work with though, as he's more or less nocturnal. It's no wonder he finds it hard to get work.'

But it was more than just joinery, Harriet could see. Signs of May's personality were everywhere. The pictures she liked, the books she read, the cups of tea had she left to get cold, combined to a homogeneous whole, harmonious, comfortable and warm.

'One bit of toast or two?' called May.

'Two please, if I may,' said Harriet.

'Are you sure you won't have any, Sally?'

'Oh go on then, just a few.'

When the baked beans were eaten, and several pints of tea

drunk, Sally uncurled her long legs, stretched and got to her feet.

'I really must go. It's been lovely meeting you both and everything. If it wasn't for the thought of telling Piers, I'd be quite looking forward to being a cleaner.'

'I know what you mean.' said May. 'My brothers'll tease the life out of me when they hear.'

'Teasing I could cope with,' said Sally. 'But Piers'll think I didn't try hard enough to get the play about Chernobyl.'

In a way, he would be right, she thought. If she'd worn her grey sack dress, clumpy shoes, and an earnest expression, she might have done better. Except that she hated her grey dress, didn't have any clumpy shoes and wasn't quite happy with her earnest expression. She felt it made her look like a mother whose child's socks aren't really white, not someone who cares about global issues.

'Still, there you go.' She picked up several sheets of paper scrawled with directions back to civilization and some neater ones on how to prepare a meal in five minutes, said goodbye to her new friends, and exposed her legs once more.

'More tea?' May asked Harriet.

'No thanks. I'm awash as it is.'

'Did I tell you how to work the loo?'

'Yes thanks,' said Harriet, vowing in future to perform as many bodily functions when she had access to proper plumbing as was physically possible. 'Now I'm going to wash up.'

Worried about her water supply, May tried to dissuade her. 'No, don't! Come and sit down and we can have a good talk. I'm sure you need to – I mean, you did say you'd run away . . .'

She cleared her throat and started again. 'You cleaning up last night's supper dishes will make me feel horribly guilty.'

Harriet shook her head. 'Please don't feel guilty, and let me do them. Washing up helps me relax.'

Finding this hard to believe, May perched on the stove, which was at the perfect temperature for sitting on. 'You must be dreadfully tired. You can't want to start washing up now. Sit down and have a chat.'

'I'm not much good at chatting, I'm afraid. I'd rather

23

clean your kitchen.' Harriet smiled. 'I'll tell you the whole gory story sometime, but not now. I promise I won't waste water,' she added.

May grinned, pleased that her lodger had grasped the basics of boat life so quickly. 'I'll go and see Mike then, and see if I can sort out my mooring problem. But I'll find you some bedding first, and then if you want to go to bed you can.'

Some time later, Harriet heard May tiptoe past where she was stretched out on her narrow but surprisingly comfortable side-bed. She was blissfully warm inside a sleeping bag and was weighed down with as many blankets as May could find.

Her bedroom at home had been in the attic – freezing in winter, stifling in summer. Apart from a few minor points, she thought boat life would suit her well. But although she was so tired, she knew she wouldn't settle until she had performed one last ritual.

She emerged from her cocoon of bedclothes and ferreted inside her bag for a torch, a lined A4 pad and a pen. Having retrieved what she wanted, Harriet started to write.

Dear Matthew, How is school? I am writing this by torchlight because I am staying on a boat and I don't want to run down its batteries. The boat is on a canal in London . . .

CHAPTER THREE

The flat was cold. The heating wasn't timed to go on until half-past six, an hour before Piers was due home. Elephant grey, bare floored, and minimalist, it was a stark contrast to the cosy environment Sally had just left.

Of course, it was marvellously stylish not to have curtains or ornaments and only books if they were behind the flush-fitting, matt-black cupboards. And it wasn't as if there weren't a couple of paintings – huge, enigmatic statements against famine or war, which had cost so much money and were so difficult to relate to. But never, even if she braved Piers's wrath and turned up the heating, would it be cosy. And it had no personality. It could have belonged to any up-and-coming young journalist.

Sally wasn't in a position to argue about the décor or the heating, so she just pulled on the brightly coloured patchwork cardigan her mother had knitted her, and went into the kitchen to cook his supper.

How was he going to react to her new job? Would he understand that being the star of West End farce didn't necessarily qualify her for a part in a play about a nuclear disaster? Would he throw her out from the sheer embarrassment of having a girlfriend who was a cleaning lady, or would the fact that she would be earning good money make it acceptable?

When she and Piers had first met she had been earning a substantial wage as the lead, albeit for the third cast, in a hugely successful farce. He'd seen her in the show, wangled an invite to a cast party, and swept her off to a restaurant on the Thames. Afterwards he'd taken her for a row on the river. She had trailed her hand in the water, watched the willows sway gently in the evening breeze and fallen in love.

Sally opened the door of the fridge and sighed deeply – because there was a mouldy tomato clinging to one of the shelves as much as for times past.

For Piers, an out-of-work actress was not at all the same thing as a high-kicking French maid in a short skirt and frilly apron. The romantic gestures which had so enchanted her had ceased at about the same time as the show had folded. He no longer sent her roomfuls of flowers, or hid presents in her food. Now, he stuck Post-it notes to her mirror reminding her to pick up his dry cleaning and forgot her birthday.

'Never mind,' said Sally, cutting the rind from a lump of Brie which was well past its best, as per Harriet's instructions. 'I'll soon earn enough to get a place of my own. Then I can paint the walls pink and have the heating on whenever I like.'

The next morning, Sally was late – and not only because it had taken her a lot of time deciding what to wear until the fuchsia-pink jumpsuits materialized. It was because Piers had reluctantly agreed to give her a lift. And having done so, demanded that Sally cook him breakfast – three rashers of Canadian back bacon, and a 'grown for flavour' tomato, grilled and served on the wholemeal, multigrain bread he bought from Harrods.

Dawdling over his Cuban coffee was his rather unsubtle way of punishing her for taking such a lowly job. He had been impressed by the money, and was pleased for *her* sake that she had a job and could therefore make a contribution to the household. But he didn't want people to know that his girlfriend cleaned for a living. Not that he put it in so many words, of course, but Sally got the message.

May and Harriet were waiting patiently outside the tall Victorian house when she dashed up.

'God! I'm so sorry. I got held up. Did Slimeball notice?'

May shook her head. 'He hasn't turned up himself yet, and as he's got the key we can't get in until he arrives.'

'And he's supposed to be bringing some sort of overalls to wear until our jumpsuits are ready,' said Harriet. She looked, thought Sally, a lot less stressed than she had yesterday.

Just then, a very flashy black car swung into a parking

space across the road, mounting the pavement in order to do so and totally disregarding the 'Residents' Parking' sign. The numberplate read K81THS.

By the time the girls had worked out that this was a personalized numberplate, the Keith in question had got out, pulled three carrier-bags from the back and then locked the car by remote control.

'Morning, girls.' He flashed a much-used, ready-to-wear smile at them. 'Let's get the show on the road.'

The hall was narrow, dusty and dark, made darker by the lavish use of brown paint and purple wallpaper. The walls were high and cobwebs looped their way across them like forgotten Christmas decorations.

'It's a bit manky,' said Keith. 'It was a forced sale and I bought it cheap. Needs a bit doing to it, of course. But a bit of redecoration and I'll make a tidy profit.'

'A bit manky' seemed a vast understatement. Harriet wondered how on earth they would reach the cobwebs. May considered again the advantages of being a traffic warden, and Sally mentally started to explain to Piers why she couldn't stick even one day as a cleaner.

Drifts of dead bluebottles meandered along the windowsills like seaweed along a tideline. Broken lino covered the floor, and patches on the wallpaper indicated where things had been ripped off the walls. In estate agents' jargon, it was 'ripe for restoration'. Anyone else would describe it as a tip.

'The immersion will heat up in a bit,' said Keith, finding a switch. 'But you can boil the kettle if you must.'

'We must,' said Harriet firmly. 'Hot water is absolutely essential. Have you got cleaning materials?'

Small pearl earrings and velvet bow notwithstanding, she presented a very determined figure. She was wearing a pair of May's jeans and had rolled up her sleeves.

Keith reached for one of the carrier bags. 'I got cleanser, washing-up liquid, toilet cleaner, and a packet of cloths, what more do you want?'

'Bleach, soda crystals and rubber gloves,' said Harriet.

'And our overalls,' said Sally, emboldened by Harriet's firmness.

'Ah, yes, overalls. I haven't got them yet. I'm having 'em made. But it doesn't matter what you look like for this job, because you're not going to see the client.'

'But we'll get our own clothes dirty,' said Harriet. 'And you promised us protective workwear.'

Hearing his own words repeating on him like yesterday's curry, Keith refrained from commenting that her jeans and May's dungarees appeared to be exactly that.

'Tell you what I'll do,' he said eventually. 'I'll pay you a bit extra for getting your own clothes cleaned.'

'And the rubber gloves?' asked Harriet. 'This house is in a really terrible condition. If you want us to clean it, you'll have to give us the tools for the job.'

Keith, who was beginning to look, if not exactly threatened, as if there was something else he ought to be doing, felt in his back pocket for his wallet. He pulled out a couple of ten-pound notes.

'Tell you what. There's a shop on the corner. You buy anything you need that isn't here. I'll be along at four to see how you're getting on.'

He reappeared at five. By that time the girls were exhausted and filthy. The house, however, was a great deal cleaner. Harriet reckoned another day should finish the job.

'You done very well,' said Keith, having slid his finger along the picture-rails like a music-hall mother-in-law. 'I'll give you that.'

'But our clothes are ruined,' said May.

'Not to mention our hands,' murmured Sally, who in spite of the gloves had managed to break several nails.

'Of course we need at least another day to finish,' said Harriet.

Keith looked aghast. 'What? Just how long does it take three women to clean a house?' he enquired sarcastically.

'That depends on the state of the house,' said Harriet who was finding her emotional feet. 'We could do this one in two days. It would take most people a lot longer.'

Keith surveyed the three women who regarded him so coolly, wondering if employing people with posh accents was really such a good idea. Along with the accents came a lot of

28

uppity-dyke ideas. Fortunately for him, Sally was an expert at reading body language. She had also been programmed to ingratiate herself with men from babyhood and found it hard to break the habit. Besides, she had no particular desire to spend another day in Tufnell Park losing layers of skin and fingernails in buckets of hot water.

'You're the boss,' she said with a smile as practised as Keith's own, but a lot more charming. 'If you're satisfied . . .'

Keith shot her a relieved glance, recognizing a 'real woman' among the rabid women's libbers. 'Exactly – er – Sarah?'

'Sally.'

'Exactly, Sally,' Keith continued. 'I think you've done a fine job, and I've got other jobs lined up for you tomorrow.'

'In other words,' said May behind her hand to Harriet, 'he's got someone who'll pay him, so he doesn't have to pay us out of his own pocket.'

He produced three pale pink, deckle-edged sheets of paper with 'Quality Cleaners' printed at the top. 'You can sort out between you who goes where. But I will be asking the clients for comments, so no funny business.'

Harriet's expression took on that of her grandmother when faced with the fact that her cat had failed to digest its dinner.

Keith, recognizing just in time where his best interests lay, backtracked hastily. 'Not that I anticipate any problems, girls. I'm a good judge of character and I know you're all first class.'

'Yes,' said May.

Keith held out the pieces of paper with a somewhat desperate air. 'Yes, well, here you are.'

'Um, I don't suppose,' said Harriet firmly, in spite of the effort it obviously took her to speak, 'you could pay us for today's work? I'm new in London and I need to pay for my digs.'

Keith, whom the girls all now thought of and referred to as 'Slimeball', regarded them thoughtfully.

'I don't see why not. You've done a good job, and I pay good work well. Here.' He handed each girl a twenty-pound note from his back pocket.

'But this isn't enough,' began May.

'Something to keep you going,' he said. 'On account, as it were. After all, your contract did require you to work a week in hand.'

'Did it? Oh,' said Sally, and pocketed her money.

'Now girls, wanna lift to the Tube?'

Sally went back with Harriet and May to *The Rose Revived*. Piers was eating out that night, and so she wasn't obliged to rush back and cook for him. She recklessly bought a bottle of cider with some of her housekeeping money which they drank with the fish and chips bought on the way home. They sat in the saloon of the boat. It was wonderfully cosy after the freezing empty house they had been cleaning all day.

'I'm knackered,' said May tipping the last of the bottle of cider into three glasses. 'Totally and utterly cream crackered.'

'It was dreadful!' said Sally. 'I thought we'd be dusting a few knick-knacks, not cleaning the Agean Stables, or whatever it is.'

'How come you know so much about cleaning, Harriet?' asked May. 'All that technical detail about washing walls from the bottom up, and soda crystals? It was amazing.'

'I was responsible for keeping my grandparents' house clean, not that it was ever allowed to get dirty. And my grandmother would occasionally lend me out to the vicar's wife. She used to clean for locals who had too many children and not enough time.'

'Sounds most unusual for a vicar's wife,' said Sally. 'I thought they spent all their time on committees.'

'She is unusual. She used to give the mother enough money to take her kids to the pictures and give them popcorn and choc-ices, and then blitz the house while they were out,' said Harriet. 'She was wonderful to me . . .' She hesitated, and then went on. 'Especially when I had Matthew.'

'Matthew?' said May and Sally in unison.

'You've got a baby?' went on Sally.

Harriet shook her head. 'Not any more, he's nine, nearly ten.'

'So where is he?' asked Sally.

'At school. Boarding school.'

'How ghastly!' said Sally.

May had stiffened. 'I don't approve of boarding school.'

'Nor do I,' said Harriet bleakly. 'My grandparents sent him.'

Now she had started, Harriet felt the need to talk about Matthew, to explain the strangeness of her upbringing. She'd lived a life of secrecy for so long that the thought of telling May and Sally everything had a cathartic appeal.

Parental oppression, while not something May had actually experienced for herself, was something she knew about. She unbent. 'Your *grandparents*? Why them?'

'My mother died when I was three. She'd run off and married someone quite unsuitable, so they hadn't seen me before. They brought me up. But, as they said, bad blood will out, and I went and got pregnant after a one-night stand. At the time, I didn't like to point out it was their blood which had escaped. Anyway, now they're bringing up Matthew.'

'But why are you letting them? Why didn't you bring him up on your own?' May demanded.

Harriet looked at her, wondering if she could make May understand the impossibility of her situation.

'It's not that easy. I stayed at school to do A-levels, but they never let me learn to type, or anything useful. The only thing I'm any good at is art and it isn't a life-supporting skill – at least, not yet it isn't. Though I hope one day it might be. Besides, Matthew was happy.'

May found this highly indigestible but struggled with it. Mothers were notorious for making sacrifices for their children.

'So you're an artist?' asked Sally.

'I would never call myself that, but it's why I ran away. I think if it wasn't for my desperate need to paint, I would have just chugged along with my grandparents until Matthew was grown up. But not being able to learn more, to paint, was killing me. Which is why I came to London. I thought there might be more scope here.'

'But you didn't try and stop them sending Matthew to boarding school?' asked May, trying not to sound censorious.

Harriet sighed. 'I did, but it was no good. Besides, his going to boarding school gave me a chance. I couldn't have escaped to London if I had had Matthew with me.'

'What about his father?' asked May.

'He doesn't know Matthew exists. I didn't want him to know.'

'So you brought up a baby on your own?' Sally was seriously impressed. 'How brave!'

Harriet shook her head. 'No. My grandparents brought up my baby – as they brought me up. I was merely his nanny.'

'How awful,' breathed Sally.

'Well,' went on Harriet, determinedly bright. 'It taught me how to clean.'

There was an awkward silence. Neither Sally nor May felt able to comment on what seemed to them an appalling situation, and sensing that the last thing Harriet wanted was them both gawping at her with sympathy, May changed the subject.

'The one snag about living on a boat,' she said, usually reluctant to admit there were snags, 'is that you can't sink into a lovely hot bath at the end of a day like today.'

'What?' Sally was horrified. 'You mean you can't wash?'

'Oh there's a shower,' said May. 'But it's not terribly efficient.'

Which, Harriet discovered a little later, was one way of describing three or four jets of tepid water played to the accompaniment of the pump, which sucked the water deafeningly from under your feet almost before it got there. When she finally emerged, cleaner but not exactly relaxed, May made another confession.

'I go home for a bath as often as I can,' she explained. 'But in between times, I don't wash much. It's one of the advantages of living alone.'

CHAPTER FOUR

Harriet had been assigned to a flat in Cheyne Walk. The other two had decided that as this address was the easiest to find, it was only fair to give it to the country bumpkin, as she described herself. They had also agreed that, with the money left over from Keith's twenty quid, they should buy Harriet a London street guide.

Sally got the flat in Victoria which belonged to an ex-naval officer and his wife who had both been in hospital. She was let in by a neighbour who explained that the couple were desperately houseproud.

'In fact,' the neighbour confided, 'I wouldn't be at all surprised if it wasn't keeping everything so ship-shape and Bristol fashion which gave Captain Walker the heart attack in the first place. I've given the place a bit of a going over already, otherwise you'd never have it done by half-past ten. Their son's bringing them home.'

'What was wrong with Mrs Walker?' asked Sally, who liked to know the details.

The neighbour winced. 'I'm not quite sure, dear. But I think it was something gynaecological.'

Sally winced in sympathy.

'They were so relieved to get a *lady*,' the woman went on. 'When their own dear char retired they managed on their own rather than risk getting some frightful *young* person.'

Sally, recognizing in the word 'young' a euphemism for 'common', nodded in what she hoped was a ladylike way, grateful that she had consigned yesterday's working clothes to the dustbin. This morning she had on a dull, knee-length skirt she had bought for an unsuccessful audition for a J. B. Priestley play. Captain and Mrs Walker were bound to appreciate it. But she surreptitiously removed her large silver earrings.

She was handed an apron which had belonged to the departed char and was shown a box of cleaning materials. Eventually the neighbour left.

'Now my only problem,' she said to the row of African violets which flowered along the windowsill, 'is finding the dirt.'

May had to find her way to Wimbledon, where a harassed young woman was having her mother-in-law to visit. She glanced at her watch and saw that she was fifteen minutes late. She'd forgotten how far away Wimbledon was.

The door was opened by a pretty, untidy young woman in jeans, apparently no older than May. There were stains down her shirt and on her jeans. Even the toe of her shoe had a mustard-coloured blob on it. A cluster of children clung to her legs, one of whom was richly covered in spots.

'You have had chicken pox, haven't you?' the woman asked anxiously. 'I did tell the man that mine all had it.'

Of course, Keith hadn't said a word about chicken pox. 'Oh that's all right. I think I remember an itchy summer holidays.'

'Oh good,' said the woman. 'Do come in. You are . . .?'

'May Sargent, Quality Cleaners. God, that's so embarrassing to say!'

The woman laughed, and backed slowly into the hall, allowing her children time to get into reverse. 'I'm Natalie Gwyn-Jones, but do call me Natalie. I've been married four years and have three children, but I still haven't learnt to relate to the Gwyn-Jones bit either.'

May followed the trail of children – there seemed to be four – into an extremely untidy kitchen. Re-counting the children, she wondered for a moment if Mrs Gwyn-Jones had actually miscalculated the number of her offspring.

Natalie noted May's confusion. 'Oh, it's all right. These aren't *all* mine. Heaven forbid! We're just having Damien for the day so his mother can go to the hairdresser. God! What I wouldn't do for the time to just wash my own hair! Coffee?'

'Yes please,' said May.

Natalie Gwyn-Jones put the kettle on, talking non-stop. 'I had to get a cleaner because my mother-in-law is coming. What beats me is why I let her in the house! I tried to put her off because of the chicken pox, but she wouldn't take no for an answer. Milk? And I know whatever I do, even if I had the house entirely rebuilt, redecorated, and sterilized it wouldn't be good enough. Biccy?'

Natalie absently unwrapped a biscuit for May and handed it to her, half the paper still on so May could hold it without getting her fingers chocolatey.

'Of course,' she went on. 'She's only coming to confirm what she's always known, that I'm a hopeless mother and not nearly good enough for darling Sebastian.'

Natalie slumped down into a chair and the children fell away, satisfied that Mummy wasn't going to move for a while. 'Of course I'll clean as much as I can too, I'd feel so guilty if you did everything, but the children are so *clingy* just now, so I probably won't be able to do much. Why can't she understand that with three children under five the place is bound to be a tip?'

Sipping her coffee and eating her biscuit, May looked about her. She was not by nature tidy, but she had never lived with small children. And the addition of infants to people with an already higher than normal tolerance to clutter linked the word 'tip' to icebergs, and the huge amount of them which remained hidden. What was needed, May decided, was a domestic dumper-truck, to scoop it all up.

She remembered what Harriet had said about the vicar's wife.

'Why don't you take the children out and let me blitz the place? I'm sure I can manage on my own.' She was also sure it would be easier to clean without the presence of several small people, who were now charging round and round on their tricycles, cornflakes flying in their wake like autumn leaves.

Natalie sighed. 'I wish I could, but there's really nowhere I can go with Octavius so spotty, and quite frankly, even if he wasn't, taking four children out when you haven't got a car is a bit of a nightmare.'

Natalie looked dreadfully tired, and May suddenly yearned quite desperately to be Harriet's vicar's wife, a fairy god-mother to harassed mums.

'Well, why don't you go up and have a bath and wash your hair, and let me and the children see what we can do down here?'

'Have you had any experience of small children?'

'No,' admitted May.

Natalie sighed. 'That might be an advantage.' She got up and stretched. 'I'll leave the bathroom door unlocked.'

If Cheyne Walk was easy for Harriet to get to, the entrance to the flat was less so, particularly as the inhabitant was not going to be there and she had to collect the keys from another tenant.

Eventually, with a bunch of keys in her hand separated from each other by her fingers and chanting under her breath the order the locks were to be opened, Harriet made her way up a terrifying metal fire escape to the back entrance. By the time she had let herself in she was convinced that, no matter what the advantages of living in a big city, they couldn't possibly offset the inconvenience of having to climb so many stairs and having to barricade your home so strongly against intruders.

When she had eventually negotiated the two locks, the padlocked bar and a swollen door-jamb which provided its burglar-proofing for nothing, she found herself in a small, badly designed kitchen. The faint odour of prawn vindaloo made her wrinkle her nose and find her way to the hall, dumping her bag en route.

In terms of rooms, it was a small flat. Four closed doors confronted her, and she opened one, feeling like a burglar. But not apparently the first. The room looked as if it had been ransacked. Had there indeed been a burglary that very morning, and was she the first to discover it?

Then, partly relieved and partly dismayed, she realized that the room was just very untidy.

A bedroom, it was taken up almost entirely by a rumpled double bed, duvet trailing. An upright chair was piled so high with clothes it threatened to tip over backwards. What clothes wouldn't fit on the chair appeared to be on the floor. The door of the fitted wardrobe was open; not surprisingly, it was empty. A chest of drawers, every drawer of which was open, was heaped with papers.

She knew the flat belonged to a man, but Slimeball had omitted to pass on his name. Whoever it was lived alone, and either never invited anyone home, or was totally unembarrassed about the thought of his dirty underwear being exposed. It was not part of her job to do his washing, but it ought to be part of somebody's – he obviously took very little interest in the matter himself. And as his empty wardrobe revealed, he had run out of clothes.

The next door threatened to vomit its contents on to the floor. It was to a cupboard and she shut it hastily before it could do so. A small bathroom, tidy but for a heap of towels on the floor, was behind the next door. It was thick with dust and a quick glance at the lavatory pan told her either it was regularly used for the disposal of tea-leaves, or it had been a long time since anyone had even poured any sort of disinfectant down it, let alone cleaned it. Her client probably had no sense of smell.

But the last room made up for everything.

Instantly, she realized it belonged to an artist. And this thought on its own was enough to cause bubbles of nervous excitement to well up in her stomach. Any resentment for his slovenly ways that she might have been developing melted away. It was such an astounding coincidence that practically her first job in London took her into the home of an artist. And the second glance told her it was an artist who taught.

The studio was vast, and had probably originally been the attics of at least two houses. The dull parquet floor was large enough to accommodate a small formation dance team, but instead of dancers, several easels were spaced out to face a focal point, now empty.

What had they been painting? A still-life arrangement of apples, oranges and a milk jug? A shivering model, naked or draped? And just how accomplished were the pupils?

37

It would have been easy to lift a sheet and find out, but Harriet was too aware of the tenderness of her own artistic ambitions to risk treading on anyone else's. She had done A-level art and had been considered brilliant by her teacher, but that was in the country. These aspirants would probably be intimidatingly good and send her into the depths of depression. It was far better not to know.

The canvases propped up against the wall – finished work – were even more tempting. For it was likely they belonged to the owner of the flat, the teacher, the artist.

Harriet turned abruptly away from temptation and considered the studio from an artist's point of view. Two sets of dormer windows opposed each other along the room. There were skylights in the ceiling, which, by the look of the damp patches on the floor, let in more than light. But it was the studio of any artist's dreams. Particularly one who had previously only painted in the shadowy seclusion of a badly lit bedroom. She wandered across to one window and stood on tiptoe to look out.

It could have been the view that inspired Wordsworth when he wrote 'Upon Westminster Bridge', except that the skyline was totally different and Westminster was over a mile away. But for Harriet it held that 'Earth has not anything to show more fair' quality which, country girl as she was, went some way to making up for the inconvenience of city living.

Irregular lead-lined roofs and platforms under webs of cables led her eye to the river and Battersea Bridge. Factory chimneys probably polluting the air with noxious gases took on a grandeur endowed to them by distance. Skyscrapers, hideous at close quarters, stood bravely under the autumn sunshine. Harriet had not expected to find such loveliness in an industrial skyline.

Turning into the room, away from the distracting view, Harriet took a professional look at the job before her. She wouldn't let herself peek under the sheets to see the standard of the pupils who used this magnificent space, but the smell of oil paint and turpentine which hung in the air was immensely positive. A less down-to-earth person would have seen it as a good omen. After all, she had come to London to learn to paint.

She retrieved a pair of May's dungarees, rubber gloves, and box of soda crystals from her bag and switched on the radio. She would start with the kitchen, and make sure she did as good a job as she could in her two hours. That way the unknown artist would ask for her again.

It would be hard to make much of an impression in such a short time, she realized. Polishing the studio floor properly would probably take at least that. She would have to do what she could in the time.

When her two hours were up, she wrote a note.

I have discarded everything in the fridge which was likely to give you food-poisoning. The milk at the back is sour, but it will make excellent scones. I have done my best in the time. All the clothes in the black plastic bag are dirty. You badly need to visit the launderette or contact a laundry. If you would like me to come again, could you provide some floor polish for the studio. I haven't looked at any of the paintings.

Quite why she added this when she was certain he wouldn't be remotely interested she couldn't begin to work out. But she wanted him to know. She wanted him to trust her not to pry. In spite of the health risk his flat presented, she wanted to come back.

She staggered down the metal staircase, posted the keys through the letter-box of the neighbour as instructed and made her way to the Tube station.

The Tube wasn't so bad outside the rush-hour, and if you had time to work out how to get where you wanted to go. It would be better for her to learn the Underground by herself. Otherwise she would just follow the others, sheep-like, and never build up the confidence to travel on her own.

She found the Quality Cleaners office and made her way slowly up the stairs, hoping it wouldn't be a wasted effort. With so many irons in the fire, Keith might well be out.

The door was open, and she could see Keith talking hard on his mobile phone. At his elbow a cigar sent smoke curling insidiously into the atmosphere.

She knocked and waited. He looked up, indicated the chair

39

in front of his desk and went on talking. He seemed to be about to close a deal which depended entirely upon his charm and salesmanship. Harriet took the offered seat and pondered on people who liked making money for the sake of it.

The deal concluded, he switched off the phone and smiled at Harriet. Harriet returned the smile and wondered if it were her duty as an employee to tell him there was a bit of parsley stuck to one his front teeth. She decided not.

'Harriet! What's the problem?' he demanded affably. The deal was obviously greatly to his advantage. 'Find your assignment all right?'

'Yes thank you. But I was wondering if it was a regular job, or just a one-off?'

'Regular, once a week, I hope. Why?'

'I'd like to be the regular cleaner. For the sake of continuity.'

Keith took a long drag from the cigar. 'Yes, continuity. Well, I think we can arrange that, Harriet.'

'Thank you. And where do you want me to go tomorrow?'

Keith looked down at a notebook which was lying open in front of him. He looked up at Harriet again, as if deciding where to send her. 'Yes, well,' he said. 'I haven't got any-where for you to go tomorrow.'

'What? I thought you promised us regular work?'

Harriet was not really surprised when Slimeball replied, 'Once a week is regular.'

'But I mean work every day.'

'All in good time, girl. We've not been in business long, have we?'

'Well, I haven't, but I thought you had . . .'

Keith smiled patronizingly. 'Quality Cleaners is a new branch of my business. It'll take a little while to build up. Unless . . .' His significant pause was spoilt by the chirrup of his mobile phone. 'Yes?' he snarled into it. 'Oh. Yeah. Well?' He was silent while the caller made some sort of explanation. 'So he didn't have the money?' Another pause. 'Well, you know what to do then.'

Harriet found her mouth suddenly dry. Of course the

phone call was probably perfectly innocent. It just sounded like the script for a gangster movie because she'd only heard half the conversation.

He turned off his phone. 'Well now, where was I?'

Harriet was halfway out of her chair, feeling that wherever he was she didn't want to be there with him. He motioned her to sit down again.

'I remember. I was wondering if I could interest you in another of my little businesses.'

Harriet was sure he couldn't, but didn't like to say so. 'Oh? What?'

'It would need a bit of capital. I like my girls to feel more like partners than employees . . .'

Harriet felt not so much a partner as a lettuce-leaf about to be eaten by a slug. 'I haven't got any capital . . .'

'You haven't any savings you could fall back on?'

She had, but no way was she going to tell him. She shook her head.

'Pity. It's an easy way to make money, if you have enough to set up in the first place.'

Harriet cleared her throat. 'Well, as I haven't any money, perhaps I could collect this week's wages? I know we're supposed to work a week in hand, but I really need some money now. I have my lodgings to pay for.'

Keith regarded her narrowly. 'I could offer you other work, not cleaning.'

'No!' Harriet tried to keep the panic out of her voice. 'No, really, I'm very happy cleaning. I just want to do it regularly, every day.'

'And I'm sure you will be soon, my dear.'

'But what can I do until then?'

Slimeball shrugged. 'Well, the system doesn't allow me to pay you before the proper time.' He paused long enough to increase her stress level to just under bursting point. 'But as you're such a good worker, I'll lend you some money, from my own pocket, just to tide you over.' He felt in his jacket for a wallet from which he produced a twenty-pound note.

Harriet had lowered herself this far, another inch wouldn't make any difference. 'I'm afraid I need more than that.'

The avuncular expression on Keith's face hardened, as if he'd paid Harriet's gambling debts more than once. He produced another note. 'That will have to do. But next week, you'll get two weeks' wages – less this forty quid and the twenty you got yesterday, of course.'

'Thank you,' said Harriet, not feeling at all grateful. 'I'll ring on Monday, then.'

'You do that. I'll be sure to have a nice little job for you.'

Sally was suffering from the particular fatigue which only trying to look busy can create. She had spent three hours cleaning a flat which had no dirt in it. Even the silver, which she had cleaned out of sheer desperation, looked no better when she'd finished, because whoever had done it before had used long-life polish. A few toast crumbs under the grill were the only evidence that the flat had ever been occupied.

Captain and Mrs W. J. Walker, RN, had duly returned from hospital after Sally had been cleaning for a couple of hours. In that time she had vacuumed, dusted and polished everything in sight, and by the time her clients had been tenderly delivered by their son, the flat was gleaming. Sally felt her job was done, but the son had fussed round them, reassuring them that Sally was going to stay for a while.

They were delighted to have a Quality Cleaner and Captain Walker asked if she could go in every day.

'We had a marvellous housekeeper – an absolute treasure – but she had to go and live with her daughter. She came in daily.'

The rheumy blue eyes which had once scanned the oceans so assiduously for the enemy contained just enough of a plea for Sally's soft heart to soften further. They would never create enough dirt to warrant so much attention, but, as the son had told her in an immensely audible stage whisper, she was 'someone in the house'. And as a 'lady' could obviously be relied on.

Sally spent the rest of her time being told how Mrs Golding had done things, and being instructed, oh so nicely, to do everything exactly the same. (She always sterilized the tin-opener on Thursday mornings, and defrosted the fridge on Fridays – it's better to get into a routine, don't you think?) Captain and Mrs Walker were kind. They appreciated her decorative, ladylike presence.

Piers's flat felt particularly cold and minimalist after the genteel clutter of the Walker's flat. Nor was it heated to such a flush-making temperature. Sally shivered violently and pulled on her cardigan. What she really needed was a hug, a rib-cracking, breath-expelling, life-threatening hug. Piers had never been any good at those.

She turned on the immersion heater for a bath and vowed that when she had a flat she would have the sort of system where you just turned on the tap to get hot water. But even knowing that, unlike the girls on the boat, she would eventually be able to immerse her aching limbs in hot water did not cheer her much. Piers was being so distant.

Usually, he liked sex almost every morning and evening. But for some reason, since she had joined Quality Cleaners, he had gone off it. And as he was a man who could only be intimate, either physically or verbally, if sex was the ultimate objective, he hadn't done more than kiss her cheek for days. He was probably on the lookout for someone with a career you could actually tell your friends about.

She should have felt devastated at the thought of Piers in the arms of another woman, but she felt more anxious about the two fillets of red snapper which lay on a sheet of grease-proof paper in the fridge, waiting to have something imaginative done to them. If Piers was getting his end away elsewhere, she would be able to just go to sleep when she got into bed, instead of having to do something imaginative to Piers. It was a marvellous relief. Piers was wont to lie on the gunmetal-grey satin sheets with just the same air of impatient expectancy as the fish. And after she had performed the required acrobatics, she had to go into the bathroom and use the bidet, while he just fell asleep with never even a word of love or comfort.

She had just added the out-of-season new potatoes to a pan of boiling water and was about to put the grill on, when the telephone rang. It was Piers, explaining with enormous self-importance that he was eating out, 'on business'. Sally needn't wait up.

Sally made a face at the fish, put it back in the fridge and turned off the water under the potatoes. Then she went into the sitting-room, switched on the television and prepared herself for an evening's viewing free from documentaries, re-enactments, and current affairs. When she finally left Piers, she would only watch *Blind Date* and *Gladiators* – things Piers would never let darken the screen of his slim Nicam television.

It would be wonderful, thought Sally determinedly, suppressing the thought that it would be more wonderful if there was someone, preferably male, to share it with. That way madness lay.

CHAPTER FIVE

May rang the bell and waited for a few minutes, Although she had worked for Quality Cleaners for six weeks now, she still hated going into other people's houses when they were out.

'There must be an easier way to make a living,' she muttered, finding the key, which, as she had been told, had been left in the smallest gumboot in the porch. 'And if Slimeball doesn't pay us what he owes by Monday, I'm going to find it!'

Gingerly, certain a thousand decibels were about to rip through the air any moment, she opened the door. There was a blissful silence. Ever since someone had forgotten to turn off their burglar alarm, and she had not only maddened every neighbour within miles, but had unwittingly summoned three police cars, she had hated this part.

'Hello!' she called. 'Sorry I'm late!'

But the house echoed emptily back at her and she made her way into the kitchen. Her morning cleaning job had involved an acre of parquet flooring which needed polishing on hands and knees. There had also been a painful visit to Mike-the-Boatyard who was becoming increasingly impatient for his money, which was only coming in dribs and drabs. Still smarting from this, she had to wait for ever for a Richmond train. Consequently, she was a lot later than she had expected, and a lot more tired.

'Good, I'm alone,' she muttered. 'Where's the kettle?'

The kitchen was done out in limed oak. All the cupboard doors, the dishwasher, even the oven, were uniform. The one exception was the fridge, which was white. May spared a moment to wonder why this was. But then she realized that, if the fridge door had been wooden, there would have been nowhere for the ubiquitous magnetic letters and numbers

45

which, she had discovered, were not so much *de rigueur* as essential. No middle-class family with children was without them.

This family had children, and they had obviously rushed out in a hurry. The table had the air of the *Marie Céleste*, with a meal abandoned before it was eaten. Bowls still half full of milk and brown bits, slices of toast with crescents bitten out of them, and half a dozen jars with their tops on askew. According to the number of mugs, there were fourteen of them in the family.

Nestling between several mega-sized packets of sugar-encrusted cereal and printed with coffee-circles, was a foolscap pad, covered with toast crumbs and what was presumably her client's writing. It was abundant and loopy, with greek 'e's and little circles for dots over the 'i's. The exclamation marks, of which there were many, looked like hot-air balloons. She, it had to be a she, had used a green felt-tip pen.

May sat down, feeling this perhaps was better faced seated. She cleared herself a space among the plates of toast and marmalade with her elbows, and read. *Dear Cleaning Lady (so sorry, I've forgotten your name). Something frightful's happened! My husband's aunt looks as if she's dying! She's been on her deathbed for years, but my husband thinks we should be there. With luck, she should be either dead or better before tonight! She'd better be! There's a hot-shot lawyer coming, who might make Marcus (my husband!!) a partner.*

May had by now ceased to be surprised by the intimacies people told their cleaning ladies. She read on. *The thing is, would you mind cooking the dinner?'* (May gulped. This was serious.) *The man at the agency told me you can work wonders! I have left a menu and money for food. You can get everything at Sainsbury's and take a taxi back. I've also written down the names of the books where you can find the recipes. (Most efficient for me!) The house isn't too bad, so if you could just give the dining-room, downstairs cloakroom, and drawing-room a lick and a promise and concentrate on the food! A neighbour (bless her) is keeping the kids and dog for the night, so no need to worry about them. I will of course pay you more for cooking!*

You must let me know how much when I get there. Will you mind staying on to serve? Tell me at the time if you do. Thanks a million, Clorinda Stockbridge.

May was strongly tempted to go home. She was perfectly justified. Slimeball had no right to let Mrs Stockbridge think she could cook. She had been employed as a humble domestic, not as a chef, and to have to produce a grand dinner party was asking too much. But the word 'extra' stopped her. It had a satisfying, cash-in-hand sort of ring to it. It implied that May might get the money direct, without going through the office.

Mike had made no bones about it – another hundred quid, pronto, or he would insist on her putting her boat up for sale. If she wouldn't do it, he would. Which, he pointed out, would be worse. Cash in hand could mean cash in the nick of time.

But May had never cooked a proper meal in her life, let alone anything approaching 'cuisine'. All her meals revolved around toast, cheese and baked beans, with the occasional bacon butty to ring the changes. And it was already half-past three. Even to May, who had a very hazy idea of how long these things took, it seemed to be a pretty tight schedule, given she had to shop and clean as well as cook.

She rested her face in her hands to give herself a moment to think without the remains of breakfast to confuse her. By the time she emerged she had made a decision. She would dash round the shops, start anything that might take a long time, clean the house, and then finish cooking at her leisure. It wouldn't be easy, but it would be possible. She would make a shopping list.

She cast about on the table for the menu and the money. The menu was reposing under a plate of bacon rinds and congealed scrambled egg but there didn't seem to be any money. The panic which May had just argued herself out of began to creep back. She searched the table, the work surfaces and the cupboards, but eventually came to a terrifying conclusion: there was no money.

May had barely enough cash for her Tube journey home and a minus amount in her bank account. Nor did she have a credit card. Since she could hardly pop round to a neighbour and ask to borrow fifty quid or so, shopping was out of the question. Well, that was one part of the job ticked off, now for the cooking. May read the menu. Clorinda was obviously a devoted fan of *Masterchef*.

Smoked trout pâté (easi-peasi!); Melba toast; lamb steaks in lattice pastry cases (lattice roller in the drawer by the cooker) with mange-tout; rosti potatoes and red wine sauce; lemon syllabub (use the glasses in the big cupboard).

Well at least she had a cast iron excuse for not following that particular flight of gastronomic fancy. It would have been incredibly difficult for a novice cook like May, even with the ingredients.

May found a teabag and made a cup of tea. She could ring her mother for advice. She was also a fan of television cookery programmes and would be full of tips and wrinkles on how to produce a gourmet meal for eight out of a few leftovers. Or she could ring Slimeball, explain the situation, and let him decide what to do. No, anything but that. If she involved Slimeball, any hopes of seeing a bit of actual money would vanish.

Besides, May didn't want to take the easy way out. She had a stubborn streak which made her reluctant to ask for help. If Clorinda had left the ingredients ready, or even a pile of ten-pound notes, she might have felt differently. But as no one could possibly blame her if she didn't make a go of it, May was doubly determined to do so. Quite how was a problem yet to be addressed. Convinced that some sort of plan would occur to her she decided to get the cleaning out of the way.

Once she had filled the dishwasher with the breakfast things, a rummage under the kitchen sink produced a box of cleaning materials, very tidily arranged. May remembered that she was there because Mrs Stockbridge's usual cleaning lady had broken her leg. Well, she might have brittle bones but she was obviously efficient and organized. 'Which is good,' said May. 'Because, unless she broke it months ago, it'll mean everything will be fairly clean already.'

Heartened, she picked up the box and made her way into

the drawing-room. Apart from a few newspapers in a heap on the armchairs, May felt it was in perfect order for entertaining. She sprayed a bit of polish in the direction of the tables and chair legs, dusted between the ornaments on the mantelpiece and plumped up the cushions. The newspapers she folded neatly and put on top of a pile already formed in a wicker basket.

Apart from being cold, the dining-room was even tidier than the drawing-room. But to make some sort of gesture, May polished the lovely mahogany table which, she was pleased to see, was antique and therefore past being a threat to the rain-forest.

The downstairs bathroom contained a lot of chrome and glass in the form of the most super-deluxe shower May had ever seen. It was all spattered with water droplets, but responded well to a rub with a damp rag. The washbasin and loo could have done with a bit more serious attention, but as May was environmentally opposed to most of the cleaning agents on the top shelf, she could do only surface wiping. If Mrs Stockbridge wanted May to take over until her regular cleaning lady's leg mended, she would have to shop more thoughtfully.

May looked at her watch. She had four hours to cook in. Being unable to go shopping had gained her hours. All she had to do was to devise an alternative menu, using the ingredients already to hand, and get cooking. There was bound to be something in the freezer she could defrost in the microwave.

Clorinda's house was blessed with a large, old-fashioned larder and in it was a vast deep-freeze. 'It's big enough to take a whole corpse, let alone enough to food to feed eight people,' said May out loud and opened the lid.

May didn't really expect to find a whole corpse, but not to find a whole leg of lamb, or a chicken, some steak, or even some pork chops was somewhat discouraging. Mrs Stockbridge might have been able to make most of her house a child-free zone but her freezer was full of ready-made products designed to tempt pernickety toddler appetites. There were a few loaves of sliced white bread, some frozen spinach, and some sinister brown packages which could have been poisonous mushrooms. There were also a lot of margarine containers which had lost their lids, and therefore the identities of their contents.

Everything else in the freezer was pre-packed and pre-formed, and for all May knew pre-digested. There were burgers, pizza slices, fish fingers, chicken nuggets, and half a dozen different sorts of potato chips including alphabet shaped ones. But the nearest thing to adult food was eight low-fat chipolatas and some broken packets of filo pastry. At first sight, there seemed to be absolutely nothing May could feed eight grown-ups on, even if satisfying their hunger was the only criterion. And Clorinda was expecting quite a lot more than that. May trawled among the drifts of ice-crystals and empty boxes which covered the bottom of the freezer and brought up a packet of frozen cream-sticks. Her initial euphoria was rapidly evaporating.

Assuming that there would be a bottle of sherry and some lemon juice somewhere in the house, she did at least have the ingredients for the pudding. She shut the lid of the freezer and rummaged through a vegetable rack and discovered some carrots, potatoes and a very wrinkled red pepper. There was a shelf of tins opposite the freezer, and May scanned them briefly. By now she was no longer surprised to see that they mostly consisted of tins of alphabet spaghetti and dog food, although there were a couple of tins of soup.

It was with some despondency that she gathered her haul into her arms and returned to the kitchen. But she had yet to investigate the fridge and it might contain all sorts of goodies. May dumped her burden on to the kitchen table and opened the fridge door. Clorinda may have already made the 'easi-peasi' smoked trout pâté. And there was bound to be some lemon juice and then she could defrost the cream and get on and make the syllabub.

There was no lemon juice in the fridge, and no trout pâté. There was something which looked like a very coarse 'pâté de campagne' but it had a picture of a dog on the lid, and although May considered it briefly, she decided not to risk it. And even she realized that low-calorie lemon squash was no substitute for lemon juice. She would have to devise a totally different menu.

Shutting the fridge door, she decided it would still be a good idea to hunt out the sherry. There might be something else in the alcohol line which might cheer up the sausages, not to mention the cook. Fortunately the drinks cupboard in the drawing-room was well-enough stocked to intoxicate half of South London. If all else failed, she could make a fantastically alcoholic cocktail, so no one would notice what they were eating.

She picked up a bottle of sherry and returned to the kitchen. There were some unexplored cupboards in there, and while they were probably full of alphabet-shaped breakfast cereal, she could but hope. Some packets of ginger nuts amongst the stale crisps and broken biscuits stirred a long-forgotten memory. She began to smile. Yes, she would give Clorinda's guests that old standby, ginger biscuits soaked in whisky or sherry, layered into a cylinder with whipped cream, and coated with the remaining cream. The recipe, in the voice of her home ec. teacher, floated comfortingly back to her down the years.

At half-past seven, Clorinda and her husband burst through the front door with a welter of apologies.

'Darling! I'm so sorry! Did you manage to do everything? Too ghastly, Aunt Maud is still alive. But I suppose if she had died, we might never have got away. How did you get on?'

May had prepared a dignified, put-upon little speech explaining how she had done her best in the circumstances, and describing in detail exactly how difficult the circumstances were. But it no longer seemed appropriate.

'Well,' she began. 'It wasn't easy . . .'

'Wasn't it? I tried hard not to make things too complicated for you. But I assumed you were a far better cook than I am . . .'

'Actually, I can't cook . . .'

'I mean, it takes me *ages* to cook for a dinner party. I meant to start –'

'Let the poor girl speak,' said Clorinda's husband. 'How do you do, I'm Marcus Stockbridge.'

May took hold of the hand offered to her. 'I'm May Sargent. The thing is, I don't cook. It's not one of the things I do.'

'What?' Clorinda's pretty face crumpled in confusion and disappointment. 'You mean, there's no dinner? But what's that delicious smell?'

'Oh I have cooked a meal,' explained May. 'But I couldn't follow your menu because you didn't leave any money.'

'Oh, Marcus!' Clorinda turned on her husband, all her anxiety and pent-up tension converted to anger. 'How could you forget to leave poor – poor May any money? You invite all these important guests and –'

Her husband interrupted firmly. 'You never asked me to leave any money, and as the important guests are due to arrive in approximately half an hour, I suggest you go and get changed.'

Clorinda made a noise which was a cross between a dog's whimper and a sneeze and flounced out of the room.

From the sidelines May witnessed this display of masterfulness, and wondered if it would have been so successful if Clorinda hadn't been more anxious to address the important issue of what she should wear than to discuss May's problems.

Marcus turned to May, obviously expecting to work the same magic on her. He was handsome in a grey-templed, prosperous way, with the beginnings of a paunch emerging above the waistband of his trousers.

'I'm so sorry about the mix-up. We could of course send out for some food.'

This easy solution hadn't occurred to May, who had overlooked the benefits of affluence, but nor was she having it, not after the effort she had put in. 'No, no. I have prepared a meal, although it's probably not what you or your guests are expecting.'

'I don't suppose there's any wine chilled?'

May, who had the gravest misgivings about her meal, had put as many bottles of white wine as she could into the fridge and had opened several bottles of red. 'A whole fridgeful,' she replied triumphantly.

Marcus relaxed visibly. 'And did my wife ask if you could stay on and serve? You can charge anything you like.' He laughed. 'You're a legitimate business expense.'

'Well, I am awfully tired. But could you pay me direct? In cash?' Suddenly all her hard work looked like being worth while.

'Of course. And I'll give you money for your cab fare home afterwards.'

'But I live in Central London.'

'No matter. We'll arrange a cab to pick you up the moment the pudding's on the table. You won't even have to clear up or make the coffee. That's settled then.' With that, he strode into the downstairs bathroom.

A couple of minutes later, May heard a noise like thunder accompanied by torrential rain. As a boat-dweller, this sound made her panic for an instant, before she realized it was not a lock-gate that had breached, but only the super-duper power-shower pounding relaxation and cleanliness into Marcus Stockbridge's manly shoulders.

May resignedly donned a plastic pinny which made her look as if she were wearing a basque with stockings and suspenders. It was all she could find that was cleaner than her own, grease-spattered jeans. She longed for a really hot shower herself. It would be hours and hours before she got home, and even when she did, she could only look forward to a trickle of lukewarm water which would hardly make her wet. But the thought of the money gave her strength. If they gave her fifty quid, she would actually be able to give Mike the hundred, only a day after he asked for it.

Clorinda floated into the kitchen. She was wearing a sophisticated black two-piece and had swept her hair into a perfect chignon.

'You look lovely,' said May, partly to be polite and partly because it was true.

If her stand-in cleaning lady was feeling more than a touch like Cinderella, Clorinda was determined not to play the ugly sister. 'Darling, you've been fab. Marcus did want you to serve, but if you just put the first course on the table while we have drinks, then serve the main course, I'll do the rest. I feel a real meany letting you do everything.'

'Perhaps I should explain . . .'

'Have a drink. I'm having one. Gin and tonic?'

May gave up trying to explain. She accepted the drink which Clorinda gave her and took a sip. It was extremely strong.

There was a ring at the door. Clorinda gulped her gin, gave a discreet but audible belch and went into the hall to answer it.

May downed her drink in a similar fashion. 'Here goes nothing!'

It had been such a long time since Clorinda Stockbridge's guests had eaten tinned tomato soup that few if any of them recognized it for what it was. But they all thought it delicious and supped it up hungrily. May was not reassured, however, by the success of her first course. She had known everyone liked tinned tomato soup. She had an aunt who had spent years perfecting a recipe using her own, home-grown tomatoes which tasted as nice. Using Clorinda's electric can-opener had been the hardest part.

It was the second course which had tested her ingenuity to the limit and was now testing her nerve. With a heavy heart, but no alternative, she retrieved the first two plates from the oven. At least she wouldn't have to see any of the diners ever again. Each portion consisted of two chicken nuggets, some potatoes, grated and hashed into brownness, some carrot sticks and some spinach and a few frozen peas scavenged from the bottom of the freezer. But in order to give this unexciting menu some pizazz, she had arranged the food into people, a man and a woman for each person.

In the end no *chef d'honneur* could have composed a plate of *nouvelle cuisine* with more care. As she arranged spinach dresses, carrot limbs and potato hair, she almost fancied that each figure developed its own personality. And feeling so personally involved in her creations, she gave the prettiest little girls to the men who smiled at her as she made her way round the table. The rather cross-looking boy, whose pea eyes gave him an aggressive squint, she put down in front of the man she judged to be the 'hot-shot lawyer' Clorinda had mentioned in her note. It was his fault there was a dinner party.

As each guest received a plate they fell silent. As she left the dining-room to the resounding echo of her Doc Martens on the parquet floor, May was convinced that Clorinda's dinner party was doomed to failure. Surprisingly for one who thought she couldn't care less about such frivolous issues, she found this conclusion deeply sad.

And even more surprisingly, as she reached the kitchen, she heard clapping. It started as the faintest splatter, like the first drops of rain on stone, and built up to a crescendo of table-thumping, whistling and yahooing. They were applauding her. May exhaled slowly and smiled. Then she punched the air with a clenched fist, and said, 'Yes!'

In theory she could now go home. But having been promised a taxi, May was reluctant to face the Tube, particularly after the huge gin Clorinda had poured her. Also, having decided to purloin her wages for herself, giving a cut to Slimeball only if Harriet insisted, she wouldn't go home without her money.

No, she would stay until Marcus or Clorinda came up with some cash. She would work out exactly how much cash while the guests ate their little people on plates. May had adjusted the amount up and down and sideways, but still gales of laughter emerged from the dining-room. The plates of food had a certain droll appeal, but were they really worthy of such hilarity? I shouldn't have opened so many bottles of wine, she thought. They're probably getting drunk as skunks. They'll be hours. I should have done a plate of sliced white bread and butter as blotting paper. They'd have loved it.

Boredom, rather than a sense of duty, drove May into stacking the dishwasher and tidying the kitchen, then she retired to the loo in search of some pleasant-smelling soap and some handcream. While there she had an idea which greatly lifted her jaded spirits. Why have a lukewarm, pathetic, dribbling apology for a shower on the boat when she could have a real humdinger here, saving time and precious water into the bargain? She felt perfectly entitled. She had cleaned the wretched shower, after all. It owed her one.

Quickly, before she could change her mind, she stripped off her clothes and stepped under the foaming stream. She could have stood there for hours while a hot Niagara massaged her scalp, her shoulders, her back, her calves. Through the thunder she became aware that someone was trying the door. But she took no notice. She wouldn't get out until her skin was hanging off in shreds, perhaps not even then. Whoever said that showers were quicker than baths had either never really needed to get clean, or hadn't experienced one like this. Eventually, reluctantly, her skin the colour of ripe strawberries and tingling exquisitely, she turned it off, and stood dripping in the silence.

The thunder of the shower was replaced by the thunder of someone banging on the door. They had obviously waited until the water was turned off before renewing their onslaught. May ignored it. There was a perfectly good bathroom upstairs, she was sure. She hadn't actually checked this out personally, but there was no way a house this size would have been satisfied with a single downstairs loo.

She rubbed a little Egoiste talc for men under her arms. Yes, this was obviously where the brisk, masculine showering got done. There would be a bath, probably pink or 'champagne' for lounging in upstairs. It would have a bidet as well as a loo. So whoever it was could bugger off up there and leave her alone.

The thought of having to drag her dirty clothes back on to her clean, damp body was horrid, particularly when she had left them on the floor, and they were wet. As she blotted herself with the handtowel, May toyed with the notion of raiding Clorinda's wardrobe. But, flexible though her morals were, they baulked at this. Besides, Clorinda's clothes wouldn't have suited her. She gathered her own into a bundle and had a brainwave – she would put them into the tumble-drier. This would at least warm them, making them slightly less unpleasant to put on.

The handtowel being far too small, May wrapped herself

in Marcus's damp one and emerged, clutching her clothes, her skin pink and her hair curling like a baby lamb's. The hot-shot lawyer was waiting, his expression easily as bad-tempered as his chicken nugget boy. Untouched by guilt, May smiled breezily at him. He may have been desperate, but she'd had the shower of a lifetime.

'Sorry, did you want the bathroom?'

'The upstairs one seems permanently locked.'

May shrugged, a foolish response given that she was wearing only a bathtowel. She gave the towel a hitch, wishing she'd knotted it more securely.

'Well never mind. I'm out now.'

The man's expression told her it was only just in time.

As the bolt went home behind him, May's towel slipped alarmingly, revealing most of her rear half. Just in time for me, too, she thought, chuckling, and tucked it back.

She had been dry and dressed for a long time when Clorinda and Marcus found her, sitting at the kitchen table with her head on her arms, fast asleep.

'Gosh, darling, I'm so sorry, we forgot all about you! How awful! We must call a cab.'

May demurred blearily but Marcus was being masterful again.

'Won't be easy to get a cab at this time of night, not to go into Central London. But I'll try. I'd take you myself, except I'm well over the limit.'

The hot-shot lawyer hove into view. He was in his early thirties, tall with black hair and blacker eyebrows, and his temper had not improved since May had kept him waiting for the loo. The effect, no doubt, of being stone-cold sober when all around him had long since lost the ability to walk a straight line.

'Whereabouts do you live?' he asked May.

'Paddington, sort of.'

'That's not much out of my way, I'll take you home.'

'Hugh, that's uncommonly kind of you.' Marcus appeared embarrassed. 'I would drive her myself . . .'

'It's all right,' May interrupted firmly. 'I'm not a parcel, I can perfectly well take the Tube.'

57

'Not at two in the morning, you can't,' said the lawyer. 'I suggest you find your coat.'

When May reappeared in her leather jacket, most of the gushing goodbyes and darling-it-was-wonderfuls had been said. Only the lawyer, who was wearing a long blue overcoat which emphasized his height and gave him a sinister resemblance to Christopher Lee as Dracula, remained.

Clorinda, who had gone along with the plan before, glanced at Hugh and suddenly put her hand on May's sleeve. 'You could easily stay the night, if you don't want to . . .'

Politeness prevented her from finishing her sentence. She could hardly suggest that May might feel uncomfortable going off in a car with a strange man, not when the man in question was in a position to further Marcus's career.

May smiled at her reassuringly. She had a low opinion of her own sex-appeal, and a high opinion of her ability to deliver a foot in the groin if it became necessary. Besides, she had had quite enough of the Stockbridges and badly wanted to go home.

'I'd be very grateful for a lift if this man is really going my way,' she said.

'Then come on,' said the man irritably.

May felt cold as they walked to where his car was parked. She hunched her shoulders and pulled up the collar of her jacket. The door clicked unlocked and she climbed in quickly, before he could do anything embarrassing like opening the door for her. As he got in and switched on the ignition she realized that he had had no intention of doing anything of the sort. She smiled into the collar of her jacket.

'Please don't feel obliged to entertain me with mindless chatter,' he said. 'I suggest you go to sleep. I'll wake you when we're near and you can give me directions.'

May shrugged, snuggled into the soft, leather upholstery and drifted into sleep.

'Whereabouts in Paddington do you live?'

May, who had been dozing happily, pulled herself together. 'Oh, if you drop me by the station, that will be fine.'

It was dark in the car, but May was very aware of her

companion's disapproval. 'I offered to take you home. Just tell me where you live.'

You asked for it, she thought. 'I live at Bryanston Moorings, on a narrowboat, on a canal. You can't actually get a car in there at night, the gate is locked.'

The man harrumphed, reminding May of her father, and drove on in silence.

'There's a car park over there where you can drop me.'

'I would prefer to see you safely home.'

May sighed. 'I will be perfectly safe. Really.'

Hugh shrugged off her thanks and winced as she slammed the door, but it was only after she had clambered aboard *The Rose Revived* that she saw the lights of his car move off.

'A true gent,' she chuckled, and opened the door of the boat.

CHAPTER SIX

May had realized Harriet was still up when she had seen the light shining across the water. She was glad. Marcus had written a cheque out to her without a murmur, unaware or uncaring of the fact that Quality Cleaners would send an invoice. She had hardly been able to believe her eyes when she saw it was for two hundred pounds.

Elated by this, and refreshed by her two naps, not to mention her wonderful shower, she longed to talk over her triumph. Harriet was making a cup of cocoa. She smiled when May appeared, but May instantly saw that she had been crying.

'Hi! What's the matter?'

'There's something I ought to tell you.'

'What?'

'We've been sold down the river.'

'What? By Slimeball?' May's heart began to sink.

Harriet nodded. 'He's completely ripped us off. He employed us under false pretences.'

'But how? How do you mean?'

'I mean that we all signed a contract which said he was taking us on for a probationary period of six weeks.'

'I didn't know that!'

'Nor did I. But we would've done if we'd read the contract. Apparently we agreed to be paid two-fifty an hour –'

'Two pounds fifty!'

'– for six weeks, and then we'd get paid the ten pounds an hour we were expecting.'

May was beside herself. She sat down on the side-bed, spluttering incoherently. Her gibberings became clearer as she remembered something. 'And I promised Mike I'd have some money by Monday, Tuesday at the latest! God! Why didn't we read the contract? I would never have agreed to those terms! They're tantamount to slavery!'

'We none of us would have signed if we'd read the contract, which is why he very cleverly manipulated us into *not* reading it. And what's more, although we've actually been working for him for seven weeks, he maintains he has the right to extend the probationary period for another six weeks. Because it's "subject to the discretion of the management".'

'Shit! Shit! Shit! Shit!'

'In other words, he can go on and on paying us two pounds fifty an hour, for as long as we put up with it. He has no intention of ever paying the wages he promised in the ad.'

'Oh bloody hell! What are we going to do?' May turned to Harriet, prepared to take on Slimeball single handed. But she sensed that, although she'd had time to get used to the idea, Harriet seemed even more upset.

Seeing her friend's distress, May calmed down a little, searching for something cheering to say. 'I did earn two hundred pounds tonight!' She pulled the cheque out of her pocket. 'And it's made out to me, and Slimeball's not going to get a penny!'

'That's wonderful,' said Harriet bleakly.

'It means I can give Mike more than the hundred he asked me for yesterday. And you won't have to worry about rent this week, or housekeeping. Oh Harriet! It'll be all right. I know it's an absolute bugger, but we'll sort something out. We can get other jobs . . .'

'I know, but it's not only Slimeball, though God knows, that's bad enough . . .'

'Well, what else has gone wrong? What else could there be?'

'It's Matthew,' she said.

May felt her knees go weak. Here she was railing about being swindled, when Harriet's son might be at death's door. 'He's not ill is he? Or had an accident?'

Harriet shook her head. 'No. No, it's not as bad as that. But I haven't seen him for over a month.'

There was obviously more to this than just Harriet missing

her child. 'Well, why don't you see him? If that's not a stupid question. Is the school far?'

'No. You get the train from Waterloo and either walk, or take a taxi.' Harriet had worked out how to get to Matthew's school almost as soon as she arrived in London.

'So what's the problem?'

'The school won't let me see him. I rang earlier.'

'What do you mean?' demanded May. 'They can't stop you seeing him! You're his mother.'

'My grandparents have told the school that I am not to be allowed to see Matthew. If I am, they'll take him away. They told his headteacher that I'm liable to abduct Matthew and so mustn't be allowed to see him.

'Surely, your grandparents can't be so cruel!'

'Yes they can. Apparently they are in the process of making Matthew a ward of court, and they have strictly forbidden the school to allow me to visit. They rubbed in the bad publicity the school would get if I did.'

'What did the school say, exactly?'

'It said – or rather the headmaster said, "I'm sorry, Miss Devonshire, we've had strict instructions from Mr and Mrs Burghley-Rice that you" – and he emphasized the "you", "are not to be allowed to visit Matthew."'

It was nearly three o'clock in the morning, and May was reeling with tiredness, but her ingenuity had had a very thorough workout. If she could just re-activate it, she might be able to be constructive. A good night's sleep would help, but knowing that Harriet wouldn't get any sort of a night's sleep if she didn't think of something, she went into the galley to make a hot drink.

Harriet remained silent. She had got her tears under control, but now depression had swamped her like a blanket, weighing her down, making it impossible to have a single positive thought. She declined May's offer of another cup of cocoa.

'I'm sure it can't be legal, you know.' May returned to the saloon, a crust of bread and butter propped on top of her mug. 'A school can't keep a child away from its mother.'

'You're not suggesting I roll up with half a dozen police-
men and take him by force?'

'No, no. It's just I'm sure there must be a way round it, if
it isn't absolutely legal.' May sipped her cocoa. 'Sorry, I was
given a lift home by a lawyer. He must have put the law into
my mind.' She chewed on her crust. 'I wonder why he said,
"you". I did get that right? The man definitely emphasized
the word "you"?'

Harriet nodded. 'Oh yes. It was definitely me.'

May swallowed. 'It's not the sort of word you'd emphasize
without reason.'

'Oh, he had a reason. He was emphasizing that I am not
allowed to see my child,' said Harriet.

'I know,' said May. 'But doesn't that mean that someone
else *could* see Matthew?'

'What do you mean?'

'I mean, I think its possible that if *I* rang the school, and
said I was Matthew's aunt, or godmother, or something, that
I could visit. And before you ask what good would that do
anyone, I could take him to the nearest sticky-bun shop.
Then you can give him a slap-up-feed, or whatever it is
mothers do on Saturday afternoons.'

Harriet bit her lip. 'I don't know – I mean – it seems a bit,
well, unlikely.'

'But worth a try?'

'Definitely, if you wouldn't mind ringing up and lying.'

'Oh, I don't mind lying in a good cause. But not now. It's
the middle of the night, I'll do it tomorrow.'

'That's awfully good of you, May. I'll be eternally
grateful.'

'And so you should be,' said May through a mouthful of
bread and butter.

Harriet almost smiled. 'And what about Slimeball? He
owes us all hundreds of pounds.'

'Well he doesn't owe me quite as much as the rest of
you, but I refuse to think about that now. Let's get you
and Matthew together first, and worry about Slimeball
later.'

Harriet opened her mouth to speak, but May's raised hand

stopped her. 'Please, Harriet, I know how grateful you are, and I really must get some sleep! Thank me in the morning!'

'Who do I ask for?'

'Mr Buckfast. Better make yourself Matthew's godmother. My grandparents might well have told the school that Matthew hasn't any aunts.'

'OK.'

'I'll dial,' said Harriet. 'I know the number by heart.' As soon as she got a ringing tone, Harriet stepped out of the phonebox, out of earshot.

May hardly had time to feel abandoned before the phone was answered. 'Can I speak to Mr Buckfast, please?' She waited while the secretary put her through.

'Buckfast speaking.'

'Um . . .' May's confidence dipped momentarily. She rallied it. 'I'm ringing to enquire if I could take Matthew Devonshire out for tea this afternoon. I am his godmother.'

'I'm sure that can be arranged. What did you say your name was?'

'May – Miss Sargent.'

'Well, Miss Sargent, the boys are allowed to be away from school from two in the afternoon until five-thirty. If you care to come to my office at two, he'll be waiting. Will that be convenient?'

'There is just one thing,' May dismounted rapidly from her high horse. 'Matthew doesn't know me very well – in fact, he may not remember me at all . . .'

'I understand, Miss Sargent. You wish me to tell Matthew who you are, and to reassure him about the strange lady taking him out to tea.'

'Yes,' May replied, not quite liking his use of the word 'strange' and mystified by the man's keen understanding of the situation. 'That's exactly what I mean.'

'Miss Sargent?'

'Yes?'

'I'm sure you understand that, as a school, we are in a delicate situation in matters of – security.'

Oh God, wasn't the plan going to work after all? 'Yes?'

64

'And therefore I may ask my brother to accompany you and Matthew to – wherever you decide to take him to tea.'

'Your brother?'

'Yes. He's visiting me today. Will that be acceptable to you?'

'But if your brother's going to see you, he's not going to want to spend his visit escorting me and Matthew to the local tearoom.'

'That needn't concern you, Miss Sargent. He'll be very happy to help.'

May shrugged, an action audible down the telephone wires. 'Whatever you say, then.'

May came out of the telephone box and was swiftly joined by Harriet who had been staring vacantly into the window of a shop called Underground Uglies.

'Well?'

'I think it's all right.'

'What do you mean? Did he suspect anything?'

'He certainly did. But he obviously thought that not letting you see Matthew was wrong, so he's fiddled it. I've got to take his brother along, to make sure I'm not a child molester, but otherwise, everything seems to be fine.'

For Harriet's sake, May had decided she needed to look respectable, to dress as a suitable companion for a bright nine-year-old to take tea with. But doing so presented a few problems inasmuch as all May's 'respectable' clothes were still at her mother's. She ended up borrowing one of Harriet's skirts and her black patent leather court shoes. She found a pair of navy tights which only had a small hole on the inner thigh, and put on a white shirt under the Fair Isle sweater which her mother had bought for her at an Oxfam shop. All she needed were some discreet pearls and a black velvet headband and, she was convinced, she would be the perfect Home Counties girl.

'Well? Do I look like someone's godmother?'

Harriet regarded her. In fact, May looked very appealing in her borrowed clothes. They enhanced the vulnerability which was usually hidden behind bib-and-braces straps and clumpy shoes. And she had nice legs. But though Harriet greatly appreciated her friend's efforts to conform, and although the elements were there, they didn't quite add up to the image of respectability May was seeking. Yet she doubted if Matthew's housemaster would be so accommodating if Matthew's fictitious godmother turned up in dungarees and high-laced boots.

'Well, far be it from me to say you look like a fairy.'

May threw a cushion at her.

CHAPTER SEVEN

They discussed tactics the entire journey. May, who had taken full credit for the plan up to now, had suddenly developed cold feet. How did a respectable girl go about luring a headmaster's brother away, so that a boy and his mother could be alone?

Harriet, who didn't care what May did so long as she had a chance to hug her son, was treating May's misgivings with less than her usual sympathy.

'You'll think of something. I have implicit faith in you, May.'

'Why?'

'You'll be OK when you're actually there. You've just got a bit of stage-fright. It's probably a good thing.'

'You've been spending too much time with Sally.'

'I'll go back to Churcham with the taxi . . .'

'But how am I supposed to get back to Churcham? You'll have to wait.'

'I can't come up to the door, or they won't let Matthew come. And I can't ask the taxi driver to lurk behind a hedge or he'll think he's participating in an abduction.'

'He is.'

Harriet took a deep breath. 'If you'd rather not go through with this, I'll pretend I'm the godmother. But the trouble is, Matthew and I are terribly alike, they might guess . . .'

May pulled herself together. 'Of course I want to go through with it. I'm just a bit nervous. God knows why. If the headmaster's brother hasn't got a car, I'll phone for a taxi,' she said. 'And pray the same one doesn't come to fetch me,' she added.

'Unlikely,' said Harriet as they walked out of the station and saw two rows of taxis waiting for the London train.

May shrugged and smiled and made a 'here goes nothing' face. 'Come on then,' she said, and led the way to a cab.

The driver knew exactly where Matthew's school was. May wondered somewhat grimly how often he had driven shivering little schoolboys sobbing for their mothers there. She pleated the hem of Harriet's skirt between agitated fingers, then noticed how dirty her fingernails were and turned her agitation to them. They'd been clean yesterday. How could she be a convincing godmother with filthy nails?

To Harriet, the drive seemed to last for ever. She couldn't believe that she would actually see Matthew, be able to put her arms round him and feel his small, lithe body again. Although she had survived nearly two months without him, the next few minutes would be like a lifetime in purgatory.

For May, it seemed only moments before she had been dropped at the end of a long drive, bitterly regretting not wearing her Doc Martens. Harriet's shoes were hell to walk in. But her stumbling progress up the gravel drive gave her plenty of opportunity to admire the building. It appeared to be a perfect Tudor manor house. She wasn't expert enough to tell if it was genuine Tudor or Stockbroker, but if the beams which segmented the building were fake, at least they had been left their natural grey-brown colour and hadn't been picked out in black.

It was small for a school, and built of soft pink brick which looked warm even in the chill of autumn. A huge rambling rose reared up the side of the building and a couple of scarlet buds still bloomed in the protection of the outer twigs. The only thing which spoilt its *Country Life* appearance was the lawn, which instead of being bowling-green velvet, had more in common with a moto-cross course. If May hadn't known how extremely unlikely it was, she would have thought it had been used for riding bicycles. But there must be some other explanation.

A boy wearing a baseball cap back to front appeared round the corner of the house on a skateboard. He slowed to a halt as he hit the gravel, sprang off, jumped on the end, caught the board as it flipped upwards and ran off with it tucked under his arm before May could speak. He was wearing jeans which gaped from thigh to ankle and were filthy. Excited screams and the sound of wheels thundering up and down echoed from around the corner. May recognized the noise of a skateboard ramp. She was more than a little surprised to find one here.

Unlike the ramp, the bell, when she finally reached the huge studded faded-oak door and pressed it, made no sound at all. The silence was unnerving. Should she assume the bell didn't work and bang the the huge, lion-headed knocker instead? But if the bell did work, she would annoy whoever was on their way to answer it. She should have kidnapped the skateboarder and demanded he take her to his leader.

She emptied some gravel out of Harriet's shoe, which had acquired a new scuff mark. If only helping Harriet hadn't involved so much pretence. She'd never been any good at acting at school. Tell the truth and get a hundred lines had been her motto. Did they still give lines, she wondered? Didn't they still cane little boys? Supposing Matthew told Harriet he was totally miserable, and they had to steal him? Oh why didn't somebody come?

She had just raised her hand to knock when she heard footsteps, keys being turned, and muffled instructions to get the hell out of the way. Hurriedly, she stepped back and a moment later a swarm of Labradors, some black, some golden, came out of the house. They were followed by a large man in a tweed jacket and green corduroy trousers. He had a reassuringly lived-in face, somehow familiar, with deep-set blue eyes and a generous, curling mouth.

'Bloody dogs,' he muttered before raising a politely enquiring eyebrow at May.

'Good afternoon,' said May, trying to feel haughty and dignified while the dogs frisked about her, thrusting their wet noses up her skirt. 'I'm May Sargent.'

'Go away, you horrible hounds!' said the man, and gestured across the churned-up grass to some distant trees.

As the dogs bounded away, May felt lonely and more nervous. Without the dogs to dilute the man's attention, she felt uncomfortably scrutinized.

'Sorry,' he said. 'Who did you say you were?'

'May Sargent. I've come to collect Matthew . . .'

With total horror, she realized she had forgotten Harriet's surname. Praying it would come back to her before she made a complete fool of herself, she smiled rather tightly. 'Can you tell Mr Buckfast I'm here?'

'I'm Tom Buckfast. Matthew is waiting in the office with my brother.' He put two fingers in his mouth and let forth a piercing whistle. The dogs, of which there were actually only five, came pounding back. Mr Buckfast smiled. 'It works on the boys, too.'

May's tightened throat relaxed a little. 'It must be nice for them, having the dogs.'

Mr Buckfast grunted. 'It's nice for the dogs having so much attention. And nice for me having so many willing walkers, but they can get rather much.' Another gesture and an 'off you go' and the dogs all careered down a passage, which to May's newly sensitized eye looked decidedly grimy. 'Come this way and I'll introduce you to Matthew – no, sorry, I mean I'll introduce you to my brother. Matthew you know.'

As it happened, Mr Buckfast had it right the first time. May had never seen Matthew before, but Mr Buckfast's brother – younger, thinner and far less approachable – was the hot-shot lawyer who had driven her to Paddington just over twelve hours earlier. His face and clothes were less in need of ironing than his brother's, and he got to his feet with a formality the headmaster lacked as May entered the room.

She recognized him instantly. It was the worst kind of nightmare – like waking up to find you really are walking naked down the High Street. But after a moment's blind panic she realized he was unlikely to recognize her. He had hardly seen her in a proper light, and in Harriet's clothes rather than a bathtowel, or her own dungarees, he would never make the connection even if she did seem familiar.

'Miss Sargent, this is my brother, Hugh Buckfast. Hugh, this is Miss Sargent, who's taking Matthew out today. My brother's kindly volunteered to stand in for Matthew's house-master, who's having a weekend away.'

May didn't hold out her hand and gave him the briefest conventional smile before turning her attention to Matthew who had risen politely.

'Hello, Matthew, I'm sure you won't remember me, but I'm May, an old friend of your mother's.'

Matthew had dark hair and fair skin, liberally freckled. Apart from different colouring, Harriet had been right, he looked exactly like his mother.

May inspected him for signs of bullying and demoralization but found none. His jeans weren't ripped and his sweatshirt was reasonably clean, but he still looked surprisingly up to date for the inmate of an institution. May was expecting hairy shorts, a sports coat, long socks, a tie with some sort of stripe in it, and shiny brown shoes. The runny nose and tearstained cheeks were missing too. He smiled shyly, but without surprise. 'My mother's talked about you lots.'

It occurred to May that Matthew had probably perfected the art of the white lie and half-truth in his cradle. May knew that Harriet wrote to Matthew every night, and phoned him sometimes. Of course she would have been mentioned.

'I hope you understand the need for my brother's presence,' said Mr Buckfast. 'In Matthew's case particularly. We've had very specific instructions. But he will be able to take you into town in his car, so he's not entirely useless.'

'I'm sure the security of all your pupils is equally important.' She gave Mr Buckfast junior, (or should that have been minor?) a brief, non-eye-contacting smile.

He didn't return the smile and didn't speak, but she felt his eyes on her, boring through her disguise like an X-ray. If only she had borrowed her parents' car, she could have taken charge. Having to cadge a lift from someone who thinks at any moment you might perpetrate a tug-of-love scandal was difficult. Sally, with her long legs and abundant charm, would have managed it far more easily.

Without looking at him, she could hardly deliver the significant glances which would give their chaperon the hint that it was time they left. His silence was killing her and she became more and more convinced that he had recognized her and was about to expose her at any moment. What he would

71

expose her as, she wasn't sure, but it was bound to be unflattering as well as a death-blow to the plan. A grandfather clock ticked with agonizing slowness, seemingly putting whole minutes between every tick and tock.

The headmaster seemed content to survey the people filling his study for as long as it took them to move.

'Are you hungry, Matthew?' May asked in desperation. Short of demanding to be led out to the car, this feeble ruse was all she could think of to get Buckfast minor to shift.

Matthew gave his pseudo-godmother a smile which told her he was still full of cowboy hotpot, but would be hungry if she needed him to be. 'Sort of.'

May, wondering how on earth a free-thinking young woman like her could possibly find herself in the headmaster's office of a boys' boarding school, even one as pleasantly scruffy as this, smiled back. Why didn't that wretched brother put everyone out of their misery and either expose her as a quasi-punk cook of dubious ability, hell-bent on kidnap, or let her take Matthew out to tea?

'If we could have a word in private, Miss Sargent,' said the headmaster. 'Hugh?'

Hugh detached himself from the wall and nodded to Matthew, who got up.

'Just wait outside a moment please, chaps,' said Mr Buckfast.

May, trembling slightly, had to remind herself that she had left school, and any outstanding prep was not this particular headmaster's responsibility. Also, unless they were extraordinarily telepathic, Hugh couldn't have passed his doubts on to his brother without even speaking.

He smiled as he shut the door. 'Miss Sargent, do sit down.'

May perched on the edge of a much-scratched leather chair.

'I'm sure I don't need to tell you how sensitive the situation with Matthew is. His great-grandparents are insistent that his mother isn't allowed to see him and I want to keep their confidence. If they think we're not backing them up, they'll take him away, and he'll have all the upset of another . . .' he allowed himself a smile, 'perhaps less unconventional school. And for his sake, I don't want that.' He raised a hand to silence May's interruption. 'Personally I feel it's barbaric, which is why I'm prepared to allow Matthew to go out with you. You are meeting his mother in town?'

May nodded, blushing furiously. It had seemed such a clever plan. And this man had seen through it, probably from the first moment he spoke to May on the telephone.

'But provided I have your word that you've no intention of taking Matthew, that you do intend to bring him back here, before half-past five, I will allow it.'

'Of course we'll bring him back. Harriet and I live on a boat. We've nowhere to put Matthew even if we did intend to steal him. Although how a mother could be accused of stealing her own child, God knows.'

Mr Buckfast put out a hairy, comforting hand. 'I'm spending every moment I can trying to persuade Mr and Mrs Burghley-Rice – Matthew's great-grandparents – not to make him a ward of court. They've overreacted badly to Miss Devonshire leaving home. I have a little influence over them. Let me stay in a position to use it.'

May returned his friendly smile and hoped he had children of his own. 'I promise you, Harriet only wants to reassure herself that Matthew's all right.'

Mr Buckfast rose to his feet in a way guaranteed to rid his study of any lingering parent. 'That's what I thought. I appreciate your help in this matter. Matthew is a delightful boy, but he needs to reassure himself about his mother's happiness as much as she does about his. My brother will drive you into town now.'

He opened his office door. 'Well, if you lot go and hit the high spots,' he addressed his brother and Matthew, 'I can get on with some work. Don't eat too much, Matthew, you know how I feel about blokes chucking up in the dorm.'

May watched Matthew respond to this combination of slang and solicitude and realized that while the whole concept of prep schools was anathema to her, this one could have been a lot worse.

'After you, Miss Sargent,' said Hugh.

73

Trying hard not to scuttle, May and Matthew preceded Hugh down the corridor. May was convinced that Hugh had recognized her, but had decided not to say anything. The thought of spending an afternoon in the company of one who had probably given him violent indigestion the night before was probably as agonizing for him as it was for her.

His car was parked in a stable-yard at the back of the building. The skateboard ramp was now deserted, but the dogs were all there, frolicking about. They woofed respectfully at Hugh Buckfast, but fell on Matthew as if he were a Sunday joint.

'Don't you mind being savaged by those greedy hounds, Matthew?' asked Hugh. 'Personally, I think they're a bloody nuisance.'

Matthew was indignant. 'But they're very well trained. If you tell them to buzz off, they do.'

'Really?' said May. 'Show us.'

'Yes, do,' said Hugh. 'Otherwise they'll be in the car ripping the upholstery the moment I open the door.'

Matthew used the same sweeping gesture with his arm that his headmaster had used. 'Home, dogs, go home!' The dogs rushed off obligingly.

'Where have you sent them?' asked May, extremely impressed. 'To their kennels?'

Matthew shook his head. 'They don't have kennels. They've gone to the kitchen to see what's left from lunch.'

'Thoroughly unhygienic, if you ask me,' said Hugh. He opened both front and rear passenger doors. 'Do get in, Miss Sargent.'

Matthew and May climbed into their respective seats, Matthew less unnerved by Hugh's brusqueness than May, who had a childish desire to giggle. Now she and Matthew were actually on their way to Harriet, she felt skittish with relief.

'Now, Matthew,' she said, turning round to check that Matthew had managed his seatbelt. 'Mr Buckfast minor doesn't like mindless chatter while he's driving. It distracts him. So no talking till we get there, please.'

Hugh looked at May in bemusement and horror. 'Whatever makes you say that?'

May smiled cheerily at him. 'You made it quite clear last night. Or have you forgotten?'

Hugh's mouth opened and closed again and settled into what in anybody else would have been a smile. 'So you're the Stockbridges' cook. I knew I'd seen you somewhere but couldn't work out where.'

May nodded, surprised at his description of her. 'I'm also Matthew's godmother.'

Hugh now definitely smiled. 'The one not invited to the christening, I assume?'

May narrowed her eyes at him. 'I can't think why you should say that.'

'From what I've heard about Matthew's great-grandparents, you'd be the last person they'd allow to sponsor their beloved great-grandchild.'

'You're very rude, considering we've only just met.'

He turned to look queryingly at her. 'You're not the model of conventional good manners yourself.'

May was indignant. 'Yes I am! Well, sometimes.' Huffily, she fastened her seatbelt. 'Can be if I want to.'

Hugh's eyebrows crinkled into an expression of amused disbelief.

May sighed. If only she'd kept her mouth shut. Now he would probably refuse to be lured away on the grounds that she was an irresponsible person and therefore her friend probably was too. Sally would have been far better at this. If she was bent on seduction, she wouldn't let herself get sidetracked into being childish.

'I assume Matthew's mother is waiting at the Comfy Pew?' He jerked an interrogative eyebrow at May.

'Er – I think so. Probably.' Please God. Harriet had told May that there would be a place where the parents always took the boys and she would find out which it was and do likewise.

To May's intense relief, the patron saint of dubious exploits had smiled on them and Harriet was in the café, nursing a pot of tea. She rose to her feet when she saw

75

Matthew, who ran between the clutter of tables into her arms. There was an uncharacteristic lump in May's throat as she and Hugh slowly followed.

'It's all right, Mum, really. I'm fine . . .' Matthew was saying.

Harriet bravely blinked away her tears and grasped the menu. She was clutching it to her when May introduced Hugh.

'This is the headmaster's brother, Hugh Buckfast.'

Hugh put out a hand, crushed Harriet's and then dropped it. 'How d'you do? You won't need us, I'm sure. We'll pick you up outside here in a couple of hours.'

'Hello, yes, thank you,' said Harriet, almost forgetting the conventional responses in her joy at seeing Matthew.

Hugh took hold of May's arm, as if he imagined she might suddenly declare a yearning for a plate of egg and chips, and marched her out.

'Do you want to see if we can find a pub, or shall we go for a walk?' he said. 'Unless you want to go shopping. In which case, you go alone.'

May didn't particularly want to spend the afternoon with Hugh Buckfast, but she hated shopping and the thought of spending two hours gazing into shop windows at things she couldn't afford even if she had wanted them was even less appealing.

'No thank you. A walk would be fine. But not too far,' she added quietly. 'Harriet's shoes aren't designed for hiking, not with my feet in them, anyway.'

The traffic in Churcham High Street was fairly heavy and she had spoken more to herself than him. Hugh, who was threading his way decisively through the Saturday afternoon shoppers, must have had the hearing of a cat. He stopped and turned to look at May. 'Why on earth are you wearing Harriet's shoes?'

May shrugged and smiled. 'It's a long story.'

Hugh frowned questioningly. 'One that I need to hear?'

May allowed a woman with a pushchair and two satellite toddlers to get past her. Perhaps the school, via Hugh, should hear Harriet's side of things. The headmaster had

76

sounded sympathetic. If he knew about Harriet's unloving upbringing, her flight to London and her struggle to become an artist, he might bend the rules for her.

'Possibly. But it's Harriet's story, not mine.'

'Let's go to the park then.'

Muttering to the absent Harriet that if her shoes were ruined, it had been in a good cause, May set off after him, struggling to keep up. Hugh guided them to a park which was surrounded by the tallest yew hedge May had ever seen.

'Apparently they collect the clippings for some cancer research thing,' said Hugh.

'Oh.' It was all May could think of to say.

'So, you were going to tell me why you were wearing Harriet's shoes.'

May made a dismissive gesture. 'That's just dressing up, really. We thought I'd look more like a godmother if I looked more – well – respectable.'

May couldn't be sure, but she had a feeling that the cough which suddenly afflicted Hugh was actually a rude guffaw. 'You mean, less like a punk moonlighting as a dustman?'

May managed to look extremely offended. 'You mean a sanitation engineer. In a word, yes.'

Hugh chuckled. 'Well, I can't blame you for thinking that, but actually my brother would have probably preferred the dungarees and Doc Martens.'

'I'll remember next time.' She kicked at a pile of dead leaves and nearly lost Harriet's shoe in the process.

It was going to be a long afternoon.

CHAPTER EIGHT

'So go on. Harriet has a tale of woe and you're anxious to get it off your chest?'

May considered complaining about his reference to that particular part of her anatomy, but decided against it. There were more important issues at stake.

'Harriet's not the only one with a sob story. And I'm not particularly anxious to tell you Harriet's life history. But I do think your brother ought to know.'

'Know what? About her repressive childhood, unwanted granddaughter who produces an illegitimate son who becomes the apple of his great-grandparents' eye? It's fairly standard stuff. I think I know most of it.'

May ran a few steps to catch up with him. 'Not the bit about Harriet running away to London to become an artist, you don't.'

'Oh, no. I didn't know about that. I don't read much romantic fiction.'

May's indignation came out as a strangled mew.

'But now that you've told me, I can't say I'm surprised that her grandparents weren't thrilled by the idea. Couldn't she have learned to type or something useful?'

'She tried to. If her grandparents had let her, she'd have gone to secretarial college or something. But they wouldn't hear of it. They insisted that her place was at home, skivvying for them.'

'Slavery in the Home Counties?'

'It does happen! Harriet had to teach herself to type on an ancient portable she bought at a jumble sale . . .'

'I'm surprised she didn't write a Booker Prize winner, while she was about it.'

'You're being incredibly obtuse and unsympathetic.

Harriet works like a demon. Honestly, she's been treated like Cinderella all her life!'

'I haven't been to the panto for a while, but I'm sure that last time I went, Cinderella didn't have an illegitimate child.'

May's sense of humour pushed its way past her frustration. 'No? I've never been too sure where Buttons fits in myself.'

'Buttons is the boot-boy,' said Hugh sternly. 'He helps Cinderella. But you're getting off the point.'

'Not really. It's because of all those years of cooking and cleaning that Harriet got so good at it. Which is how she got involved with Slimeball Slater – or should I say, Quality Cleaners.'

He shot her a querying glance. 'And how did you meet Harriet?'

May smirked. 'I'm a Quality Cleaner too!'

'Is that what you do? You're a *cleaner*?'

'For my sins.'

'Then what were you doing cooking dinner for the Stockbridges?'

With everything that had happened since, May had managed to blot most of last evening out of her mind. Now, the chicken nugget people, with their frozen pea eyes and potato hair rose up to haunt her. 'You may well ask!'

Her expression made Hugh wish he hadn't.

'I arrived at the house, all prepared for a couple of hours ambling about with a duster, to discover I was expected to cook for a dinner party!'

'Why didn't you ring your employer and get him to send someone else?'

'There isn't anyone else! Me, Harriet and Sally are the sum total of Quality Cleaners! Besides, it was a challenge. Mrs Stockbridge left a menu and meant to leave some money, only she forgot. So there was I, forced to cook a posh meal for eight when I can't boil an egg. But even if I had been a *cordon bleu* chef there was still damn all to cook with that wasn't letter-shaped. I had to do the best I could.'

She stopped, giving him an opportunity to tell her what a marvellous job she'd done in the circumstances. He didn't.

'I see.'

'And when I got home – when you'd *driven* me home – I found Harriet crying. It turns out that our slimeball of a boss got us to sign a contract agreeing to be paid a tiny amount for a probationary period . . .' she paused momentarily, '. . . which somehow we'd overlooked. Anyway, although we've been working longer than the six weeks, he can continue the probationary period as long as he likes.'

She had time to wonder what it was about Hugh which had made her tell him all their innermost secrets before he asked the inevitable question.

'I gather you didn't read the contract before you signed it?'

'No.'

He didn't seem surprised. 'But you must have noticed you weren't being paid what you expected when you got your wage slips?'

'Wage slips! That's a laugh! He never actually paid us at all! He just gave us little bits of money, going on about "administrative hiccups". And I feel really bad, because Harriet has given me almost every penny she got out of Slimeball for rent. She's my lodger.'

'But I thought you lived on a boat?'

'I do. I bought it in the summer but only just discovered there were thousands of pounds owing on mooring fees.'

He would have done really well as an interrogator, thought May. He wouldn't even have to torture people. Something about him made you confess all your sins, your life history, with him hardly even asking a question. For someone who was a lot less sympathetic than most bank managers when being asked for unsecured loans, it was quite an art.

'And then, to cap it all,' she went on, unable to stop. 'Harriet told me how she'd rung the school and heard she wasn't allowed to see Matthew.'

She glared in way which implied she held him personally responsible. He was responsible for letting her blurt out not only Harriet's problems, but her own, as well.

'So you thought of a wizard wheeze which would make everything all right?'

May felt incredibly deflated. She had wanted so much to

help Harriet, and all she had succeeded in doing was getting this odious man to laugh at them. 'It was silly of me to imagine that a man like you would understand. You just don't have the imagination.'

'Oh?'

'No one as straight as you are, who probably votes Conservative and supports the re-introduction of capital punishment, could possibly understand how hard it is to have to stifle your dream and make cheese straws for your grandparents' bridge parties!' Forgetting what nearly happened last time, May kicked at a Coke can in her frustration. Harriet's shoe landed several feet away and there was a muddy puddle between it and May's foot. May wanted to howl.

Hugh picked up the can and fetched the shoe. 'You're making a lot of sweeping assumptions, considering we've barely met each other.' He supported her while she found her way into the shoe.

'Anyone who drives a big black car and has a brother who runs a prep school is bound to be like you.'

'And what am I like?'

May knew she was using him as the butt of her anger and frustration, but she couldn't stop herself. 'Oh how should I know! Right-wing, overbearing, sexist,' she threw in, remembering his remark about dustmen.

He was surprisingly unoffended. 'Well, in order to avoid being called mean as well, I'd better buy you an ice-cream.'

He wasn't at all the sort of person to eat ice-cream with, but as she was terribly aware of how badly she was behaving, she couldn't refuse this peace offering. 'Thank you, that would be very nice,' she said meekly.

Hugh, who hadn't bought an ice-cream for himself, handed her hers, and said, 'So what are you going to do about this man who's been defrauding you?'

May shrugged. 'Oh, I don't know. We'll think of something. But I'm sorry for burdening you with it. It's none of your business. I had no right to chew your ear off.'

May was not good at apologizing, and that was one of her best. He took no notice.

'I assume you're not qualified to do anything more sensible than cleaning?'

'Cleaning is sensible! If we'd been paid what we'd been promised, I'd have paid off a chunk of my debts, and both Sally and Harriet would have had deposits for flats by now.'

'So it's sensible. Is it satisfying?'

'It's all I can do!'

'Rubbish, you just haven't found your vocation, that's all. What about the other girl,' he went on, not giving May a chance to argue. 'Sally, did you say her name was?'

'Sally is an actress. But only sometimes.'

'Oh. Well, you'd better set up in business for yourselves. That way you can charge people less but you can keep most of the money you earn. Presumably, this Slimeball person charges quite a lot?'

'Oh I expect so.' May had filed this piece of advice away, but didn't want to discuss it now. 'Is there no way we can get the money that Slimeball owes us?'

'I think it's very unlikely, if you signed a contract. But I'll have a look at it for you if you like.'

May, having eaten her ice-cream, wiped her sticky fingers on Harriet's skirt. 'Oh, I'd hate to put you to so much trouble.'

'No trouble. I could call at your boat tomorrow, if that's convenient.'

May looked up at him. He was the archetypal establishment figure, representing everything she rejected and rebelled against. Why was he offering to do them a favour? It was probably something to do with caring for the peasant classes. For Harriet's sake, she would have to endure it. 'That would be very kind.'

'You do have a copy of the contract?'

If you haven't, Harriet, she swore, silent but fervent, I will personally keelhaul you. 'Of course.'

'Good. Shall I call about six, then?'

'Fine,' said May, through gritted teeth.

'I shall look forward to it, Miss Sargent.'

It was only with an enormous effort of will that May managed not to stick her tongue out.

★

'Once Matthew knew that I was all right,' Harriet told May on the train going home, bumping her teeth against a polystyrene cup of coffee, 'he reckoned that school wasn't too bad at all. He really likes having so many companions his own age, and he loves the dogs. I gather the school is pretty messy, not at all like home.' Harriet took another gulp. 'Mr Buckfast told them all that only wimps are ashamed of crying, and that he cries whenever he sees *Goodbye Mr Chips*, and that his wife cries during *Neighbours*.'

'Golly.'

'My grandparents would die if they knew Matthew was allowed to watch Australian soaps.'

'Yes. I was wondering, why on earth did your grandparents choose such an unusual school for Matthew?'

Harriet sighed and smiled. 'Because it's incredibly expensive. The Buckfast family have owned that house for generations. Tom Buckfast set up the school so they could afford to keep it on and because he loves children. But they've an entry in Debrett as long as your arm, and all sorts of very grand children get sent there. Matthew's there because my grandparents are such crashing snobs.' Seeing May's horror, Harriet chuckled. 'Funny how things turn out, isn't it?'

'Hilarious,' May agreed. 'Especially when I tell you that Hugh Buckfast is a hot-shot lawyer and has agreed to look at our contract with Slimeball for us. And if you haven't got a copy of it, I shall swing for you.'

'It's all right, I have. I insisted on taking it away with me. But that's wonderful!'

'He wasn't very hopeful that we'd be able to do anything, but he did make a suggestion which I thought was rather good.'

'What?'

'That we set up our own business. We can charge less than Slimeball, but take most of the money for ourselves.'

'I suppose so.'

'There is a lot of money in cleaning. Slimeball has proved that. If we actually got the money we earned, or most of it, we'd soon have enough to do what we want to in life.'

'Mmm.' Harriet stared out of the window wondering if this was true.

'And if we worked for ourselves, we could work when we want. If you need time to paint, or Sally got offered a part, we could accommodate each other.'

'Could we?'

'And think of the people we've worked for. Most of them would probably employ us direct, especially as we'd be so much cheaper. I bet he charges way over the odds.'

'Wouldn't that be illegal? Taking his clients?'

May ruffled her hair. Now it was slightly longer, it was starting to curl, taking the edge off the severity of the cut. 'Don't suppose so. But so what if it is? He's diddled us, it's only right that we should diddle him.'

'But it takes money to set up a business. We'd need some sort of office, all sorts of things.'

'I've *got* money,' said May smugly. 'I've got a cheque made out to me personally, for two hundred pounds. And why do we need an office when we've got a perfectly good narrowboat? All we need is a mobile phone.'

Harriet sighed. 'Two hundred won't be enough, and I thought you had to give a hundred of that to Mike? But I've got some savings, and I dare say Sally has too.'

May suddenly realized what she was asking of Harriet. She was asking her to put all her dreams on hold in order to set up a cleaning business, when what Harriet wanted was to paint.

'I don't think you should use your savings, Harriet. I mean, why should you?'

'I'm not qualified for anything else, May. I might as well get paid properly for cleaning.'

'We'll ask Sally what she thinks,' said May. 'But if either of you dislike the idea, we'll have to make a plan B.'

Sally had confirmed that Piers was out when May telephoned, but was crying when she opened the door. She tried frantically to disguise the fact with a cough and ended up choking. By the time she had been thumped firmly on the back by May, the tears had dried up.

She sniffed loudly and wiped her nose on her sleeve. She was wearing one of Piers's white shirts without cufflinks, and had plenty to wipe it on. 'Oh God, sorry about that. Come in.'

'What's the matter?' asked Harriet, who in spite of the coughing had recognized tears when she saw them.

'Nothing really. It's Bastard Piers. He's left me – or thrown me out. One or the other.'

'Oh Sal, I'm so sorry,' said Harriet.

'On a Saturday night too! I meant to bloody well leave him!'

May seemed confused. 'The end result's the same, isn't it?'

'No,' said Sally, having found a ball of tissue, 'it's not.' She stuffed the tissue into her capacious sleeves. 'But I suppose it's only a technical difference. Come in.'

'So what happened?' asked May.

Sally led the way into the kitchen and put the kettle on. 'He told me when he finally got back here last night that he's got another woman, and was going away and that he didn't want me here when he gets back. He's going to be gone for a month.'

Harriet bit her lip. 'Poor you. You must be devastated.'

'But you didn't love him, did you? I mean, he was a complete pig.' May sat herself down at the breakfast bar, prepared to back up this statement.

Harriet dug her in the ribs. 'May!'

'Oh it's all right,' said Sally. 'May's right. He's a pig and I knew it. It's just being dumped for another woman I don't like. But it had become a dreadful strain living with him. Is tea all right? He bloody well locked the cupboard under the stairs.'

'Tea's fine,' said Harriet, not quite grasping the significance of the cupboard.

'Oh – that's where we keep the booze,' Sally explained. 'Herb tea or ordinary?'

'Ordinary.'

'Assam, Earl Grey or Darjeeling?'

'Just make the tea!' said May. 'We've got a proposition.'

85

'But if now's a bad time . . .' said Harriet.

'Oh no,' said Sally. 'It's as good a time as any, I expect.'

'At least you won't have to rush home and cook his meals now,' said May, realizing, a few minutes too late, that she'd been rather unsympathetic about Sally's broken heart.

'I won't have anywhere to rush to,' said Sally, rummaging in a cupboard for something to eat with the tea.

May waved her hand. 'Oh, you've got a month! Plenty of time to find somewhere else. And if all else fails, you can come and live with us.'

Sally was warmed by the offer but a little chilled at the prospect. 'That's sweet of you. I certainly won't be able to afford the flat I was saving for, although it was tiny. Let's go through to the sitting-room. I want to hear this proposition.'

'It's Slimeball Slater,' said May, when she had sunk almost out of sight into the grey leather sofa. 'He's conned us.'

'I thought as much. How?'

Harriet, who hadn't sat down, said, 'You tell her, May. I think I'll go to the loo.'

By the time she returned, Sally had been fully informed of their day in the country and Slimeball's perfidy.

'And there's no way we can get our money?'

'Hugh Buckfast – you know, the headmaster's brother? – is coming round tomorrow evening to look at the contract, but I don't suppose we can. So we thought –' May went on, 'well, actually, it was Hugh who suggested it, – that we'd set up our own business. We could charge the clients less than Slimeball does but pocket the lot.'

'That's not dishonest, is it?' Sally sat with her legs slung over the arm of a chair. Harriet's fingers longed for a piece of charcoal.

'I dunno. But I've already got a cheque made out to me. Two hundred pounds. Once you've started on the path of dishonesty, it's a swift glide down to the bottom.'

'And if he's diddled us,' said Sally. 'We're entitled to diddle him.'

Harriet was not convinced. 'We'll have to speak to the clients, explain what we're doing. If they choose to break off their contract with Slimeball and come with us, that's OK.

86

But we're not,' she looked reprovingly at May, 'to just tell them to give us the money direct.'

'Oh OK,' said May. 'It was a one-off. I had to cook for a dinner party, Sal. It was ghastly.'

'But we'll need a phone,' said Sally. 'And now Bastard Piers has done the dirty on me, we can't use this one.'

'We thought we'd get a mobile, so we can use the boat as an office,' said May.

'Aren't we going to need working capital, or something? Will two hundred pounds be enough?' asked Sally.

'It should be, to begin with,' said May. 'I mean, we use their cleaning materials.'

'There's advertising,' said Harriet.

'I shouldn't think we need to advertise much,' said Sally. 'If we just tell our loyal clients what we're doing, they're bound to pass the word round.'

'I think some leaflets would be a good idea,' said Harriet. 'Not all that expensive, and they would make us look more official. I could put them through the other doors in the Cheyne Walk building, for instance.'

'The trouble is, we need to start now,' said May. 'We can't afford to have a period when we're not earning anything.'

'There's no reason why we shouldn't start now,' said Sally, considerably more cheerful. 'Piers has got a photo-copier. We could do the leaflets now and put the telephone number on when we've got one.'

'Diddling Piers and Slimeball in one easy movement,' said Harriet drily.

'You're the artistic one, Harriet,' said May ignoring this. 'Design something!'

'I may be artistic, but I'm also dead beat,' Harriet yawned. 'And I told Matthew I'd ring him.'

'You can ring from here,' said Sally. 'In fact, why don't you both stay the weekend. We could do the leaflets in the morning.'

May saw that Sally needed the company, but she badly wanted her own space. 'I suppose I could stay if you really want me to,' she said. 'But I can't even write so people can read it. You two would be far better off without me.'

'If I can use the phone and have a bath,' said Harriet, 'I'll be as artistic as you like.'

May, suddenly pleased at the prospect of having her boat to herself, picked up her jacket and put it on. 'Then I'll leave you two to play with felt-tip pens and go home. Just tell me where the contract is, Harriet. I've got a hot-shot lawyer to see. Not to mention a boatyard owner to sweet-talk.'

CHAPTER NINE

Mike-the-Boatyard was not impressed with May's news.

'Working for yourselves isn't easy. It's not just a matter of taking the money,' he said. 'You've got to keep books, you've got tax, insurance, VAT – all kinds of things you need to think about.'

'I know. But working for someone else hasn't been a barrel of laughs and if Slimeball can do all that, we can.'

'You haven't got any capital, for a start.'

May was about to tell him about her two hundred pounds, but realized just in time that if Mike knew about it, he would claim it. 'We don't need much. Harriet and Sally are doing some leaflets. Sally's boyfriend's got a photocopier.'

May didn't describe Piers as being an 'ex' boyfriend, either. She was operating a need-to-know policy.

'What does he think of this idea?'

She didn't want to lie, though. 'He's away. But I'm sure he'll be in favour of such enterprise.' She got up, a confident smile adding to the impishness of her expression. 'So, I'll let you have the hundred at the end of the week, OK?'

'It was supposed to have been for the end of last week. I can't go on like this for ever. You'll find, when you're running your own business, that it's people who won't pay what they owe that give you all the grief.'

'Well, circumstances alter cases. But I must go. I've got our solicitor coming over soon, to advise us.'

'That's something, at least. But I've only put up with the situation because it's you, May.'

'What do you mean, because it's me?'

He paused for a long time. 'A lot of people round here seem very fond of you. But the fact you're the local problem-solver won't protect you for ever.'

May laughed at what she supposed was a joke and clattered back to the boat feeling less buoyant than she had sounded. Setting up in business was bound to be difficult. And if she had to give Mike half their capital, they would be drastically underfunded. And while she may have earned her reputation as a problem-solver, it was either with physical things, like wood and tools, or people. Anything that involved maths was way out of her area. Still, Harriet was bound to able to keep books and things. It couldn't be that difficult, could it?

Although Harriet and Sally both had a little money, she was determined to use it only as a last resort. It was her boat which was at risk, after all. The thought of borrowing money from her parents flitted into her mind and flitted out again. They would pay for her to run away and join a travelling circus if they thought that was what she wanted, and would certainly sponsor her in her own business, but she refused to involve them. She was twenty-four years old. If she didn't stand on her own two feet now, she never would.

Her brothers both had good jobs and no commitments, but the hell they would put her through before lending her money made asking them only a slightly more attractive option than living in a cardboard box. No, they would have to convert Slimeball's clients, find new ones, and work their way out of trouble.

She stepped aboard *Shadowfax*. Jed would be stirring soon. It was a pity she got to see him so seldom. He was a kindly, supportive vegan, who smoked roll-ups in special cigarette papers he had to send away for, because ordinary ones used animal products. He kept body and soul together in a casual, laid-back way, which didn't involve getting heated, but got the work done.

But her company for that evening would be far less congenial: the hot-shot lawyer now standing on the far bank. He was bound to be critical, and as Harriet was still at Sally's she would have to face him alone.

Thanks to Harriet's recent presence, the boat was fairly tidy. Just as well; if Hugh Buckfast found the boat in a shambles, he was bound to make one of those dry, under-stated little comments he specialized in. He was also bound to use words like 'tax', 'insurance' and 'VAT' in the same irritating way that Mike had. The need-to-know policy would have to remain in operation.

'Hello!' May called. 'If you cross the lock, you can walk round. I'll meet you.'

Hugh raised a hand and stepped on to the lock gate. Ivan, a young man who lived with his dog on a converted lifeboat, and made his living as a drummer in a jazz band, a sign-writer, or a welder, depending on how the work went, joined her.

'Hi, May! How are things?'

May made a face. 'Not wonderful. I owe Mike loads and loads and my boss has been ripping us off. Me and my friends are going to set up in business together to try and get some cash. What about you?'

'All right. Got a gig up West which pays quite well.' Ivan suddenly noticed Hugh, making his way along the pontoons. 'Who's this geezer?'

Hugh was wearing cord trousers, a navy-blue guernsey and waterproof jacket more suited to sailing than to narrow-boats. In spite of this relatively casual gear, May was certain everyone could tell just by looking at him that he spent most of his time in a suit. While not exactly embarrassed by his arrival, she did feel obliged to explain his presence to Ivan, who wore a bandana round his head and three earrings in one ear.

'Um, he's a solicitor, actually,' she explained to Ivan.

Ivan was impressed. 'Jesus! Mike's not hassling you, is he?'

'I hope not. Why? Does he do that sort of thing?'

Ivan nodded, but before he could say more, Hugh arrived and he drifted away. May noted Hugh's eyes follow Ivan's slight, anarchic figure as he leapt on to his lifeboat, and felt instantly defensive. She forced herself to remember that Hugh had come for her benefit, not his own.

'Hello. It's very kind of you to come.'

His eyes crinkled as if he might be amused, but didn't want to commit himself. 'You don't sound as if it's kind.'

May pulled herself together. She must not be churlish. He

was on their side. He was helping them. 'Don't I? Sorry. I'm just a bit worried.' She forced a smile. 'Come aboard. See the headquarters of our new business.'

He climbed aboard *Shadowfax* and from there, on to *The Rose Revived*.

'It's a lovely boat.'

May's resentment evaporated; she felt like a mother whose baby is being admired. 'Yes it is, isn't it? I've done a lot of work on her. I'd hate to lose her.' She opened the doors. 'Do go in.'

Hugh bent and angled his body through the opening. Once in the saloon, he straightened up only partly, to avoid hitting his head.

May chuckled. 'You'd better sit down. You're too tall for narrowboats.'

Hugh sat. 'Some might say narrowboats don't have enough headroom.'

May laughed again. 'Well, yes. Some of them do have a bit more than this. Would you like a cup of tea, or something?' She should really be offering him a gin and tonic or a glass of sherry, but the commissariat didn't run to it.

'I'm fine, thanks.'

May perched on the stove opposite him.

'Have you got the contract?'

'Oh yes. It's here.' May handed him the wad of paper which Harriet had stuck to a picture with Blu-Tack so that May wouldn't lose it.

Hugh spent agonizing minutes reading it. Eventually, he looked up. 'There's no earthly point in trying to fight this. You've been suckered, like many before you. Your best bet is to put it down to experience.' May nodded. 'Are you sure you really want to work for yourselves? It's not as easy as it sounds, you know.'

'Oh yes, definitely. We need to earn a lot of money, fast. I couldn't do that with my qualifications. Nor could the other two, unless Sally got an acting job. She might get lucky, but you can't depend on it. We know we can clean, and we know there are people willing to pay for cleaning. By cutting out Slime –, Slater, we'll be quids in.'

Hugh continued to look doubtful, but said no more. 'Well you won't need to worry about registering for VAT for a while. Can you do basic bookkeeping?'

May crossed her fingers behind her back and nodded. 'Harriet can.'

'Keep a record of everything you spend, and everything you earn, and don't lose any sort of receipt, even if it's just a scrap of paper. If you never throw anything away you shouldn't go too far wrong.'

'Right.' May tried to picture herself as the sort of person who kept receipts but the leap of imagination was too much for her.

'And you must register with the Inland Revenue and the DSS.'

'Right,' May said, again mentally delegating this task to Harriet. Just the words 'Inland Revenue' were enough to bring May out in spots.

'You must open a separate bank account for the business, of course.'

'Well, of course we'd do that!' This notion had genuinely crossed May's mind and she was indignant that he was treating her as if she were completely stupid.

'And you should have a proper partnership drawn up, by a lawyer.'

'Um . . .'

'I'll do it if you like.'

'It's very kind of you to suggest it, but – I don't think that will be necessary. We're all very good friends.'

'It just that if you don't, if any debt is incurred, any one of the individual partners could be held liable. If it's the cost of drawing up –'

'No! No. It's nothing like that – it's just we trust each other, and have no intention of running up any debts.' But he had guessed right. May had no intention of using a penny of their precious capital on legal fees. Besides, she didn't want him knowing just how shoe-string their budget was.

She got up, and was about to thank him and indicate it was time he left, when instead, she found herself renewing the offer of tea. Rather to her surprise, he accepted. She was in the galley making it, when there was a knock on the door and Ivan appeared.

'Hi!' he said to Hugh who had got to his feet. 'May?'

May called through, 'Hugh, this is Ivan, Ivan this is Hugh. Do you want tea, Ivan?'

'I'd rather borrow your big wrench,' said Ivan.

'Engine seized again?' May came through carrying a couple of mugs with a tin balanced on them.

'Yeah. Is it all right if I help myself?'

May nodded. 'You know where it is.'

When Ivan had gone, Hugh asked. 'Do you always lend your tools so freely?'

May shook her head. 'No. But Ivan just came to check up on me.'

'Oh?'

'Because you're here.'

Hugh's eyes widened in mocking surprise.

'Oh yes,' said May. 'It's difficult to explain, but we're sort of interdependent. We do things for each other, keep an eye out, share our skills.'

'And what's your particular skill?'

May grinned. 'Mending broken fences.' As she had hoped, an expression of bewilderment disturbed Hugh's features, raising his eyebrows into a peak of curiosity. 'Figuratively speaking, of course,' she added.

Hugh's mouth twisted in a rueful smile. 'Funny, it's not a role I can easily imagine you in, somehow.'

'How did you get on with the hot-shot lawyer, then?' Sally ushered May into the sitting-room where Harriet was sitting cross-legged on the sofa, mending a pair of jeans.

May suddenly found herself resenting this description of him and flushed as she wondered why. 'He says we've no chance of getting our money back and we must register with the tax people and the DSS. I thought you might do that, Harriet. You look right.'

'Thank you very much.' Harriet bit off a length of thread. 'I'm flattered.'

'He also said we ought to get a legal agreement drawn up,

for the partnership,' May continued. 'That would cost money, but if you feel –'

'Oh no,' said Harriet. 'We don't want to bother with anything like that.'

'Are you sure? It's something to do with all of us being responsible for debts, I think.'

'We're not likely to fall out, and I hope we're not going to run up any debts,' said Sally.

Harriet shook her head. 'I shouldn't think so. When we've saved *The Rose Revived*, and Sally and I have got luxury flats to live in, we'll think about legal agreements. But until then, we'll just have to trust each other.'

'At least we *can* trust each other,' said May. 'Unlike dear Slimeball.'

'When are we going to tell him?' asked Sally. 'Or shall we just leave?'

May shook her head. 'I think we should do all the assignments we have for this coming week, handing out leaflets. And then on Friday, we'll march on Slimeball's office and ceremonially throw our dirty rubber gloves in his face.'

'Oh brilliant,' said Sally. 'Shall we fill them with something vile before we do?'

'Sally!' said Harriet. 'What a suggestion!'

'It's since I met May,' Sally explained. 'I've become much more assertive.'

May grinned, secretly wondering if 'assertive' was always such a good thing to be.

On Monday, when Sally had gone to her elderly convalescents, detailed to tell them about their decision to go it alone, Harriet decided she had time to deliver a leaflet, minus telephone number, to the house in Cheyne Walk. As she didn't yet trust herself to use the buses, she walked, and spent the entire journey debating whether she should ring the doorbell or just post the pamphlet and run. She had reached the address and had firmly decided on the latter course when someone came out of the house.

For some reason she felt foolish slipping her scrappy bit of paper into the postbox while this man was looking at her, so she went upstairs, trying to remember if the artist's flat door had a letterbox. She had no idea if the artist was in or not. She had never cleaned for him on a Monday, nor did she know his name. They communicated through notes, which he had signed with an unreadable hieroglyphic. His reply to her first, tentative little missive had been a simple, *Next time, make scones.*

His writing was strong and artistic and he used thick, black charcoal. Her reply, *I have no time to make scones in the two hours I have to clean*, in pencil, looked unbearably prissy under his scrawl. He had answered, *I have now hired you for three hours. Do what's needed and don't make excuses!*

Since she had made scones, he had ordered her to make other things. His favourite was flapjack, but last week she'd been too busy scraping years of accumulated grease off his kitchen shelves to make any. Now she was perhaps on the verge of meeting the man in person. It was with a mixture of hope and dread that she went up the stairs. If it had been possible to fall in love with someone because of their handwriting, Harriet felt she might have done so.

His flat door was in dire need of a good wash-down with hot water and soda crystals, but it did have a metal flap you could post things through. She shoved her paper into it, pushing her fingers into the opening to ensure its safe arrival. Just then the door opened, pulling the flap shut on her ring and trapping her hand.

Frantically she tried to free herself, but as the door opened, the flap tightened its grip. By the time the door was pulled wide, she was over the threshold, trying to find the words to stop whoever it was increasing her torture.

'Ah! Help! Please stop!'

A tall man with thick grey hair and black eyebrows stood there, holding the door and scowling at Harriet, panting on his doormat, her hand firmly attached to his door. The artist looked just like his handwriting.

'Sorry. I've got my hand stuck.' She freed herself quickly, resisting the temptation to suck her fingers.

'Well?' said the man crossly, demanding an explanation.

Before Harriet could think of one, he went on, 'It's tomorrow.'

'What is?'

'The art class.'

'Oh. What time?'

'Ten o'clock.'

He still had his hand on the door as if he might close it at any moment, whether doing so would squash Harriet or not. Harriet felt she must take avoiding action.

'May I join the class?'

'Presumably that's what you came to find out?'

From somewhere, Harriet found some backbone she didn't know she had. 'Actually, no. I'm your cleaning lady. I came to give you that.' She pointed to the screwed up leaflet which was lying on the mat. He ignored it.

'*Who* did you say you were?'

'Your cleaning lady. The one you write notes to. About the laundry and things?'

Some light dawned. He had a craggy face which had probably never been handsome, but had gained attractiveness with every decade. Harriet judged him to be in his mid-forties.

'Oh. You'd better come in. Why didn't you make me any flapjack last time?'

Harriet picked up the ill-fated screw of paper before following him into the kitchen, which still smelt of curry. It was probably all he ate.

'I didn't have time, for one thing. And for another, I'm a cleaner, not a cook.'

'Are you due to clean today?' the man asked. 'That's handy.'

'Actually, I'm not. I came to give you this.' She spread it out and tried to smooth out some of the creases. He picked it up and put it down on the working surface without looking at it.

'My colleagues and I,' said Harriet, realizing he probably read little, if anything, which came through his door, 'have decided to set up our own business. We can do it for a lot cheaper than Mr Slater is charging.'

'Who is Mr Slater? Coffee?'

'Yes please,' said Harriet, feeling she might need some

sustenance. 'He's the man who owns the agency who sent me to you. The man you presumably write cheques to.'

'He's your boss?' His eyebrows beetled alarmingly at her.

'Not for long. He pays us only a tiny percentage of what he charges the clients. We can do it for less and earn more. I'd be grateful if you'd use me directly, rather than going through Mr Slater.'

The man waved a milk bottle at Harriet. Recognizing it from her visit last Thursday, she shook her head.

'If I can rely on you, I don't suppose it makes much difference to me. What do you charge?'

'That's our hourly rate.' She pointed to the leaflet, making sure he took in what he would have to pay her.

'Now I've started giving art classes, I need the place kept in order. Women are so neurotic about cleanliness.'

Harriet nodded, sympathizing with the women. 'About the art classes, how much do you charge?'

He told her.

'Do you really get people willing to pay that?' asked Harriet, shocked.

'Dozens of them. London is full of women with time on their hands and aspirations to great art. They won't contribute much to the art world, but they will pay my alimony and my mortgage.'

'Oh.' Harriet looked down, noting that the lino badly needed replacing. 'I'd like to come, but unfortunately, I haven't got that sort of money.'

'Can you paint?'

'Yes.' This was no time for false modesty.

'I'm not a charity. I can't afford to take people for nothing. On the other hand, we might be able to do a little barter.'

'I couldn't really swap cleaning for art classes. It wouldn't be fair on the other girls.'

'I didn't mean cleaning.'

A chill settled over Harriet.

'I sometimes need a model. For the life class.'

'Oh.' Harriet's racing heart slowed down, but only by a notch. She may have led a sheltered existence, but she knew that 'life' meant 'nude'.

The man's mouth curled into a smile. 'I'd appreciate the opportunity to teach someone with some talent. Bring me your portfolio tomorrow, and think about the modelling. I'm sure we can work something out.'

'That's very kind . . .' she began.

'But don't short-change me with the cleaning. If my clothes need washing, do something about it.'

'Very well. I'll do whatever needs doing. But I'll charge you the hourly rate for it. The art class thing will be separate.'

'What's your name?'

'Harriet Devonshire.'

'My name's Leo Purbright.'

Harriet took too large a gulp of coffee. It was hot. Leo Purbright was one of the few names in the art world she knew. She loved his huge, figurative creations. She was almost sure she'd read that he was the principal lecturer at one of the major art colleges. Somehow she had found her way into this great man's kitchen and from there, his art classes. She cleared her throat.

'I've heard of you. But I didn't know you taught privately – I mean, I thought . . .'

'You thought I taught at our nation's "most prestigious font of artistic learning"?' Sarcasm and bitterness edged his smile. 'Well I did, until they decided they didn't want me any more. Which is why I'm teaching idle women to do flower painting.'

Harriet shuddered. 'How ghastly for you.'

Surprisingly, this time the smile was sincere. 'No, in fact, it's not. The women who come to me may not have enormous talent, but they are willing to learn. And here I am actually allowed to teach.'

'Didn't you do that before?'

'Oh yes, but it was against the ethos of the college. Which is why we parted company.'

'I see,' said Harriet, who didn't.

'Now you're having second thoughts about coming to my classes?' Harriet had been examining her toe with unusual intensity. She looked up. 'You're a nice girl. You're nervous of getting mixed up with an artist who might shake up your ideas a little and wants you to take your clothes off?'

He was not mocking, but his eyes, strangely light against the blackness of his lashes and brows, seemed to read her life history: her small village upbringing, her respectable, overbearing grandparents, the stifling 'niceness' of her education. He didn't judge, he just observed.

Harriet cleared her throat. 'Of course I'm nervous at the thought of being a life model. I've never done it before and your studio is dreadfully cold. Besides, I thought your students did flower painting.'

'My students do what I tell them. But I'm not a bully, I wouldn't ask you to do anything you felt uncomfortable about.'

'Well . . .'

'Look, just bring along your portfolio, and if you're any good you can join the group. Then you can pay your way with a little modelling. We'll start off with some figure work. Ten-minute poses, fully dressed, heater on.'

What portfolio? thought Harriet, panicking. 'Thank you. You're very kind,' she said.

He shook his head. 'No. I may not be a bully, but no one who knows me would accuse me of being kind. I'll see you tomorrow at ten.'

CHAPTER TEN

'Hi! Where have you been? What's all that?'

Harriet staggered through the door of Sally's flat, weighed down with artist's materials, tins of emulsion, huge sheets of paper, and a bundle of household paint brushes.

'You've got to help me, Sally. I've got to produce a portfolio by ten o'clock tomorrow.'

'Of course, anything I can do. What's a portfolio?'

'A folder of work, drawings, sketches, things like that.'

'But, Harriet, I can't draw to save my life!'

Harriet smiled for the first time that morning. 'You don't have to, twitto! I want you to model.'

Once Sally understood Harriet's problem, she threw all her energies into helping. All day she lay on a sofa in various states of dress and undress. She took up yoga positions, pretended to serve at tennis, do ballet or anything else that Harriet asked for. When she became stiff from holding the same position for too long, she primed sheets of paper with the white emulsion, leaving Harriet to create meaning out of a black banana, an unripe kiwi fruit and a half-empty bottle of Perrier.

Harriet had to abandon her tidy, water-colour habits. Time was short, and working at such a furious pace forced her to be bold. Swift, curving lines slashed across sheets of white paper, blocks of white chalk created patches of light on sheets of black, in a frenzy of creativity. When May appeared in the evening, Harriet laid her brush down for a moment.

'Well here we are,' said May. 'The proud possessors of a mobile phone and a telephone number.'

'Was it awfully expensive?' Unconsciously, Harriet wiped paint on her face with the back of her hand.

'No, it's all right as long as we don't use it. They charge us for incoming as well as outgoing calls. If we have to ring anyone, it's better to use a phonebox if we can.'

'We've got Piers's phone for a bit,' Sally reminded her.

Harriet nodded, her mind back on her painting. She had stopped doing lightning sketches and was using acrylics, working on a composition using the many sketches she had of Sally's naked body, some fruit, and a cat drawn from memory which, if she were honest, looked a little like an owl.

Sally made her stop for something to eat. May made appreciative noises, and they both plied her with glasses of wine. Eventually, May went back to the boat and Sally went to bed. At three in the morning, Harriet abandoned her painting and lay down on the sofa.

'I'll just close my eyes for a moment,' she promised, and fell asleep.

'Harriet?' Sally stood over her with a steaming mug. 'It's half-past eight. You've got to be at your class at ten. I'm doing your cleaning job, remember?'

Sally's voice seemed to come from a long way off. Harriet dragged herself away from the kaleidoscope of confused images which had been her dreams and into the present. Sally poked at her with a scarlet-tipped finger.

Harriet pushed her hair out of her eyes. Whatever was in the mug smelt faintly medicinal.

'What is it?'

'Camomile. It'll do you good. I've run your bath. I'll get your pictures together while you're in it.'

'You've been wonderful, Sally. Thank you so much.'

Sally, whose maternal instinct had been suppressed during her relationship with Piers, shrugged off Harriet's gratitude and went to cook something nourishing for Harriet's breakfast.

While Harriet was still asleep, Sally had fashioned a portfolio cover from a dress box and some wrapping paper. When Harriet emerged from the bathroom, pink-cheeked and sick with anxiety, Sally was hunting down the scattered sheets which littered the sitting-room.

'Shall I put this in?' Sally held up a pastel drawing of a boy asleep which Harriet had brought with her. Harriet shook her head. She had drawn it shortly before Matthew left for prep school. There had been no point in asking him to sit for her as he couldn't keep still for longer than a minute, so she had done it when he was asleep. Although she thought it was far better than anything else she had done, it was private. She couldn't bear to have it criticized as a mere work of art.

Everything else went in though. Even the most tentative sketches were needed to pad out the body of work, which was still extremely thin. But the one painting which Harriet had worked on so long into the night, would make up for everything, Sally assured her.

Sally then telephoned her favourite mini-cab driver and ordered him round. 'You can't struggle on the Underground with that thing.' She gestured to the William Morris papered portfolio. 'Besides, if you don't take a cab you'll be late.'

Meekly, Harriet agreed, and put on the patchwork cardigan knitted by Sally's mother.

'It's folksy,' said Sally. 'But it's warm.'

Between them, the mini-cab driver and Sally got Harriet to the house in Cheyne Walk at nine fifty-five precisely. Harriet felt a little woozy. In spite of the herbal tea, the bath and the boiled egg with soldiers, she still wanted to go back to bed and catch up on her sleep. Her nervousness also made her inclined to yawn. She took a deep breath and went up the steps.

Her breathless introduction into the intercom was dismissed by the rude buzz of the front door being released. Hurriedly she pushed it open, certain it would change its mind and shut again any minute. She was panting when she reached the flat door, flushed by her exertions and the patchwork cardigan.

Leo Purbright was anything but the dreamy artist Sally would have imagined. He was alert, incisive, with a tongue as potentially cutting as a laser. He regarded Harriet intently before speaking.

'Good morning, Harriet. I'm glad you've got leggings on. It's good if the model's limbs are clearly defined.' He took a sip from the mug he was holding. 'And I see you've got your work with you.'

Harriet's stomach suffered a minor earthquake. Sweat broke out under her clothes. She nodded. 'You want me to model today?' Somehow the words came out in the right order and with only the faintest tremble.

'Yes please. If your work turns out to be no good, I'll pay you for it in the normal way. You can go through to the studio. The other students are just setting up.'

The thought of joining them fortified only by camomile tea overcame her natural shyness. 'Actually, could I have a cup of coffee first?'

Leo raised a black, interrogatory eyebrow. 'Of course. Help yourself.' Leo's rather formal smile had a penetrating edge to it. Harriet removed herself from under it and took refuge in the kitchen.

Clutching her mug of coffee, Harriet braved the studio. She was aware of low-voiced chattering as the students, all of them women, adjusted easels, stretched paper, and pulled on paint-spattered shirts. At the end of the room was a low table in front of a sheet. Leo was beside it, waiting impatiently for Harriet.

'Good. You just hop up on to the table and we'll get going.'

Harriet felt unable to hop. She climbed somewhat unsteadily, wondering if it was vertigo, lack of sleep, or sheer terror at what Leo would make of her work which was making her feel dizzy. She could see her portfolio, leaning up against the wall, as yet unopened.

Leo regarded his class. As one, the women stopped what they had been doing and gave him their full attention.

'This is Harriet. It's time we did some figure work and she's going to be our model for today. When she gets used to us we might persuade her to take her clothes off so that we can do some life work. But to break her in gently we'll start with some two-minute poses.'

'Two minutes!' Protest erupted from the group like champagne out of a bottle. 'What can you do in that time?'

'You'll be surprised. Your hand and eye have to work as

one, with no time to think.' He looked expectantly at Harriet.

Obligingly she raised her arms behind her head as if about to yawn.

'That's nice,' said Leo. 'Feet apart, head back. Raise your elbows slightly. Can you hold that?'

'Yes,' said Harriet, who had no idea if she could or not.

'Good. Can everyone see? Right. You've got two minutes. Don't worry about getting the whole figure in but keep what you can fit on the paper in proportion.'

As the class drew, Harriets' arms began to shake with the effort of keeping them raised.

'Time's up.'

Harriet could almost hear her muscles heaving a sigh of relief as she lowered her arms. She caught Leo looking at her with some amusement.

'Even two minutes can seem a long time in some positions. Take off your cardigan and stand like this.'

Moving her limbs about as if she were a lay-figure, he placed her in a position which was interesting to draw and bearable to hold.

'Artists don't think of their models as people, merely objects,' he told her. 'If you take up a position which is exciting to draw, they'll draw you in it, no matter how excruciating it is for the model to maintain.'

Harriet smiled stiffly at him.

'Right,' he went on. 'Everyone should have loosened up a bit by now. We'll have one more, and then I'm going to come round and have a look at what you've been doing.'

Harriet sensed the women's heightened tension as he said this. She studied the class as the class studied her. They were mostly on the safe side of forty, and not planning to cross over. What nature had withheld, grooming and expertise had provided. Harriet envied their chic and their confidence. But even more than their elegance, Harriet envied their materials. Between them, they could have set up a creditable art shop. The whole spectrum of pastels taking up three drawers in a varnished wooden box; a similar box containing squares of watercolours; a picnic basket full of tubes of gouache or oil paints: fistfuls of brushes; small trees worth of charcoal; oil crayons – everything an artist could possibly need or desire.

One of the women was different, though. Her hair was unashamedly grey and she was very thin, wearing faded denim jeans and a navy-blue fisherman's smock. Her eyes matched her clothes, and her skin was clear and fresh without the use of make-up. She could have been thirty or fifty, an heiress or on a student loan.

A margarine carton containing a grey substance which Harriet guessed was rice held her pastels. She didn't protest or chatter when the pose was changed, but just got on with the next one, dipping her hand into the box without apparently caring which colour her fingers closed on. She either had a lot of talent or a lot of nerve. Harriet suspected the former and tried to stop hankering after the materials which the other women owned. Talent was all you needed, and if you didn't have that, spending a fortune on equipment was pointless.

Harriet's stomach churned in a fresh wave of anxiety. What if she didn't have talent? What if Leo Purbright thought she was only fit to be a model and a cleaning lady?

'Relax your jaw,' said Leo. 'Not long now.' Harriet made a supreme effort. 'Better,' said Leo. 'You look less tortured.' He glanced at his watch. 'Stop, please,' he called. 'We'll try a seated pose next.'

Stiffly, Harriet stumbled down from the table and slumped into the chair intending to use her forced inactivity to catch up on her lack of sleep. Leo strode purposefully towards her and Harriet was sure he was going to move her into some less-relaxed position. Instead, he produced a ball of string from his pocket, picked up her hand and tied the string round it. His fingers were warm and firm against her wrist as he tied the knot and she was certain he must feel her pulse which leapt about like a captured fish. As he replaced it casually on her knee she could still feel the imprint of his touch. Nerves had made her fanciful and oversensitive.

He led the string to a point on the board behind her and stuck in a drawing pin. He did the same to one ankle, both knees, and from the string on her wrist, he attached another length, going in the opposite direction from the first piece. When he moved away, her body was quartered by the string.

'This will help you see how the lines of the body relate to each other and to the chair. It should help you with your foreshortening. Put the strings in and see what happens.'

Harriet watched as he moved round the room, standing for a moment behind each easel, murmuring comments, occasionally taking the charcoal, pastel, or crayon and putting in a line. His stalking seemed to have the same effect on the women as a lion would on a happily grazing herd of gazelles. Would he have been so leonine if his name had been Wilfred, she wondered?

In spite of her relaxed position, Harriet felt anything but, as she watched Leo leave his students and pick up her portfolio. She wished she'd fixed her gaze on the view from the window, and then she wouldn't be forced to watch as he untied the shoelaces and opened the sheets of cardboard covered in wrapping paper.

One by one her works were extracted, scanned and replaced. The picture of Sally naked with a still-life arrangement he looked at for slightly longer, but he offered her no word or smile of reassurance.

'We'll break for coffee now,' he said. 'And while we're having it, there's something I want to show you.'

Harriet got up from her chair feeling like an old dog. She wondered if Leo had expected her to bring a flask, which she hadn't. She was desperately thirsty.

One woman took pity on her. 'Would you like a cup of my coffee? It's black, with sugar.'

Harriet, whose usual preference was the exact opposite, accepted gratefully.

'I sat for Leo once and I was absolutely starving. You're a wonderful model,' the woman said. 'So still.'

Harriet smiled.

'If I could sit still I'd be the model myself – at least you don't get Leo breathing sarcastic nothings into your ear.'

Harriet shuddered. 'No . . .' She nodded to where Leo was taking one of her sketches from her portfolio. 'Not into my ear perhaps, but he's been looking at my work just now and I've a feeling he's going to tell the whole room how bad I am.'

Leo regained the room's attention merely by wishing for it. 'You've all been wondering how you can be expected to produce anything in two minutes,' he began. 'Well, let me show you Harriet's work.'

Scarlet, Harriet felt under greater scrutiny than when she had been posing. In fact, when she looked up, no-one was looking at her at all. Everyone was looking at a drawing of Sally. She was in a deep lunge, a yoga pose that Sally had described as a martial stance. Sally also told her it was agony to maintain, even for a short time.

'Here, Harriet has managed to get the feel of the posture in a very few lines, some of them in quite the wrong place.' Leo looked up at the blushing Harriet. 'I think I'm right in saying this was a two-minute pose?'

Harriet nodded, longing to press herself into the floor-boards she had struggled to polish.

'And here . . .' Leo went through every one of Harriet's sketches, explaining how he could tell that they had been done extremely quickly.

Harriet couldn't decide if he was using her as a shining example or as a ghastly warning. 'So you see,' he concluded, 'you have to be brave – or desperate – and make the first stroke. The Prince wouldn't have found Sleeping Beauty if he hadn't raised his cutlass and plunged into the wood. Thank you, Harriet.'

Harriet spent the rest of the session trying to work out if he thought her work was good or bad. The women also looked at her with questioning eyes as if they didn't know either.

'OK, everyone, time's up. Harriet, you can relax now.'

The irony of it was almost funny. How could she possibly relax knowing she would have to confront Leo and find out if she had any talent or not?

At last everyone had gone. Leo turned to her, a quizzical, humorous expression in his light eyes. His amusement provoked Harriet into speaking first.

'Well? Are you going to pay me off? Or let me join the class.'

He smiled in a way that made Harriet want to hit him. 'Don't be silly, Harriet. You know perfectly well that you're better than almost everyone who comes. But you'll never be really good until you shake off all those middle-class inhibitions you cling to so stubbornly.'

Harriet, who thought she'd shaken them off extremely well in the circumstances, was indignant. 'Oh? And what gives you the –'

But he wouldn't give her the argument she craved, as a release for twenty-four hours' built-up tension.

'Come on Friday. At ten.'

Harriet exhaled, ashamed of her anger. 'Thank you so much . . .'

He made an irritated sound and thrust his hand in his pocket. Then he stuffed something into her hand. Harriet looked down and saw it was a twenty-pound note.

'What's this for?'

'You were a good model. That's the going rate.'

'But I thought . . .'

Leo looked as if he were about to throw Harriet out bodily. 'Put it towards materials, woman. And don't look a gift horse in the mouth.'

Harriet left the flat with more haste than dignity.

CHAPTER ELEVEN

The Walkers were surprisingly calm about Sally's announcement that they were setting up business for themselves. 'Mr Slater' had struck them as 'rather a vulgar sort of fellow' when he had rung up about a misdated cheque, and Captain Walker described them as having 'plenty of pluck'.

And, here Mrs Walker became pink with excitement, 'I even have a job for you! Fancy that! What a coincidence!'

It transpired that Mr Flowers, who had lived upstairs for thirty years had died, discovered dead in his bath by his nephew.

'Apparently the flat is *filthy*, but the nephew, whose name I can't remember for the life of me, said he was desperate, and would pay whatever it cost. I was going to get in touch with Mr Slater, but it would be much better if your new firm could have the business.'

'Gosh yes. Does he want me to do it now?'

'Whenever it's convenient. Although I mentioned you, I didn't commit you to anything without having spoken to you.'

Sally glanced at her watch. She had Harriet's assignment to do, but it was only a bachelor pad and the work was mostly a matter of removing the empties and changing the sheets.

'I could just pop up and have a look at the place when I've finished here, so I can get an idea of what's required.' Sally was surprised but pleased to hear such businesslike words coming out of her mouth.

'That would be wonderful, Sally. He said the matter was truly *urgent*.'

The moment she opened the door to the flat, Sally wished fervently that she hadn't been so keen. It was like the scene in *Great Expectations* when Pip meets Miss Haversham. Everything was filthy. Years of dust had settled on years of grease, creating grime which would take all Harriet's expertise to remove. Where the grease was only a yellowing smear, flies had left sepia coloured spots, the size of pinheads.

Only the refrigerator, growling away like a motorbike in the corner of the kitchen, seemed to have any connection with reality. But even that had the cream-coloured burgeoning door of the nineteen fifties. Sally opened the fridge door and discovered a bottle of milk and small loaf sharing the space with what had once been a freezer compartment and was now a white block of ice. The bread and milk might well have been there since the old man died, and Sally shut the fridge door hurriedly.

Next, she peeped into a bedroom. A sleeping-bag lay on top of the striped ticking mattress and she realized the nephew must be staying in the flat. She shuddered. It was all so foul.

The bathroom was worse than either the kitchen or the bedroom; she didn't think the post-match ablutions in a rugby club could possibly create a worse smell. She fled, hoping that the reception rooms would be better.

The curtains in all the other rooms were drawn, but she identified the dining-room by the unmistakable smell of bone-handled knives and port. The drawing-room was draped in dustsheets – obviously Mr Flowers didn't use it. The last room was his library.

Glass-fronted bookshelves filled with unreadable leather-bound books covered one wall. A leather-topped desk stood under the window, and a leather chesterfield, its back turned unsociably away from the room, took up the third wall. This room smelled of cigar smoke and, while it was just as dusty as the rest of the house and was probably home to a thousand spiders, the dirt had a more superficial feel to it – as if it might respond to gentler treatment than a hammer and chisel.

She crossed to the windows and had dragged back one of the maroon velvet curtains, coughing from the clouds of dust, when she heard a noise behind her. The blood rushed away from her brain, almost making her faint with terror. She opened her mouth to scream, but her throat muscles were paralysed. She stood, her hand on the other curtain, her ears straining.

The noise came again. A sort of snuffling groan which could only come from a soul in torment. Perhaps Uncle Flowers was here in the room with her, back from the grave in a wormeaten shroud, his head an eyeless skull. The snuffling turned into something like a growl, causing a fine sweat to break out over her body. She must make herself move. She must get to the door and get out. Time expanded infinitely. It seemed like years since she had crossed the room and first heard the sound.

At last, Sally's brain began to unfreeze. Very, very slowly, she inched herself round until she could see the room behind her. She saw, above the top of sofa, a bearded head with two dark eyes which surveyed her from under white, bushy eyebrows.

A dog, she thought, relieved. But then her panic returned at full blast. The expression in the animal's eyes was hardly welcoming, and judging by the size of its head, it must be enormous. A scuffling sound indicated claws on leather.

She opened her mouth to make some sort of remark which might pacify the monster, but the words wouldn't come. There was something so prehistoric and ancient about the animal's face that nothing less than a quotation from Beowulf seemed adequate.

Her brain was working at twice the speed of light and she suddenly remembered an ancient, black-and-white film of *Macbeth* she had seen at drama school. These hounds had lounged about in front of fireplaces in which entire oak trees burned. Sally realized she was exchanging meaningful looks with an Irish Wolfhound.

She cleared her throat and, lacking the necessary degree in Anglo Saxon, said, 'Hello.'

If she'd hoped the beast would rise up from its bed and lay its grateful head in her lap, like a unicorn from Arthurian legend, she was disappointed. The dog just sighed deeply and replaced his head on its resting place, out of sight.

Sally tiptoed forward to peer over the back of the sofa. The animal obviously wasn't vicious, but it was incredibly large, taking up the entire length of the sofa. What was it doing here? Had it been here since the old man died?

Sally returned to the window and drew back the other curtain, then went back to look at the wolfhound in the improved light. She loved dogs, and usually they loved her. This one apparently remained uncharmed.

'Oh well,' she said aloud. 'I've got a job to go to, even if you haven't.'

The dog seemed to take offence. With a sound which lay in that dangerous no-man's land between a groan and a growl, it rolled off the sofa and came round to peer at Sally. With all four feet on the ground, its head came up to her chest. On its hind legs it would have been much taller than she was, and it was considerably heavier.

The dog sneezed violently, and Sally hoped it was not intelligent enough to realize it was her fault he needed to. Then he sniffed her. His beard tickled her clenched hands and his nose was cold. She kept very still. One false move and her face could become hamburger steak. Then he rose very slightly on to his back legs and kissed her cheek.

Sally stopped being frightened. She flung her arms around the dog's neck and hugged it. Somehow all the affection Piers had never given her was made up for by that one lick. The dog gave a little woof in return, and then suddenly spun round and knocked Sally over in its rush for the door.

Sally heard it skid on the hall floor, a noise which coincided with the sound of the door being opened. From her low vantage point, Sally observed the dog rise on to its back legs and put its front paws on the shoulders of the man who had just entered, totally obscuring him.

'Get down, Clodagh,' the man said gently, removing the dog's paws from his shoulders. Then he spotted Sally. 'Oh.'

Sally was still lying on the floor where Clodagh's enthusiasm had sent her. Usually, she had scant regard for her own dignity, but now she felt remarkably foolish, and consequently angry. It didn't help matters that the man was good looking in a hairy, rough-hewn sort of way.

'Hello. You must be the cleaner Mrs Walker told me about.' He spoke to her with the same tone as he had used to the dog, only with a touch of amusement which added to Sally's irritation. 'Did Clodagh knock you over? I'm so sorry.' He held out a hand to help her up.

Sally ignored the hand and scrambled to her feet. If she hadn't been feeling at such a disadvantage, she could have brushed herself off and smiled with a friendly, devastating charm. But even though she was no longer scrabbling about on the floor, she couldn't deal with the matter gracefully.

'You really shouldn't keep a dog that size in a flat. It's cruel.' Even to her own ears, she sounded incredibly aggressive.

The man, who was a fair size himself, nodded. 'I know, but if I leave her at home, she pines.'

'Even so . . .'

'And that means she howls at night. No one can put up with it, so I have to bring her with me.'

Sally brushed at her skirt, momentarily surprised to find herself wearing a knee-length tweed instead of her usual thigh-high Lycra, or ankle-length linen. Her gesture to Mrs Walker's notion of what nice young ladies wore to clean in added to her feeling of being out of kilter. She longed to swear. Instead, she pursed her lips and looked sourly at Mr Flowers's nephew.

'This flat is incredibly dirty. It must be months since it was cleaned.'

'Years, I should think,' he said cheerfully. 'But I thought Mrs Walker said that you were part of a firm who could deal with big jobs? Quality Cleaners? Some such name?'

'Not any more. My friends and I are in business for ourselves.'

'Oh? And what are you called now, then?'

Sally was totally at a loss. She opened her mouth, hoping inspiration would bypass her brain and go straight to her lips.

Light suddenly dawned on the man. 'Ah ha! The doorman thrust one of these under my nose.' He pulled a crumpled leaflet from his pocket. 'You must be – Cleaning Undertaken!'

Until that moment, Sally had been unaware that they had a name, and was fairly sure that Harriet and May were equally ignorant.

'Er, that's right. You will be needing our Spring Cleaning Service.'

The man nodded. 'As long as I don't have to wait until spring for it. I need to get this flat habitable as soon as possible.'

'It's just a figure of speech,' said Sally haughtily. 'I'm sure we'll be able to fit you in early next week.'

'Not before then? It is in an awful state.'

'But you've been sleeping here.'

He nodded. 'If you've ever tried to find a hotel willing to accept an Irish Wolfhound as a guest, you'll know why.'

'I see.'

'Perhaps I'd better introduce myself. My name's James Lucas.'

This time Sally accepted the hand which he held out to her. It was warm and large and rather rough. 'Sally Bliss. How do you do?'

'And I gather you've already met Clodagh? She's not very sociable, I'm afraid.'

'She licked my cheek.'

James Lucas's brows drew together in puzzlement. 'Did she? How very – unusual.'

Sally looked up into his coffee-brown eyes and gave him her very best smile. 'Is it?'

James Lucas returned the smile, but his brows, which were very thick, crinkled questioningly, as if he were uncertain why she had smiled so warmly.

Well, why did I? Sally asked herself as she clip-clopped down the marble stairs into the foyer of the building. He's not at all my type.

When she had dealt with the bachelor pad and returned to Piers's flat, she found Harriet and May already there and a bottle of wine already open. As Sally appeared, they poured another glass.

'Here, have this,' said May. 'You look as though you need it.'

'I do. I need it and deserve it. I've got us an assignment, one which has nothing whatever to do with Slimeball.' Sally flopped on to the sofa. 'It makes that first house we did seem like a show-home, but it should earn us a few quid.'

'And Leo Purbright has agreed to teach me art,' said Harriet.

'And I've managed to convince her that she must take time off for classes,' said May. 'So all in all, things seem to be going quite well.'

'So, here's to Cleaning Undertaken!' Sally raised her glass.

'What?' said the other two.

'It's the first words on our leaflet, and our new client thought it was what we were called. But I suppose we ought to think of a proper name.'

There was a contemplative pause.

'What about "Second Quality Cleaners"?' suggested Sally. 'It's a sort of pun. We're the second –'

'Yes, I think we get it,' broke in May. 'Or we could go for "Harsalmay", a subtle combination of our names, as in the best tradition of naming boats and houses.'

'No,' said Harriet, who for a hideous moment had appeared to be actually considering these suggestions. 'I think "Cleaning Undertaken" is a good name. We can answer the telephone with it. And, when we become a huge success, and want to take on more people, we needn't change it.'

'OK with you, Sal?' asked May.

Sally nodded. 'If you don't mind, I'll slope off to the bath.'

'Mm. Come to think of it, you're *filthy*, what happened?'

'Oh nothing much. I was just rolling round in the dust with a dog the size of a donkey. I'll tell you later.'

Sally wasn't as concerned to wash away the dust as the thought of James Lucas, which was proving remarkably tenacious. Try as she might, she couldn't banish James Lucas's large, shaggy form from her mind.

She tipped the last of her Floris bath-oil into the steaming water. Her trouble was, she took male appreciation for granted, like other people took oxygen. She only noticed it when it wasn't there. Had he stuck in her mind because she obviously hadn't stuck in his? It must be the reason. He wasn't her type at all.

She picked up her tweezers and her hand mirror from the side of the bath and inspected her eyebrows closely. James Lucas's eyebrows would need an electric hedge trimmer to get them into shape. There was definitely something in the saying that people looked like their dogs. James Lucas didn't have a beard, and his eyebrows weren't grey, but give him a few years, he and Clodagh would be indistinguishable on a dark night. Both pairs of eyes shared a strong gentleness, but in neither gleamed the speculation, the spark of interest which Sally was accustomed to seeing.

She plucked at a stray hair and winced. Had she lost her touch? Immediately, she chided herself for her vanity. Why should she assume that every man she met would instantly fancy her? Why should she care if they didn't? Why should the absence of the slight narrowing of the eyes, the curl of the mouth, the predatory flare of the nostrils, seem like a rejection?

Sally put down her tweezers and mirror and allowed herself to relax back into the steam. She inspected her right foot. Only a small bulge at the joint of her big toe, a legacy of three years of pointe work at her after-school ballet lessons marred its beauty. But that bulge seemed to symbolize her life – her failure to be a ballet dancer, her failure to be a proper actor, and now her failure to attract a tall, shaggy man with rough hands.

May would say she was mad to be even thinking about another man so soon after Piers. But some women needed men, however much they wished they didn't, and Sally was one of them.

'Not him, though. He was too straight for words,' Sally told herself. 'Positively rustic. Besides, there are dozens of great-looking men who fancy you rotten.'

But her mind kept going back to tweedy, countrified James Lucas, who didn't fancy her at all.

CHAPTER TWELVE

'I'd have had to let you go, anyway,' said Slimeball, who had listened to their faltering excuses for leaving with no change of expression at all. He opened a drawer and took out a couple of envelopes which he tossed to Sally and Harriet. 'It's easy enough to get women who know what they're doing.'

'We knew what we were doing,' said Harriet indignantly. 'We were very good cleaners.'

'There were complaints.' Slimeball bared his teeth, no longer trying to make his smile seem good humoured. 'About watering plants so they overflowed on to the first editions, for example.'

May flushed. The plant had been near death, but now she wished she'd let it wither.

'So don't bother answering my ad again, will you?'

'We'd die, rather,' muttered Sally under her breath.

'But you,' he turned his attention to May. 'You owe me quite a lot of money.'

It was a relatively simple statement, spoken quietly, but the hairs on the back of May's neck rose. She was suddenly terribly aware that she was a young woman, out of her safe, middle-class environment, away from her supportive male friends, being confronted by a man who could pick up a phone and call on a wealth of heavy, illegal, backup to deal with any little problem he might have. She swallowed hard but shook her head. He was a bully. She would not be intimidated.

'Not as much as you owe me. I worked extremely long hours, in very difficult circumstances, and I'm keeping what I've got.'

'It's my money. You were behaving dishonestly when you took it for yourself.'

'You were behaving dishonestly when you told those people I could cook! If you want it, you'll have to sue me.'

'There are other, much simpler ways of getting money out of people, you know.'

May did know. It was called GBH, but she put her chin up. 'I'm sure there are, but I'm also sure you wouldn't want to get involved with the police.'

Slater got up. 'And would you? You always stay strictly within the law, do you? You always tell the DSS exactly who's who, and what's what, do you?'

As one, the girls got to their feet, resolving to a woman, to register the business immediately.

'And if I should discover,' he went on, in the same, conversational tone, 'that any of my clients are now employing you direct, I won't be pleased.'

May licked her lips. 'It's unlikely,' she croaked. 'If we're so bad at it.'

'Just remember what I said. If any of them do, I shall take steps . . .'

Quite what steps, he didn't need to specify – the girls took the steps down to the street as fast as they could.

'You were brave,' Sally's heart was still thumping after their flight. 'I'd have handed over the money the moment he got nasty.'

They had collapsed, panting heavily, at one of the tables of the greasy-spoon café where they had first got to know each other.

May picked up her coffee with a shaking hand. 'I couldn't. I haven't got it. Besides, he was always nasty.'

'Did it all go on the phone?' asked Harriet.

May nodded. 'Some of it. I've got to give the rest to Mike. I can't go on avoiding him for ever.' She rested her head in her hands for a moment before saying. 'I'm sorry, I know I shouldn't. It's Cleaning Undertaken's money . . .'

Harriet broke in. 'You earned it. You should have it.'

May shook her head. 'No. If we're going to be in business, we must work as a team, pool our resources. From each according to her abilities . . .'

'Yes, and to each according to her needs,' said Harriet.

'But we must give ourselves a basic salary, which has to be enough to keep a roof over our heads.'

'If we earn enough.' Now the adrenalin rush was over, May felt desperately tired, and the fear that Slater had stirred still lingered. He was dangerous, and they did plan to do the very thing he warned them not to do. 'We probably won't earn enough to pay for food, let alone luxuries like bills.'

'May, we're bound to! Think about it!' said Harriet. 'I managed my rent before, when we were earning about a quarter of what we should have been. We'll be heaps better off now!'

'I suppose so.'

'But we must work it out fairly,' Harriet went on. 'I mean, I spend time painting, so it wouldn't be fair if I had the same wage . . .'

May lifted a decisive hand. 'No! I insist we all get the same. If you need to paint, or if Sally needs to go to an audition, you must do it. Cleaning's only a stopgap in our lives. We mustn't let it come between us and the real thing.'

'But we must be businesslike,' said Harriet. 'We all need money for various reasons, and we won't get it if we don't commit ourselves wholeheartedly to the project. Painting's a luxury.'

'It's why you came to London, Harry. And Sally's acting is her career. Besides,' May tried to inject a little humour into a very unfunny situation. 'Can you really see me committing myself wholeheartedly to cleaning? I mean, really?'

Harriet smiled. 'Well, as wholeheartedly as we can.'

'You do the books, Harriet, which will more than make up for the time you spend painting, and if Sally gets an audition . . .'

'Yes?' Sally asked, trying to look useful. 'What shall I do to make up the time?'

May exhaled. 'We'll cross that bridge when we come to it, shall we?'

Sally stirred her black, sugarless coffee. They probably never would come to it. She hadn't had a call from her agent since the Chernobyl interview. Perhaps she'd never get one again and she would end up being a cleaner for ever. She sighed deeply, 'I say, Slimeball couldn't really do anything, could he? If we took his clients? I mean, they're not property, are they?'

'Oh, I shouldn't think so,' said May, feeling far less confident than she sounded.

'You could always ask the hot-shot lawyer,' suggested Harriet.

May was reluctant to involve Hugh, in spite of his offers of help. She wasn't frightened of him in the same way she was of Slater, but without saying anything he seemed to challenge her lifestyle and she couldn't afford any negative influences just now.

'I could, but supposing he said we couldn't take our clients with us? We might not have any clients. And we can't afford to be without income, any of us.' And especially me, she added silently.

Sally thought about her small accumulation of wealth at present living in a drawer under her knickers. There was at least a hundred pounds less of it than she needed and she only had a home for another couple of weeks. The thought that she could move in with Harriet and May was not particularly reassuring. They would have to take work where they could find it.

Harriet too thought about her dwindling bank balance. She'd brought precious little money with her to London, all of it earned through painting pictures of people's houses when she lived with her grandparents. There wasn't much left. May was right. They couldn't afford to be fussy. 'I still think you should mention it, if you see him,' she said.

'I will,' said May, confident that she wouldn't see him. 'Promise.'

'We've got one client,' said Sally, finishing her coffee, 'who's never had anything to do with Slimeball! Let's go and clean James Lucas's flat.'

May looked at her watch. 'I've got to see Mike. I didn't realize it would take us so long to tell Slimeball what to do with his job. I'll have to meet you later.'

'We could start, and you could join us,' suggested Sally.

May shook her head. 'Together we stand, divided we fall. You two go to Sally's and I'll meet you there. I shouldn't be long with Mike.'

'Would you like me to come with you to see him?' offered Harriet. 'If we can't clean a flat on our own, should you be tackling Mike alone?'

May shook her head. 'No, Mike's my problem exclusively. Besides, he's not like Slater. He's –' Once, she would have described him as nice, reasonable, kind even, but he didn't seem like that any more.

'Yes?' Harriet persisted. 'What is he?'

'Honest,' said May definitely. 'I'm sure he's honest.'

Honesty didn't make him reasonable though.

'Fifty quid is no good to me, May. Fifty quid is less than a week's mooring fee. You're supposed to be paying back fees.'

Mike hadn't asked her to sit down for a cup of coffee, or performed any of the pleasantries she once could have expected. Now he stood over her, hands on hips, and was all but shouting.

'I know your friends are all very fond of you, and look on you as if you were some sort of mascot. But, quite frankly, I'd like to get rid of the lot of you – you narrowboat dropouts! The sooner I can clear my yard, get some decent boats, which aren't seventy bloody foot long, the better I'll be pleased. And if fifty quid is the best you can do, I'll sell your boat over your head right now.'

Without a word, May fumbled in the bib pocket of her overalls and produced another hundred pounds.

Mike hesitated for the merest second, then snatched it and stuffed it in his back pocket. 'Thank you! And I'll have another hundred and fifty next week.' Then he turned and stormed into his inner sanctum leaving May, shocked and bewildered, in the outer office.

'What's *wrong* with that man?' she demanded of Ivan, who was lugging a gas bottle along the pontoon. 'Has he had a personality transplant, or something? He threatened to sell my boat over my head!'

Ivan halted the gas bottle. 'He's got greedy, that's what. He's found out how much money he could earn from this place if it was full of nice short plastic boats. He's got it in for all of us.'

May, whose teeth were starting to chatter, nodded. 'You're not kidding!'

'And as *The Rose* owes money, he's got it in for you most of all.'

May tried a smile. It didn't come out too well. 'I think I'll buy a lottery ticket.'

It was only afterwards, while she was on her way to Sally's, that May identified the strange expression which had flickered across Mike's face as she gave him the extra money. It was *disappointment*. Far from just wanting his money as quickly as possible, he wanted her to fail. That way he could get her off his moorings.

With the aid of Capital Radio, an arsenal of cleaning materials, and Mrs Walker's vacuum cleaner, borrowed for the occasion, they restored to the late Mr Flowers's flat some of the old-fashioned dignity it had a right to. It took the three of them all day.

'Well, I think James Lucas ought to be delighted,' said Sally, bending backwards to ease the ache in her spine. 'You can hardly smell the urine now.'

'What's worrying me,' said May. 'Is how we're going to get paid for the job.'

Sally looked down at her shoe. It was splashed with creme cleanser. 'I'm afraid I never thought of that.'

May chewed her lip. This was their one genuine client. If they didn't get paid for this job, how would she give Mike his next instalment?

'I suppose this James Lucas is trustworthy? He won't just change the locks on the flat and never be seen again, will he?'

'I'm sure he's honest,' Sally insisted. 'I mean, he arranged it all through Mrs Walker. She wouldn't get taken in by a confidence trickster.'

'She signed up with Keith Slater,' said May.

And so did we, thought Sally. 'He seemed a very *solid* type of man,' she said aloud. 'He wore a tweed coat.'

'Never mind,' said May, trying to conceal her disappointment and frustration. 'We can send him an invoice through the post. What's his address, Sal?'

Sally shook her head. 'I don't know.'

'What?' May was too appalled to be angry.

Sally was nearly in tears. 'I'm sorry, I've blown it. We've done a day's hard labour for nothing. And spent all that money on materials.'

'We needed the materials anyway,' said Harriet quickly. 'And Mrs Walker might have his address. Ask her when you take the hoover back.'

Sally returned looking more doleful than ever. 'She hasn't got it, and she doesn't think he'll be back in London for a month.'

May bit back a nasty word. 'Well, take the keys, Sally. And if he comes back, Mrs Walker can send him to you to fetch them. Then you can ask him for the money.'

Sally briefly considered demanding money with menaces from someone the size of a small yeti. 'No problem,' she said brightly. Compared to facing an angry May, it would be a doddle.

May regarded her colleagues. 'In the meantime, we'll get an accounts book, design some invoices, and offer a whacking great discount for cash on the nail. And while we're about it, let's start a fund to buy an industrial vacuum cleaner. I'm fed up with using ones that push out more than they suck in.'

CHAPTER THIRTEEN

May poled *The Rose Revived* out of its mooring, and was just walking over the roof to the bow-end to get the boat pointing in the right direction when she heard a voice from the towpath.

'Do you want a hand?'

It was Hugh Buckfast. May's brain moved rapidly. In fact a hand would be very useful. Harriet had gone to look at art galleries and was going to stay with Sally. May had decided to charge both the boat's batteries and her own with a trip down the canal. Boating single-handed was tricky, but would accepting Hugh's help oblige her to ask him about stealing clients and things?

'Um . . .'

Before she'd reached a conclusion, he'd pushed the bow off, so the boat was headed for the zoo, and stepped on board. Like it or not, May had a passenger.

May ducked down into the engine-room and started the engine. It took three tries. She would have to go on a long trip if the batteries were to be properly charged. But she'd planned to be alone.

'I don't remember inviting you along for the ride,' she said, as Hugh joined her. But as he showed no sign of leaving and she could hardly just push him into the canal, she aligned the boat, adjusted the throttle and resigned herself to his presence.

'You can come, but don't bother me with mindless chatter.'

Hugh appeared to be in an incurably good mood. 'You really have held that against me, haven't you?'

'Not at all. I just expect you to understand my need for quiet.'

'I'll understand it later, but first I must tell you why I'm here.'

'So it's not just the pleasure of my company? My sparkling conversation, my witty repartee?'

'My brother asked me to come.'

'Oh, God! Matthew's all right isn't he?'

'Yes of course. He's fine. My brother says he's a credit to his mother.'

'Good.'

'Tom wants you to do a job for him.'

'Tell him if he wants us to clean the school, it will take all three of us and several days. And we want the money in advance.'

Hugh seemed amused by this. 'Do you indeed? No, the school is fine. He wants something else.'

May's hackles of suspicion twitched. 'What else is there?'

'Something perfectly respectable, I promise.'

'Then why didn't he ring me himself?'

Hugh chuckled again. 'He imagined that, because we know each other, it might come better from me,' He sighed. 'Tom is terribly optimistic.'

May found it hard not to smile too. 'So what is this perfectly respectable thing your brother wants us, to do?'

'He wants to hire your boat to take a party of boys out for a trip.'

May had slowed down as the boat passed a chain of moored craft.

'How on earth does he know about my boat?'

May lifted a hand to greet a head which had risen from the hatch to see who was moving on the canal. 'Did you tell him?'

'No. Matthew did.'

'Oh?' It seemed a bit unlikely to May.

'Yes. Under torture, they do usually confess.'

The disturbing thought that he might actually have a sense of humour entered her head. She ignored it.

'Tell me what you want, exactly. And remember that hiring the boat as well as me will be very expensive.' If the Buckfast family were screwing thousands of pounds a year out of people uncaring enough to send their boys to boarding school, there was no reason why Cleaning Undertaken shouldn't get some of it.

'Every term a few boys are taken to London for a visit. It's usually the boys who don't get taken out because their parents are abroad or something. It's considered quite an honour.'

'What fun.' May was on the lookout for supermarket trolleys and other hazards which often ended up near bridges. She didn't fancy having to get the weed hatch off to unwind a mattress from her propeller with Hugh as an audience.

'They visit some exhibition or museum or something, to make the trip vaguely educational, and then Tom usually takes them to a film and McDonald's, something like that. But he wanted to do something different this time.'

'I see.'

'All you have to do is take Matthew and five other little boys, Tom, and possibly me, for a trip up the canal, much as you're doing now. And give them tea.'

'But I don't cook . . .'

'I know you don't. But you don't have to. They'll be quite happy with burgers and chips.'

May was hurt that he should regard her *tour de force* at the Stockbridges with so little respect.

Hugh didn't notice. 'They eat terribly healthily at school, so they'd be grateful for an E-numbers fix.'

'I see.'

'Will you work out a price and ring me?'

May shrugged. Cleaning Undertaken couldn't afford to turn down any job that might be lucrative. 'Wouldn't it be better for me to ring your brother direct?'

'I told him I'd handle it. He's got a lot on his plate at the moment. And I am more or less on the spot.'

May resolved to make boat hire very, very, expensive. 'You'd better give me your number, then.'

'I'll give you my card. It has my home and office numbers on it.'

'OK. I'll get back to you. And if you stay there, you'll get knocked in as I go round this bend.'

Hugh moved just as May swung out over the canal, leaning on the tiller, making the boat nose its way round the corner. Only when the boat was straight again and May was once more upright did he speak again.

'Far be it from me to make suggestions, but don't you think you should be a touch more conciliatory with your paying customers?'

She narrowed her eyes at him. 'You didn't pay. You just got on.'

Hugh laughed, unabashed.

They travelled on in silence for another few minutes. 'So how is working for yourselves working out? Any problems?'

'Not really.' There was, of course, the massive burden of feeling responsible for not only her own debt, and her own living, but for Harriet's and Sally's too. But she wasn't going to share that with him. Nor was she going to keep her promise to Harriet and mention their stolen clients. She couldn't afford for him to give the wrong answer.

'Getting plenty of work?'

'Why? Do you need a cleaning lady?'

'No. I've got one, she's very good and I've had her for years. And I won't sack her. Not even for you.'

'Well that's not very supportive!' May's eyes twinkled as she imagined his sterile bachelor flat. How he would hate having her clean it. 'If you changed your mind –'

'But I will give cards to my colleagues and friends,' he broke in.

'Jolly decent of you. But being poor char ladies, we can't afford cards. We've only got leaflets.'

'Well, give me a handful of leaflets then.'

'I'll have to get some more from Sally. She's got the photocopier.'

'For goodness' sake, May! You should be a bit better organized.'

This criticism got under her guard because it was justified. 'I know. And perhaps we ought to have cards as well. There's just so much to think about.'

He nodded. 'So, what is it about canals that makes you so determined to keep your boat?'

May thought carefully how best to explain. 'I love travelling along. Every bend, every bridge hole, is like a new page in a book, you don't know what you'll see, or what the country will be like. On the cut you can be passing the most sordid part of a town one minute, and be in the countryside the next. And at boat pace, you actually see the things you pass, not like in a car.'

'You're obviously very passionate about them.'

'I am. When I get out of this mess, I plan to move about much more.'

'That would be difficult if you had a job, wouldn't it?'

May shook her head. 'Not necessarily. If I don't go too far away from London, I could travel to any job I had from where the boat was. There are so many canals, you see.'

'I see.'

May felt suddenly embarrassed. She had gone on about her favourite subject. 'I'm sorry to bore on about it.'

'Not at all. You make canals sound fascinating.'

May looked up at him at the same moment as he looked down. Their eyes met and May suddenly felt extremely weak, as if she were going down with flu. It was something to do with how his hair curled very slightly on his neck, or how his throat emerged from the collar of his coat.

May cleared her own throat hurriedly. 'Would you like to steer? I think I'll make some tea?' Leaving him with the tiller, she bobbed down the step into the engine-room, then bobbed back up. 'You know how to steer with a tiller? You push it the opposite way to the way you want to go.'

'I know.'

In her own, familiar galley, designed and built by her own fair hands, and away from Hugh's unsettling presence, she felt better. It's pheromones or something, she told herself as she filled the kettle. It's been months since you've had a man's arms round you. Any unattached man under forty, with the right number of limbs and features more or less in the right place, would have that effect. She tipped a potful of cold tea and tea bags out of the window and into the canal, satisfied with her explanation. She managed to overlook the fact that Jed fitted that category and was a nice person to boot. But he never had the slightest effect on her heart rate.

Convinced she had the problem sorted out, she took up a tray of tea and a packet of biscuits. But as she handed him his tea she caught a whiff of his aftershave and her knees went weak again. You're as bad as Sally, she chided herself, detaching a digestive biscuit from the packet, any unattached man and your hormones take over. And perhaps he wasn't unattached. Perhaps she should find out.

'I'll take over now,' she said.

He relinquished the tiller and sat on the roof so his legs swung in the space over the engine.

She eyed him speculatively. Could she just ask him if he was married? Possibly. But if he said no, she couldn't probe further, and ask if he had a live-in lover, or anything. Or, heaven forbid, he might think she was making a pass at him. Picturing his horrified reaction if she did was extremely funny. She yearned for the courage to ask him out for a drink, just to see his face.

'What are you laughing at?' he said.

'Oh – nothing really. Doing anything nice for Christmas?'

'Yes, actually. I'm going to sit by my fireside and read my book, drinking some rather good port. I'm looking forward to it enormously. You?'

'Oh I shall go home. We'll all fight. Mum will work herself into the ground, but we'll all enjoy it really.'

They lapsed into a companionable silence, the gentle pace smoothing out their differences.

'Are you ever tempted just to sail away down the canal?' he asked.

'I would be if it would solve anything,' she said. 'But running away never helps. And if I left my mooring, Mike would give it to someone else, then I couldn't get a licence. It's a vicious circle.'

'You could get another mooring, couldn't you?'

May shook her head. 'Residential moorings in London make hens' teeth look like pebbles on a beach. They cost all the bombs in NATO. I owe Mike a bundle for mine, but it's very cheap compared to what most people charge. That's

why he wants me out, so he can bump up the price. If I stay
there, he can only put the rent up by a certain amount. And
that's bad enough.'

Hugh nodded. 'I have a friend who's got a warehouse on
an arm of the canal.'

'Well if he's short of a few bob, tell him to rent it out as a
marina.' She sighed, sounding to her own ears uncomfortably
wistful. 'We'll have to turn now. The next winding-hole isn't
for miles.'

'What a shame. I was enjoying myself.'

So was she. In spite of the bickering that went on between
them, she did feel he had picked up a little of the magic of
canals. He had seemed to understand when she had explained
her love of them.

'Would you mind getting down from there? We have to
wind here, and I need to concentrate.'

She made the manoeuvre perfectly. It took every ounce of
concentration, using the engine to turn the seventy-foot boat
without knocking into any of the craft on the other side of
the towpath.

They were facing the other way and motoring for home
before Hugh spoke again. 'Look, if you're not busy tonight,
we could go out and eat.'

Was he making a pass at her? A quick glance set her mind
at rest. And she was hungry. She and Harriet had an incredibly small housekeeping budget. Without Harriet to do something magical with an onion and a tin of tomatoes, May
would have to make do with copious amounts of toast and
Marmite. But financially, it was out of the question.

'I'm afraid I really can't afford it.'

Hugh was taken aback. 'I meant you to be my guest. I'm
inviting you out to dinner.'

It was May's turn to be taken aback. She hadn't been
asked out to dinner in ages. Feeling thoroughly flustered, she
tried to backtrack. 'I don't like restaurants much.'

'No, well, I don't suppose they're too keen on you, either.'
He looked pointedly at her dungarees and big boots. 'But
we – I could get a takeaway.'

The glands under May's ears started to hurt.

'It's against my principles to accept . . .'

'For crying out loud! Your principles can be so *boring*! You've given me tea and biscuits, I've accepted your hospitality. Why, by all that's holy, can't you accept mine! If you'd feel happier, I'll put it on my expense account!'

'Why would that make it better?'

'Then you can tell yourself you're getting a free meal off the bloated plutocrats!'

May and her principles crumpled. She was being ridiculous. If there'd been anything half decent to eat on the boat, she'd have offered to share it with him. If she'd known him better, she would have shared the heel of cheese and the bread. She was being gauche and churlish. 'Sorry. I do get a bit rabid.' She smiled ruefully up at him. 'If the invitation's still open, I'd be delighted to accept.'

A flicker of emotion crossed Hugh's stern features, but he kept his reaction down to a small smile. 'Well, what would you like? Chinese, pizza, fish and chips . . .'

'Curry?' She was really hungry now and had to keep her mouth shut in case she actually drooled.

'Is there a good Indian locally?'

She nodded. 'Just round the corner. I can give you directions.'

'Curry it is, then.'

The thought of plunging a fork into a steaming heap of chicken korma and saffron rice made her grin suddenly. 'Wonderful! Now be an angel and jump ashore with a bow-rope – but don't, for goodness' sake, pull on it. Just hold it firm.'

He was remarkably adept for a beginner, and honesty forced her to tell him so. He shrugged off her grudging praise. 'I sail. It helps.'

May found knives and forks and cleared the clutter from the table while Hugh went to the Indian. She hoped they wouldn't take too long, and that he'd remember the poppadoms. When she thought she wouldn't last another minute he appeared, his arms full of carrier bags and chilled lager. I could get to like this man, she thought.

May was far too hungry even to pretend to make small

talk, but as the food went down, she felt better and better disposed towards its donor . . . until he started to nag.

'Is there really nothing else you can do apart from cleaning?'

May wiped her plate with a bit of naan bread. 'No! Yes! It's hard enough trying to establish a business, without the likes of you coming along and asking damn fool questions.'

He ignored this. 'Have you thought of everything?'

'Yes! Get off my case, will you? I'm quite happy being a cleaner.'

'You don't look happy. You've lost your carefree, devil-may-care attitude.'

She glared at him. So would you if you had my problems, she thought. Out loud she said, 'Nonsense!'

Hugh put down his fork and stacked his plate on top of May's. 'Tell me about *The Rose Revived*. Was it like this when you got it?'

May relaxed. The boat was her favourite subject. 'No! It was more or less a shell. I fitted it out. I had help. Jed, on *Shadowfax*, is a brilliant joiner, and he showed me what to do. But I did it.'

Hugh got to his feet and gathered up the plates, keeping his head carefully lowered so as not to hit it on the beams. 'Well it's not very good. Look at this joint.' He poked an accusing finger into an angle. 'It doesn't fit properly.'

May leapt up, cut to the quick. 'What do you mean?' She examined the joint. 'There's nothing wrong with that, it's just a little out of true! God! I'd like to see you do as well!'

Hugh shook his head. 'You'd be disappointed. I'm hopeless.'

'Then don't criticize my work then!'

'Don't get all indignant, I was just making a point.'

'What?' she demanded, eyes sparkling, squared up for a fight.

'That you can do other things besides cleaning.' Hugh put his hand on her cheek, then took it away again rather quickly. 'You are very talented. You're just totally unfocused.'

His touch seared her. It was all she could do to summon

133

up a retort. 'People who don't know what they're talking about often take refuge in jargon.'

'And people who know they're cornered often take refuge in aggression.'

May drew breath to deny she was being aggressive but instead had to swallow hard. The lager made her want to belch. By the time she'd got her bodily functions under control he'd taken the plates and glasses through to the galley and put his coat on. May barely had time to thank him for a lovely meal before he had gone.

'That's wonderful!' said Harriet. 'Matthew is always asking me about the boat, and now he'll have a chance to see it! Mr Buckfast is *such* a nice man.'

May was about to argue when she realized Harriet was talking about Matthew's headmaster. She felt a twinge of unease. She hadn't been rude enough to put Hugh off, had she? She'd feel dreadful if Harriet had missed an opportunity to see her son.

'You work out the food, I'll work out a price.' She grinned ruefully. 'It's about time *The Rose* did something to earn her own living. We've been supporting her for long enough.'

CHAPTER FOURTEEN

Sally awoke at ten o'clock with a familiar grinding pain in her back which said she was about to have a bitch of a period.

It was Saturday – the day of the boat trip for Matthew and his friends. That was good. She'd offered to help but they'd said they didn't need her. And Piers wasn't there to grumble at her. Sally sank back into her pillows. Perhaps there was something to this living alone after all.

Piers had behaved as if she had periods on purpose. She would find herself apologizing as if the whole female reproductive system was designed by her to get out of having sex and to draw attention to herself. Perhaps, she mused, his new woman had found a way to avoid menstruating. If she also managed not to grow hair under her arms or on her legs, she would render herself totally perfect. Like a Barbie doll. Sally slithered out of bed and staggered to the bathroom. On the other hand, she thought, a doll which came with a bottle of red fluid and tiny, looseable tampons who said, 'I can't go swimming today, Ken,' when you pressed a button in her tummy, might be a big seller.

The bottle of aspirin, which she had hoped to find in the bathroom cabinet was missing. Piers had probably taken it. Sally was indignant. They had been her aspirin, bought with her money. He had no right just to take them.

Her reflection in the mirror did nothing to lift her mood. Her hair was greasy, there was a spot in the crease of her nose which had ambitions to become Vesuvius and there were shadows under her eyes, emphasizing the paleness of her skin. Not only that, but she was down to her last two panty-liners. Now she would have to venture out into the cold and not spend the entire day with her back against a radiator. She was not surprised, it always happened. But she was annoyed.

'Still, I've got a couple of hours before I need worry,' she told herself bracingly. 'I'll have a bath, wash my hair, floss my teeth, put on some make-up. I might feel better by then.'

She switched on the immersion heater, went into the kitchen and heated the last of the milk. Then she fetched her duvet from the bedroom, made herself comfortable in front of the television and settled down for a spot of mental chewing-gum while she waited for the water to heat.

Saturday-morning television was all cartoons and bouncy, white-toothed presenters, who either didn't have periods at all, or were more organized about them. None of those tanned young things would ever run out of 'sanpro' or aspirin. The programmes they presented seemed to be aimed at the under-tens, which suited Sally's present mood perfectly. She watched uncritically and automatically. Scrappy-doo was just rescuing his Uncle Scooby from the maw of some particularly frightful monster when the television and all the lights went off.

For a moment Sally thought how nice it would be if she could just burst into tears. But it would be more useful to find the trip switch and reset it. At least with Piers away, she wouldn't have to flap about resetting the multitude of digital clocks which would flash at her from every electrical appliance bar the toaster the moment the power went back on. Piers felt insecure if he couldn't tell the time at least three ways in every room and caused an almighty fuss if any two clocks differed.

The trip switch was solidly in place. Sally peered out of the window to see if everyone's lights were out or if it were just hers. But no, the rogue street light which shone all day and was dark all night was twinkling merrily in the morning sun.

Sally contemplated tears more seriously. If only she could have rung May and Harriet. May would have made jokes about feminists and light bulbs, and come round with a screwdriver and fuse wire and sorted out the problem. But she couldn't bother them today, when they would both be so busy.

Without much enthusiasm, she dragged out the Yellow Pages and looked up electricians. It was Saturday, and anyone who was prepared to come would charge extra and want to be paid in cash. Sally hadn't any. But she had to do something. Mentally, she trawled through her past boyfriends, but there was no one she could ring up who'd be remotely useful. She was on her own.

She padded back to her bedroom to get dressed and pulled on an ancient pair of leggings, several T-shirts, a couple of baggy sweaters and her worn-out trainers. As she scraped her greasy hair into a scrunchie, she wondered if she could face washing it in tepid water. She would have to towel it dry, which would take for ever and make it stick out at funny angles, but it might make her feel better. Then again, it might make her catch cold. She decided against it.

Sally found her handbag and opened her purse to see if she had enough for a family pack of Mars bars and some magazines as well as tampons. If you're going to be self-indulgent enough to have a period, she reckoned, you might as well do the thing properly. There wasn't nearly enough.

'Oh sod, sod, sod, sod!' she said aloud, and went to see if there was any money lying around in Piers's desk. It was a faint hope. He kept a close eye on his loose change, but not even living with Piers for six months had cured Sally of optimism.

All she found were loose paperclips and letters. Harriet had stacked his post, mostly bills, in date order. It hadn't occurred to Sally that she should open them.

Now, for want of anything pleasanter or more constructive to do, Sally took them over to the window so that she could look through them. There was a bill from the electricity board which turned out to be for quite a large amount. It was also dated from before Piers left. Another riffle through produced the red one.

'Very unlike him!'

Her flicker of satisfaction at having caught him out in incompetence was swiftly edged out by an unwelcome suspicion. Were these unpaid bills part of a deliberate ploy to get her out of his flat? How long had he told her she could stay? Grimly, she went on examining envelopes, searching for a love letter to complete her orgy of misery. Instead, almost as painful, was another letter from the electricity board. It thanked Mr Fox for his cheque and arranged to terminate the supply. Sally peered at the calendar. The date mentioned was today's.

Putting her hysterics on hold, Sally opened every envelope, confirming her worst suspicions with each one.

There was the letter from the telephone company confirming that the phone would be disconnected, but not saying when. There was one from the landlord accepting Piers's final payment of rent and confirming that the flat would be vacant by next Monday. Only the water company was keeping to itself as to whether that was going to be cut off too.

Sally sat very still. She had to think, and quickly, but if she wasn't careful she would go off into a tailspin of panic, which wouldn't help her.

Her mother would always take her in, but only as a stopgap, she couldn't stay there long. And she wasn't the sort of person who could squat. Even if she could manage without heat, electricity and mains water, she couldn't live with the feeling that men with crowbars might evict her at any moment.

Since being with Piers, she'd rather lost touch with her friends. And anyway, those of the type and vintage which she could have rung and said, 'Sorry I haven't been in touch for ages but my boyfriend's thrown me out. Can I sleep on your floor?' were scattered round the country.

May and Harriet were the only ones in London she could call on in an emergency, and with her luck the phone would be cut off before she could reasonably ring them. And what could they do, apart from inviting her to live with them. She sighed. At least she wouldn't be homeless, although, having heard Harriet's description of the plumbing arrangements, she might become dependent on public conveniences.

The telephone announced that it was still in working order with a piercing chirrup. She picked it up, hoping it was

Piers. She had several months of anger and some recent moments of pure rage to communicate to him. And for once she was confident that she would get it all out without stumbling over her lines.

It wasn't Piers. It was a nicely spoken girl, whom Sally couldn't possibly shout at, telling her that a firm was arriving on Monday to pack and store all Piers's possessions. She wanted to know where the men could collect the key.

'I'll leave it under the mat,' hissed Sally through clenched teeth and slammed down the receiver.

Wondering simultaneously if Cleaning Undertaken should offer that service and if the packing firm would swathe her in bubble wrap if she were still here on Monday, Sally slumped back on to the sofa. Once, in this situation, she might well have walked out of the flat into the nearest department store and made full use of the ladies' powder room, sprayed herself with free samples of scent and tried on clothes. But having had May and Harriet as an example, even for a short time, this no longer seemed the way to go. She would have to do something more positive and constructive.

Thus resolved, she went into the bedroom to pack her clothes. But pack them into what? All her suitcases, apart from a sports bag and a vanity case, were at her mother's house, and Piers had selfishly taken all his.

'He's turned me into a bag lady. A designer bag lady,' she amended, pulling out the pile of glamorous carriers from under her chest of drawers. But although they would make her the chicest derelict in town, they wouldn't hold nearly enough. She must supplement them with something more practical. She fetched some bin-liners from the kitchen.

With the resolve to be sensible firmly in mind, Sally determined to weed her wardrobe, to have a good clear out. It was the sort of task best undertaken with a strong-minded friend who would be frank about items bought in sales because they were half price and had a good label and not permit the snatching back of shrunken sweaters from the rubbish pile because they're riddled with memories of some really sweet man as well as moth holes. But Sally was alone and at a hormonal disadvantage. It was only when it dawned on her that she still had eight plastic sacks full of clothes to transport across London without the wherewithal for a taxi that she decided to go through everything again.

It was back-breaking work, especially to a back already racked with pain. Sally had a deeply ingrained resistance to drinking before twelve o'clock caused by her mother's insistence that it was the first step on the road to alcoholism, but the moment it struck noon, she was going to finish Piers's gin. It was supposed to be good for what ailed her.

Unfortunately, the heel-tap in the bottom of the bottle didn't take a lot of finishing, did little for her throbbing ovaries, and with low-calorie orange squash, tasted disgusting.

She kept looking at her travelling alarm clock, the only timepiece in the house still functioning, counting the hours before May and Harriet would be free. It was a race between the boat trip's return, and the telephone company terminating its contract.

She found her coat. She surely must have enough small change to buy something. She left the building wondering what women did before Tampax and cursing the government for putting VAT on them.

In the shop, she dithered between buying a six-pack of Mars bars and a copy of the *People's Friend*, or a roll of loo paper and a packet of ten own-brand tampons. Eventually she made the adult choice and put back the chocolate and the love stories. They were false friends anyway. One made you fat and the other made you believe in happy endings.

Regretting her decision, she walked slowly back to the flat feeling drained. Huddled on the sofa under the duvet to keep warm, Sally tried to sleep. There was nothing else to do.

She had just dozed off, after reciting at least half of the old counties of England and Wales to herself, when the doorbell rang. Jolted awake, she ran to answer it, sure it was Harriet and May come to visit her. She realized it wasn't them immediately she opened the door, but disappointment and a fading light left her at a loss as to who had woken her. She blinked vacantly at the huge man. He was looking expectant, as if she ought to know who he was.

'Miss Bliss?'

The voice did it. Recognition flooded back. James Lucas. Sod's law dictated that he would appear on her doorstep when she was looking worse than she hoped to look in her coffin.

'It's you.'

'I've come for the keys. Mrs Walker said you had them.'

'The keys? But I thought the flat was mine until Monday?'

'What are you talking about? Are you all right?'

Piers had always said that so crossly. This bear-like person sounded genuinely interested, if not actually concerned. Sally developed a lump in her throat and hoped he wouldn't notice that she wasn't wearing a bra.

'Yes. No. I've just realized what keys you mean. Would you like to come in while I find them?'

She was fairly sure that the keys were in her handbag. Where that might be was another set of worry beads. He followed her into the sitting-room as she hunted round in the gathering darkness, cursing Piers for renting a flat with so few windows.

'Why don't you put a light on,' he asked.

'Because I've no electricity. It's been cut off.'

'Why? Didn't you pay the bill?'

'Someone else didn't pay the bill.' She swung round to look at him. 'Talking of which, you haven't paid us for cleaning your uncle's flat.'

'I know. If you tell me how much, I'll pay it.'

'In cash?' Sally brightened considerably.

'No. I'm afraid it'll have to be a cheque. Is that a problem?'

'Frankly, yes.'

'Well, how much money do you need? I've got a little.'

'I couldn't possibly borrow money from a complete stranger.'

'You wouldn't be, even if I were a complete stranger. You'd be borrowing it from your firm. How much do you need?'

Sally did not have many inhibiting feminist principles about being subsidized by men, and those she did have were swiftly overcome. 'Enough for a taxi to my friend's boat in Paddington.' The little boys must have gone by now.

'I could lend you the Tube fare . . .'

'I can't go on the Tube! I've got all my clothes in plastic sacks! Plus a few carriers!'

'But why do you have to take all your clothes to go and stay with friends? Surely you could just choose –'

'You don't understand. I'm being evicted. I've got to get out of this flat, with everything in it that's mine and go and live on a boat! And now I can't find my bloody handbag!'

Sally sniffed and wiped her nose on the back of her hand. Now she had started to cry, he would flee, with or without the keys to his flat. She huddled herself away from him so she wouldn't see him leave.

'I'm sure there's nothing broken that can't be mended,' he said gently.

Sally swallowed hard. She would be able to get herself under control if she didn't have to speak. If she could just find her bag, give him the keys, take his useless cheque and get him out of there, she would be fine.

'Is this your bag?'

Sally snatched it, realizing too late that, when she gave him the keys and had been paid, she would be left alone in the cold and dark again. Angrily, she emptied it on to the table, searching for the keys more by feel than by sight. At last she found them.

'Here you are!'

'Thank you very much. Now, how much do I owe you?'

If she'd ever known, Sally had now forgotten. And right now, the thought of trying to work it out was worse than the thought of what May would say when she confessed to being within inches of payment, only to let it slip through her fingers.

'I don't know,' she said dolefully. 'Give me your address. We'll have to send you a bill.'

She watched him as he wrote his address on the back of the envelope he handed her. Now, she wouldn't even have him while he wrote out a cheque and she fudged together some sort of receipt. She stuffed the address into her bag and gulped.

James had put the pen and the keys in his pocket but otherwise didn't move.

'I don't think I should leave you here. You don't seem very well.'

'I'm perfectly all right, I just happen to be having a period. It's a perfectly natural process you know.' Then she burst into tears.

James Lucas had broad shoulders, strong arms and a very hairy tweed jacket which smelt of old rope and grass. Sally had plenty of opportunity to analyse this smell as he clasped her sobbing figure tightly to him, patting her back as if trying to get wind up from a baby.

'I'm so sorry about this,' she sniffed.

He didn't reply, but stuffed a hanky into her hand.

'I don't usually cry on strangers.'

'I'm sure you don't,' he murmured.

Sally wanted to stay in his arms for ever, but tried to wrench herself away. He was probably dying to escape from this weeping, crazy woman. He tightened his hold. 'Just stay where you are. You'll feel better in a minute.'

Sally already felt better. But the thought that he would put her down in a minute was devastating. 'You're very understanding,' she mumbled into his coat.

'I have two older sisters,' he said. 'Both of whom suffer from extreme PMT and cramps. They didn't think my being a boy entitled me to be spared the gory details.' He was still holding Sally with the firm but gentle hold which animals were supposed to respond to.

'Oh.' Having failed to free herself, Sally stood passively in the circle of his arms.

'What you need is a hot bath, a hot water bottle and a hot toddy. Have you any hot water?'

'No.' Comforts beyond the dreams of avarice, and all out of reach.

'Then you'd better come with me.'

CHAPTER FIFTEEN

James helped her find the bag with her night things in and
led her down the stairs and into the car. It was an old estate,
muddy and smelling of dog, but marvellously warm.

'Clodagh's in the back,' he said.

The back seats were folded down and, turning round,
Sally saw the dog, taking up the entire space. She lifted
her head to greet Sally, who sensed empathy in the dark
eyes.

James Lucas's car may have been a touch bucolic but there
was nothing countrified about his driving technique. He
snaked through the traffic as if he were a taxi driver and
drew up in front of an all-night chemist, ignoring the double
yellow lines.

'I won't be a moment,' he said. 'I just want to get some
analgesics and a hot water bottle. Should I get anything
else?'

She shook her head. In spite of his sympathy and his
sisters, Sally didn't feel able to mention her most pressing
need. 'I've got my toothbrush and everything in my vanity
case.'

'I didn't mean that.' He smiled, and she noticed that there
was a tiny chip off one of his front teeth. 'Don't be embarrassed. What do you use? Super?'

Her cheeks burning, Sally nodded.

'I won't be long.'

Sally was just starting to look furtively up and down the
road for traffic wardens or wheel clampers when he returned
and put a carrier-bag on her knee. Peering inside, so she
wouldn't have to look at him, she noticed it contained chocolate and bubble bath as well as a furry hot water bottle,
aspirin and the dreaded Tampax.

'I thought you didn't have much cash. You've bought all sorts of things.'

He started the car. 'I used my credit card. I don't suppose Cleaning Undertaken accepts them, does it?'

Almost, she wished he would be cross with her for putting him to all this trouble. His niceness was making it so hard not to lapse into wimpishness. No one had looked after her so well since she'd had glandular fever and her mother, who was also an actress, but 'resting', had nursed her. They'd spent the happiest three months together that either of them could remember. But when she saw that they had reached the flat she and the others had cleaned so assiduously, she found her voice.

'Look, I don't think this is a good idea. I mean, supposing the Walkers saw me go into your flat? They'd be horrified. Just the sight of my leggings would send them into apoplexy.'

'You could always put my coat over your head,' he said, and opened the tailgate for Clodagh.

Sally wasn't in the mood for jokes. She got out of the car and kept her head well down as they climbed the stairs to his flat.

'Welcome home,' said James and opened the door.

The flat smelled faintly of soda crystals and disinfectant and was cold. But the lights went on at a flick of a switch.

'You know where the bathroom is,' he said, 'and then I suggest you come into the library. There's a heater in there.'

Robbed of embarrassment by his matter-of-fact attitude, Sally did as she was told. The library was already warmer than the rest of the flat. An ancient electric fire which had three bands of electric coils glowed crimsonly above some crinkling artificial coals pushed out a faint smell of burning dust along with waves of glorious heat.

Clodagh had claimed the sofa, but James ordered her off, insisting that Sally's need was more pressing. Gingerly, Sally stretched herself out, anxious lest Clodagh decided that soul-sisters could share, and suffocate her.

'I'll find a cover to put over you and when I've got my things in from the car I'll make you something to drink.'

The man's a saint, thought Sally, kicking off her shoes.

He came back with a travelling rug which smelt of moth-balls and covered her tenderly with it, tucking it in round her feet.

'You're very good at this,' said Sally.

'So I ought to be. As a farmer, I'm used to looking after sick stock.'

It took Sally a millisecond to grasp the enormity of this statement, but while it was very unflattering to be treated like a cow, the effect was very soothing. Before she could think of a suitable reply, grateful yet reproving, James had left the room.

Sally lay with her eyes closed. She heard the flat door open and close several times as James fetched his stuff from the car. If she was a good guest she'd help him. But she wasn't a guest, she was a poorly cow. He probably took in sick lambs and lame dogs, too. She was just another stray he happened to come across.

He came in with a pillow and a steaming mug. The pillow smelt faintly of maleness, the mug smelt strongly of whisky and lemon. One could do a lot worse than be one of James's cows, thought Sally, sipping the scalding toddy. What price feminism?

The alcohol in the drink had just dispersed itself to her extremities, when James reappeared wearing a suit. It was an unpleasant shock. The severe tailoring and white shirt made him suddenly handsome and strange looking, as if the hairy son of the soil had a smarter, urban, twin brother. In other circumstances Sally would have considered it a vast improvement, but it meant that he was going out, and she would be alone again.

She smiled as brightly as she could. She was at least warm and had Clodagh for company. 'You look extremely smart. Are you going anywhere nice?'

'Tea with my ancient aunt, and then dinner with some old friends. But I'm going out to get you a video first, so you won't be lonely.'

'I won't be lonely unless you take Clodagh,' she protested, not quite truthfully.

'Bored then. She's not much of a conversationalist. And my uncle's got no books published after nineteen ten, so there's nothing much to read. Unless you fancy Trollope?'

'Joanna or Anthony?'

'Anthony.'

She shook her head and bit her lip.

'A video then.' He whisked himself out of the room before she could say any more.

Her lack of culture must be obvious. He had known at a glance that she never read a book more than two inches thick unless it was written by Jilly Cooper. Perhaps Piers had been right: she was an air-head.

Sally was beginning to feel that if she had made a start on *The Warden* she would have got quite well along the way, he was being so long, when Clodagh suddenly clambered to her feet and went to the door, whining softly. Sally rolled off her sofa and let her into the hall before looking out into the street for James's car. But there was no sign of him getting out of any of the larger vehicles already parked.

Clodagh probably needed to go out. 'Now I'm going to be fined for letting a dog the size of a donkey foul the footpath. Oh hell!'

She had just found her shoes when she heard a key in the lock. A moment later she saw Clodagh with her paws on her master's shoulders. 'Sorry I was so long,' said James. 'It took me a while to find a shop. Can you take Clo while I bring them in?'

'Of course.'

Clodagh seemed quite happy to return to her place in front of the fire, and Sally, who didn't want James to get too much opportunity to see her in such dreadful clothes without underwear, returned to hers. Once there, she had several minutes to wonder why he needed to go back to the car when he'd only got a couple of videos.

When he did come into the library, he was carrying a television.

'What on earth . . .' Then light dawned. 'You didn't go out and buy that, just for me?' Sally was appalled.

'I hired it. And it's for me,' he said, dumping it next to the heater. 'I'll just go and get the video.'

He returned with a video recorder tucked under one arm and a clutch of tapes in his hand. He handed the tapes to Sally. 'Have a look at these while I get this lot set up.'

Part of Sally wanted him to have chosen something artistic and intellectual, but no, her blatant empty-headedness had led him to hire three of the most romantic films about. And, as Piers refused to watch anything that wasn't about war in some form or other, she hadn't seen any of them.

'Right, which one shall I put on first? Or would you rather watch the box?'

'I'll watch a video please,' she said hastily, before he homed in on the fact she was addicted to *Blind Date*. 'Here, this one had really good reviews.'

James smiled and slotted it in. 'I'm sorry I have to leave you so early, but this is a special occasion. It's why I came back to town again so soon. Do eat something when you feel like it. There's all sorts of things in a box in the kitchen.'

'I'll be fine. Don't let me make you late.'

'No. I'd better go. Clodagh, you'll be all right with Sally. She'll look after you.'

He squatted down and caressed the dog's head with such tenderness, Sally felt a pang of jealousy. If her hair hadn't been dirty she'd have liked those sensitive fingers soothing the tension away from her own scalp. She smiled up at him, willing him to kiss her goodbye – even just a peck. But probably put off by her spot, he didn't. He just straightened up. 'I'll let her out when I get back.'

Then she heard the flat door close and he was gone.

Sally woke up as James tucked a duvet about her. On the floor were the remains of her evening's self indulgence – chocolate wrappers, empty mugs, the videos (out of their cases), and a magazine face down.

'I didn't mean to wake you, but since I have, would you like the bed?'

Sally blinked at him, not properly awake. 'The bed? Sorry – er what's the time?'

'Two o'clock in the morning.'

'I must go home! I can't spend the night with you.'

Something – sternness? disapproval? – flickered across his features under his now-tousled hair. Sally was too dazed to work out what she'd said wrong. 'You've been so kind and everything, normally I'd . . .'

James appeared to bite down on his emotions, but before his normal calm returned, Sally recognized a flash of pure anger.

He interrupted her automatic apology. 'If you're quite comfortable here, I'd be glad of the bed. This sofa's a bit short for me.'

'The sofa's fine. Here, have your duvet.'

'No, thank you. I've got a sleeping-bag. Goodnight, Sally, I'll see you in the morning.'

Alone in the dark, Sally realized she'd made a dreadful mistake. Her experience of men had not led her to expect the proverbial free lunch. On the whole they didn't lavish care and attention on you unless they expected something in return. And that something was usually sex.

Of course she hardly knew James, but he had been extremely kind to her and the thought of spending time in his bed was not what she'd think of as a fate worse than death. But it seemed that her feelings were not reciprocated. The very idea of even touching her was obviously totally repellent to him.

When she was feeling less awful, when her hair was clean and her complexion clear and she had on something decent, she would try again. He wouldn't refuse her if she was really concentrating on seducing him.

Sally got up early the next morning, had a bath and washed her hair, drying both hair and body on James's towel. She felt fine again and was determined to give James a really good impression of what she was like when firing on all four cylinders. When he and Clodagh appeared in the kitchen she was cooking eggs and bacon and had made fresh coffee. She flashed her freshly brushed and flossed teeth in a smile that was shy yet enticing, with a hint of domestic efficiency thrown in. Sometimes she hated herself for being so shallow. Now she was grateful for being able to act.

'Good morning, James. Did you sleep well?'

He pushed back his hair from his face and confirmed that he had.

'I hope you can eat breakfast at this ungodly hour, but I felt I must repay some of your kindness by cooking it for you.'

James glanced at his watch. 'I usually have breakfast about nine, when I've done the feeding. On a farm, this wouldn't be considered early.'

'But I daresay on a farm, you usually go to bed before two o'clock in the morning.'

'Very true. I'll just take Clodagh downstairs, have a quick bath and then join you.'

'Fine.' Sally turned back to her frying-pan, hoping she'd left him some hot water, and wondering if a woman was responsible for his late return.

'So, are you going to sell this place then?' asked Sally, being wifely with the coffee pot.

James nodded, his mouth full of toast and marmalade. 'Eventually. I've got to wait a while, though.'

'Why?'

'Stipulated in the will.' He finished his mouthful. 'I had very eccentric twin uncles. They hated each other. The first one left me the farm, which I love and was born to look after. The other one, Joshua, who lived here, was determined not to let the farm, left to me by my uncle Isaac, benefit from his estate.'

'So why leave anything to you? Why not the local cats' home?'

'Sometimes I wish he had, honestly. But he had too much of a sense of duty to let the money go out of the family completely, so he just made things difficult for me.'

'He could have left the flat to your sisters, couldn't he?'

James shook his head. 'He left them all the available cash, lucky things, but land has to pass down the male line, even if it's only a few square feet in Victoria and several floors up.'

'Can't you ever sell it, then?'

'Oh yes, Joshua wasn't totally off his head, but I've got to wait a year. He doesn't want good money being poured into "that bloody eccentric's miserable little parcel of land he doesn't even know how to farm", and I quote. Isaac was into organic farming before it was either profitable or fashionable. Now it's fashionable, but we'll be waiting to be the other thing for some years yet.'

'Oh. Why?'

'The farm's too small, too full of hedges, wildflowers and Cotswold stone walls which cost a fortune to maintain.' He grinned suddenly. 'Or they would, if we did maintain them.'

'You could sell the farm, then?'

James shook his head. 'I couldn't. It's my life.'

The cold hand of disappointment clutched at Sally. She would never have him for herself, he was already married to his farm. A moment later she realized that if she wanted James, she would have to take the farm too. 'I've always liked the country,' she said encouragingly. 'But I don't get into it enough.'

James regarded her steadily. 'The country's not all downy ducklings and sweet little lambs, you know. Most of it's mud and icy winds.'

'Even in the summer?'

James's mouth curved in a smile which was more ironic than humorous. ''Fraid so.'

Sally saw that he had finished his toast and leapt to her feet before he could bring their conversation to an end. 'Shall I make some more toast?'

'No, thank you. What about you? You've hardly eaten a thing.'

Sally, who found it difficult to eat anyway when she was excited, had forced down more breakfast that morning than she'd had in the previous two years. 'No, I'm fine. I'll just wash the dishes.'

He didn't argue. 'If you wouldn't mind. I've got some papers to sort out. And then I'll take you wherever you want to go.'

With luck, Sally's mumbled thanks hid her disappointment that he hadn't offered to let her stay in his flat.

To soothe her feelings of rejection, she offered Clodagh a piece of bacon rind. Clodagh accepted it with extreme delicacy and then dropped it on the floor. Sally felt more rejected than ever.

CHAPTER SIXTEEN

While Sally was suffering and powerless, Harriet and May were preparing for an onslaught of small boys and their minders.

May, who was never too particular about the standard of her housework, insisted that her boat should gleam as if for a royal visit. The brass bands round the chimney were transformed from greeny-grey to the brightest gold, as was her brass tiller-bar, extricated for the occasion from under her bed. The white paintwork was scrubbed and, in places, renewed, and she had used furniture polish on the boat's bright blue sides. She had even gone so far as to polish the outside of the windows, which she did lying face down on the roof with a wodge of newspaper. She nearly fell in.

Inside, Harriet had swept and dusted almost as hard, so the interior of the boat was as immaculate as the outside. Harriet knew that for May there was a lot at stake, more than she'd admit, even to herself.

When May had rung Hugh with what seemed a fair price for a day's outing on a boat, including food, he had snorted rudely. Expecting this, May had been fully prepared to quote overheads, say what they'd have to pay anyone else, and generally justify herself. But then it turned out that Hugh thought they were charging too little.

Since then, May had put herself through hoops in an effort to give value for money, and as far as possible, there not being time for a total refit, turn her comfortable narrow-boat into a luxury cruise liner.

'I don't suppose I've got time to re-do the name,' said May. They had spent the entire morning polishing everything that moved and painting everything that didn't, and were collapsed in the saloon, panting slightly.

'No.' Harriet was prepared to be very firm, when they heard a shout.

'Narrowboat ahoy!'

'Thank God for that,' breathed Harriet, and rushed with May to the window where they could see Tom Buckfast, his brother Hugh, and six little boys. They were all waving like mad from the other side of the canal.

'Matthew!' Harriet rushed through the boat, over *Shadowfax*, and jumped ashore, like a dog after a rabbit. She was streaking over the lock with no regard for safety before May could get out into the well-deck.

May saw one of the boys being picked up bodily and hugged until his ribs seemed endangered. His face was entirely obscured by Harriet's shoulder. May knew that Harriet would be crying and that she would be determined not to let anyone see.

She followed, more slowly, suddenly nervous. It seemed likely that Harriet had forgotten she was supposed to lecture the party on how to cross a lock gate safely, and generally remember that canals were wet and could drown the unsuspecting.

May's eye caught Hugh's as Harriet apologized profusely to her son for such an open demonstration of feeling. Matthew shrugged and smiled and seemed quite unembarrassed.

'How do you do, again?' said May, holding out her hand to Tom Buckfast, trusting he would recognize her without her disguise.

Matthew's headmaster crushed her hand fondly. 'Very well, thank you. It's very kind of you to let this rabble take over your boat for an afternoon. We've got a splendid day for it, haven't we? Now let me introduce you. You haven't a hope of remembering their names, but it's good practice for me to see if I can.'

Tom Buckfast solemnly introduced the boys, each of whom shook hands with May and Harriet. 'Miss Sargent is very kindly going to take you for a trip on her boat,' he said.

'Oh is she?' murmured Hugh over May's shoulder so only she could hear. 'Very kindly? Who'd have thought it.'

May tried to step back on to his foot but he was too quick

for her. She had found to her surprise that she'd been looking out for him, and acknowledged, reluctantly, that if he hadn't been there, she would have been disappointed. It was, of course, only because she knew she could trust him to do the right thing with a rope.

'Now,' said May, capturing the party's attention by holding her arm in the air. 'We have to cross a lock gate to get to my boat. This is a very dangerous thing to do! It is only possible if you go slowly, and hold on to the rail all the time. If you fall, you might not drown, but you will definitely have to have your stomach pumped. This they do by putting a thick tube down your throat into your stomach. Then they pour salty water down the tube which makes you throw up.'

She actually had only the haziest of ideas about how stomachs were pumped out, but she knew instinctively that gory details were more likely to sink in than more conventional strictures about safety procedures. She didn't want the cabin full of wet clothes.

She watched as each boy carefully crossed the lock, clinging to the rail, and then followed, having to force herself to be as slow and not skip over as carelessly as she usually did. She didn't concern herself with Hugh and Tom Buckfast's crossing. Harriet was still talking to Matthew.

'Now,' she said as the party assembled on the pontoon. 'To get to my boat, you have to cross this black one, it's called *Shadowfax*.'

'Out of the *Lord of the Rings*,' said a boy behind his hand to his friend.

'That's right, Eric,' said May, after a brief tussle with her memory. 'And when we cross other people's boats, we have to be *quiet*, otherwise they drop stink bombs down our chimneys.'

This was a bit of a slur on Jed, the most placid soul, who was unlikely to be disturbed by anything less noisy than an air-raid siren. But it was important for the boys to learn good boat manners.

'Harriet – if you'd like to get on board first, we'll go across one at a time. That way, if Mr Shadowfax decides it's time for a snack, he'll only get one of you.'

The boys were laughing nervously, but obviously enjoying themselves hugely. May found she was enjoying herself too. Her audience were so appreciative. It dawned on her as she swung herself aboard after them that perhaps she liked children. It was a revelation. She had always assumed that children were someone else's nuisance.

'In a minute, we'll set off,' she announced. 'We'll be away for about an hour. Keep your hands inside the boat when we go through bridges or locks. And if you decide to end it all and jump in the canal, remember, you'll get stuck round someone's propeller and cause them awful problems. Er um – Mr Buckfast?'

Both Hugh and Tom looked at her expectantly. How was she to distinguish between the brothers? Could she call Hugh Hugh in front of the children? She couldn't possibly call Matthew's headmaster Tom.

'Could you please go one each end of the boat and cast off when I yell?'

'Don't you use terms like "bow" and "stern" on canal boats?' said Tom Buckfast as he passed her to go aft.

May smiled briefly but didn't reply. She was too busy trying to get the engine to start first time. If it didn't, her tiny engine-room would be full of Buckfasts giving advice before she could spit on her hands.

'Thank you, thank you,' breathed May as the trusty engine turned, and began thumping sturdily. She liked Tom Buckfast so much, she didn't want him to patronize her, and so make himself an enemy.

'Cast off at the front there please, Mr er – Buckfast,' she bellowed.

Hugh, who had been standing on *Shadowfax*, the rope coiled, but still held round the pin at the bow, lifted it off and leapt neatly on to the bow of *The Rose Revived* as she nosed her way into the main canal.

'And now, you?' May smiled at the headmaster, who unhooked his line just as efficiently and joined her on the counter.

'You're very handy about a boat,' said May, adjusting her tiller. 'I know Hugh sails. Do you too?'

'Oh, yes,' said Tom. 'But Hugh sails seriously. The Fast-net, and all that stuff. I don't have the time. And do call me Tom. The boys are used to it.'

'And I'm May.' She grinned. 'I was wondering how to distinguish between you.'

Tom returned her grin. 'Is there a way to the cabin through the engine-room?'

May nodded, secure in the knowledge that, for the first time since they were built, her bedroom and the bathroom were tidy.

'Then, if you don't need me, I'll see how Miss Devonshire is getting on with the brats.'

'I'm sure she'd prefer it if you called her Harriet.'

Tom Buckfast smiled his agreement and disappeared down the hatch into the boat, while Hugh made his way along the two-inch gunwale to where May was standing on the flat stern of the boat, her shiny brass tiller-bar under her hand.

When they had passed the complications of boats moored on both sides of the canal and were out into the main stream, May suggested to Hugh, silent and watchful, that the boys might like to try steering.

'I notice that you're not offering me a go.'

'You've had a go. Besides, it must be dull stuff after sailing.'

'Not necessarily,' said Hugh.

May made a face at him. 'You're only saying that to be controversial. I know perfectly well you sailors consider travelling by canal as ditch-crawling, and utterly beneath the notice of anyone with a drop of British seafaring blood in their veins.'

'Now are you saying that in the hope that I'll agree with you? Or do you want me to argue fervently to the contrary?'

May muttered something rude under her breath. 'Are you going to let the boys come up, two at a time, for a turn at the tiller?'

The way he looked at her made her wonder if he'd heard her incantation. 'Only if you let me steer too.'

'You just want to show off in front of all those little boys.'

Hugh grinned.

Tom Buckfast had to have his go too. While everybody else was busily eating tomato soup, 'hogies' (which, Harriet told May, were filled French sticks) and tortilla chips, he came up to join May.

'It's good to see Hugh having such a nice time. He enjoys being with the boys if he lets himself.'

'He is rather –' May sought for a polite word for it.

Tom laughed loudly. 'He told me you called him a right-wing reactionary.'

'Well, he is.'

'Don't be misled by his appearance. He might surprise you.'

'Not if I can help it,' said May. Then, suddenly realizing that this sounded rather rude, she fell back on her seasonal change-of-conversation gambit.

'So, what are you doing for Christmas? Anything exciting?'

'We'll scoop up any boys left over after the end of term and go skiing. Hugh usually comes with us, but he's not this year.'

'Why not?'

'Says he's got to go away on business soon after and can't afford to break anything, but I don't think that's really the reason. He never does break anything, he's first-class at it.'

'Oh?'

Tom nodded. 'He brought his fiancée last year.'

Ah, so there was a woman in his life. 'I didn't know he had one.'

'Oh he hasn't now. She upped and left.'

Damn! If he had a nice solid fiancée, she might be able to stop thinking about him. 'I hope she didn't leave him broken hearted,' she said.

'Oh no. She'd have clung on for ever if there'd been any chance of them actually getting married. But I think Hugh likes the bachelor life too much to give it up. I think the reason he's not coming skiing this year is because my wife is inclined to match-make. He's frightened she'll introduce him to every spare female intent on finding a husband.'

'I know how he feels. The idea of getting married makes me thoroughly depressed.'

Tom laughed. 'Wait until you fall in love. You'll feel differently then.'

May scowled. 'You sound like my mother.'

'So why is it called "winding", like the stuff that blows, instead of "winding" like you do a clock?' Matthew asked his mother. 'It's much more like "winding" round something.'

Harriet looked questioningly at May.

May, who had just 'winded' the boat with enormous panache, didn't know. 'It's just called that. The turning places are called winding 'oles. Canal people were illiterate on the whole. They had their own reasons for calling things what they did. They called guillotine locks "gullentine" for example.'

'Surely,' said Hugh, 'that implies some degree of literacy. Otherwise, why would they even think of having a "u" there? If they'd just heard the word, they'd invent a word like "gillingteen", wouldn't they?'

May, who'd wondered about this herself, glowered at him. 'It's not too late to push you in, you know.'

Matthew was shocked. 'But May! He'd get stuck round your propeller and you'd have to take off the weed-hatch to get him out of it. Then some other poor soul may run aground on him.'

May, aware that Matthew had taken in much more of what she'd told him about canals than she'd suspected, nodded agreement. 'I suppose you're right. But there is still the mop.'

She indicated a rag mop with a handle painted like a barber's pole which she had used to swab down the roof of the boat, spinning it neatly to shake off the surplus water.

'How true,' said Hugh. 'Perhaps I'll go and give Harriet a hand.'

Without him, May felt a little lonely.

The trip was voted by all as a tremendous success. The boys were all delightful – polite, and yet relaxed enough to make jokes with each other and with the adults. Both men were enthusiastic and appreciative. And Tom Buckfast wrote out a cheque having added somewhat to the bill, with a grateful smile.

'We'd love to do this again, May. Have you ever thought of taking a boat out of London somewhere?'

'Well, there are camping boats, which take groups of children on canal trips.' She remembered passing boatloads of children, hanging over the side of unconverted narrowboats.

'Mmm. I know. I wondered about taking a small party in the summer term, say eight boys and a couple of adults? We'd make it worth your while.'

'I'd have to borrow a butty,' said May, and even as she said it, remembered who she could ask.

'If it hasn't got bacon in it,' asked Hugh, 'what's a butty?'

'It doesn't have an engine and you tow it along behind. It's a Welsh word for "mate". As in friend.'

'Ah, so you couldn't be my butty then?'

'No. I certainly could not.'

'But you could conceivably be my mate?'

'Not in even in my worst nightmare.' May glared, but there was laughter in the back of her eyes.

Sally could see May washing down the roof of *The Rose Revived* as she and James drew up in the car park opposite the mooring. They had been to Piers's flat and the boot was full of black plastic sacks.

'There's May. Come and meet her.'

Sally sounded cheerful, but she was disappointed in James. He had missed all but one of the many cues she had flung in his direction. She should by now be unpacking her things into his chest of drawers and thinking up a story explaining her presence for Captain and Mrs Walker. However, she thought, if you've the tiniest drop of theatre in your blood, you don't give up at the first refusal.

'I'll just get your stuff out of the boot and help you over with it, but I can't stop. I've got to have lunch with my solicitor.'

'On a *Sunday*?' Hastily, Sally covered her indignation with a quick dab of surprise.

James smiled somewhat ruefully. 'Fortunately, he's also a friend, otherwise I'd never get out of this mess.'

'Well, I don't know how to thank you for rescuing me. You were so kind and sympathetic.'

His kind and sympathetic eyes should have held at least a glimmer of a baser emotion by now, but they were still brown, crinkled with smile lines and utterly uninterested in Sally as a woman.

'That's perfectly all right. Now, let's get these bags across the lock.'

Sally was aware of his Volvo reversing out of the car park even before she had hefted the last plastic sack into the well-deck.

'Well you won't be homeless,' said May, who, with her share of their Saturday's work and Harriet's rent, had had great satisfaction in slapping a pile of used notes into Mike's hand.

Sally sipped the mug of tea placed in her hand by Harriet. 'That's wonderful of you, but there's all my stuff! It's so maddening of James not to offer to let me live in his flat when it's going to be empty most of the time.'

'How do you know?' Harriet, who had put down her cup and picked up a piece of charcoal and a scrap of paper was drawing Sally, long legs in a knot, body hunched in disappointment.

'He told me. He has a farm in Gloucestershire which he's just inherited, as well as the flat.'

'Lucky guy,' said May from the galley. 'Who wants a biscuit?'

'Really, May, I don't know how you keep so slim. You're always eating,' said Sally, momentarily distracted from her woes.

'I don't know either.' May came back into the saloon with a packet of Rich Teas. 'So how come he's inherited so much, then?'

By the time Sally had told May and Harriet about the organic farm and the mud, Harriet had half a dozen useful sketches.

'So do you think you'll see him again?' May, convinced that Sally had fallen in love with James already, needed to know if they would be supporting six plastic sacks and a case of unrequited love for long.

Sally smiled ingenuously. 'Oh yes. I left my watch in the bathroom and one of our leaflets. He's bound to ring to see where to send it, if he doesn't bring it round himself. Anyway, what are we going to do about my stuff?'

'I think you should go through everything again and have a car boot sale or something,' said May.

'I couldn't. I can sell ice to Eskimos, but not for me.'

'You could give the money to charity,' suggested Harriet. 'Then it wouldn't be for you.'

'Don't be daft! I'm desperately short of money! Anyway, it seems madness to sell my vital assets when I might need them.'

'We didn't mean you should go on the street, Sal,' said May. 'Just that you should get rid of a few surplus clothes.'

'None of my clothes are surplus. I was ruthless before. I'll ask the Walkers if they've any space I could borrow.'

And they may mention to James that they're looking after my stuff, and he might eventually think of suggesting I keep his flat warm for him, she added silently. But she kept her plan to herself. It was bad enough feeling manipulative without being accused of it by her best friends.

CHAPTER SEVENTEEN

Harriet was struggling. Her paper was so black she could hardly see her latest set of marks over the hundred other scrubbed-out ones. The man lay, naked and unadorned except by a single gold earring, entirely relaxed and unaffected by the half a dozen women who were struggling to draw him.

Harriet, who had hardly ever seen, and certainly never studied, male genitalia before, found herself getting it alarmingly out of proportion. She could almost hear May commenting that the model must have been hung like a dinosaur. Harriet had so little experience she didn't know if this man was normal or especially well endowed. He certainly seemed a lot bigger than the men who adorned the ceiling of the Sistine Chapel. She made a note to inspect any naked statues that came her way more carefully.

With luck, Leo wouldn't guess the struggle she had had with herself to make her confront this man's sexual organs, and not seat herself so she could only see his muscular back and curved buttocks. Most of the women had chosen this comfortable option. It was only Harriet and the grey-haired lady, who was called Elizabeth, who had braved this angle. Typically, Elizabeth, who had arrived late, but unflustered, was drawing this man with the same detached confidence with which she drew everything else. Harriet gritted her teeth and carried on.

The side of her hand was already black. Leo's old shirt, which she wore back to front as an overall, was also severely streaked. She smudged at the place again, leaving only a suggestion of shape. Then she shifted slightly, so the troublesome articles were in shadow, so when Leo came back from his cup of coffee, he might think that was all she could see.

Leo's attitude to her was hard to fathom. He said little about her work and what he did say was hardly complimentary. On the other hand he seemed to expect her to be encouraged by his acid remarks about 'water-colourists' and 'lady-painters'. Harriet's experience of men, including one brief, life-changing occasion, was limited. No-one like Leo lived in the village where she grew up – or if they did, she never met them. She had no tools to deal with Leo's worldly ways apart from common sense, which wasn't always enough.

Leo was cynical, demanding and arrogant and although he never bothered to be with Harriet, he could be charming. His entire class, with the apparent exception of Elizabeth, were in love with him.

None of these characteristics was particularly endearing. To be fair, he did little to encourage the women except toss out the occasional, bitingly sarcastic criticism of their work. But Harriet knew that he had had affairs with at least two of them, and might well currently be sleeping with another.

Harriet tried hard to dislike him. But just when she was convinced he was, in May's terminology, 'a complete shit', and it was only his stature in the art world, both as teacher and perpetrator, which kept her within a barge-pole's length of him, he did something undeniably kind, like offering a tramp the takeaway curry he had just bought. (She learned this from the tramp, who accosted her on the steps of the building, not to beg, but to send his regards to the 'governor'.)

Harriet wiped her hands on her overall and picked up her charcoal again, determined to capture the model's strongly defined Adam's apple. She was just enjoying the deep curve it formed before gliding into the neck, when she remembered it was a tertiary sexual characteristic. Leo knew how to pick a model.

And he was a superb teacher. If only he wouldn't dismiss her cleaning as a triviality. He couldn't be made to understand that she was part of a team. She owed it to May to do her bit. He expected her, which from him was more like a command, to spend more and more time working at her art, and less and less time doing anything else.

Therein lay Harriet's problem. Cleaning Undertaken was beginning to take off, even after only a month. They were popular among their clients, and their reputation, and with it their workload, was steadily growing. So far, none of Slime-ball's threats had materialized.

But even with no gaps in their diary, they could none of them earn for much more than six hours a day. None of their clients wanted anyone cleaning at the crack of dawn, or in the evening, when they came home from work. The obvious solution was to clean offices, either early or late. But as Harriet knew she wouldn't have the energy to do this and paint, she had avoided suggesting it to May, who would undertake it all herself, and end up exhausted.

They also needed some form of transport which would cut down the dead hours spent travelling from one job to another. Without an injection of capital, Harriet feared they were just too small to survive. Which was something else she didn't want to confide to May. It would be dreadful if, after all their hard work, May's boat still had to be sold.

And Harriet wasn't even managing her six hours a day, although she was the only one who worried about this. The other two knew she kept the accounts, advised on trickier cleaning problems, and that they couldn't manage without her. But Harriet felt guilty that she was spending more and more time on her art and less time cleaning. Since she had seen Matthew, she had attended several of Leo's classes which took up a whole morning or afternoon.

Harriet took a piece of tissue from her pocket and put a fine gleam on the model's earring with her fingernail. Just in time, as it turned out.

'That's it,' said the model. 'You've had half an hour, I need a coffee.'

A roomful of women sighed and put down their pencils. The young man climbed into a pair of boxer shorts, some jeans and a jersey before going to the kitchen in search of a hot drink. Harriet, on whose shoulders had fallen the role of coffee and tea maker for the models Leo had taken to importing, followed him. Leo met them at the door, mug in hand.

'Will you make Jake a cup of coffee, Harriet? I'll have a look at what you've all been doing.'

As always, these casual words made Harriet's heart race with anxiety, but she managed to smile calmly enough at Jake.

'Do you mind instant? I suspect Leo's finished all the real stuff.' It was Harriet's most important task in the morning, making Leo a large vacuum jug of strong, Costa Rican coffee. It was always gone by ten o'clock.

Jake shook his head. 'Anything as long as it's hot.'

'You must get awfully cold, doing what you do.'

'Yup,' he said cheerfully. 'But the money's good, so what do I care?'

'Oh?' Not for the first time, Harriet wished she was May and could ask direct questions.

Fortunately, Jake was proud of what he could earn with his beautiful body and announced his hourly rate with pride.

'Golly.' Harriet poured on the boiling water. I ought to do it, she thought. If I modelled for Leo, and put my earnings into the kitty, I needn't feel so guilty about spending so much time painting. I could earn twice as much modelling as cleaning, which would bring my earnings up to what May and Sally bring in.

But even the thought of it sent a deep blush up from her neck to her hairline. She knew she wasn't fat or anything, but she hadn't learnt to like her body. Living on the boat, she never had an opportunity to see it. Keeping it clean was difficult enough.

'There wouldn't be a biscuit, would there?' Jake had either not noticed the blush, or was accustomed to having that effect on women.

Harriet blinked for a moment and then pointed to a tin. 'Flapjack, in there.'

Jake took a bite out of the biggest piece. 'It's good.'

'It should be. I made it.'

Jake raised his eyebrows. 'So, are you and he an item?'

'God! No! Why should we be?'

'Well, you seem fairly handy round his kitchen.'

'I'm his cleaning lady,' said Harriet severely. 'I'm fairly handy round his U-bend, too.'

They both laughed. Harriet made herself a cup of black coffee and followed Jake back to the studio. Her cleaning had become limited to an hour before the class in the mornings and as much time as she could fit in before Leo sent her home. She had arranged a laundry service for his washing, and packing and unpacking the parcels was now part of her routine. The flapjack she made on the boat and brought in. Her grandmother would not have been satisfied by the standard of cleanliness, but thanks to her attention the contents of Leo's fridge were no longer likely to give him ptomaine poisoning.

Harriet achieved quite a lot by way of the cleaning that morning while Leo talked to Jake, more indeed, than she felt she had achieved at her easel. But eventually Jake went home and Leo got fed up with the sound of the vacuum and switched it off at the plug. Harriet, knowing a murmured request to 'just let me finish in the bedroom' would be a waste of breath, wound up the cord.

'Leo? Can I talk to you?'

Leo turned to look at her. For a moment their eyes locked and Harriet thought he was going to refuse. Then he brushed his hair out of his eyes and nodded.

'But not in the passage, come through to the studio.'

Harriet would have preferred the kitchen. The studio was too full of stressful vibrations. She didn't want to have difficult discussions in it as well as struggles with her charcoal.

'Well, what's your problem?' Leo sat on a high office stool, twirling it round with his feet. His shoes were badly in need of cleaning.

Harriet sat on the model's chair. 'I'm not doing enough cleaning for the amount of tuition I get.'

'So?'

What he should have said was, 'Oh yes, Harriet, of course you are,' but Harriet had given up expecting Leo to say the right thing.

'And I'm not doing my share for Cleaning Undertaken.'

'Who?'

'The firm – the other girls I work with.'

'So?'

'I thought if I did some figure work for the class, I could pay you back for the tuition. Also, I'd contribute more to the business.' The blush returned, hotter and more widespread than it had been in the kitchen. Unlike Jake, Leo paid it close attention.

'OK,' he said slowly. 'If you think that's what you want to do. Take your clothes off and arrange yourself in a suitable pose.'

If Harriet had been embarrassed before, now she was dying. In theory the idea was bad enough, but actually doing it was a million times worse. Her body felt on fire. Her hands went to the neck of her shirt and fell away. She stood up, took hold of the bottom of her jumper and then dropped it. Her fingers trembled too much for her to make any impression on the button of her jeans. She felt shaky and desperately sick.

No real artist would be so embarrassed about taking her clothes off to be a model. She knew that, once posed, the model became a series of lines and planes and ceased to be a person. She might have managed it had the class been present, but she just couldn't do it for Leo alone. She licked her lips, took a deep breath and tried again. Then she shook her head.

Leo regarded her agony with folded arms and an uncomfortably knowing expression. 'So you've been talking to Jake?' he said, after a lifetime's silence.

'Yes.'

'And he told you how much he earns?'

'Mmm.'

'And you thought you'd jump on the bandwagon?'

'Hardly – I just thought . . .' She was glad when he interrupted her.

'But I wouldn't pay you that.'

Relief covered her body in a cold sweat. She crumpled on to the chair again. 'Why not?'

'Because you're a girl. Men are more interesting to draw – harder to sell – but more exciting for an artist.'

'Oh?' She had been willing to put herself through torture to earn an honest living, and she wouldn't earn as much as a youth who'd strip off without a second thought and lie about in shameless attitudes. 'That gives you the right to pay them less for the same work?'

'I pay what I want, to whom I want, and at the moment, I want a male model.'

'Isn't that a bit limiting?'

Leo shook his head. 'I love female nudes. If you can capture the texture, the glow, of a woman's flesh on canvas, it's glorious. But we're concentrating on drawing. For that, the greater delineation of a man's muscles are more interesting. Artistically speaking.'

'Oh.'

'Besides, Jake's a professional. He doesn't move, he doesn't get cold and he puts the artists at their ease. If I offered you the same money, you'd feel obliged to do it. You wouldn't have enough time for your own work, you'd hate it so much that what work you did fit in would go to pieces.'

'I might get used to it . . .'

Leo shook his head. 'No. I don't know what's happened in your past, but I know it's affected you deeply. You have a great potential for beauty, but you won't come into it until you've sorted your life out. One day I might ask you to take off your clothes for me again, but not for a while.'

Paradoxically, Harriet found this reassurance disappointing. And also tantalizing.

'So just keep doing what you're good at,' he added, 'which is cleaning. Leave modelling to the professionals.'

Emboldened by her lucky escape and his talk of her potential beauty, she asked, 'Aren't I good at drawing, too?'

'You might be, one day.' And his expressive mouth curled into a smile, both challenging and reassuring. His cynical, even slightly sadistic face became suddenly boyish and intensely attractive. 'If you give up the day job.'

In vain, Harriet fought to resist. She knew the water was deep and dangerous, yet something inside her flipped over like a pancake. Her heart started to thump and another of

Leo's pupils fell in love with him. Except she knew she always had been. She'd just put off admitting it.

'I think you set out to be as offensive as possible.' Somehow she thought of something to say which sounded like their usual level of badinage.

'Of course I do. If you're nice to people, they never leave you alone. Now are you going to clean my bog or aren't you?'

'I aren't,' said Harriet, but did, anyway.

Sally was finding boat life difficult, and although Harriet and May did their best to make her as welcome and comfortable as possible there was simply not enough space in it for three people on a permanent basis.

On Friday night, after a gruelling week, they calculated the week's earnings. Even the fact that they could all have a bigger cut after the expenses had been accounted for failed to improve their collective mood. When they had brushed aside Harriet's regular apologia about painting when she should be cleaning, the weekend stretched before them, long, cold and grumpy.

May wanted to take the boat for a run, for the sake of her own batteries rather than the boat's. Harriet, aware of this, badly wanted to spend her weekend between the Tate, the National and the Serpentine galleries, and as much of Cork Street as she had the legs for. But she knew that if she didn't offer to help May with the boat, Sally would feel obliged to, in spite of May's protests that she could manage alone. It was perfectly possible that Sally would prove to be adept at hurling dripping ropes at distant bollards and getting them to loop satisfactorily, but it was unlikely. Harriet feared that by Sunday night no one would be talking to anybody else.

As the silence was most uncomfortable for Sally, sitting on an inadequate cushion, she was the one to break it. 'This boat is blissful for two . . .'

'It's Bliss-full with three, now you're here,' said May.

Sally strained to hear if there was acid in May's tone as she made this pun on her name and decided there wasn't, but that there would be soon. 'But there are only two comfortable places to sit. I'm going to have to find somewhere else to live.'

Harriet and May, though they refused to look at each other, heartily agreed. But they knew that if Sally had to pay a proper, commercial rent, she couldn't manage on what they were paying themselves.

'You can't afford it on what you're earning, Sal,' said May.

'I could tell the council I'm homeless and get a council flat,' she said.

May shook her head. 'It wouldn't work unless you were pregnant.'

'Oh. I would find that rather difficult.'

Harriet sighed. 'Yes.'

'Perhaps I should go on the dole, get housing benefit, and moonlight?' This suggestion was no more appealing to Sally than getting pregnant had been, but she felt obliged to make it.

'No,' said May. 'It's not worth the hassle.'

Silence fell again.

'If we had our own transport, we could cut down on the time spent getting from one job to another,' said May. 'Then we could fit in more jobs and earn more. I got off at the wrong bus-stop today and had to walk miles. A dreadful waste of time.'

'So?' prompted Sally.

'The trouble is, we're dreadfully under-capitalized . . .'

Harriet sighed. It had been too much to hope that May wouldn't reach this conclusion. The other two regarded her, hoping she had a solution ready.

'What about motorbikes?' May went on. 'We could nip in and out of the traffic like couriers. Sally would look wonderful in black leather.'

'I might,' said Sally. 'But I won't ride a motorbike. Sorry.'

'No,' said Harriet firmly. 'There's no point in getting a vehicle we can't carry stuff in, like our industrial hoover, when we get it. Besides, I won't ride a motorbike, either.'

'It was just a thought,' said May. 'We won't even be able to afford the cleaner for ages. It's going to be hard to find enough for Mike.' She smiled ironically. 'But I don't think I'll get another lodger, however badly we need the money.'

'Perhaps if we tidied up a bit,' Harriet suggested. 'It wouldn't seem so cramped.' She picked up May's boots with one hand and a pile of Sally's magazines with the other. 'I'll try and find somewhere to put these.'

At that moment, they felt the boat tip as someone heavy put their foot on the gunnel.

'Oh God! Who's that?' May instantly ran through her extensive selection of male friends who would sit and talk all night. If it was any of them, she would be firm and not let them across the threshold.

Sally started stuffing things under cushions as they heard footsteps climbing down into the well-deck. Harriet retreated with the boots and magazines and threw them into the bedroom. Then she returned to the galley and put the kettle on. She suddenly felt terribly vulnerable, and needed to occupy herself with meaningless tasks. Besides, if, heaven forbid, it was Leo, he would need coffee. 'Oh please don't let it be Leo,' she prayed, swiping madly at the work surfaces with a rather grubby cloth. 'Or if it is him, don't let him fall in love with Sally.'

When the knock they were waiting for came, Sally answered it. Although only a small section of him could be seen through the narrow frame of the door, she knew at once it was James Lucas.

'Good evening. Oh, hello Sally. I've brought your watch round.'

Sally smiled her most seductive smile, thus concealing the 'about time too' which was her first thought. 'Do come in James, and meet the others.'

James squashed his body through the door, but even when he was through, he had to remain hunched to avoid hitting his head. For a fanciful moment Sally wondered if the boat was actually wide enough for his shoulders.

'May, come and meet James. He owns that flat we cleaned, you know?'

May smiled and shook the paw offered to her, pretending she didn't know a lot about James's life he would prefer her not to know.

'Have a cup of coffee or tea or something. I'm afraid we've nothing stronger at the moment.' May's father's supply of red wine had taken a hammering. The only bottle left was being saved for the direst emergency.

'Tea would be wonderful. I'm just off back to the country, so I wouldn't want anything alcoholic.'

'Do sit down, James.' Sally manoeuvred him into a chair, which effectively cut off one half of the boat, as his feet stretched almost the entire six-foot width. Fortunately, most of the business end was the other side. 'Harriet, come and meet James.'

Harriet, who was making a big deal of making the tea, was forced out of the galley.

James tried to get to his feet but was prevented by Sally's hand on his shoulder. 'Don't. You'll hit your head.'

'Hello, Harriet,' he said, awkward about having to forgo good manners.

'Hello, James.' Harriet thought James Lucas had the kindest eyes she had ever seen and wished she could fall in love with kindness. Still, perhaps it only took practice.

By the time Harriet had returned to the kitchen and come through with a tray of tea and the ubiquitous flapjack, Sally had settled herself endearingly at James's feet. But no one could have accused her of doing it on purpose – there was just nowhere else for her to sit.

Harriet handed James a mug and the flapjack. 'Sugar?'

'No thank you.' He took a piece of flapjack.

Harriet smiled and tried to think of something to put him at his ease. It was difficult, especially when physically he must be extremely uncomfortable.

May, as owner of the boat, tried next. 'What do you do, James?'

'I've a few acres in Gloucestershire which I farm organically.' He smiled. 'Or perhaps they farm me. I certainly seem to put more in than I get back out.'

'Have you had it long?' May went on.

James shook his head. 'Only a year. Long enough to fall in love, not long enough to get disillusioned.'

Sally squirmed uneasily at his mention of love, in case it drew attention to her feelings. She was grateful that she'd been to a client who was a BBC producer. She was never in when Sally went to clean, but Sally made a point of wearing her best clothes, just in case.

'So what did you do before that?' Harriet hoped she didn't sound too much like her grandmother.

'I was an estate agent. But I was very bad at it. I kept telling people that with children they really needed more garden and that the road got dreadfully busy at about five o'clock. It was only ever a stopgap.'

'Oh?'

'My uncle had always told me I would inherit the farm.' James laughed. 'But he didn't tell me there was no money to go with it. The farmhouse is a bit spartan.'

'I'd love to see it,' said Sally, shamelessly.

'And I'd love to show it to you. Unfortunately . . .'

'I haven't been to the country for ages. I could come back on the train on Sunday night.'

Harriet and May held their combined breaths. It would be marvellous to get Sally out from under their feet for the weekend. But they could neither of them approve of her inviting herself to stay with a man they hardly knew.

'That wouldn't be necessary. I've got to be in town on Monday, but . . .'

'Do you mean I can come?' Sally gazed up at him with an expression strongly reminiscent of Clodagh.

Harriet wondered how any man could resist Sally. Her eyes were as large as saucers, she looked as long-legged and vulnerable as a newly born foal. May decided that James needed saving from himself.

'Really, Sal, you can't go inviting yourself for weekends like that,' she said, sounding shocked.

James nodded. 'My house is totally unsuitable for guests. You saw my other uncle's flat? Well, the uncles were twin brothers. They had a lot in common.'

'The country's always freezing at this time of year,' said

Harriet, who couldn't see Sally coping with country life in winter.

'And terribly muddy,' put in May, in spite of her desire to have Sally out of the way.

'Honestly! The way you all go on, anyone would think I'll melt if a drop of rain falls on me. I am washable, you know.' Sally clambered to her feet, using James's knee to pull herself up. 'I'll just go and fling some things into a bag.'

May and Harriet regarded James helplessly. 'If you don't want her to stay, just say so,' said May. 'You only need be firm.'

Harriet realized that part of James did want Sally to stay, but he didn't want her to be wildly uncomfortable and complain. 'But Sally's a sweet girl. In spite of being an actress, she isn't a bit prima-donnaish.'

'She's an actress?' James's shaggy eyebrows went up. 'I suppose it figures.' He got up awkwardly. 'She'll be miserable. I'll tell her she can't come.'

'I won't be miserable,' said Sally, appearing from May's bedroom. 'I'll help you clean up.' She had a sports-bag over her arm, and felt just then that if he told her she had to stay on the boat for another ten minutes she would burst into tears. 'I just need to get away. I won't moan about anything, I promise.'

'Really, it's dreadfully primitive . . .'

'I've stayed in some frightful digs in my time. Unless you've actually got bedbugs . . .'

'Good God, I hope not!'

'Then please, I would very much like to come with you.'

James looked down into Sally's eyes. They shimmered with unshed tears of entreaty. She may have been acting, or she may have been sincere, but he was not the sort of man who could put out a dog on a cold night. And Sally was no dog.

'Right. I'll bring you back on Sunday night, then.'

A moment later, May and Harriet had the boat to themselves. They pulled back the curtain in time to see James carrying Sally's bag while she tottered over the lock gates.

'She hasn't got the right sort of shoes or anything,' said Harriet. 'We should have helped her pack.'

'She's completely shameless. Imagine just inviting yourself for the weekend like that. James didn't want her at all.'

'Oh he wanted her,' said Harriet drily. 'But not for the weekend.'

'She manipulated him dreadfully.'

'That's how women have survived up until now.' Wistfully, Harriet wished she knew how to manipulate men. Although she knew in her heart Leo would be proof against the most talented persuasion. She sighed sharply, earning herself a look from May. 'On the other hand, it does give us some lovely space,' she went on, to deflect the look. 'And we can think about Sally finding somewhere permanent to live when she comes back.'

'I think Sally's already found something permanent,' said May. 'I'll be very surprised if she's not ensconced in the other uncle's flat before the end of next week.'

'Well, I have to admit, much as I love her, it's been a dreadful strain having her live here. This boat is fine for two, but it's just not big enough for three.'

'No,' May agreed. She knew Harriet was waffling on to cover something up. 'So what about you, Harriet? Have you fallen in love with Leo?'

Harriet didn't waste time asking May how she knew. She just shrugged. 'Well why wouldn't I? I was brought up without a father, he's older and terribly kind to me, not to mention devastatingly attractive. Of course I've fallen in love with him. But I'll get over it. There's no space in my life for love.' But she didn't sound convinced.

CHAPTER EIGHTEEN

Sally began to regret her impulse before they'd been on the road ten minutes. She had greeted the sleeping Clodagh like an old friend, and had been rewarded by a brief flicker of her long tail. But since then hardly a word had been said.

She was such a fool for wishing herself on him when having her to stay for the weekend was the last thing he wanted. She opened her mouth to speak and shut it again several times. She couldn't think of anything to say. She ought to ask some leading question about farming, but as what little she knew about it she had gleaned from *The Archers*, it was a bit risky. She hadn't heard it for weeks.

And she would freeze to death. The tights she wore under her short skirt were thick, but they would be no protection against the icy blasts which no doubt blew over the Cotswolds from September to May. If only she'd packed some jeans, but she couldn't remember which plastic sack they were in, and hadn't dared start rummaging in case James left without her. By now, she was convinced that's what he would have done if she'd been out of the room for more than five minutes.

She had been so desperate to get away. James's enormous figure had seemed to represent escape, safety, an alternative to a weekend being cooped up on the boat with May rapidly losing her patience. He had been so incredibly kind when he had rescued her from Piers's flat that she saw him as her knight in shining armour. But she didn't remember him being such a silent knight.

She wasn't going to chatter. May's experience with men in cars tied in with her own; men hated chattering. Some music would help, but even after six months with Piers, she had never managed to work the tape-player in his car. She either put the tape in upside down, or back to front, and he would sigh, and snatch it from her and do it himself. James was totally different from Piers, of course – he was practically a saint. But even saints got irritated with technophobics.

'Would you like some music?' James's voice made her jump.

'Er – sure, if you would.'

James rummaged among the muddle of tapes which were scattered about the floor of the Volvo. 'Van Morrison?'

'Fine, yes.'

Sally would have agreed to Wagner's *Ring* cycle if James had suggested it.

'Here,' he said, handing it to her.

Sally took it, head bowed in defeat. 'I'm dreadfully sorry, I know it's frightfully stupid, but I can't ever –' She was only half way through her rambling apology when he interrupted her.

'Oh. Right.' He took the tape back, slid it into an invisible slit, and a moment later, the car was filled with sound.

Desolate, Sally looked out of the window at the lights of London where Westway became the A40, wondering if she should ask to be dropped off now, while she could still hitch back to the boat. She must have sighed loudly, because James glanced at her.

'It's only a couple of hours. Why don't you close your eyes and have a nap?'

Men were obviously the same the world over, they would do anything to avoid being talked to.

'You don't want me to map-read, or anything?' Pretending to sleep would be an easy option for her, but she didn't want to fall down on her duties as passenger, albeit unwanted.

James chuckled. 'I've been coming up and down to London several times a week ever since my uncle died. Besides, it's almost impossible to map-read at night. The street lights keep whizzing off, just when you've found your place. You just snuggle down and get some sleep.'

Sally was almost sure he wasn't being sarcastic. 'Yes.'

Piers had been difficult to navigate for even in broad daylight. The few times they had ventured out of the capital together, to spend weekends with friends who had country cottages, they had arrived with Piers refusing to speak to Sally. The moment any of her directions went wrong, he would pull over, snatch the map, look at it, and then snap it shut. Sally had to pray that she had found the page again before the next turn-off.

She regarded James's profile for a moment, but she wasn't rewarded by another smile. So she closed her eyes, thinking how long it had been since she'd been held by a man. Too long, she decided. But this weekend should put that right. If she couldn't get James into her bed (or herself into his) she would forswear men for ever, and take the veil.

Although she was tired, Sally didn't actually doze off until they were deep into Gloucestershire. She awoke from a five-minute nap when the car stopped in front of a five-barred gate.

'We're here,' said James.

Sally blinked at James and then at the gate. 'Shall I open it?' She knew enough about country life to know that it was the passenger's duty to open all gates.

'I shouldn't . . .' said James.

But it was too late. Sally had already opened her door and sunk her suede loafers with gold bars into a deep puddle. This bad start was made worse by her going to the wrong end of the gate. Dreadfully embarrassed, she stumbled over the ruts to the end with the catch. She had just realized she couldn't make head or tail of it, when James joined her.

'The binder twine is tricky when you're not used to it,' he said, lifting the gate, and doing something clever with a spring and a lever which was designed to take the fingers from unwary city-dwellers.

Sally plodded towards the car, and then, remembering she should at least shut the gate, she plodded back again.

'Just slam it hard and loop that twine over the top,' said James, who had had to pull shut the passenger door before he could drive through.

Sally slammed and looped and eventually found her way back into the Volvo. James drove on without speaking. Sally couldn't speak for the chattering of her teeth and convulsive shivers.

As the car drove up, the security light went on, and a terrific barking started up, giving the farmyard the appearance of a prison after an axe-murderer had escaped. Sally hoped the dogs weren't really Alsatians and bloodhounds.

'The farm dogs,' explained James. 'They're awfully noisy, but they don't often bite people.'

'They don't *often* bite people,' Sally repeated under her breath. 'Great.'

By this time she would have given her right arm plus a kidney to be to driven straight back to London. There were no takers here, though. Her only option was to get out.

Still shivering, she climbed out of the car on to another yielding surface, which she desperately hoped was mud, and prepared to be savaged. A collie, regarding this townie intruder with intelligent eyes, barked sharply at her. Another slunk along the ground towards Clodagh, whom James had released. There were at least two others, who either ignored Sally, or growled faintly at her.

Oh, for Clodagh's dignified aloofness, thought Sally as she watched the dog stalk long-legged to the door, ignoring the yapping and fuss which surrounded her. Sally decided to follow Clodagh's example to reduce the possibility of being bitten, or going down with hypothermia.

James loomed up behind her as she huddled out of the wind and handed her a bunch of keys. 'Here, you let yourself in. I'll bring the stuff in a moment.'

By the time James reappeared, his hands full of suitcases and Sally's sports-bag tucked under his arm, she had at least got the door open. An efficient person would by then probably have lit the range and drawn water from the well, and had a three-course meal simmering on the hob, thought Sally. She gave James an apologetic smile, and followed him inside.

In the house it seemed to be just as cold as outside, only quieter. James switched on lights as he led her through a series of dusty rooms to the kitchen. At first glance, it looked like the set of *Cold Comfort Farm*, but at second, Sally noticed a gleaming red Rayburn and became aware of its warmth. 'What a lovely stove!'

'It's beautiful isn't it? My uncle hardly left any money, but what he did leave, I spent on that.' James dumped down the suitcases and Sally's bag where he stood.

'Goodness, why? I mean – didn't you want to spend it on something farmy, like a – a –' *The Archers* came to the rescue, 'a forage harvester?'

James smiled. 'Well there were so many things I needed, I couldn't decide what was most pressing. And my sisters refused to come and help me out unless there was some sort of central heating and something to cook on. This was the cheapest combination.'

'Ah.'

'When I told the girls I planned to get a solid-fuel stove, they forced me to make it a gas one. Otherwise, they said, and they were quite right, the damn thing would always be going out when I wasn't here to see to it. It's bottled gas, of course. We're not on the mains here.'

'I see.'

'I expect Lucy'll be over first thing in the morning. She'll be surprised to see you.' Sally waited in vain for him to add the words, 'and delighted.' Instead, he slid the kettle over from one side of the Rayburn to the other. 'She will have been in today and put stuff in the fridge, bless her. And possibly made a casserole.'

Sally hated Lucy before Lucy even knew of her existence. Thanks to her busybody efficiency, Sally was deprived of showing James how well she could make Welsh rarebit, and of proving that she knew it was not the same as cheese on toast.

'Now,' said James. 'Would you like to make some tea or something, while I dump these?' He indicated the pile at his feet. 'It's all stuff from Joshua's flat. Or, if you don't want tea –' he stepped over a leather case much stuck with ancient travel labels. 'The whisky's in here.'

And so it was, in with the cornflakes. Sally, who went for months without ever drinking anything stronger than Campari and soda, got out the bottle. She allowed herself about ten seconds to find a glass before abandoning her search and tipping some whisky into a mug. It tasted disgusting, but went straight to her head. Sally began to feel better.

James was gone for ages, and after the whisky had restored some of her self-confidence, Sally found a teapot, some teabags and some milk and assembled a tray. She was just about to pour on the boiling water when James came back.

'Would you like tea?' asked Sally.

James shook his head. 'In a minute. Right now I need a huge drink. Would you like one?'

James interpreted her hesitation for disapproval and poured two fingers into a glass produced from a cupboard. 'Come on. It'll do you good. You'll like the guest bedroom better if you're slightly slewed.'

He poured a similar amount into another glass and added water from the tap before turning back to Sally. 'Sorry, I forgot to put anything in that. Lucy always drinks it straight.'

'It's fine.' Anything Lucy could do, Sally could do better. 'I like it like this.' And surprisingly, it tasted less foul with every sip.

'Do sit down, Sally. I'll get us something to eat in a moment.'

Sally was tipsy – not so tipsy that she couldn't see how dreadfully tired James was, but drunk enough to get herself into trouble.

'You don't have to look after me, James,' she heard herself saying. 'I'll get us something to eat. You have a power-nap.'

'What the hell's that?'

'I heard about it on *Oprah*. You go to sleep for ten minutes. When you wake up, you feel marvellous.'

James chuckled. 'It's worth a try, I suppose. In my day, it was called forty winks.' He slumped into his Windsor chair, looking decidedly less comfortable than Clodagh did on her sofa, which took up the entire window embrasure, closed his eyes and seemed instantly to become unconscious.

There were no curtains. If there had been, Sally would have drawn them. She hated having the night looking in at her, particularly now it had started to rain. Hard, unhospitable raindrops were hurling themselves at the glass, saying 'Go home, townie'. But seeing that James actually seemed to be asleep, she began to find her way round. The fridge was in the larder and the sink, the twin of the one in the London flat, was in the scullery. What, Sally wondered, made philosophical with whisky, makes a kitchen a kitchen? The room where James was now snoring in harmony with his dog definitely was one. But the Rayburn, and a row of surprisingly new-looking saucepans which hung over it, were the only kitchen appliances in it.

The furniture, perhaps? There was a table, which had once been scrubbed, a collection of chairs and a long, built-in dresser, with deep, half-moon handled drawers, all obligatory in a Cotswold farmhouse. As an avid reader of 'house mags' Sally recognized that they would have been much sought after by the hundreds of people who were ripping out their fitted cupboards. Perhaps it was her recent change of career, or perhaps it was because she'd been living on a boat, with no scope for home-making, but something made Sally long to tidy and polish the dresser, and put the plethora of jars and pots into some sort of order. She itched to put the papers somewhere else, and put bowls of apples in their place. But the dresser obviously doubled as the farm office, and couldn't be touched.

Sally pottered about opening and shutting cupboards and drawers, searching for the makings of Welsh rarebit. To hell with James's sister's casserole. She found the bread, the heel of a very home-made wholemeal loaf, in one of the dresser drawers. The cheese was under an upturned bowl on the top shelf of the larder. An ancient grater took the skin off Sally's knuckles as she made breadcrumbs and grated cheese, but if she hadn't wanted James to sleep undisturbed, songs from the shows would have issued merrily from her lips. Whisky was wonderful stuff.

She gently laid two plates of Welsh rarebit on the table and either the sound, or the appetizing aroma which wafted up, awoke James.

'Gosh, that smells good. Did you make it?' He picked up a

piece of toast and bit out a huge half-moon. 'Tastes even better than it smells.'

Sally nibbled daintily at her slice.

'We can have tea in a minute,' mumbled James, his mouth full. 'After I've shown you upstairs.' He tipped more whisky into both glasses. 'Then I'll find out what Lucy's left us for supper.'

Sally sipped her whisky and chewed her toast. It must be working in the open air all day, she thought, that makes him so hungry. She thought Welsh rarebit *was* supper.

'Come along, then. I'll bring your bag.'

Sally got to her feet, swaying slightly, and followed James out of the room. Refreshed by his nap and his snack and unhampered by a lot of neat whisky, he was taking the uncarpeted stairs in threes. Sally hastened after him.

The upstairs of the house was as primitive as the kitchen, but without its charm. The single, unshaded bulb which lit the corridor cast unfriendly shadows into every corner, making them appear even dirtier than they really were. Sally put all thoughts of spiders firmly out of her mind as she followed James, who was opening doors.

'You can't sleep in here. The bed's quite comfortable, but there's a hell of a draught from the window.'

Sally barely caught a glimpse of the room before he opened the next door.

'This room's OK in summer as it has a view of the garden, but it's a bit bleak at this time of year.'

And that damp patch on the floorboards doesn't look too healthy either, Sally thought as she listened to the rain pounding on to the obviously leaky roof above.

'That's my room at the end.' James didn't open the door, but merely pointed, then opened the next and final door. 'You'll probably be happiest in here.'

'Here' was a fairly small room with a high single bed and a little fireplace. The only other furniture was a Lloyd-loom chair painted in the same drab green as the corridor.

'It's directly over the kitchen, so it's warmer than the other rooms. And the roof doesn't leak, and I had to replace the window frame in the spring.'

Sally regarded it dolefully. James hadn't been simply making excuses when he told her his house wasn't fit for guests.

'There's not much in the way of furniture, I'm afraid. My uncle sold it off bit by bit to pay his bills. There were some fairly decent antiques here originally.' James smiled ruefully. 'My uncle used to send me up to Phillips's with them, to sell at auction. My sisters were always furious when they found out. They thought my uncle had no right to sell family heirlooms.'

'Didn't *you* mind?' asked Sally.

James shook his head. 'No. It was only furniture, after all. When I was an estate agent I saw too many people making themselves miserable over it. There was a woman who bought the most God-awful house, no view, no garden, no nothing, simply because she could fit her mother's antiques into it. Talk about the tail wagging the dog. I'd rather have junk and be happy.'

The nearest thing Sally's family had to an heirloom was a cracked toby jug which had supposedly been given to some distant female relation by Sir Henry Irving. As the relation-ship was unblessed by the church and undocumented any-where, they didn't talk about it much.

'Well, there's a chair, at least,' said Sally.

James smiled. 'Yes, but don't sit on it. It's probably rotten as a pear. It's just there for show. Now,' he went on, as if he had just shown Sally to the guest suite complete with its own bathroom, sitting-room, and every other concession to com-fort, 'the airing cupboard is just along the hall. Help yourself to whatever you need. I've got to pop out and look at the beasts.'

The whisky was wearing off. Sally was now sufficiently sober to realize that James had tried to prevent her coming for the noblest of reasons. His house was barely habitable. He only managed because he was one of Britain's Hardy Sons, and inured to discomfort. May might have been able to cope with such surroundings, but Sally was not so tough. On the other hand, May didn't have exclusive rights to the pioneering spirit, Sally could be just as adaptable if need be.

It was only a matter of being positive, after all, and Sally had lots of practice at that.

She found the airing cupboard and opened the door. It was stacked with blankets, ticking-covered pillows and old-fashioned Paisley eiderdowns. The sheets must be kept somewhere else. She pulled down as much as she could carry in her arms and staggered back to her room. Her backbone suitably stiffened by bracing thoughts and whisky, she told herself that, provided the bed wasn't too damp, she'd be quite warm enough. And with luck, she wouldn't be sleeping in her little room over the kitchen for more than one night, anyway. All she had to do was to be nice and he would succumb to her charms and sweep her into his arms.

There was no point in making up the bed until she had some sheets, so she dumped the blankets and eiderdown and took advantage of James's absence to have a look at his bedroom. This was hardly more comfortable than any of the other rooms. There was a huge double bed, a bedside table covered with books and dusty glasses of water, and a chest which looked large and ancient enough to conceal any number of brides. So not all of the antiques had vanished, then. For a moment she was tempted to open the chest and see what was in it, but thought better of it and went downstairs to the kitchen instead. After all, once she had succeeded in seducing James, she could just ask what was in it, or look.

She had made the tea and was reading a three-year-old newspaper which covered an enamel-topped table when James came in.

'Everything all right?' asked Sally, handing him a mug and feeling pleasantly wifely.

James took the tea. 'Thanks.' He frowned and said, 'No, not all right. I'm a bit worried about one of the cows. I might have to get the vet to her. But he'll want to stuff her full of antibiotics and then I won't be able to sell the milk for ages.'

Sally nodded sagely. She remembered Pat and Tony Archer having similar problems. 'Might she get better on her own?'

'She might. Flying pigs have been spotted in the area.' He

smiled kindly down at her. 'I'm sorry. I've no right to burden you with my problems. You've come down to the country to get away from it all, not exchange one lot of stress for another.'

Sally bit her lip. 'I did invite myself. The least I can do is express an interest.'

James gave her an indulgent look which said plainly, 'Don't bother your pretty little head about things you don't understand.' What he said out loud was, 'I hope you won't think you made a mistake.'

Sally, who had known for certain she had made a mistake even before she had ruined a hundred pounds' worth of Kurt Geiger footwear, said, 'Oh no. It's terribly kind of you to let me come.'

'Let's find something to eat, shall we?'

The promised casserole was produced and James set about peeling potatoes. Sally watched him until she could bear it no longer.

'Let me do that. I'm sure there's something you'd rather be doing.'

James dropped the knife into the muddy water. 'Well, actually, I could do with having another look at that heifer. I hate to take advantage of you.'

Sally protested. 'You're not! I asked myself! Let me peel a few potatoes. And cook them, if you want me to.'

James gave her a smile of such encompassing warmth, Sally wondered if there were any lengths to which she wouldn't compromise women's emancipation to earn another. 'Thank you, Sally. You're a star.'

Being cast in the role of 'star' gave Sally confidence. She discovered a deep-freeze in another of the various still-rooms, dairies and pantries with which the farm was supplied so generously, and in it some frozen peas. She chopped a white cabbage and put it on to cook with milk and salt and pepper. She mashed at least twice as many potatoes as she thought they could possibly need with a lavish quantity of butter and resolved not to eat any herself. By the time James came in again the stew was hot and the vegetables were waiting in the warming oven of the Rayburn.

As she burrowed about in a drawer for some knives and forks while James opened a bottle of wine, she realized how much she was enjoying herself. What she needed was a small part in *Emmerdale* to get all this farming nonsense out of her system.

They ate at the kitchen table, which Sally had cleared by putting everything on it on to one of the chairs. She had found a box of household candles and had stuck one in a candlestick. She didn't eat much herself, but James ate enough for both of them.

'Delicious potatoes!' he said, adding another small mountain of them to his plate. 'And the cabbage. I would have made do with the frozen peas.'

There wasn't any pudding. Although Sally strongly suspected that James would be a nursery-puddings-and-custard man, there wasn't time for her to drag out a recipe for roly-poly from her supply of childhood memories. Tomorrow night, she would make something wonderful.

James made coffee, but fought back enormous yawns while he drank his. Sally refused a second cup and gathered the dishes together.

'I'll do these in the morning, if you don't mind,' she said.

James forced himself to his feet. '*I'll* do them in the morning! Can't have you spending your entire weekend in the kitchen!'

Sally smiled. 'We'll argue about that tomorrow. In the meantime, I don't suppose you've got any sheets? For my bed?'

'Oh.' James looked abashed. 'I'm afraid I've only got one set. My uncle's bed-linen all disintegrated. I keep meaning to buy some more, but you know how it is. You get out of bed and forget all about it.' Seeing Sally's expression of distaste, he hurried to explain. 'I do wash them! I just have to do it on a fine day, or leave them folded up on the Rayburn. It's a bit of a bind, really.'

'Oh. Then have you got a pair of pyjamas? I've only brought a T-shirt to sleep in, and the blankets will be a bit scratchy. But if I had a pair of pj's . . .' She pictured them in her mind's eye. Large and stripey, a set of bed-linen in themselves.

James shook his head. 'I'm terribly sorry . . .'

'You don't wear pyjamas?'

'No.'

He obviously wanted her to be comfortable so badly, and she wanted to spare him the embarrassment of thinking she wasn't going to be, but neither of them knew how to put the other out of their misery.

'There's a perfectly simple solution to this,' said James after a moment. 'You must sleep in my bed.'

CHAPTER NINETEEN

May had counted sheep, done some deep breathing and had tried to remember the names of the girls in her class at school, but still sleep wouldn't come. She was just wondering for the hundredth time how Sally was getting on in the country, with no proper clothes and a reluctant host, when she heard a loud knocking on the roof of her boat.

Instantly, she was alert. Who on earth could it be? But the next moment she heard her name.

'May? Are you awake? It's *Curlew*. She's leaking again.'

She recognized the voice. It was Debra, part owner of *Curlew*, who, May knew well, had been in this situation before.

'Hang on. I'll be with you in a moment. Do you want the pump?'

'Yes, please. The boatyard shed is all locked up, and there's no sign of Mike.'

May had been pulling on her clothes. 'Do you want to bring the kids over?'

'That would be great.'

'Pop them into my bed then, I'll dig out the pump.'

She explained the situation to Harriet, who said she'd babysit as required, then May retrieved her wellingtons and made her way to the *Curlew*, an elderly wooden narrowboat, home to Debra and Jethro and their two children. By the time May got there, her pump under her arm, the *Curlew* was full of men. Jed was there, as were Ivan, and of course Jethro. May handed over the pump.

'Thanks, May,' said Jethro. 'Why does it always happen at night, when the yard's closed and we can't get to the proper one?'

'How much water is there?' May asked, ignoring the

aspersions cast on her pump, which had been borrowed by most of the boats at the mooring at some time.

'A couple of inches over the boards. We'd just got Spike settled, when Juno called that her boots were floating.' He had already lifted a few floorboards and sunk the pump into the space. Then he connected it to a battery with crocodile clips. 'Just as well the boat's down a bit at the back end.'

Debra arrived. 'I left the children with Harriet. Spike stayed asleep, bless him, but Juno was having hot chocolate and a story.'

'Did much get wet?' asked May.

Debra made a face. 'About three launderette trips. I'd left all Juno's clean clothes in a pile on the floor.' She made a face at her husband's back, which was bent double. 'I'm still waiting for the drawers he was going to put under the bunks.'

May chuckled. Jethro, a carpenter who often worked with Jed, was a meticulous worker, but he took his time. And he was so good-natured that if anyone else asked him to do anything, he would instantly abandon work on his own boat and build whatever they wanted.

'If you girls want to be useful,' said Ivan, 'you could stand on the counter. We could do with a bit of weight right at the back, to get the last of the water out.'

The women exchanged glances in the torchlight, and obligingly stood right at the stern of the boat. May nearly suggested that the men, who were heavier, did the standing, while she and Debra manoeuvred the pump, but she could see Debra was tired and so leaned on the tiller bar with her.

'*The Rose* doesn't leak, does it?' asked Debra.

May shook her head. 'No, she's dry as a bone.'

'So how come you're the only one among us who's got a pump, then?'

May laughed. 'When I bought *The Rose* my father gave me the pump as a boat-warming present. He assumes automatically that all boats leak.'

Debra harrumphed. 'Mostly, they do. We'll probably end up sinking at our moorings.'

'If this had happened a month ago,' said May, 'I would have said that Mike would do anything to stop that happening. Now, I'm not so sure.'

'You're right,' said Debra. 'He's changed. He wants us all off. If a boat sunk, he'd use it as an excuse to have it towed away, or something. Come on, let's go inside. I've got to make somewhere for the kids to sleep.'

'I'll see how the pumping's going on, then check on Harriet. But I expect she's enjoying having Juno.' May made her way to the back of the boat, lining up behind the queue of men who were all giving Jethro advice. She was about to ask brightly how it was going, when she realized that the water was up to her ankles and changed her enquiry to, 'Anything I can do?'

'This pump isn't up to it. The leak's much worse than usual.' Jethro sounded worried. 'You may have to break into the yard and borrow Mike's, May.'

'Oh, thank you. And why should it be me?'

'You're lighter than any of us. We can heave you over the wire.'

This idea was not appealing. 'Wouldn't it be better to do something about the hole, rather than just pumping the water out?'

'It's difficult,' said Jed.

'Well you'll have to do something,' said Ivan, with the ill-concealed satisfaction of a man whose own boat isn't sinking, 'or she'll go.'

May's pump was sucking its heart out, but the water level was still rising. Debra appeared.

'I'd better sort out some things to take,' she said resignedly. But May knew she wasn't feeling as matter of fact as she sounded.

'It may sound awfully silly,' said May, having cleared her throat. 'But I read something once that may be worth a try.'

'Go on then, tell us,' said Jethro. 'And if it doesn't work, we'll put you over the fence.'

'Well, what these people did . . .' Should she confess the book she'd read was *Hornblower*? '. . . was to drag a sail under the ship – er, boat – with ropes, and when it gets to the leak, it gets sucked into it, and stops it. At least, it did in this book.'

'We haven't got a sail,' said Ivan.

'No, but there must be some plastic lying around somewhere,' said Jethro. 'Anyone got a bin-liner?'

'You think it might work?' May was touched that they should be taking her idea seriously. 'I'll get a bin liner,' she said, and hurried back to *The Rose Revived*.

She pulled out one of Sally's sacks and emptied it on to the bed. 'Sorry, Sally,' she muttered, and did the same with another. 'It's in a good cause.'

May arrived back at the *Curlew* breathless. Jethro opened out one of the bags, then tied the corners with ropes and took it all to the stern before stripping down to his underpants. 'These are my last dry clothes,' he explained.

Lying face down on the counter, which was already under two inches of water, he coaxed the plastic under the rudder while Ivan and Jed pulled gently on the ropes.

After much muttering and bad language, Debra called from inside that she could see the black plastic through the gap in the planks. 'I think it's worked,' she called.

'Yes!' Jethro clapped May's palm with his. 'It's worked! You're brilliant, May!'

'It won't last for ever, of course,' she said, rubbing her palm.

Jethro shook his head. 'No. I'll slap on some quick-setting cement in the morning.'

'You should do yourself a favour and put this boat in dry-dock,' said Ivan, who was single.

'Why, are you offering to pay?' Jethro asked with good-natured sarcasm.

'Sorry,' said Ivan, somewhat abashed. 'But I can put you up on *Titan*, if you like.'

'I think I'll go home and see how Harriet is getting on with the children,' said May, suddenly tired.

'I'll come with you,' said Debra. 'Thanks, Ivan. We would appreciate somewhere dry to sleep.'

Harriet, Juno and Spike were all sound asleep in May's

bed. Debra took Spike, but at May's suggestion left the sleeping Juno.

'I'll bring her over in the morning,' said May. 'I think Harriet's got an art class, so don't disturb her now. I'll sleep on the side-bed.'

After all that activity, sleeping was no problem now. 'Bin bags. I must remember to buy some,' she muttered, just before she became unconscious. 'Or Sally won't speak to me again.'

A hundred miles away, Sally was preparing to accept James's offer to share his bed. I thought you'd never ask, she said silently, and was about to say something similar but less brazen out loud when James continued, 'I'll be perfectly happy in your room.'

'But . . .' She gulped back her disappointment.

'You needn't worry, I'm not the seducing type.' He smiled his heart-stopping smile.

Sally felt tears of frustration and embarrassment gathering in her throat. She had obviously been right about him from the very first: he didn't fancy her.

'But I can't push you out of your own bed – when you didn't even invite me . . .'

'Really, it's all right. Now, did I show you the bathroom?'

Sally, who'd found a downstairs lavatory full of ancient leather riding boots and spiders the size of dinner plates, shook her head.

'I thought not. It's so foul, I usually avoid showing it to people until it's too late.' He put his hand on her shoulder for an all-too-brief moment. 'Poor Sally, you're really seeing the country cold in tooth and claw!'

Sally trailed up the stairs behind him. It needn't be cold, she silently pleaded with his back. If only you'd take me in your arms and into your bed. It was typical. When it came to a man she really wanted, for all the right reasons instead of all the wrong ones, all those techniques learned at the charm school of her mother's knee were useless.

Since Piers had gone, she hadn't missed sex. But although she did want James, what she needed so burningly was the security he represented. She wanted his arms around her, strong and bear-like, crushing her against his massive chest. She wanted him to keep her warm and safe.

The bathroom was draughty and comfortless, very like the one in Uncle Joshua's flat. Only the gaps between the windows and the frames prevented the smell from being so strong. The lavatory seat was cracked and the basin was stained with verdigris, but with a great deal of cleaning, painting and possibly a couple of stencilled shelves it could easily be converted into an authentic country bathroom.

'There is at least loads of hot water,' said James. 'If you have a really hot bath, it should warm you up.'

So he had seen her shivering. 'Mmm.'

'If you run it, I'll put a hot water bottle in your bed. When I get round to it, I'm going to put a radiator in here, to run off the Rayburn. It wouldn't be difficult . . .'

'It's just there's so much else to do,' Sally finished for him.

James grinned. 'Exactly. I'm so glad you understand.'

And in that moment Sally did understand. She saw how hard James had had to work, struggling to keep the cattle alive and thriving, to put the farm buildings in order, when the farm was desperately under-funded. Getting the house into a fit state for visitors, let alone self-invited clothes-horses from London, just wasn't a priority.

She yearned to put her arms round his neck and comfort him, to tell him it was all right, it didn't matter. But it was she who needed comfort, not him. He was perfectly self-sufficient.

'I'll leave you to it then, and get that HWB under way.'

The bath – deep, hot and relaxing – made up for a lot. She started to feel less desolate about the whole weekend. Tomorrow she would convince him what a smashing girl she was, and even if she wasn't his type, at least he wouldn't hate her for coming.

In spite of the sheets being clean, James's bed still smelt of James. But it was a lovely, musky, male smell. The bed was warm and so was she. Sally snuggled down feeling more cheerful than she had done for ages.

Then she noticed the mug of milk on the night-stand. She sipped it. It too was warm and tasted of whisky and honey. Sally was touched to the heart. None of the many romantic gestures that had been made to her over the years had been as considerate or as appreciated as that nightcap. Very soon after drinking it, she fell fast asleep.

CHAPTER TWENTY

With one of James's jumpers reaching well below her bottom, and a pair of his socks reaching above her knees, Sally's skirt was barely visible as she went down into the kitchen the following morning.

There was a man she had never seen before drinking a cup of coffee and talking to James. Both men looked at her, stunned into silence for a moment, before James came to his senses.

'Sally, hello. How are you? Did you sleep all right? Have a cup of something.'

Sally, who hadn't been expecting company this early in the morning, saw from the kitchen clock that it was nine o'clock. It was probably quite late in farming circles.

'I slept wonderfully.' She smiled vaguely at the man.

'Oh, this is Dave, who's come to look at my cow.'

'Oh, are you a vet?' Sally had once auditioned for a part in *All Creatures Great and Small* and felt she knew where she was with vets.

'No,' said Dave, still dazed by Sally's appearance.

'Cup of coffee? Tea?' said James. 'Then you must let me cook you some breakfast.'

'Oh, I never eat breakfast, but I'd love whatever it is you're having.'

James handed her a mug of instant coffee. 'Milk? Sugar?'

'No, thanks.' Sally took the mug and sipped gratefully, wondering if she had caught her tights on the edge of the chest, or if there was some other reason for Dave's fascination with her legs.

'No wonder you're so thin. You hardly eat and you drink your coffee black,' said James.

Sally smiled, accepting the compliment.

Dave cleared his throat. 'Yes. You need a bit of farm cooking to fatten you up.'

May, Sally knew, would have uttered a cutting retort pointing out that she wasn't a pig being prepared for market. Sally smiled inanely.

'Yes, well, if you'll excuse us, Sally, I'd just like Dave to take another peek at Blossom . . .'

Dave tore his eyes away from Sally's too thin, albeit fascinating, thighs and hurried after James. 'I never knew you'd called that cow Blossom,' Sally heard him say. She couldn't hear James's reply, but imagined it was something sexist and uncomplimentary. Sighing, she started to clear the table.

She had just finished the washing up when she saw a Land Rover Discovery pull into the yard. It had two occupied child-seats in the back, and was driven by a girl in a Barbour. She jumped out and revealed that her 501s were tucked into green wellingtons. As she came towards the house, shouting instructions at her infants as she did so, Sally saw she wore a black velvet headband and had two small pearls in her ears. It didn't take much imagination to add the missing Hermès scarf tied under the chin.

The girl, unaware of Sally's presence, came into the house without knocking and rapidly fetched up in the kitchen.

'James? Ah! Gosh! Sorry! James never said.' The girl had very bright blue eyes.

Sally smiled shyly. 'I'm Sally. I'm – er – a friend.'

The girl took in Sally's clothes and, unlike the men, realized their significance. 'You could do with some jeans. Would you like to borrow some?'

'Gosh, yes,' said Sally. 'That would be marvellous. I packed in rather a hurry.'

The girl nodded sagely. 'I'm sure. I'm Lucy, by the way, James's sister.'

'Would you like a cup of coffee?'

Lucy, who seemed more than a little put out at being offered coffee in what she considered to be her territory, nodded.

'Yes. I must just get the kids in from the car. I wasn't expecting to stay long.'

But now you've got to stay until you find out what on earth your baby brother has got up to, and how you can rescue him, thought Sally despondently.

With any luck, James would have returned from worrying about Blossom before Lucy arrived with her offspring, but luck must have been attending to more important matters. Lucy reappeared in the kitchen looking determined, followed by two bewildered children. 'This is Gina,' she said, bringing forward a little girl with straggly blonde hair, blue eyes, and a complexion to die for. 'And this is Augustus.' Augustus looked almost identical to his sister, only his hair was shorter. Twins obviously ran in the family.

'They're twins,' said Lucy, in case Sally had missed this. 'And we're fighting against Augustus being called Gus, tooth and nail, but people will do it.' Lucy regarded Sally accusingly, as if she had called him Gus already.

'Oh.'

'Now sit down,' Lucy said to Gina and Augustus. 'And I'll get you a drink.'

Sally made a cup of coffee for Lucy while she found some orange juice and diluted it heavily for her children. Then she got out a biscuit tin and gave them each a dry Ryvita. Sally was impressed. Those children would be as slim as their mother when they grew up. But let's hope, she went on cattily to herself, that they don't get their mother's broken veins. The outdoor life did do terrible things to the skin. Perhaps she should take Lucy aside and offer some advice about skin-food.

Lucy sat down and sipped her coffee. 'Do you know where James is?'

Sally sat opposite her, nursing her own mug. 'Looking at a sick cow with someone called Dave.'

Lucy made a gesture which consigned Dave to insignificance. 'I came over to see if James has had a letter?'

Sally shrugged. 'I've no idea. I've only just got up.'

'Of course. Well I have, and it's not good news.'

'Oh?' What did one say to express interested sympathy without seeming curious?

'Ya.' Lucy may have lived in the country, but she spoke Sloane like a native. 'Aunt Sophie. Dreadful old bat. Only one in the family who's got any money.' Lucy eyed Sally. 'James hasn't got a bean, you know.'

Actually, Sally did know, but she felt that Lucy wouldn't appreciate her knowing, and so just smiled. 'Oh?'

Lucy nodded. 'We had twin uncles. Hated each other. One lived in London, in frightful squalor, I gather. The other lived here. They were each determined that the other wouldn't get any of his money.'

'Oh.' Sally wondered if there was one-woman show where the woman just sat on the stage saying 'Oh' a thousand different ways. If there was, she should try for it.

'Which left this place totally under-capitalized.' She drained her coffee with an expression of distaste. 'I'd better go and find James,' said Lucy irritably. 'He could be in the cowshed all day.'

Fortunately for Sally, who dreaded having to look after Gina and Augustus, James came into the kitchen just then. His hands were covered with something unpleasant-smelling and his boots were covered with mud.

'Oh, hello, Luce, Gina, Gus. When did you get here? Have you met Sally?'

'Of course I've met Sally, and can't you take your boots off before you come into the house?' snapped his sister.

Lucy was a fraction of the size of James, but was obviously used to bossing him into the ground and protecting him fiercely from the Sallys of this world. Her tirade slithered unnoticed off James's broad back. He bent and kissed his sister's cheek.

'Goodness me, guys!' he said to the children. 'Couldn't Sally find you anything more exciting to eat than that? That's not food for a growing bloke, is it, Gus old man?'

Lucy sighed.

Clodagh, who had come in with James, investigated the Ryvita, which the children hadn't actually eaten, but only crumbled up and mixed with their orange juice. Her beard, which hovered several inches above the plates, dislodged much of the food on to the table, but she didn't eat any of it either.

'Can't you keep that dog out of the children's food?' Lucy spoke rhetorically. 'And have you had a letter from Aunt Sophie?'

James pulled out a stool from under the table and sat down, preparing himself to be harangued. 'No – well, I don't know. I haven't looked yet.'

Lucy hissed disapprovingly. 'Well look now. She wants to come down for Christmas.'

'So what's new? You always have her for Christmas.'

'She wants to come *here* for Christmas,' Lucy snapped. 'Do you read me? *Here!*'

'Well, she can't,' said James, seemingly unaffected by this bombshell.

'James! You can't say she can't! She'll cut you out of her will!'

'She's always cutting me out of her will. What do I care?'

Lucy exhaled, glanced at Sally as if deciding whether she was safe to discuss private family business in front of, and clenched her teeth. 'Well you *ought* to care, the state our bloody uncles left their affairs in.'

Sally, feeling extremely *de trop*, got up. 'If no-one minds, I think I'll have a walk round and stretch my legs.'

'They look quite long enough to me,' said James, probably to annoy his sister.

Lucy ignored him. 'I'd borrow some boots, if I were you, Sally. There are a whole lot in the little room at the end, behind the door.'

'Thanks.' Sally slunk out of the kitchen and went in the direction indicated by Lucy, followed by Clodagh.

'Where did you find her?' Lucy's tones rang embarrassingly loudly down the corridor.

'In London.'

Lucy tutted expressively.

'Clodagh likes her,' James replied.

'Odd, that,' said Lucy. 'Now listen, James. It's no good being high-minded about this . . .'

Sally, having taken the precaution of shaking them care-fully first, thrust her feet into some ancient size sevens before she could hear more private family business. Then she let herself out of the door into the yard. She had forgotten about the farm dogs. They all barked at her, but Clodagh's presence seemed to prevent them from rushing up and tearing her to shreds.

'I should never have come,' she said to Clodagh. 'You're the only one who likes me.'

Clodagh woofed gently at her and set off at a steady pace along the side of the house to where a small gate led to a garden. Sally followed. She would be safer letting Clodagh take her for a walk than wandering about on her own.

It was obviously a regular route. They went through the very overgrown garden and into an orchard, into a field and over a stile to a lane. The lane took them back to the house.

Lucy and James were still talking when they came back.

'It's no good, Sally,' said James benignly. 'Lucy's con-vinced me I've got to have Aunt Sophie. Which means that everyone, the whole darn family and all the hangers on, for Christmas Day. How am I going to manage?'

Somewhat to her surprise, Sally heard herself speak. 'Oh, no problem. I'll come down and do everything for you.'

Lucy choked and instantly chided Augustus. James started to laugh.

'You couldn't! I wouldn't ask my worst enemy to entertain Aunt Sophie, especially not at Christmas. She's a red-hot traditionalist and the place has to look like Birnam Wood under the greenery. It's all right for Lucy, but I'll have to paint the house first.'

'All it needs is a thorough clean,' said Sally, sounding to her own ears impressively like Harriet. 'A good scrub down with soda crystals, and you won't know the place. You won't have time to redecorate if you've a farm to run.'

Lucy put her head on one side. 'What exactly is it you do, Sally?'

Sally smiled airily. 'Oh, I'm an actress. But I'm also part of a cleaning agency. In London. Which is how I met James,' she added for Lucy's information.

'And you really think you could sort this place out for Christmas?' Lucy asked.

'It would take some days, of course.'

'And I would need you to stay over the Christmas period,' said James quickly. 'You'd have to cook and everything.' His eyebrows were raised in a half-questioning, half-hopeful expression.

Sally's hands made a delicate, dismissive gesture. 'Of course.'

Lucy closed her lips contemplatively. 'Come along, kiddy-winks. It's time we weren't here. I've got to drop you off with Liz and then go and do dried-flower arrangements for the church bazaar.' She smiled at Sally. 'I'll bring you some jeans on my way back.'

When James had seen his sister and her children safely into the Land Rover he came back to the kitchen and rested his hands on the back of the chair opposite Sally.

'It's awfully sweet of you to offer to help me out, but I can't take you up on it. I couldn't afford to pay you. Money is frightfully tight. I could only pay you before because I have to let that flat. Until I'm allowed to sell it, there'll be nothing over for extras like Fairy Godmothers.'

Sally swallowed and looked up into his eyes. 'Fairy God-mothers are free. All you have to do is invite me, James.'

James looked back helplessly. 'But I can't ask you to give up your Christmas – to drag you down here in the depths of winter, with all my unspeakable relations – for nothing. You ought to get double time for unsocial hours and triple for putting up with the cold!'

'Really, Christmas is a bit of a non-event for me anyway. I'd love to help you organize a traditional country Christmas.'

'Well it would get me out of a God-awful hole. Lucy's right when she says I can't afford to turn up my nose at Aunt Sophie's money. She might leave everything to my sisters anyway, but if I don't let her come and see the place, she certainly will. She more or less said so.'

'Is she very old?'

'Nearly ninety, but age has not withered her – she was

always withered. Actually, I'm extremely fond of the old duck. But this coming for Christmas lark is a total nuisance.'

His attitude was rather deflating. In Sally's mind's eye, snow was already gently falling, and the twins were singing 'Away in a Manger' around the piano. A real live crib scene, with baby lambs and a donkey was probably expecting a bit much, seeing as it was winter, but Sally, like Aunt Sophie, had very romantic ideas about Christmas.

James glanced at the kitchen clock, ticking noisily and slightly slow, on the wall above the Rayburn. 'Right. I've got to see a man about a feed bill after lunch. But now I'd better go and see to Buttercup.'

'She was called Blossom earlier.'

James shrugged. 'I've got a terrible memory for names.'

'So why don't you think up a number?' suggested Sally sweetly.

'How was the farm then?' asked Harriet, when James had dropped Sally off late on Sunday night.

'Absolutely grim!' said Sally gleefully. 'But I managed to wangle an invitation for Christmas!'

Talk of Christmas made Harriet's heart lurch. In spite of the plethora of Christmas decorations and muzak carols which filled every shop, she had been putting it out of her mind. The thought of spending it without Matthew was tearing her apart. His first term at prep school was about to end and she was no nearer having somewhere suitable for him to live than she had been when she first arrived in London. But as was her habit, she said nothing.

'So did you and James, you know – get off?' she asked.

Sally shook her head. 'Not so much as a pat on the knee or a kiss on the cheek. I did kiss him goodbye in the car, but he sort of reared back in horror. He obviously doesn't fancy me at all.' She sighed deeply. 'And he's so wonderful. I know I could make him happy, if only he'd let me.'

'He didn't suggest you lived in the flat in Victoria Mansions then,' said May, ever hopeful. 'Just to keep it aired?'

Sally shook her head. 'No. He's got to let it for a year before he can sell it. He needs every penny. His sister was there and she made quite sure I knew exactly how hard up James was. Honestly! I mean, do I look like a gold digger?'

Neither May nor Harriet had the heart to tell her that quite possibly, she did.

'Never mind,' said May, who felt better from a weekend without Sally. 'I'm sure we'll rub along somehow.'

Harriet yawned. 'I must go to bed. If I get to Leo's early, I can get most of the flat done before he wakes up.'

Sally regarded her anxiously. Harriet was obviously working herself into the ground over-compensating for the time she spent painting. And what she had to say probably wouldn't help. 'I say, girls.' Sally paused in arranging the cushions which were her mattress. 'My helping James out over Christmas means I'll need to go down a couple of days earlier, the place is in such a state. But it means I won't be around for the Christmas Cleanup deals we're doing.'

May exhaled. 'That's all right, Sally. We agreed that cleaning shouldn't come between us and our careers.'

'It's not – James isn't . . .'

May suppressed a sigh. 'James is important to you?'

Sally subsided. 'Yes.'

'Well then, you follow your dream. Harriet and I will cope with the Christmas Cleanups.' May pushed Sally affectionately. 'We haven't got many booked, anyway.'

CHAPTER TWENTY-ONE

'The Chinese say you should draw with three things,' said Leo, 'the hand, the eye and the heart. Two out of three is not enough. You have all the skills, all the technique, but your heart isn't in it. You've made poor Jacqueline look like a depressed Mrs Mop caught without her clothes on.'

'It's because *I'm* a depressed Mrs Mop. It's called transference.' Harriet tried to inject a lighthearted note into this sad conclusion. Unfortunately, it didn't fool Leo.

He glanced at his watch. 'It's nearly time to pack up anyway. Go and make some coffee. We must talk.'

Harriet didn't want to talk, at least, not about herself, but coffee would help. As she went, she passed Elizabeth's easel. She had captured all the model's vitality and inner beauty. Her picture, done in pastels, glowed like a Rubens nude.

Leo poured the last of the cafetière into his mug. The class had finally gone, and they were alone. 'Put the cloth down and tell me about your life, Harriet.'

'Why?' Harriet was determined not to drag out her miserable, middle-class life story for his cynical inspection. He mocked her enough as it was.

'It's blocking you. Is it your job? Where you live? Or what?'

Harriet turned round. 'It's not *life* that's blocking me. It's sodding Christmas!' Then to her extreme embarrassment, she burst into tears.

Leo watched patiently while Harriet found a piece of the kitchen towel which she had recently introduced into his life and blew her nose.

Harriet, grateful that he hadn't tried to take her in his arms, dabbed at it again. 'Sorry. I don't know what brought that on.'

'Probably your unaccustomedly bad language.'

'Nonsense! I may not often swear, but when I do, it's because I mean it.'

'So why is Christmas making you swear?'

'Because I won't be spending it with my son. It'll be the first time. He's nearly ten. He's at boarding school. It's nearly the end of term and he'll go home to my grandparents for Christmas. I probably won't see him until he goes back to school.'

Chopping up her problems into neat sentences should have minimized them. But the thought of Christmas without Matthew still tore at her.

'Why won't you see him?'

'Because I've run away from my grandparents' house. They looked after me all my life, but they were dreadfully oppressive and restricting. I couldn't go on living there after they sent Matthew away to school.'

'Well, that's the life story out of the way. Now all we need to do is address the happy ending.'

Harriet smiled bravely. 'There is no happy ending, I'm afraid. I'm stubborn, my grandparents are stubborn – even Matthew can be stubborn. They might take me back if I begged forgiveness for my ingratitude, but Matthew would still be at boarding school. And I couldn't go back now, anyway.'

'That doesn't mean to say that the situation is unalterable. When does Matthew's term end?'

Harriet told him.

'We'd better go down as soon as possible, then.'

Harriet tried to protest, to thank him, to be coherent. They were all three beyond her. It was only when she had been through several sheets of kitchen towel and turned her nose Rudolph-red that she could speak.

'I don't know why you should involve yourself with my troubles just so Matthew and I can spend Christmas together.'

Leo smiled his usual sardonic, crooked smile. 'I don't care where you and your brat eat your festive turkey. I just want you to be a half-decent artist.'

★

Harriet and Leo were seated in Leo's car parked at a steep angle at the edge of the village green, so tenderly cared for by the Village Green Committee, of which Harriet's grandfather was a member. Leo had telephoned the grandparents and told them that he and Harriet were coming for lunch. They were expected at half-past twelve. It was now twenty-five past.

'If we walk from here, we'll be exactly on time.' Harriet felt extremely sick.

'Shall we go into the pub for a stiffener? You look a bit green.'

Harriet shook her head. 'God, no! Someone would see us! Besides, we'll get a glass of sherry when we get there and it always goes to my head.'

'That might help.'

Harriet, her teeth clenched together to stop them chattering, shook her head. 'No. I've got to keep my wits about me.'

Leo, who felt that Harriet's wits had gone begging long before they reached the village, refrained from comment. 'Come on. We'd better go.'

He took her arm and pressed her close to his side as they walked along. She was shaking so much, he put his arm round her and held her tighter. It made walking almost impossible, but it felt better. She shook him off as they reached the gate.

The house looked exactly the same. Harriet had expected it to be smaller, but remembered that only happened when you left places as a child and returned as an adult. The neatly clipped golden privet still surrounded the small front garden. The tiled roof still came down over the upper windows like eyebrows, and a berberis, like razor wire, still repelled boarders from around the bow-windows. The small lawn had turned to slime, as it always did at this time of year. Claustrophobia covered her like a blanket over the head of a kidnap victim. She clutched Leo's free hand as he rang the bell.

Her grandfather opened it. He was looking outraged in readiness, in the assumption that Leo would be outrageous. For a burning moment, Harriet wished that Leo had dreadlocks and the glazed expression of a drug addict. Seeing her grandfather's surprise made her wonder if he wished it too. Being presented with Leo, who was admittedly much older than Harriet, but who was wearing his suit (taken to the cleaners by Harriet) and had recently had his haircut, might have been a severe disappointment.

'Hello,' said Harriet. In theory, Harriet called her grandfather 'Grandpa'. In fact, she'd avoided calling him anything for years. She leaned forward and kissed the reddened bristly cheek. 'Let me introduce you to Leo Purbright. Leo, this is my grandfather, Anthony Burghley-Rice.'

'Well let the man in, Harriet. You're blocking the doorway!'

Her grandfather's characteristic snap stirred the familiar stifling feelings. I've changed so much since I was last here, she thought, but I still can't fight them. Until I have the money to give Matthew a home, they still have all the power.

'Come in, Leo.' She tugged his arm gently. 'Where's Granny?'

'In the drawing-room,' said her grandfather, indicating with his head. He was a handsome old man, white-haired, white-moustached and stiff-necked. He was wearing a tweed jacket, cavalry twill trousers, a Viyella shirt and a cravat. He felt it very important to wear the right clothes for the right occasion. Given a chance, he would have changed for dinner, even in the jungle.

'Shall we go through?' asked Harriet tentatively. It was fatal to rush her grandfather. If there was some other ritual, like horsewhipping Leo, that he felt should have been carried out in the hall, it was important to let him observe it.

He was in an awkward position, thought Harriet. He can't really condemn Leo as a cad and a bounder, not good enough for his granddaughter, when the granddaughter has blotted the family escutcheon along with her copy-book. Mr Burghley-Rice harrumphed.

'Yes. Y'grandmother is waiting.'

Harriet's grandmother had also dressed carefully for the occasion. She was wearing a pale-blue suit with a pale-pink blouse and a string of very good pearls round her neck. She didn't get up when they entered, implying she was too overcome to do more than tremble genteely on the edge of the sofa.

Recognizing this emotional blackmail and the tyranny of the weak as old enemies, Harriet remained nervous but was unmoved. She knew behind her grandmother's watery blue eyes and trembling fingers lay a heart of granite.

Leo crossed the parquet floor, avoided tripping on the rug, and shook hands with Harriet's grandmother.

'This is Leo Purbright,' said Harriet.

'Oh yes? Would that be the Yorkshire Purbrights?'

Harriet's toes curled in her shoes with embarrassment. She knew her grandmother assumed that Leo belonged to some lesser Purbrights and merely wanted to highlight his lowliness. Her snobbishness was extreme, even for one of her background, generation and temperament.

'Yes,' said Leo. 'My uncle is Lord Westwood.'

Harriet shot him a look of disbelief which was met by a bland little smile. It took Lavinia Burghley-Rice but a moment to adjust her expression into something more suitable.

'Sherry, Anthony! Do sit down, Mr Purbright. And you, Harriet. Oh, and Anthony – the *good* sherry.'

Harriet sat down on the sofa next to Leo. Her grandmother hadn't even said hello to her. But Leo, with his grand connections, had been offered the *good* sherry, which her grandfather would have to fetch from the cupboard under the stairs. Leo's enormous confidence diminished their power over her. All their petty tyrannies now seemed rather pathetic.

'Now, Mr and Mrs Burghley-Rice,' said Leo, when everyone had taken diminutive sips out of their diminutive glasses. 'We've come to discuss Matthew.'

Everyone stiffened. Harriet felt sweat break out under her hairline.

'Although you have behaved both foolishly and illegally in preventing Harriet from seeing him while he is at school, I've managed to persuade her not to sue if Matthew spends his holidays with her.'

His words were like an explosion. Harriet almost expected

the glasses to shatter, the ceiling to come down. The effect wouldn't have been much greater if they had.

'Now listen to me, young – er – Mr – er. Harriet has behaved in a totally reprehensible way. We have supported her and Matthew out of the kindness of our hearts ever since they were both born.' Anthony Burghley-Rice, having altered the truth in order to improve the story, got to his feet. He rose somewhat more slowly than he would have liked, but he was no longer a young man. 'Matthew is a fine boy,' he went on. 'A credit to us. And we have no intention of letting him live in some sordid digs with his mother,' he shot Harriet a look of loathing, 'who has shown her extreme ingratitude – not to say complete irresponsibility – by leaving the home we have provided for her all these years. She has absolutely no rights over Matthew.'

'I hate to contradict you,' said Leo, obviously loving it, 'but a mother has very strong rights over her child. She could get Matthew away from school and living with her, in her "sordid digs", in a very short time indeed.'

Lavinia gave a little shriek. Harriet wondered if Leo knew what he was talking about or was just making it up.

'Of course, it would be better for everyone, particularly Matthew, if we could keep this out of the courts. There's bound to be very unpleasant publicity. It's just the sort of scandal the gutter press would love. However, if you refuse to agree to some sort of compromise, that will be Harriet's only choice.'

Leo paused dramatically. His connection with Lord West-wood, whoever he was, had obviously made him extremely haughty when the occasion demanded. Harriet could almost see her grandparents shrink under the effect of his quasi-noble birth and his horrifying words.

'However,' Leo went on, 'she is very reluctant to ex-pose her son to anything like that unless it's absolutely essential.'

Anthony Burghley-Rice cleared his throat, obviously think-ing that this man had held the floor for long enough, whatever his connections. But Leo hadn't finished. 'She would, of course, like Matthew with her for the entire school holidays.

It will give her an opportunity to let him visit some of the schools in the area which he might be called upon to attend. Foxmoor Comprehensive is the most obvious choice. Matthew would benefit from sharing the cultures of several ethnic minorities, and gain an insight into the needs of children less fortunate than himself. Despite their social disadvantages and the school's lack of resources, many of the better motivated pupils do manage to come away with some GCSEs.'

Harriet thought her grandmother was going to faint. She could almost see her groping for the smelling salts an earlier era would have provided for her. Harriet would have felt like fainting too, if she hadn't known that Foxmoor Comprehensive, if it existed at all, was nowhere near either Paddington or Chelsea.

'Of course a boy with Matthew's background, fresh from a private prep school, might not fit in with the rougher elements initially, but I'm sure he'll soon toughen up. At least being the son of a single mother will give him something in common with most of his classmates.'

'Now listen here,' said Anthony. 'I'm sure that none of this is really necessary.' He shot his wife a concerned glance – the heart of granite seemed to have taken a knock. 'We would hate the boy to have to suffer . . .'

'Then perhaps you should give some thought to what you have made Harriet suffer, and make some reparation?'

Harriet drained her glass, got up, unasked, and fetched the bottle of sherry. Nobody refused a second glass.

'Er – what do you have in mind?' Lavinia Burghley-Rice asked tentatively.

Harriet felt that at that moment, Leo could have demanded a king's ransom and it would have been delivered in used, non-sequential notes. Perhaps Leo could see it too, because he hesitated, as if considering the monetary value of a dewy-skinned prep-school boy.

'I think Harriet might be persuaded to leave him at Buck-fast's for the time being. If she has visiting rights and plenty of opportunity to see him in the holidays.' Leo smiled the crooked, cynical smile he usually reserved for particularly ghastly paintings. 'Including the forthcoming Christmas period, of course.'

Harriet's grandmother's eyelids fluttered, as she realized that *she* might be spending Christmas without Matthew, instead of Harriet.

Reading the expression in the pale eyes, Harriet suddenly felt a compassion she could not afford just at the moment. The tiniest weakness on her part now, and she would lose everything Leo had gained for her. She redirected her pity. The lunch was bound to need some attention. She got up.

'Would you like me to make the gravy, Granny?'

'Oh! Er yes, dear. Thank you.'

Harriet withdrew to the kitchen where, as she had known there would be, a leg of lamb was steadily overcooking. Her grandmother had actually thanked her!

By the time Harriet and Leo had been ushered out of the front door, having eaten lunch, and drunk pale tea out of bone-china cups, Harriet felt giddy with success. Her grandparents had invited Leo to join them all for Christmas, and Leo had accepted. Afterwards Harriet was to take Matthew to London, to stay at Cheyne Walk. Somehow Leo had led them to understand that this was where Harriet lived, and a very swanky address it was too. Had they known that the swank was a front for a flat only a couple of degrees up from sordid, they would not have agreed. But Leo had wooed them with his masterful manner and his aristocratic connections.

'Well,' said Leo, as they reached the car, 'what do you want to do now? I think some sort of of celebration is in order.'

'I should think so! You were wonderful! You bewitched them. Are you really a relation of Lord Westwood? That was a master stroke.'

Leo smiled. 'Yes, I really am. So, what do you want to do?'

Harriet regarded him. What Harriet wanted to do was to be taken to a hotel, be made just drunk enough to lose her inhibitions, and be made love to, with all Leo's undoubted skill and expertise. Unfortunately, she couldn't possibly say so.

'I feel so *tired*,' she said, suddenly overcome with it. 'All those years that pathetic old couple ruled my every waking moment. Now, instead of doing all the things they'd disapprove of most, like digging holes in the village green, or vandalizing the telephone box, all I want to do is sleep.'

'Let's find a cosy pub with a fire and sit by it for a while. I don't want to go back to London just yet.'

Harriet shook her head. 'I haven't kicked over the traces to the extent that I'll go into pubs at five in the afternoon.' She held out her hand. 'Let me show you where I grew up, Leo.'

Leo took the hand. 'Harriet, you're adorable. You want to kick over the traces and yet can't bring yourself to have a drink before six o'clock.'

They set off across the village green to a footpath which led to the river. Across the flatlands, a football match was going on. Small boys in shorts being egged on by parents, freezing in the biting wind. For the first time Harriet was almost glad that Matthew was at boarding school. She was hopelessly unsporty, and would let him down dreadfully.

'Have you got any children, Leo?' Harriet pulled up her collar, hunching her shoulders against the wind.

'No.'

'Then why do you have to pay your ex-wife alimony?'

'I may not have to any more. She's getting married.'

'Oh. So will you keep the classes going?'

He heard the edge of panic in her voice. 'Don't worry about that now. I've other plans for you. Tell me how you came to have Matthew.'

It was such a boring, overtold story. But if he really wanted to hear it – 'Oh, the usual. You know. I went to a party without my grandparents' permission. Got drunk. Got invited upstairs by a boy and thought it would be all right to go with him.'

'But how could you . . .'

'How could I have been so silly? He was the only person at the party with the same accent as I had. I thought he would be safe. But of course, he only wanted one thing . . .' Her voice trailed away on the sad little cliché.

'And that was the only time? You were terribly unlucky to get pregnant.'

Harriet shook her head. 'No. Not unlucky. Terribly, terribly lucky. Think how empty my life would have been without Matthew. I'd have withered away and died. He forced me to keep going.'

'But telling your grandparents . . .'

'Was dreadful, of course. But I was so pleased to be having a baby.'

'Did you tell the boy?'

Harriet shook her head. 'I didn't know his surname, and I utterly refused to tell my grandparents anything about the party, or they would have had private investigators tracking him down.'

'But Harriet, you were so young! Didn't you think of having an abortion?'

Harriet studied a willow pulled into the river by last year's floods. She wanted to paint it. 'Only to reject the idea out of hand. It was what my grandparents wanted, of course, but I made sure it was too late before I told them. I don't think I will ever forgive them for trying to force me into one.'

'They probably thought it was best for you. You were so young to be a mother.'

'Seventeen is not particularly young to be a mother. And they didn't think of me, they only thought of themselves, how it would be having an illegitimate great-grandchild. Matthew was a public statement of their failure to bring me up properly.' She sighed deeply. 'I suppose I can see their point of view now. And they do love him very much, in their way.'

'But how did you survive? It must have been hell, living with them.'

'It was, but the vicar's wife was wonderful. She convinced them that what was done was done, and they had better put a brave face on it and pretend to the world that they were thrilled.' She chuckled. 'And having decided the vicar's wife was right, my grandmother went the whole hog. Little

215

Cherub vests, Viyella nighties, a broderie-anglaise swathed crib. The poor little thing wasn't allowed into Babygros for months, until someone with a title gave him one. Then she insisted on calling them Growmores, like the fertilizer.'

'It must have been terrible at times.'

'Most things worth having are terrible at times. But I loved him so much, and he loved me. It was the first time I felt loved.'

'Not the last, I hope.'

Harriet saw that he wished that he could say he loved her, that he saw that she loved him. But she was glad he didn't lie to her. She looked at her watch.

'I think if we walk slowly, my Calvinistic principles might allow us to find a pub.'

CHAPTER TWENTY-TWO

May was wrapping Christmas presents, cursing herself for not doing it sooner, when Harriet or Sally would be around to help her. But they had both gone to their respective Christmases in the country. She'd have been gone herself by now, if so many people hadn't wanted their houses cleaned for Christmas. At the last minute, the Christmas Cleanups promotion had taken off.

She took another gulp of her tea. Harriet had infected her with Christmas spirit by making things for Matthew's stocking. Rashly, May had decided to do stockings for her parents and brothers.

Most of the gifts were home-made and/or edible. Harriet, for many years a stalwart of her church's Christmas Bazaar, had a vast repertoire of easy, economical ideas involving either condensed milk and pounds of sugar, or gold spray and pine-cones. A local open-air market had provided both the girls with a multitude of stationery. All in all, May thought that both Matthew and her family would be pleased with their stockings. She may be poor, but she could still hold her end up at Christmas.

It was just the wrapping-up which was a bind. If the glass jar which she had bought at a junk shop and filled with Smarties for her father broke out of its paper once more, she would damn well eat the Smarties herself. Her father was supposed to be on a diet anyway.

The familiar sensation of someone stepping across from *Shadowfax* to *The Rose Revived* lifted her flagging spirits. It couldn't be either of the girls, but it might be Jed, or Debra. Then she remembered that the *Curlew* had been taken to be near relatives for Christmas, and Ivan had gone to his parents. With luck, Mike had gone away too. She really didn't feel like an argument with him.

Whoever it was knocked, instead of yelling, which was a bad sign and ruled out Jed. At least half the salutations and exchange of news had usually gone on before whoever it was actually came in through the door. This person, or persons (there seemed to be two of them) hadn't said a word.

May went to answer the door with some misgiving. Having Sally and Harriet to live with her had knocked off her independent edges. Some of her sang-froid about letting strangers into her space had left her. She unlocked half the double door.

Only partly visible through the narrow space, stood two men. They wore overcoats and carried briefcases. May might have taken them for solicitors, except that they were too heavily built and weren't quite smart enough. Something about them, the one at the door, the other standing in the well-deck, made her nervous.

'Miss Sargent?'

'Yes?'

'Is this the premises of a business known as Cleaning Undertaken?'

'Yes.'

'And you are one of the partners?'

'I suppose so.'

'I think you'd better let us come in. We need a word.'

'Um. Who are you?'

'We're from the West London Register of Businesses. We've come to check your registration is in order.'

Her mind worked frantically. They had registered with the tax office and the DSS. Was there something else, that Hugh hadn't known about, they should have done? Only one of the men spoke, she noticed. The other was a silent Chorus, observing everything, so he could report later. 'What is that? Something to do with VAT?'

'That's right. We need to come in.'

'Can I see some form of identification?'

The man reached into his pocket and produced a plastic-covered photograph attached to a card. As he held it out to May, she couldn't suppress the thought that it looked wrong

218

in his hand, as if his fingers were more accustomed to larger, heavier things than mere scraps of pasteboard.

Her eye skipped over his name to the legend underneath. It said, West London Register of Businesses, VAT Office.

'And what is that?' May pointed to the words.

'It's a register of business you have to join. It's to check everyone's paying the correct Business Rates, VAT and so on. It's for the protection of legitimate business. If anyone is operating without paying what they owe, it's not fair on the businesses that do, is it?'

'Umm. I suppose not.'

'So, would you kindly allow I and my partner in? We need to look at your books.'

May regarded them. She wasn't exactly nervous but they did make her feel uncomfortable.

'I'm sorry, I would prefer to wait until one of my partners is at home . . .'

'No need for that. We won't be long.'

And before May had grasped their intention, the door was pulled out of her hand and the men were in the boat, their feet tangling in tubes of Smarties and Father Christmas wrapping paper. She opened her mouth to protest, but before she could, the spokesman grinned at her.

'Can we have a couple of teas, please love? Milk, two sugars? Ta.'

May retreated to the galley to gather her thoughts. Would ill-wishers really demand cups of tea in such a peremptory way? Surely not. Their grammar was bad and their manners worse, but were they sinister? Sinister or not, they were in now, and she couldn't get them out. She made the tea, chiding herself for paranoia.

The two big men filled the saloon. May invited them to sit down, which they did awkwardly. The thought flashed through her mind that, if it came to a chase, she could escape through the back of the boat and out through the engine-room. They would get stuck in the narrow space between her bunk and the door. At the best of times it could only be negotiated by thin people. Now, it was further obstructed by Sally's black plastic sacks. But why was she thinking like that?

She handed the men their mugs. 'So what do you want, exactly?'

The one with the speaking part produced a clipboard from his briefcase. 'I'd just like to ask you a few questions. Where do your partners, Miss Bliss and Miss Devonshire, reside?'

'Here.' 'Reside' was as good a word for their hugger-mugger existence as any.

The man looked incredulous, as well he might. 'You don't have their addresses?'

'*They* don't have their addresses. They live here.'

'And where are they?'

'Away. It's Christmas.'

'And do you have the addresses of where they are at present?'

'No. And if I did, I wouldn't give them to you. Why do you want to know? If this is a business matter, what do their holiday addresses have to do with anything?'

The man shook his head. 'There's no need to be like that about it. When we're asked to investigate a new company, we do it thoroughly. We don't want any unfortunate mistakes.'

'You say you were *asked* to investigate. Who by?'

The silent man had unhooked a plate which May had hanging on the bulkhead. The speaker looked at him and nodded before shaking his head. 'Confidential information, miss. And we do need those addresses.'

Please dear God, she prayed silently, let one of these men turn out to be Jeremy Beadle. Let this whole thing be some ghastly practical joke. But she knew it wasn't. It was real. She'd never felt so alone in her life.

She tried hard to sound accommodating. 'I'm really not withholding information, but they are both away for Christmas, and I haven't got their addresses.'

'So you're in charge while they're away?'

May nodded, wishing passionately she'd managed to get away a day earlier herself.

'Can I see your business registration forms?'

The palms of May's hands began to sweat. They had done everything they should have done, hadn't they? But she didn't know for sure. 'What business registration forms?'

The man looked at her as if she were deaf or stupid and then exchanged another, almost smug look, with his silent companion. 'You did register with the council, didn't you?'

May's mouth went dry. Should she just say that there weren't any forms? Or should she say they were somewhere else?

'I think they are with our accountant.' That sounded good. But only for a moment.

'You do know *his* address, I presume?' The man's pen was poised, waiting for a name and address.

'I'm not sure. I don't deal with the business end of things. Miss Devonshire does that.' Forgive me, Harriet. You're not here, and I'm desperate.

'But you run the business from here?'

May nodded.

'Then you keep your books here?'

May chewed on her lip. What should she say? Surely she didn't have to let these apes see their books? Surely their books were confidential?

'You do keep accounts?'

'Of course.'

'Then show us.'

It took her a lifetime to find them. At last, she hauled out the big red book which she had heard Harriet curse over, in her refined, Home Counties way. Oh where are you, Harriet, now that I need you?

'Here you are.'

The man put it on the table and opened it.

'I want to see your client list.'

'That's confidential.'

The man sighed with exaggerated patience and exchanged another glance with the silent partner, who was now fiddling with an antique lace plate, which had been her mother's boat-warming present. 'I need to know if you've got enough people to go on the register,' he explained, when he had received the nod.

'We don't have a client list as such . . .'

'You must have something.' He smiled. It was more threatening than his gruff demands had been.

May bit her lip. There was the little notebook with their clients' telephone numbers in it. She produced it. It wasn't up to date, but they wouldn't know that. 'There's this.'

The man almost snatched it from her.

May couldn't bear to look as he went through their earnings, checking down the columns of figures, referring to the notebook. Blast Christmas, sending all her friends away, leaving her here alone with these two. She stared out of the windows, but because they were high, she could see nothing but the darkening sky. This added to her growing despair. She turned her gaze to more comfortable things and noticed some garment of Sally's which had fallen behind the stove. Then she spotted the mobile phone.

She could ring someone for help. Because it was so expensive, they rarely used the phone for outgoing calls, and she'd practically forgotten she had it. She could get someone to come along and sit with her while these men did their business. Or, even better, throw them out.

Hugh leapt into her mind in an instant. He had offered to draw up their agreement, he would surely help her out now. He was bound to be at one of the numbers she had for him. Then she thought again. She didn't know him well enough to impose on him like that. She couldn't ask him to drop everything and rescue her.

Her father, of course, would come running. But she couldn't remember his office number, and by the time she'd rung her mother, thought up why she wanted her father's daytime number and got through to him via his secretary, these thugs would have done whatever they planned to do.

Her brothers? No. They wouldn't stir until they'd had hours of explanations, by which time it would be far too late. She would be lying in a pool of blood or have been carried off to jail for failing to keep her address book up to date long before they got there.

'And these are the only people you work for?'

May had long since stopped assuming they were bona fide officials. They had 'Friends of Slimeball' written all over them, from the flashy suits to the sausage-like fingers. But she didn't see how she could accuse them without getting hurt.

'Er – yes.'

'And do you keep receipts?'

May retrieved a shoe-box which was full of nasty little bits of paper. One of them caught her eye. It was the sheet which had the details of the boat trip for Buckfast's School on it. It also had Hugh's home and office telephone number.

It had to be Hugh. Maddeningly, the tune of an ancient song came into her head. She focused on the number. She couldn't retrieve the paper, she would have to learn the number by heart. Thank goodness she had a good memory. But even as she recited it in her head, her hands shook.

'Hang on a minute. I'm not sure this is the right box.' She laughed in a very Sally-like way. 'You don't want to look through all my clothes receipts.'

'Not immediately, no.'

Fear stabbed her, scrambling her brains, until she doubted her ability to remember Hugh's name, let alone his telephone number. Frantically, she fitted it to the tune of 'It Had to Be You,' and at last it stuck. She repeated it silently a couple of times to make sure.

'It is the right one,' she said, handing it over.

The man almost snatched it.

Now, how to get the phone and herself into her bedroom without the men seeing her go. She crossed the boat in a casual stride, sinking down on her hunkers next to the stove, as if she were cold. She *was* cold, or certainly shivering. But that was mostly due to fear. She tucked her shaking hands under her armpits. She was wearing the big patchwork cardigan which Sally's mother had knitted, and Sally had lent to Harriet. Somehow it had gravitated to May and she had been wearing it more or less ever since. Its baggy sleeves suddenly gave her an idea.

The phone was on the bookcase. If she could scoop it into her sleeve, she could tell the men she was going to the loo. A casual arm thrown across the front of the bookcase accompanied by a sigh got her within grasp of it. Keeping her eye on the man rifling through the box, her fingers closed on the phone. A moment more and she would have it in her sleeve, and then all she had to do . . .

'Who are you planning on ringing?'

'Ringing? Me?' God! She sounded like Miss Piggy! 'Oh! I want to ring my boyfriend. I was due to meet him, now I'll be late.'

The speaker looked towards his mate, who considered for a second and then nodded.

'OK, ring him.'

How on earth could she alert Hugh to her situation without them suspecting her? She pushed down the keys. Oh Hugh, please, please, be in. Oh please let the number be a direct line. Don't make me go through the switchboard.

'Yes?' a voice barked.

'Hugh? Is that you?'

'Who is this?'

'Darling!' She sounded wildly theatrical. 'It's me, May. I'm just ringing to say I might be a little late for our date. I've got these men on the boat and they're looking at the books and things.'

'May? What on earth are you talking about? And why are you calling me "darling"? Are you in some sort of trouble?'

May giggled seductively. 'You always guess exactly right. You could come over.'

'Can you speak freely?'

'Of course not, you silly man,' she cooed.

'Are you frightened?'

'Mmmm. I'll say. I'm *longing* to see you.'

'I'll get there as soon as I can.'

'You're so sweet.'

By the time May put the phone down she felt giddy with relief, and just like Sally. It was something of a comedown to see her own Doc Martens appearing from under her dungarees. How convincing could she have sounded when she looked like that?

'My boyfriend's coming in a couple of hours,' she said casually. 'Will you be finished by then?'

The man shrugged. 'That very much depends, young lady, on what we find. But I should think so.'

May was slumped on the steps under the side doors, which, during the summer, opened to let in light and air and people. In winter, they formed what May referred to as her 'conversation area'. There was precious little conversation going on in it now. May felt miserable. It seemed ages since she'd rung Hugh and still he hadn't appeared. She felt desperately lonely.

At last she heard his step in the well-deck. The door opened without anyone knocking and Hugh came in.

May's first, irrelevant thought was that he was right about the headroom in her boat, and that if she did something different about the ballast, she could get another couple of inches. Her second was how quickly the men jumped to their feet. They both hit their heads and looked extremely guilty. Be like Sally, she commanded herself.

'Darling!' May threaded her way rapidly through feet and legs and Christmas presents to Hugh, and flung herself into his arms. 'You're early, how lovely!'

What was unexpectedly lovely was the feel of his very strong arms round her, holding her extremely tightly. She clung to his lapel, no longer sure if she was imitating Sally, or just holding on to something safe. Gently, he put her from him.

'Who are these people –' he hesitated only for the tiniest second, 'darling?'

'Oh, they're from the council. They're looking at all the books and things from the business. Apparently we should have registered or something. They'll show you their cards.'

The talking man put his hand in his pocket as if to produce a card, coughed and said. 'I think we've pretty well finished now, young lady. You'll be hearing from us, no doubt.'

'Will she? Then perhaps you'd like my card? I am Cleaning Undertaken's legal adviser. You may need to get in touch with me if there are any problems.'

The talking man looked at May with disgust. 'I thought you said you was ringing your boyfriend?' His accent and manner had become distinctly rougher.

'This young lady is my fiancée,' said Hugh stiffly. 'Naturally, she would look to me for legal advice. I may have come here for purely social reasons, but if I find a situation where I am needed, naturally I will act.' He hesitated just for a moment. 'And I mean, act.'

His meaning was sufficiently clear for the silent man to nudge his friend and indicate the door of the boat.

'Well, we'll be getting along then,' said the spokesman. 'Ta for the tea.'

They thumped their way out of the cabin, into the well-deck, on to the adjacent boat and away. May sat down by the stove, shaking. 'Thank you so much for coming. I don't know how I could have been so frightened of such clowns, but I was. And that bit about being our legal adviser was brilliant.'

Hugh grunted. 'Do you know who they were?'

'They said they were from the West London Register of Businesses, VAT branch, but I've a good idea they were from Slater. They were very interested in the client list.'

'Oh? Why should they be?'

May ruffled her hair with her fingers. 'Because Slater told us that if we pinched his clients, he'd "take steps".'

'But why wait until now? You must have pinched his clients ages ago.'

'I don't know for sure, but it could be because usually there are half a dozen friends with windlasses about. Now, everyone's gone away for Christmas, except Jed, and he's asleep.'

'They didn't hurt you? Threaten you?'

May shook her head and smiled to reassure him. 'No. They just went through the books and the shoe-box, where we keep all the receipts and things.'

'Why did you let them in, May?' He was angry now, and trying not to show it, but it was revealed in the tightness of his expression.

'I didn't, really. But I did ask for identification, and they had proper cards . . .'

'Doesn't mean a thing. You can get cards printed in motorway service stations . . .'

226

'Anyway, I didn't let them in, they let themselves in. I couldn't stop them.'

His anger was well past his guard now. 'Are you here on your own?'

'Yes. Until tomorrow, when I'm going home for Christmas. Why? You don't think they'll come back?'

Hugh stayed standing in the middle of the cabin, his head slightly bowed to accommodate the lack of space. 'If Slater wants to scare you off, and doesn't think those goons did a good enough job, this boat would be a good place to start.'

May put her head between her knees, feeling violently sick. 'Oh God.' She was trembling from head to toe.

'Would you like me to come and boat-sit for you?' Hugh said. 'Keep an eye on things over the holiday?'

May looked up. She wasn't sentimental, but she suddenly wanted to cry. It was the shock of Slimeball's heavy mob coming to visit her, no doubt.

'No! I couldn't possibly ask you to do that! It's Christmas!'

'I know. What I'm saying is, do you want me come and live here while you're away? It should keep the boat safe.'

May, who had been thinking, shook her head. 'No. I've got a better idea.'

'What?'

'I'll move the boat. There's a place a little way up the cut, opposite the towpath, where you can fit a narrowboat. But there are trees and things hanging over, so you can hardly see it.'

'Oh?'

'The only trouble is, you have to climb up a brick wall to get off once you've put it there. But it's the perfect hiding place.'

'How do you know about this place, if it's so inaccessible?'

'A friend hid there when he thought his ex-wife's boyfriend was after his manhood. I used to row along with supplies. But those men would never find it.'

'I see.'

'I'll put it there tomorrow, when I'm ready to go home.'

He shook his head. 'Not tomorrow. Now.'

The fear which had begun to recede came back like recurrent toothache. 'Why now? Do you think they'll come back tonight?'

Hugh deliberated for so long that May could only think the worst. 'I just don't think,' he said at last, 'there's any point in taking unnecessary risks.'

May inhaled deeply. 'OK. I'll start the engine.' It didn't occur to her that she'd taken Hugh's help for granted until the engine was running and she had untied the back-end. She saw him at the bow, the mooring rope in his hand. As she saw him step back on to *The Rose Revived* she silently thanked him.

There was little pleasure in their short trip down the cut but there was satisfaction. They worked well together, and working as an efficient team was pleasing. When both ends of the boat were secure and the engine noise had ceased, May joined Hugh in the saloon.

'Would you like to come home with me for Christmas?' she asked bluntly.

Hugh looked up sharply. He obviously hadn't been expecting that. May hadn't either. It took them both by surprise.

'I couldn't possibly. But it's awfully kind of you . . .'

May shook her head. 'It's not kindness, it's self-defence. If I come with a man – any man – even if there's nothing whatever going on, it'll give me family cred. My brothers won't tease me about being such a rampant feminist who no man'll come near. And my mother would be thrilled.'

Did she really have to tell him why? But then brutal honesty was probably the best policy with Hugh. He was in the legal profession.

'She will, of course, think you are my boyfriend, however much I try and tell her that you're not. But she'd really like to have you. She says it's important to have non-family members at Christmas, to stop me and my brothers quarrelling. You'd be doing us a favour, really.'

'I'm sure you'll all get along without me.'

Suddenly it became very important to May that he accept. 'Of course we will! But I really would like you to come. Please.'

Hugh regarded her for so long that May felt sympathy for all those documents he scrutinized.

She broke the silence. 'My mother is an awfully good cook. Her Christmas dinner would be some consolation for having to rescue me.'

Suddenly Hugh smiled. 'In which case I shall be very happy to accept.'

Relief took away the last of May's energy. 'I'll ring my mother, and tell her, then.'

'Are you sure she won't be put out?'

'No, no, of course not. We've two spare rooms, if you include my father's study. And I don't think anyone else will be staying the night. My aunt and her family always walk.'

'When are you going?'

'Tomorrow.'

'Would you like a lift?'

May grinned. 'My father usually picks me up, but today's his last day in the office, so he'd have to drive up specially to collect me.'

Hugh's expression became resigned. 'I'll pick you up about four.'

'Thank you.'

'May?'

'Mmm?'

'Would you like me to stay tonight?'

May swallowed hard but shook her head. 'No, I'll be OK.'

'Are you sure?'

'Quite. I'll be fine. I'm used to being on my own. I like it.'

He took out a pen and one of his cards. 'If you're sure, I'll go. I've got a dinner engagement. I'll just jot down my mobile number, so if you get nervous or anything happens you can get in touch.'

'I won't be nervous and nothing will happen.'

He studied her face seemingly for ages, and while he did so, May concentrated on keeping her expression serene. He looked at his watch. 'In which case, I'll go. I'm half an hour late.'

May's serenity took a dive the moment she had seen him off the boat. She went to bed late, and took the phone and his number with her. She didn't sleep well.

CHAPTER TWENTY-THREE

'Hi! Sorry I'm late, but the kids had to go to a party and the mother would talk.' Lucy was wearing a tweed hat to keep off the pouring rain, and peered at Sally from under it. She picked up one of Sally's bags. 'James did want to meet you himself, but he got tied up. A farm is like a prison sentence, if you ask me, only the better you behave, the worse your chances of parole.'

Sally smiled bravely, realizing she was going to get extremely wet. It hadn't been raining in London. 'It's very good of you to come for me.'

'It's kind of you to come. Goodness knows how James would have managed without any sort of help. Although what you'll be able to achieve in two days, God knows. Did you see the house properly last time?'

Sally shook her head.

'I thought not, or you wouldn't have offered to help out. Do you want me to bring the Land Rover nearer, or can you make a dash for it?'

Wishing she'd had the forethought to lie about seeing the house, Sally said. 'I can make a dash for it.'

'Jolly good. Come on then.'

Lucy ran across the station forecourt. Hampered by the remaining luggage, Sally followed her more slowly. Lucy had the back of the Land Rover open by the time Sally arrived.

'Just fling it in.'

Sally flung, on top of a golf umbrella, several pairs of wellington boots and a couple of riding hats. Lucy banged the door and went round to the driver's side. Outside, Sally wiped the rain off her nose, hoping that Lucy would get the door unlocked before the rain penetrated her inadequate jacket. A moment later the door opened, and Sally hauled herself in.

'Aunt Sophie will arrive at about six the day after tomorrow. Christmas Eve.'

'I know.'

'I'll pick her up from the station and bring her over.'

Sally nodded.

'It's going to be awful for you. I should never have let James accept your offer, selfless though it was.' She switched on and the engine rumbled into life.

Sally stared out of the streaming screen, now cleared by the wiper. Could it be, she thought, that James hadn't referred to his sister? One thing was certain – that notion would not please the sister in question.

'Still,' said Lucy brightly. 'If all else fails, we can ship you all over to my house.'

'I'm sure we'll manage,' said Sally, determined to have her bones ripped from her body before Christmas moved to Lucy's.

'She's a very demanding old lady, you know.'

Sally had got that impression. 'I'll just do my best.'

Lucy cut in front of a battered Ford Escort and swung out of the car park into the traffic. 'Frankly, sweetie, your best won't be good enough. If you can just get James to hang up a bunch of mistletoe for Aunt Sophie to kiss him under, you'll have done more than anyone expects.'

Lucy did up her seat belt as they negotiated a roundabout.

'And *James* appreciates your volunteering to help.' She managed to imply that everyone else considered her a complete waste of space. 'Though don't, I beg you,' Lucy lowered her tone and looked at Sally for a frighteningly long time, 'don't, for your sake, interpret his gratitude as anything else. He's a lovely man, there's no getting away from it.' She overtook the Ford Escort which had somehow got ahead. 'But even if he wanted one, which he categorically does not, he cannot possibly afford a wife.' Her eyes added the words, 'especially a wife like you'.

Sally smiled blandly and considered telling Lucy that she only wanted James for his body but decided that honesty was not the best policy on this occasion. Besides, although marriage to a farmer was not an option for an actress, a close relationship with one was not out of the question and she didn't want to damage her chances.

Lucy's assumption that she was a useless idiot and that the whole of Christmas Day was going to be a fiasco made Sally more determined than ever that it should not be. Being lighthearted did not make one a fool, and this fool's initiative and resourcefulness had been sharpened up a lot lately. She may have been there because James was too soft-hearted to tell her not to come, but he was not going to regret it for a moment.

'Of course, I wouldn't dream of saying anything,' went on Lucy, who, as far as Sally could tell, had never dreamed of doing anything except speaking her mind. 'But Aunt Sophie is bound to think you're walking out together. And will make all sorts of desperately embarrassing remarks about your bottom drawer.' Sally caught a glimpse of perfect little teeth as Lucy smiled. 'I just wouldn't want you to think that anyone except Sophie has marriage on their minds. Least of all James. He'll run a mile if he thinks that's what you're after.'

Oh will he? You may live to be surprised, Mrs Mother-of-Beautiful-Twins. You may find that the gold-digging little actress from London arranges Christmas so beautifully that you'll be ordering James to marry her at gunpoint, and begging her to have the twins as attendants.

What she said was, 'I'd better cancel my subscription to *Brides* magazine, then.'

Lucy shot her a worried glance. Had James's bimbo made a joke? Sally smiled blandly, and decided to keep Lucy guessing.

James was nowhere to be found when they arrived at the farm. Clodagh, however, was in the kitchen, and gave Sally a warm welcome, which consisted of two wags, a little woof, and a paw waved while Clodagh sat back on her haunches.

Sally, who knew when she was honoured, held the paw and rubbed the massive chest. 'Hello darling, it's lovely to see you again. How've you been then? Has James been looking after you?'

Clodagh seemed to take all this perfectly well. Lucy looked nauseated.

'I must get back. Can you sort yourself out? I expect James has left it up to you to decide where to put everyone, but you'll be glad to hear that I've bought him some sheets.' Her look was like Waterford crystal, expensive and unambiguous. 'I gather you had to sleep in James's bed last time.'

'Yes,' said Sally. 'Thank you so much for picking me up. If James had said it might be difficult, I could have taken a taxi.'

Lucy seemed to unbend a little. Perhaps she felt guilty for implying anything had gone on when Sally was here before. 'God! No need for that! My number's written on the wall by the phone. If you need anything, I'd be glad to help. Really, I will.'

'Thanks.' Sally's smile was warm and grateful, but she knew that, while Lucy would be glad to help, she would be even more glad to know that Sally needed it.

When Lucy had gone, Sally took off her sopping coat and hung it on one of the pipes over the Rayburn, but carefully, so it wouldn't drip into anything she might cook later. Then she rummaged in her bag for Harriet's Christmas present, which Harriet had insisted Sally open early. She found it, and put it on. It was a blue striped cook's apron which generously encompassed Sally's slender waist and covered her from collar to knee.

May had also given Sally clothes: a set of red thermal long-johns which went down to the ankle, and a vest which finished at her thighs. She had also lent Sally her wellingtons, which were green and the right size, and a boiler-suit, which was a little short in the body, but, as May said, she had the bum for it.

She also had all her own warm clothes. But even Harriet was surprised when she took a couple of packets of soda crystals, a bottle of extra-strong bleach, and two pairs of rubber gloves from the firm's cleaning supplies. Thus kitted

233

out, Sally felt fit for anything – Aunt Sophie in a snowstorm, Lucy in a paddy.

She had also brought with her a couple of Christmas cookery books which she had bought at a cut-price bookshop, and a notebook to write lists in. According to Harriet, lists were the answer to any crisis situation, including Christmas. If you wrote down absolutely everything you were likely to need to do, from ordering extra milk to buying spare bulbs for the Christmas tree lights, you'd get through somehow.

Sally slid the kettle across to boil and sat down at the kitchen table. She opened her notebook, found a pen in her handbag and wrote the date at the top of the page. Then she wrote, *Bedrooms – allocate.*

When James came in an hour later, he was surprised to see her. It seemed for a moment that he had forgotten she was coming. Sally, hearing him come into the room, got up from her chair and would have run towards him and flung her arms round his neck. But he held out his hands and caught hers.

'Don't come too near, I stink of cow.'

He could have stunk of the entire Royal Agricultural Showground for all Sally cared, but she didn't force herself on him, although he looked particularly gorgeous in his flat cap and worn Barbour jacket. It was no good rushing a man like James, particularly if he was wary of women who looked like wanting a white wedding, two point four children and a half-share of the farm. While Sally absolved him of reaching such a conclusion unaided, she was positive that Lucy would have sown the seeds to give him the idea. She would have to be patient. A moment later she was chiding herself for letting her imagination run away with her. She did not want to marry a farmer, so why did she keep thinking that she did?

'Hello, James,' she said hurriedly, in case her thoughts scared him off. 'It's lovely to see you. Do you want tea? The kettle's boiled.'

James dragged a chair out from under the table. 'I'd love tea. How wonderful coming in from the cows to be greeted by a beautiful woman, a warm kitchen and a cup of tea.'

Sally, her back turned to him, smiled as she poured his

234

tea. That's my boy, she thought, keep thinking along those lines.

'Lucy tells me you've got some sheets, now.'

'Yes. At least four sets, which should do us over Christmas, shouldn't it?'

'How many people are staying the night?'

'Just you, me and Aunt Sophie, I think. But we'd better make up another bedroom in case anyone drinks too much to drive home.'

'And how many people do you expect for Christmas dinner?'

James considered. 'Well, there's Lucy and Alexander, Gina and Gus – that's four – you, me, and Aunt Sophie, Liz and Peter, their two kids, and Uncle John. I don't think my cousin Rebecca is coming, though I'm not sure. How many's that?'

'Twelve or thirteen,' said Sally weakly.

'And there's Damien who comes sometimes, though I think he's supposed to be doing something else this year. We probably need to eat in the dining-room. Did you see it? It's off the hall, on the right, as you come in the front door.'

'You did offer to show me round the house when I was last here, but there was never time.'

'Really? How awful of me, I am sorry. We'll do it after supper.'

'Do you want me to cook? Or has Lucy . . .?'

James seemed apologetic. 'Lucy has been frightfully busy, what with Christmas and all. But she did go shopping for me. I can do it when I've finished outside.'

'That's fine, just as long as I know. And tell me, have you got any Christmas decorations at all?'

'No. The girls got all the family ones.'

'And are you prepared to buy any? I know money is tight, but if we just had some fairy lights . . .'

'Oh God, yes! I'm sure we can run to that. He put his hand in his back pocket and took out his wallet. 'You're going to be needing all sorts of odds and ends. Lucy can take you into town tomorrow. Buy what you think we'll need.' He handed her two twenty-pound notes. 'We'll have to do a supermarket shop tomorrow, I reckon, but Lucy's got the bird and the plum pudding and stuff. It's mostly in the larder, with at least two crates of booze.'

Money and alcohol were important, but she needed something else. 'Have you got any secateurs?'

'What?'

'You know, for me to cut boughs of holly, and stuff?'

'Of course. I thought it was a funny time of year to prune roses. I'll dig you out some.' He watched as Sally added to her list. 'You look frightfully efficient.'

'I'm planning to *be* frightfully efficient. Whether it'll work, we've yet to find out.'

A large, calloused hand covered Sally's. 'I don't suppose you could do something about the Christmas cards?'

Sally snatched her hand away. 'You're not asking me to send out your Christmas cards? Two days before Christmas?'

'Oh God, no! I haven't sent any! No, I meant the Christmas cards I've got. It's just that if Aunt Sophie doesn't see hers, she'll get offended.'

Sally wished she hadn't been so hasty with her hand. If the mistletoe failed to do its stuff, it might be all she got in the way of physical contact all Christmas. 'Of course. Sorry.'

James got up, bestowing on Sally another of his heartbreaking smiles. 'You're an angel. I hope you'll put on your tinsel halo for Christmas dinner.'

'Tinsel,' Sally murmured, adding it to her list. 'And that reminds me. Do you have Christmas dinner in the evening, or at lunchtime?'

'Evening. The girls like a leisurely morning while the kids unwrap their stockings, and they assure me that if you have it at lunchtime you have to get up at cockcrow to get it all sorted, which they refuse to do. They'll turn up here at about two, when the children get to open their presents.'

Sally made more notes, thinking as she did so that James's nieces and nephews were very well disciplined.

'I'd better get back out there,' said James, draining his mug. 'No rest for the wicked.'

'And not for the virtuous either,' said Sally. 'Where did you say the Christmas cards were?'

Eventually, Sally found some string in the feedstore. It was lying on the floor having been unpicked from the various bags of feed and left. It was just what Sally needed for the Christmas cards, and she took it all, in case it came in useful.

She hung the cards over the string which she tied to convenient nails protruding at intervals along one of the beams. Having done this, she washed and peeled a mountain of potatoes from the sack in the scullery. Potatoes were always a good start.

When she'd finished, and crossed off, *Peel spuds* she wrote, *Rationalize kitchen storerooms* in her book. At the moment, all the various little rooms, and there were six, seemed to contain something that was needed in the kitchen. If she was going to be Superwoman *par excellence*, she would need to have things to hand. As things were at present, she had to walk miles to prepare a single meal. Christmas Day would notch up a half-marathon at least.

This done, she had a look in the fridge for something to cook with the potatoes. She found some very appetizing lamb chops, and as she had noticed a huge rosemary bush when she was last here, she could show her culinary flair by sprinkling it over them.

She added *Pick rosemary* to her list, before finding some kitchen scissors and going out of the back door. The secret of list-making, Harriet had explained, was to put things on it you can cross off easily. It was no good writing *Clean house*; what you had to do was to break it up into achievable chunks: *Dust bathroom shelves*, *Empty w.p.b.'s*. 'Honestly,' Harriet had told Sally, 'When I was really up against it, I used to put down things like, *Get Dressed* and *Brush teeth*.'

When the potatoes were eye-free and waiting in their pan and the chops ready to go under the grill of the ancient electric cooker Sally had discovered in the room with the potatoes, Sally decided there was just about time to make a pudding.

She hadn't actually checked with James that he liked custard, but although she had been wrong about many things concerning James, she would stake her life on this. A jam sponge wouldn't take long to cook and was easy to make.

James came in and washed his hands in the sink. Sally imagined that Lucy would scold him for doing so. I'd scold him too, she thought, if it was my sink. As it wasn't, all she said was, 'Would you like a cup of tea?' This had gone down well before.

'Tea? James dried his hands on a clean tea-towel. 'No, I think it's time for a drink, don't you? Wine or whisky?' he said over his shoulder, looking in the cupboard with the cornflakes. 'I'll have to make sure we've got enough booze for the festivities. I don't know about you, but I can be teetotal for weeks and weeks. Then the house fills with people and I suddenly turn to drink.'

A pang shot through Sally. He had drunk whisky when she had come for the weekend. Did he think of her as 'people'?

She didn't ask him. She just said, 'Wine please, we're having chops.'

He handed her a glass into which he had fitted almost half a bottle of wine. 'I hope you'll like it. It's an amusing little number I picked up for two-ninety-nine.' James smiled. 'Happy Christmas, and thank you for coming.'

James was a dream to cook for. He ate everything, liked everything and didn't make 'suggestions'. Piers was forever saying things like, 'Can I suggest that next time you cook this in the oven instead of under the grill? It would be so much nicer.' Piers claimed it was constructive criticism and she should be grateful for having her cooking skills improved by his advice. To Sally, it felt like unconstructive nagging.

James ate two-thirds of the jam sponge. 'I haven't had a proper pudding with custard for years. Lucy says it's fattening and tries to make me have yoghurt instead.'

Mentally, Sally licked her finger and gave herself a point. 'Oh but Greek yoghurt's all right!' she said. 'It's quite creamy.'

James put down his spoon and regarded her seriously. 'I never, ever, eat yoghurt, in any form.' He sounded almost strict. 'Kindly remember that.'

Sally chuckled happily. He must like her a little if he thought it worth her while remembering his little fads and fancies.

After Sally had donned her rubber gloves and washed, while James dried, he took her on a tour of the downstairs. It was quite a large farmhouse, but most of the rooms had fallen into disuse and there was very little furniture. All three of the reception rooms were illuminated only by low-wattage bulbs hanging from short pieces of flex from the middle of the ceiling. Consequently, it was hard to tell if the rooms were musty and damp because of lack of use, or had stopped being used because they were musty and damp.

'The rooms are a good size,' said Sally, glad she could find something positive to say. 'I'm sure with a good clean. . . .'

'Replastering, repapering and a damp-proof course . . .'

'. . . I'll be able to get it looking quite Christmassy.'

Together, they went back to the kitchen. Sally wasn't as optimistic as she sounded. Perhaps Lucy had been right, and that two days wasn't nearly long enough to make any sort of impression – let alone a good one.

'You're sweet, but unrealistic,' said James. 'I shouldn't have let Aunt Sophie come – or you. You'll both get rheumatisim and freeze to death.'

'I can't speak for Aunt Sophie,' said Sally, 'but I have thermal underwear. A little cold holds no perils for me.'

James laughed. 'Perhaps that's what I should buy the old bat for Christmas, long-johns.'

'You mean you haven't got her a present yet?' Sally liked buying presents and started in November.

James shrugged and smiled in a rueful way which made it impossible for Sally to be satisfactorily annoyed.

'Christmas comes every year, you know? 'Bout this time.'

'I know. I've no real excuse except that I never know what to buy anyone, and I always manage to get just the wrong thing. My sisters won't let me buy anything any more except at Marks and Spencer's, so they can change it.'

Sally's tender heart took another blow.

'And there isn't one locally. I have to go to Cheltenham or Gloucester. I haven't had time this year.'

Mentally, Sally added, *Buy J's Xmas presents* to her list.

'I've got to go into town tomorrow. If you can't take me, I'm sure Lucy would. I'll get your presents then.' And I'll buy four pink bathcubes for you to give me, and then your sisters will think you've chosen the presents yourself, she added silently.

'Sally, you really are the sweetest girl.'

Sally fixed her eyes on his face, willing him to take her in his arms. But she was hardly even disappointed that he didn't. He probably called his cows 'sweet girls' and she could bide her time.

She would have liked a Christmas present from him, there was no escaping the empty feeling that not getting one was giving her. And she had spent a small fortune on a silver model of an Irish wolfhound. She had seen it in an antique shop, and although she couldn't possibly afford it, and would have to borrow from the business account to get through January, she couldn't resist it. Now, naturally, she couldn't give it to him. She would have to get something else. More money.

Oh well, she had already got things for his sisters and their children, and a box of handkerchiefs for Aunt Sophie. She would get some handkerchiefs for James, too.

'Would you like a hot toddy, to take up to bed with you?' asked James.

'For a moment there, I thought you said, "hot body". But failing that, a hot toddy would be lovely.'

James got out the whisky. 'I'm fresh out of hot bodies, I'm afraid.'

Oh, I wouldn't say that, said Sally silently to his corduroy-covered rear end as he bent to retrieve the whisky.

CHAPTER TWENTY-FOUR

'OK,' said Hugh. 'Are you ready?'

Hugh pushed May's bottom with more force than courtesy, but at last she got her foot into a crack, her hand on an ancient mooring ring, and heaved herself on to the side into a forest of buddleia. She was panting as she turned to look at Hugh, who was still standing on the roof of the boat.

'That's me. Now how are you going to get off?' she said.

'Give me your hand. Now grab on to something solid. Right. Hold tight!'

For a moment May thought her arm was going to be wrenched from its socket and her fingers crunched into powder, but then, with a swoop, Hugh half climbed, half leapt off the roof of the boat and was beside her. For someone who had a sedentary occupation he really was surprisingly athletic. She massaged her hand.

'Getting back on will be easier,' said Hugh, panting slightly. 'You can jump. Do you really need all this?' he went on, eyeing the two suitcases, one cardboard box, and multiple carrier-bags which had already been hauled up from the boat.

'It's Christmas,' said May. 'And some of it's washing.'

Hugh picked up the suitcases and a handful of carrier-bags. 'You should be ashamed of yourself, getting your mother to do your washing at your age.'

'If you'd ever lived on a boat you'd know how difficult these things are. Besides, I do the washing myself. I just use my mother's machine.'

She heard herself sounding defensive, and cursed under her breath. She'd vowed she'd be really nice to Hugh out of gratitude for saving her, and here she was, as prickly as ever. It was his fault. She had no difficulty being nice to anyone else.

She hurried to catch up with him as he crossed the waste ground at a terrific pace. She joined him by his car.

He unlocked the boot and put in her suitcases. 'That lot'll have to go on the back seat.' He indicated a box in the boot already. 'I bought your parents some wine. I hope that's all right.'

'You needn't have, you know. But they'll be delighted. My mother and I tend to get a bit squiffy, particularly when it really is Christmas.' She saw an eyebrow shoot up and felt she had to explain. 'We don't see that much of each other, so when we do, we get out the sherry while we do the veg. Then we always say "It's like Christmas". So when it really is Christmas, we get even drunker. I don't know why I started this conversation.'

She climbed into the car feeling bad-tempered even before they set off. So much for her good intentions. At this rate she'd be lucky if they were still speaking by the time they arrived.

'Tell me about your family,' said Hugh, when they were finally on the right road.

He'd been maddeningly stoical about her confusing directions, not tolerant, but enduring, as if having a woman who didn't know left from right as a passenger was a cross all true Brits bore with a stiff upper lip. She wanted to kick him.

'Well, there's my father,' she said, crossing her ankles firmly. 'He works for the Baltic Exchange and is a dear. He's interested in antiquarian books and frames pictures as a hobby.'

She took a breath, deciding how best to describe the small, laughing woman whom they all teased dreadfully, but all depended on for sound advice.

'My mother – well, she doesn't work outside the home, but she's always incredibly busy. She's involved in every village organization there is because she can't say no to people. She's simply longing for a grandchild but tries terribly hard not to talk to us about it, in case we feel pressured.'

'Us?'

'My brothers and I. They're both older than I am and

have proper jobs, but no wives and they both appear to be totally selfish, but aren't as bad as they seem. They say it's my responsibility to provide Mum with grandchildren.'

'You're a bit young, surely?'

This had always been May's argument. Coming from him, it was galling. 'I'm nearly twenty-five. Past my most fecund years, according to some biologists.'

'I didn't mean you weren't old enough in years, but in experience.'

This was valid too, but she wasn't going to take it from him without protest. 'How do you know how much experience I've had? We've hardly known each other five minutes.'

'I'm only suggesting you develop a bit in your own life before taking on responsibility for a new one.'

It was all exactly what she had told her mother on one of the rare occasions her mother allowed her broodiness to show. She subsided into silence.

'So what are you going to do with your life, when you've earned enough money to pay back the boatyard? You're surely not going to stay a cleaner for ever.'

May started to protest that running your own business was extremely fulfilling, and it was. But a cleaning agency? 'I don't know.'

'Still waiting to find out what you want to be when you grow up?'

'No! Yes – I don't know. I want to do *something*, I just don't know what.'

'What do your parents think you should do?'

'They're not those sort of parents. They just want me to be happy. They'd support me in anything I decided to do.'

'So what are you good at?'

'Nothing. It was the curse put on me by the wicked godmother at my christening. Don't make her stupid, but don't let her develop any special talent. And I haven't.'

'You're practical, not a bad carpenter. You're brave, resourceful. And,' he added, remembering the chicken nugget people, 'inventive.'

'Yes –'

'You were excellent with the boys.'

243

'Oh?'

'And you're bossy. What about teaching?'

'Thought of it. In fact, for a while, I quite liked the idea. But I haven't got any A-levels. And I'm not in the least bossy.'

'Well – call it manipulative then.'

May squeaked her indignation.

He ignored it. 'You're a good co-ordinator. You should get some career advice. As a mature student, you might not even need A-levels to get into college. But if you need them, you could get them.'

They were passing through an area of London which had decided to rationalize its decorations and every tree was studded with tiny white lights. They were extremely beautiful.

'There is just a small problem,' said May.

Hugh glanced at her. 'What?'

'I haven't got my maths GCSE. You can't do *anything* without it.'

May was not particularly surprised when Hugh laughed, but she was annoyed.

'I have *got* it. I mean, I passed. I just didn't get a C grade.'

'And you didn't resit?'

'What was the point? I would have got another D. I know someone who kept resitting. She ended up with fifteen GCSEs, all of them in maths.'

'You don't know you'd have got another D. And if that's all that's stopping you doing something more meaningful than cleaning, surely it's worth a try?'

'Who's to say cleaning's not meaningful! You're just snobbish about it. You don't like to admit you're about to spend Christmas with someone who cleans for a living.'

He sucked in his breath. 'You have a point. But of course, I will be very careful who I tell.'

'Shouldn't that be whom?'

'There, you see. I said you should try teaching. You love putting people right.'

'No I don't! I don't even know if I was right. And supposing I couldn't control my class. It would be dreadful.'

244

'You controlled those brats of my brother's well enough.'

May gave him a pitying look. 'But those brats, as you call them, were dear little middle-class boys in private education. They're a very different kettle of fish to real children.'

Hugh laughed, rather patronizingly, May thought. 'If you think class and education prevent little boys from behaving like savages, you've led a more sheltered life than I thought. I admit they were a nice bunch and my brother was there. But the point is, you held their attention. They didn't misbehave because they were interested.'

'Well, canals are interesting.'

'Not particularly.'

'What do you mean?' May was indignant again. 'They're fascinating!'

'To you, perhaps. Maybe even to me. But lots of people think of them as somewhere to chuck supermarket trolleys. The point I'm trying to make is,' he persisted over her squeaks of protest, 'that you *made them interesting*. You brought them alive. If you have that ability, you're halfway there.'

'I still don't think it's quite me. Anyway, according to someone I met at a party once, teaching is all form-filling now. I'm hopeless at that.'

'Well, if ever you decide that not having your C grade is preventing you from fulfilling your potential, let me know. I'd be happy to help you with it.'

May suppressed a giggle. If sweet, patient, Miss Simons couldn't get her through, it was unlikely that Hugh could. Rather than hurt his feelings, she said, 'It would be against my principles to ask a man for help.'

Hugh chuckled, and in so doing, reminded May that she had done that very thing, only yesterday.

'I mean,' she went on, 'I wouldn't ask a man for help with anything where brute strength wasn't required.' That sounded wrong too. She wanted to put him in his place, but she was truly grateful. 'Not that you used it, your brute strength, but . . .'

'I could have, had it been necessary?'

'Exactly.'

There was a pause long enough for May to remember the two men and how frightened she'd been.

'I'm very glad it wasn't necessary,' said Hugh. 'And I think I'll make some enquiries into Mr Slater and his Quality Cleaners. There may be a legal way of getting him off your backs.'

This was heaping coals of fire upon her head. 'I was extremely grateful to you. I didn't mean to sound churlish when you were so kind. And it made you late for dinner and everything.'

Instead of receiving this costly apology with dismissive grace, Hugh said, 'Churlishness is part and parcel of your personality, May.'

She made a little sound of dissent.

'But my offer still stands.'

May couldn't think of a put-down devastating enough for him, so held her tongue. But she vowed she'd spend the rest of her life practising simultaneous equations before she'd ask him for so much as the loan of a calculator.

'Mummy! Darling!' They hugged, tightly. 'This is Hugh, Hugh Buckfast, this is my mother, Victoria Sargent.'

'Hello, Hugh,' said May's mother. 'I'm so glad you could come.'

'I'm delighted to meet you, Mrs Sargent.'

'Oh goodness! You must call me Vicky. And here's Ted.'

May's father followed his wife out to meet their visitor. He was a grey-haired man of medium height, most noticeable for his twinkling blue eyes. When he had disentangled himself from his daughter, he held out his hand to Hugh. 'Ted Sargent. Very glad you could come.'

'Are the boys here?' May asked, putting her arm in her mother's and leading the way into the house.

'They'll be down after their office parties. I think Ian may be bringing a girl with him, possibly as a driver.'

'Golly!'

'I don't mind. In fact, I'm delighted. But I hope they don't expect to be put in the same bedroom. Not that I mind

246

what people do, but it embarrasses me to have to acknowledge it.'

'Well . . .' They had reached the kitchen by now. 'You need have absolutely no fears about me and Hugh wanting to share a bedroom.'

'I'm glad to hear it,' said her mother. Strangely, she didn't sound glad.

'Shall I make tea?' asked May.

'If you want it. But I expect Dad is plying Hugh with his best single malt.'

'I hope they get on,' said May.

Her mother shot her a sharp look.

May made a face. 'Only so they enjoy each other's company! If they hate each other it'll be so awkward. I've nothing in common with the man!'

Vicky Sargent took a tray of hot mince-pies out of the oven.

'Here, take these in, there's a dear.'

As predicted, Ted and Hugh were both armed with drinks and greeted the mince-pies enthusiastically.

'My wife makes the best mince-pies in the world, though I say it as shouldn't,' said Ted.

Vicky smiled graciously. 'If you feel like that about them, my dear, perhaps you wouldn't mind dropping some in to Meg Reade. She's going to the Faulkners' for tomorrow, but she'll be on her own now. You don't have to stay for more than a moment.'

Ted's expression became pained. 'Darling, do I have to?'

'I can't, I'm far too busy. Besides, it's male company she misses since her husband died.'

'Why don't you ask Hugh to go with you?' said May. 'I'm sure he's a wow with old ladies.'

'There's no need to go immediately,' said Vicky. 'Finish your drinks and mincers. Supper'll have to wait until the boys get here, anyway.'

Ted looked despairingly at Hugh. 'Would you mind? She's a fascinating old thing really.'

The men thus disposed of, May and her mother drifted back to the kitchen with drinks of their own to prepare the vegetables for Christmas Day. May, knowing her mother was dying to ask but wouldn't, gave her a detailed account of how she'd met Hugh, how helpful he'd been, and their subsequent trip on the boat with the boys. She lied unashamedly about his visit on the previous day, saying he'd called in to see if he'd left his coat.

'But you do understand,' she finished, gathering up a few stray sprout leaves which had missed the newspaper. 'There's absolutely nothing going on between me and Hugh.'

'I think I have managed to grasp that, dear. You told me at least a dozen times on the phone. You invited him because you felt sorry for him.'

'Just so long as that's clear.'

'Oh totally. He's too old for you anyway.'

'He's not *old* precisely, just . . .'

'Stuffy?'

'Not even that really. I don't know what's wrong with him. I only know he's not for me.'

Ted and Hugh chose this moment to come in through the back door. May was fairly certain that Hugh had heard nothing that he ought not, but his expression had a certain edge to it which made her uneasy.

'So, button, how's Cleaning Undertaken going?'

May took a breath, and, bowdlerizing like mad, told her parents about her business.

May's brothers appeared, as their mother predicted, late, drunk, with a girl in tow.

'Hi Mum!' Ian picked up his mother and swung her around a few times, to remind her how much bigger and stronger he was than she.

Vicky Sargent straightened her apron. 'Hello, darling. How lovely to see you. And who's this?'

'This is Saskia. She drove us down,' said Ian, drawing forward a black-clad, giggling girl with streaked blonde hair and legs up to her armpits. 'Believe it or not, she's stone cold sober.'

'I can't take alcohol at all, I'm afraid,' Saskia apologized breathily. 'It makes me come out in a rash.'

That must make you popular at parties, thought May. Particularly with my brothers.

Vicky kissed Saskia. 'Welcome my dear. Let me introduce you to my daughter. May?'

'Hi,' said May. 'You're sharing with me, I'm afraid.' She made a face at her brother. 'But unlike some people I could mention, I don't snore.'

'Hugh,' said Vicky. 'Come and meet my sons. This is Ian. And this is Andrew.'

Both young men shook Hugh's hand and would have given him penetrating stares, had they been able to focus clearly. What Hugh made of them, May couldn't begin to guess.

'Do let's get out of the hall,' said Vicky. 'Ted, take everyone into the sitting-room. I'll make the boys some black coffee.'

'Shall I take you upstairs?' said May to Saskia. 'So you can sort yourself out a bit?'

'Gosh yes. Super. Frightfully kind.'

Saskia made up for in cheerfulness what she lacked in original conversation. When May asked if her family minded her not going home for Christmas, Saskia told her without a trace of self-pity that her parents were divorced and had new families.

'So when darling Ian suggested I came here, I was thrilled. I love traditional family Christmases.'

May's heart went out to her, and she wondered if inviting waifs and strays home for the festive season was a family failing. Not that Hugh was a waif, exactly. She was sure he would have been perfectly content with his book and his port. But she hadn't liked to think of him being on his own at Christmas.

She thought about it as she waited for Saskia to finish in the bathroom. Would it, she wondered, idly at first, and then with more enthusiasm, be possible to pair Hugh and Saskia off? Saskia was obviously besotted by Ian, but he was such a pig when it came to women, it would do him good to suffer the pangs of jealousy. And if he didn't suffer any pangs, Saskia would have another man to make her feel wanted.

Hugh wouldn't be the first man to be attracted by a pair of

249

long legs and a breathy voice, particularly when the voice was unlikely to be argumentative. Saskia, young, beautiful and polite, should be right up his street. May did owe him a favour – lots of favours, in fact. And if he had a girlfriend, it might stop him wandering around in her imagination like a loose cannon. Perhaps she should engineer things a bit and give him the fairy off the top of the Christmas tree as a present.

This thought cost her a momentary pang as she considered that she might want Hugh for herself. She suppressed it. Saskia deserved an alternative to her thoughtless brother. Hugh might prove a very nice diversion. A lot of girls appreciated the attentions of an attractive older man, and Hugh certainly qualified.

When May and Saskia came downstairs again on a cloud of Saskia's scent, Ted Sargent was pouring drinks in the drawing-room. Hugh was making up the fire, while both of May's brothers sprawled across the two sofas, mugs of coffee in their hands. Neither of them got up as May and Saskia entered, and May could see her mother wince and bite her tongue.

'Come and sit by me, Sassy,' said Ian, patting the cushion next to him. 'No, not too near Andrew, he might put his hand on your knee. Sorry about having to share with my sister, but my mother's very strait-laced.'

'Not at all –' began Vicky.

'I know, I know,' said Ian. 'Only teasing.'

Ted Sargent cleared his throat and changed the subject. 'So, who's going to midnight mass? It's at half-past eleven.'

'Why isn't it at midnight?' asked Saskia.

May's brothers looked at Saskia in disbelief. 'Because, *sweetheart*, you have to be in church beforehand, so you can celebrate mass at midnight,' said Ian.

'Oh,' Saskia drooped and began picking at her tights. 'I just thought . . .'

'I know,' said Hugh. 'It should be at midnight, shouldn't it? It's rather like when you're navigating at sea. You have to find out what time noon is each day if you're going south. Surely, noon's at noon.'

Saskia gave Hugh a grateful smile which, May observed, he responded to with one of great kindness which she had never seen before.

'I'd like to go,' said May. 'Unless Mum needs a hand.'

'Do we need a driver?' asked Saskia. 'I could drive.'

'The church is a short walk through the woods,' said May quickly, fearing her brother's sarcasm. 'But come anyway. They light the church entirely with candles. It's a lovely service.'

'I've got presents to wrap,' said Andrew.

'And me,' said Ian.

'Oh you've got presents for us, have you?' muttered May. 'There's a first.'

'I have actually, *Sis*.'

'I went shopping for Ian,' said Saskia. 'He was so busy.'

'Well I hope you bought yourself something really nice,' said May. 'He's a selfish hound.'

'Do stop bickering,' said Vicky. 'The moment you children get together you start.'

'Sorry, Mum,' said Ian, who, with difficulty, hauled himself to his feet. 'Want a hand in the kitchen?'

Vicky smiled forgivingly. 'You can put the extra leaf in the dining-room table and then set it. We should be ready to eat soon.'

'I'll help too,' said May. 'Don't you move,' she said to Hugh and Saskia who were twitching with the effort of thinking of something useful they could offer to do. 'You two drivers deserve a rest. Particularly if you're going to midnight mass.'

'So who's this blokey, then?' asked Ian, putting knives and forks round the table. 'A boyfriend? Thought you'd never get one.'

'He's not a boyfriend,' said May, following behind him, turning the knives the right way round and adding spoons.

'Just good friends, eh?'

'Not at all. We hardly know each other. I just invited him for Christmas. What about Saskia?'

'Ditto. There's nothing going on beyond a bit of a cuddle – *really*,' he insisted, seeing May's scepticism. 'I'm not such a brute as to bonk a girl like Sassy. She's looking for the Real Thing. Are you sleeping with whatsisname, then? Does he make the earth move for you?'

'No I'm not sleeping with him.' May adjusted a salt cellar so it sat on a darn in the tablecloth. 'And if I want earth moved, I'll hire a JCB.'

Ian shook his head sadly. 'You'll never get a man if that's your attitude.'

May was just wondering how she could change her brother's attitude permanently, or even just his nose, when Hugh came in holding two bottles of wine.

'Your mother's ready to dish up; is it warm enough in here; and will May decant the gravy?'

CHAPTER TWENTY-FIVE

Sally had set Harriet's alarm clock for six a.m. The moment she heard it, she hurled herself out of bed before she could change her mind and staggered into the bathroom. The bath mat was damp and the mirror steamy, which told her James was already up. Blast! She'd hoped she could impress him by her early rising.

Sally liked to tackle unpleasant tasks before she could think too much about them. If she went in bull-headed, they were half done before she noticed. So, once downstairs, before even making herself a cup of tea, she found a bucket, thanked God for the Rayburn which seemed to provide unlimited hot water, and filled it. Then, with soda crystals, bleach, rubber gloves, and a slightly malodorous cloth which she found under the sink, she went to tackle the dining-room.

By the time she heard James come in, she had decided that, while her zeal told her it would be wonderful to strip the walls, pinning up the sagging paper with drawing pins would be more to the point. She carried her bucket, now full of cold, grey water, and joined James in the warmth of the kitchen.

'Hello! What have you been up to?'

'Cleaning the dining-room. And while I was in there, something struck me.'

'Not a joist, I hope.'

'There's no furniture. I know you told me about the antiques going to Phillips, but if you're going to entertain, you need some sort of table.'

James frowned. 'There are loads of chairs and stuff in one of the stables, but I haven't got a table big enough. We got five hundred pounds instead.'

Sally glanced down at the kitchen table. It would seat six at a pinch, but never the numbers James was expecting.

'I'm surprised Lucy didn't say something,' said Sally. 'She worried so much about everything else . . .'

'Lucy doesn't know. Neither of my sisters have been anywhere except the kitchen and the bathroom for ages. We'll have to improvise.'

Sally, who had spent three months in an Arts-Council-funded repertory theatre as an a.s.m, knew about improvization. 'Right,' she said. 'What do you suggest?'

'I suggest we disappear to a good hotel and leave them all to it.'

A flicker of pleasure at the 'we' fired her inspiration. 'Have you got an old door, or something? Anything as long as it's flat?'

'I might have. As I say, there are all sorts of things in one of the disused barns. I'm fairly sure there's a door.'

'It's not panelled, is it?' Sally had visions of people's plates sliding into the indentations, gravy sloshing about in the beading.

'Oh no. It's a barn door. We had to take it off to get the new combine into the shed. And I think we've got some trestles knocking about.'

Sally made a gesture reminiscent of a conjuror's assistant. 'There you are then.'

'They're probably covered in muck and paint, but I'll get them in for you, if you think you can make something usable.'

'I certainly can. And if you've got enough trestles, we can put planks across and sit on them.'

'Oh there's no need for that. There are dozens of chairs. And come to think of it, there are trunks of old curtains and stuff in the attic. You may find something up there you could use as a cloth.'

She had been prepared to sacrifice her sheet for this – she'd managed before, she'd manage again – but something underneath would be a definite plus.

'Super. I'll go and have a rummage after breakfast. What

am I going to do about lighting? I mean, a single bulb is all very well, but it isn't exactly festive.'

James shrugged. 'I could shine the tractor's headlights in through the sitting-room windows while we have drinks, then move it round when we go into the dining-room to eat. How about that? It's hellish noisy, but it would solve the conversation problem.'

Sally gave him a quelling glance. 'Come on,' she said. 'I'm hungry, give me some breakfast.'

It was only after she'd eaten eggs, bacon, tomato and several bits of toast, that she remembered she didn't eat breakfast. Life on the farm must be getting to her.

The attic, with a deeply sloping roof through which splinters of light appeared, proved a real treasure house. There were several chests, and the first one Sally opened was full of beautiful, real velvet curtains, a bit musty and mothy, but thick and in a rich, Christmassy green. There were also some satin ones, a beautiful gold colour, which reminded Sally of princely cloaks and pantomimes. The other chests might contain anything – from double-damask dinner napkins to a Father Christmas costume.

But what really delighted Sally were the dozens of oil lamps in varying degrees of elegance and antiquity which were ranged along the edges of the room. Obviously when the farm had electricity put in, all the old lamps were put up here. Some were for outside use, others were brass under the tarnish, with frilly glass shades. There were a couple of Tilley lamps. Sally's lighting problems were solved. Amongst so many lamps, there must be enough that could be made to work.

She told James about this find when he brought her a cup of tea while she washed the sitting-room windows.

'I still don't see what's wrong with the lighting we've already got. I mean, you could stick a couple of candles in bottles to put on the table.'

Sally shook her head. 'If Aunt Sophie wants a Christmas-card Christmas, she can't have it by the light of a single bulb dangling high up in the ceiling.'

'Well, if you say so. By the way, Lucy rang. She'll be round to take you shopping in about an hour. Is that OK?'

Well, she hadn't really expected that he would be able to take time off to take her. 'That'll be lovely,' said Sally, wringing out her cloth. 'I'll be waiting.'

The sitting-room was damp but clean and Sally was just setting about lighting the fire when she heard footsteps behind her. Oh hell, Lucy. And she wasn't ready. So the lu-lu was unpunctual as well as thick. She turned round with an apologetic smile.

It wasn't Lucy. It must have been Lucy's sister, for there was a strong family resemblance. This sister was older, darker and looked less affluent.

'Hi! I'm Liz. I've come to take you shopping as Lucy's hundredth tray of mince-pies aren't cooked yet, and she can't trust the au pair to take them out.'

'Oh. Are you sure . . .?'

'No prob. Lucy's au pair's got my brats with hers. I've got loads of things to get myself and would have had to drag my lot round town with me.' Liz grinned. 'I'm not as efficient as Lucy.'

Sally smiled back. Not as threatening, either. 'I'd better make myself more respectable.'

'Oh, don't bother. You look loads more glamorous as you are, with a smudge on your cheek, than any of us local yokels do, ever.'

Liz didn't appear to be teasing, or even paying her a compliment. It was more a statement of fact. 'Really?'

'Yes. Just dry your hands, grab a coat and we'll hit the high spots – as far as they go.'

Sally's coat was still damp.

'Take James's Barbour. He won't mind,' said Liz. 'If he even notices, which he won't.'

Liz talked as much as her sister Lucy, but lacked Lucy's possessive attitude towards James. Nor did she despise Sally just because she was an actress from London, and therefore, of course, completely stupid and dead set on marriage to her dear little brother. Liz gassed on about all the various relatives, and told Sally that there was a holly tree dripping with berries in one of James's hedges, and a lot of other useful evergreens.

'I'm surprised Lucy didn't mention the holly. Her au pair always takes loads for her house.'

'I expect she forgot,' said Sally charitably. 'It's a forgetting time of year.'

'Mmm,' said Liz. 'Not like our Luce.' Liz sighed, as if reluctant to explain something she felt Sally ought to know. 'Lucy married a frightfully rich man, and she tends to forget that makes a difference. It's easy to be efficient if you've got people you can delegate things to.' Lucy's money seemed to worry Liz, as though she felt it wasn't good for her younger sister to have it. 'Anyway,' Liz changed the subject. 'Dave'll cut you loads of greenery if you ask him. Have you met Dave?'

'I think so.'

'He's a dear. Very shy, but very obliging, especially to ladies. Anyway, tell him to cut down whatever you want. James won't mind. Now, what do you need in town?'

Sally's list was long and complicated. 'I'm afraid I've got to buy James's Christmas presents for him, and I haven't got much money.'

'No prob,' Liz said again. 'Not for an experienced pauper like me. There are some ace charity shops and a market. Is Aunt Sophie one of the presents?'

Sally untangled this and nodded.

'I know just the place. Follow me.'

Liz was the ideal guide, and together they found beautiful linen hankies for Aunt Sophie, (which unfortunately meant that Sally would have to find something else), a massive bowl of hyacinths for Lucy from the WI stall ('At least she won't be able to change those,' said Sally), and Liz very obligingly chose her own present, an Aran cardigan, four pounds fifty at the Oxfam shop.

But although Liz and Sally had bought everything very cheaply, by the time Sally had bought a few decorations, fairy lights, lamp mantles and wicks, she hadn't enough for a Christmas tree.

'Oh dear!' said Liz. 'Christmas just isn't, without a tree. Aunt

Sophie will be terribly disappointed. I wonder if I could put ours in the back of the car and bring it over when we come . . .'

Sally thought not. 'What sort of evergreens did you say there are on the farm?'

Liz made an expansive gesture. 'Oh everything! Yew trees, fir trees, larch trees – though they're deciduous now I come to think of it – but it's all there.'

'Yew trees,' said Sally thoughtfully. 'They're not topiary or anything?'

''Fraid not. Though I think even Dave might have a problem digging up a topiary bird to use as a Christmas tree. No, they're bog-standard trees which need trimming like mad, not smart at all.'

'Excellent!' said Sally. 'If you've finished, let's go home.'

By the time Lucy arrived at seven o'clock on Christmas Eve, Aunt Sophie and several suitcases in tow, Sally and Liz (to the fury of Lucy's au pair), had been inspired with artistic fervour, draping every unsightly corner with curtains, masking peeling paint and wallpaper with massive arrangements of greenery. Liz was furious that she wouldn't be there when Aunt Sophie arrived, but had taken photographs of every room.

'I should have taken "before" shots, too,' she said regretfully.

'Just don't think how it'll look by Twelfth Night, with everything dried up and dropping,' said Sally.

She hadn't meant to sound wistful, but Liz gave her a rallying smile. 'It'll all go swimmingly, I promise you. And I'll be over on Christmas Day to give you moral support. The good thing about Christmas is you can start drinking at breakfast without anyone looking askance.'

'But if I do that,' said Sally, 'I'll lose my timetable and then everything will go to pot.'

Liz sighed. 'Don't worry. James will get Lucy gently pissed, and no one else will mind.'

'And I'll never get all those cousins worked out.'

'Don't worry! Just smile sweetly and keep the bottles circulating.'

Sally shivered in her short velvet dress, despite the fact it had long sleeves, and for the first time in its life the house was warm. All three open fireplaces had yule logs roaring up their chimneys and candles and lamps gave out a surprising amount of heat. It was nerves, not cold, she thought. Good old-fashioned stage fright. I've created the set, learnt my lines, and I'm waiting for the curtain to go up. No wonder I'm shaking.

James was leaning against the stone mantelpiece, looking incredibly handsome in a clean white shirt under his V-neck sweater, olive-green corduroy trousers and very shiny brogues. Up until now, Sally had always liked men to be smartly dressed: dinner jackets, Italian suits, and cashmere. But James, she decided, looked quite wonderful in a tatty old sweater, filthy cords and wellington boots, the clothes he'd been wearing all day, in fact. His marvellous body and his sheer niceness made formal clothes unnecessary. He had, at her insistence, allowed Sally to tuck one of her own silk scarves into his neck. His cravat, when he found it, was black with grease and quite uncleanable. James refused to wear a tie before Christmas dinner.

Sally gave a deep, shuddering sigh, and was just about to check the oven again, when they heard a car draw up, doors slam, and voices complaining about the unclipped hedge which made walking down the path to the front door almost impossible.

'It's because we never normally use it,' muttered James. 'I should have got Dave to cut it back.'

'I thought of it,' whispered Sally, who had had a head full of decorative effects at the time. 'But box hedge smells of cat-pee, so we didn't bother. Silly really.'

James gave her a confused look then answered the peremptory knock on the door. Lucy headed the procession with a hat-box and a carpet-bag which actually seemed to be made out of carpet. Behind her came a tiny old lady, enveloped in furs. She was about four feet high with very white hair. That was all she saw before James enveloped this minute person in a hug which might be fatal for calcium-depleted bones.

'James, darling! Put me down! Let me look at the house! It looks *marvellous*! How clever you are.'

'Not me, Sally. Let me introduce her.'

Sally was all for slipping back to the kitchen, but she found James pulling her firmly forward.

'Aunt Sophie, this is Sally Bliss. Sally, this is my favourite aunt, Lady Caswell.'

Sally found a tiny, gloved claw being held out to her. She took it, fighting the desire to curtsey, and discovered the claw was encrusted with rings which bit painfully into her fingers.

'How do you do, my dear? I'm so glad James has met a nice girl at last. James, dear, do give poor Lucy a hand with the luggage.'

Sally, panic-stricken at the thought of being left alone with Aunt Sophie, frantically tried to think of something to say. But Aunt Sophie had come further into the hall and was looking about her in rapture.

The farmhouse had undergone a transformation scene worthy of the Theatre Royal, Drury Lane, and the hall was Sally's *pièce de résistance*.

Lit only by candles, lamps and the fire, it was awash with greenery. Every doorframe, windowsill and picture rail was swathed in wreaths and boughs of holly, bay and ivy, which filled the house with fragrance. Every highly polished brass lamp reflected the twinkling flames of the candles and the crackling logs in the fire. A huge yew branch was wedged into an old stone chimney pot salvaged from the barn. This, covered in fairy lights and decorations bought from a charity stall made an enchanting substitute for a Christmas tree. There was a smaller version in the drawing-room.

Lucy, who had returned with Aunt Sophie's remaining luggage, now had time to take in the scene before her. Sally saw Lucy's delicate little chin drop with amazement.

'I wouldn't have believed it was possible!' she said. 'It's a miracle!' This she directed towards Sally, who wondered, perhaps unfairly, if Lucy would have been so amazed if it had been anyone other than Sally who was responsible.

James, a cardboard box clutched to his chest, came in and

slammed the door behind him. 'Sally, why don't you show Aunt Sophie to her room? I'll bring up the bags in a minute.'

Sally picked up the carpet-bag and the hat-box. 'Yes, let me show you. If you'll just follow me.'

Sally led the old lady through the dimly lit passage and up the stairs to James's room. He had given it up with very good grace, admitting it was the only bedroom remotely suitable for Aunt Sophie.

'It's lovely, darling,' said Aunt Sophie, who Sally kept reminding herself was really Lady Something. 'And you've even found some flowers. At this time of year too. How delightful. Now you run away, I'm sure you're frightfully busy.'

Sally ran. James was in the kitchen unpacking the cardboard box. It was full of bottles. 'She's a dear old thing,' he said, lifting out a bottle of port. 'I won't hear a word against her.'

Sally peered into the oven at the lasagne. 'She is sweet. I just hope she likes pasta.'

Lucy had told her that she always gave Aunt Sophie roast beef and Yorkshire pudding on Christmas Eve. 'Then you've got the cold beef to slice all over the holiday.'

That was all very well, agreed Sally and Liz, if you could afford a joint big enough.

'And you really don't want the faff of roast potatoes two days running,' Liz said definitely.

Sally felt anxious about offering lasagne and salad, although it was easy, and would be delicious. It just seemed rather modern for someone who probably lived on lamb cutlets with frills round the bones.

James handed Sally a large, brown drink. 'Whisky and ginger wine. It's what Aunt Sophie drinks.'

Sally sipped the drink which was warming and delicious. 'I thought Lucy said she liked a little chilled Tío Pepe.'

James laughed. 'In Lucy's centrally heated palace, maybe. Here, she has to be more robust.'

Aunt Sophie did like lasagne, and in fact, seemed to like everything, from the ancient patchwork quilt which Sally had unearthed from the attic and had aired on the line all day, to the cosiness of eating in the kitchen.

James had pooh-poohed the suggestion that they eat in the had unearthed from the attic and had aired on the line all day, to the cosiness of eating in the kitchen.

James had pooh-poohed the suggestion that they eat in the dining-room. 'No. We'll keep that for tomorrow. That barn door is far too big for just the three of us.'

When James had finally helped Aunt Sophie up to bed, Sally was wishing that they could stay 'just the three of us'. She was no longer frightened of Aunt Sophie, but tomorrow there was the rest of James's family to meet.

Sally was just filling the sink with hot water when James came down.

'I don't know how to thank you, Sally,' he said.

Sally turned round sharply. 'Don't you? Isn't it time you made a wild stab?' The surprise in James's eyes made her instantly repent. 'Sorry. I'm just tired.'

'I'm not surprised, you've been a real Trojan. Not to mention a miracle worker. Even Lucy was impressed.'

It would have been so natural for her to put her arms round James and let his arms come round her in return. But it would have been just as natural for him to encircle her as she stood at the sink. They'd worked together as a team that evening, and had to again tomorrow. Yet the lack of physical contact between them was like an enormous barrier they had to peer over in order to see each other.

'Well I'm glad everyone liked what we did with the house. Now it's only Christmas dinner to get through.'

'Sally? Are you all right?'

'Actually, no. I am frightfully tired. If you don't mind I won't wash up. I simply must go to bed.'

Sally left James staring bemusedly at her. But she didn't care. She was fighting back the tears.

CHAPTER TWENTY-SIX

From May's point of view, dinner on Christmas Eve was an extremely satisfactory meal.

She arranged it so that Hugh and Saskia were sitting next to each other, and he played his part with uncharacteristic charm. He listened to what Saskia had to say, he laughed at her jokes and made jokes for her to laugh at. As none of the men of May's acquaintance, except perhaps her father, would bother to be nice to a woman they didn't fancy, she assumed this must be the case. He had certainly never been so nice to her.

May leaned across to Saskia to tell her again how wonderful midnight mass was. 'The walk through the forest is lovely. Crunchy pine needles underfoot, the stars twinkling through the trees overhead. It's like a Christmas card, really it is.'

'Twelve trees do not a forest make,' said Andrew.

'There's more than twelve trees! It's a proper wood. Like in *Winnie the Pooh*,' said May.

'Oh I love that book!' said Saskia. 'I have a Piglet which sits on my bed. Too gorgeous.'

'Hugh's brother has a school,' said May. 'I expect they all read *Winnie the Pooh*, there, don't they?'

'Actually, with boys that age, Stephen King tends to be more popular than A. A. Milne,' said Hugh. 'Who's your favourite author, Saskia?'

'Golly. I don't have time to read much, actually. What about you?'

Feeling that any more interference would be *de trop*, and still full of virtuous intent, May decided she ought to please her mother and show an interest in some of the more boring relations.

'So what's the latest on Natasha, Mum – she's our glamorous cousin in the fashion industry,' she explained to Saskia. 'Always going to Bali on shoots, and things.'

'That was only once. When I last spoke to her mother, Natty was in Skegness. And you're not usually interested in family gossip.'

'She's not usually dead set on getting everyone to midnight mass, either,' said Ian. 'I suspect an ulterior motive . . .'

May's heart missed a beat. Don't say her loathsome brother was going to expose her.

'Why is she so keen to get us all into the moonlight?'

'In a wood,' added Andrew.

'What's got into you, old girl? Face growing hairy is it? Teeth a bit on the long side?'

May kicked at her brother under the table. 'I'm just showing an interest.'

Ian continued to smirk, and although May's shoe had definitely connected with something, she began to wonder what it was. Hugh had a rather pained expression and, she remembered, very long legs.

After large helpings of alcoholic trifle, Ian, Andrew and Hugh disappeared into the kitchen to make coffee. May tried to protest that it wouldn't take three of them and that Hugh could perfectly well sit on the sofa next to Saskia and enjoy the fire. But he gave her a look which told her she was being bossy, and she gave up.

Ted disappeared to his study to 'do something', which May was certain involved sticky tape and swear words, and the three women slumped in the sitting-room, awaiting the promised coffee and liqueurs.

Vicky Sargent promptly fell asleep. May talked brightly to Saskia, managing to bring Hugh's name into the conversation fairly often, always with the rider that he and she were 'just friends'. She was determined to get them to walk to midnight mass together. If the boys said that they wanted to come, May would go too. If not, she would stay behind and sort out the kitchen.

May had completely run out of conversation and was wondering if it would be too rude to suggest turning on the television when Hugh appeared with a tray. He put it down and then handed Saskia a glass of port.

'Gosh, how lovely,' said Saskia, 'But unfortunately, I can't drink.'

'Sorry, I forgot. Perhaps you'd like it, May?'

May took the glass, aware that Hugh was displeased with her for some reason. 'I'll take some into Daddy, shall I?'

'I've already taken him some. He says he'll give midnight mass a miss as he and your mother need an early night.'

'Oh. Well, you and Saskia can go. It's a beautiful night for a walk through the woods. Very romantic.'

'You did mention that,' said Hugh.

'The boys and I will come too,' she went on hastily, in case her matchmaking appeared too blatant.

'Actually, May, I'm frightfully tired,' said Saskia. 'It's been hell in the office this week. As well as finishing up all the odds and ends, I had to organize a drinks party for the clients and do all the Christmas shopping.'

'You're obviously totally exploited, Saskia. You shouldn't be so eager to please. Your boss won't respect you if you let him walk over you.'

'What's that about Sassy's boss?' demanded Ian, coming into the room.

'I'm just saying that he exploits Saskia. Just because she's a nice person and doesn't like to say no, it doesn't mean he can treat her as a dogsbody. You must back me up on this, Ian. You can't let her be walked over.'

'But May,' said Saskia, looking confused. 'Ian is my boss.'

Andrew gave a shout of laughter. 'May charges to the rescue again. What a classic!'

May gulped. 'Exploitation is exploitation, wherever you find it. I hope you're nice to your secretary, Andrew.'

'She scares the hell out of me, and I share her with three other blokes.'

'Good. Now I suppose I'd better do something about the mess. There's no chance that you men will have lifted a finger.'

Cross for all sorts of reasons she couldn't put her finger on, May stomped into the kitchen. It was almost spotless.

The surfaces were wiped, the dishwasher was humming obligingly, and all of the pans were soaking. May rinsed out the cloth, which was in a soggy ball, and squirted some cleanser round the sink, but otherwise couldn't find anything to do. Surely her brothers wouldn't have done all this. It must have been Hugh's influence.

Deep down, he *was* a nice man. He deserved a sweet, good-natured girl like Saskia. If only she could get them together. She must have another word with Saskia. She was just wondering what word would finally do the trick, when she heard a step behind her.

She turned round to see Hugh. He had his coat on and looked decidedly cross.

'Hello,' she said hastily. 'Did you clear up the kitchen? I can't imagine my brothers doing it.'

'It was a joint effort. I just came in to tell you that everyone else has gone to bed. It's just you and me for midnight mass.'

'But – I'm really not religious, you know. I'm quite tired too, I'll have to be up early . . .'

'No you don't. You've spent all evening going on and on about the woods, the frosty air, the smell of the pine trees, the sweet singing in the choir. It's a wonder you left out the running of the deer. You can bloody well come with me and enjoy it!'

He came round behind her, put his hands on her shoulders, and marched her into the hall. He halted beside the row of hats and coats which hung on the wall, and pulled off a selection at random. He tugged a woolly hat down over May's eyes and shrugged her into one of her brother's coats. Then he tied a scarf unnecessarily tight around her neck.

'Right! That's you ready. Now come on.'

He took hold of her arm and half pushed, half pulled her through the front door and out into the night, which was indeed frosty and starlit.

May, who genuinely enjoyed this Christmas ritual and would have been sorry to miss it, unhooked herself from his hold, but didn't take offence at his cavalier behaviour. She had bored everyone to tears by going on about how lovely it was. She did owe it to them to put her Doc Martens where her mouth had been. And Hugh had, either by example or force, got her brothers to help clear up the kitchen.

Neither of them spoke as they tramped along. May decided anything she said would be classed as mindless chatter, and it was possible that Hugh had had enough of that for one evening. And Hugh was obviously not talking to May because he was a grumpy so and so.

As always, it was a beautiful service. As always, May, not usually given to sentiment, cried when a boy soprano sang 'In the Bleak Midwinter'. Even knowing that the singer was the local vandal, and his heart was the last thing Baby Jesus would want, didn't stop the tears sliding embarrassingly down her cheeks during the last verse.

Afterwards, it was less fun. Hugh had to be introduced to every one of her parents' friends who had known May since she was a wee thing and had never seen her with a man before. And they quite obviously couldn't think what a fine-looking chap like that could see in young May Sargent who dressed so scruffily, even in church.

The fine-looking chap in question took it stoically and said he looked forward to meeting them all again on Boxing Day, when May's parents had the neighbours in.

'I must take May home now,' he said firmly, taking her arm. 'She's getting cold.'

For a moment, May experienced the unusual sensation of being cherished. It was lovely, except she knew he wasn't really cherishing her, just bossing her about. If it had been Saskia, now, he might really have cared if her toes were getting numb.

'You really ought to have taken Saskia, you know,' she said when they were in the wood. 'She would have loved it. Her parents are split up, and they've both got new young families. She adores traditional Christmases.'

Hugh came to an abrupt halt. 'Don't you ever give up? Saskia is a sweet girl, if a complete ass, but she and I only happen to be guests at the same house. We've nothing else in common. And apart from putting us in the same bedroom, you could hardly do more to throw us together!'

'I thought you were getting on like a house on fire. She obviously thought you were frightfully amusing.'

'Just because I was kind to her doesn't mean I want her thrust into my arms. I do not like having my hand forced. If I want a woman I'm perfectly capable of making her aware of it without outside interference. Particularly from you.'

'Look, I'm sorry, I meant well . . .' Her voice tailed away. Hugh was advancing towards her and even in the nearly pitch dark, she could tell his expression was murderous.

Oh help, she thought, retreating nervously. He's going to strangle me. Then no one will ever walk through these woods alone again. But he didn't strangle her. He backed her up against a tree and trapped her there with his body. Then he put one hand under her chin and raised it so her lips met his head on.

At first, May made little sounds of protest. But after the initial shock, her dormant senses flared, and she found herself kissing him back with equal ferocity. His mouth was cold, but his tongue against hers built up a surprising heat. When he paused for breath, he put his arms round her, so he could crush the life out of her at the same time as he kissed her to death.

Her head lay snug against the wall of his arm and his fingers were free to caress her neck. Eventually, thoughts of murder must have left him, for he stopped fingering her windpipe with longing, and burrowed under her layers of clothes until he found her breasts. His icy, gloveless hands were incredibly exciting against her warm flesh as he lifted and massaged her breasts, spreading his fingers so both nipples could respond to his tantalizing touch.

The night air, the season, the darkness and the remnants of alcohol sharpened May's responses and sent her zinging to a height of passion she wouldn't have thought possible. She felt he could have taken her, standing, right there against the roughness of the tree with her total co-operation.

She had entirely forgotten he had been angry with her until he finally broke away. But *he* hadn't. His breath was ragged and he had been fully committed to the urgent task of kissing her senseless, but he was still livid.

'There, now we're quits. You've been forced into something, just like you forced me. And with luck I've made you
as bloody furious with me as I am with you.'

Then he took her hand and pulled her the rest of the way
home.

May's feelings towards him were in an uproar. Anger was
certainly in there, amongst the confusion, and the unexpected, unwelcome desire. But she was honest enough to
admit she wasn't angry with him because he kissed her. She
was angry because the kiss had been intended as a punishment and was not a genuine expression of his attraction.

As she stared broodingly at the stocking she had prepared
for him, and now was reluctant to let him have, she envied
the girl he did fall in love with. He would be a stupendous
lover, with just the right combination of dominance and
tenderness. But he obviously didn't fancy Saskia. Contrarily,
considering the lengths she had gone to throw them together,
she was pleased. She didn't want him herself, of course (once
bitten, twice shy), and besides he was so Hughish. What she
wanted – badly – was for him to belong to another woman,
and so be automatically out of bounds, even in her head. But
she didn't really want that sweet-but-nitty girl to have him.

In the end she was forced to be grateful to him. She was so
hopping mad that she was still awake until long after everyone
else had dropped off. Thus, she tiptoed into each bedroom
and placed a stocking on each sleeping, and in many cases,
snoring, form. By taking a tax of chocolate and stationery
from the male stockings, and one or two things from her
mother's, she even managed to cobble a stocking together for
Saskia. Tired at last, she crawled into bed and fell asleep.

May was woken by her mother. 'Happy Christmas, darling.
I've brought you a cup of tea.'

May sat up sleepily. 'Oh, Mum, you shouldn't have.
What's the time.'

'Half-past ten.'

'What! Why didn't you wake me before? You must be
frantic getting lunch. I meant to be so much help to you! Oh
Mummy!'

'Don't panic. Hugh is being a saint, and everyone else is pitching in like mad, and we all agreed you ought to have a lie-in after being Father Christmas.'

May let her mother's opinion of Hugh pass without comment. 'It wasn't me! It was Santa Claus!'

'How come you got left out then? Actually, you didn't, because I did you one. But you'll have to open it later because the family will be arriving in an hour and if you don't have any breakfast you'll get hideously drunk.'

May put her quarrel with Hugh out of her mind. She couldn't ruin everyone's Christmas by sulking, and pretending nothing had happened was probably the best way of punishing him. Any girl would go a little bit shaky after a kiss like that. Her insouciance would make him think he was off form.

As a gesture to the season, May put on black velvet trousers with a white Hamlet blouse and a velvet waistcoat instead of her usual dungarees and baggy sweater. She even borrowed a bit of Saskia's mascara. Then, as she was just about to go downstairs, she realized that Hugh might think she'd put it on for his benefit and wiped it off.

Galloping downstairs a moment later, she wondered if perhaps she hadn't. Pull yourself together, girl, she commanded, and opened the kitchen door.

'Trousers again, dear?' said her father, putting down the coffee-pot. 'I know it's frightfully old fashioned of me, but I really do prefer to see women dressed as women.'

'No one's ever seen May in a dress,' said Andrew to Hugh. 'We secretly wonder if she's got milk-bottle legs.'

'Well I've seen May in a skirt, and in a bath-towel, come to that,' said Hugh. 'And there's absolutely nothing wrong with her legs.'

There was a silence broken only by the gentle throb of the dishwasher which was doing twenty-four hour shifts. All May's relations put down their respective slices of toast, croissants and cereal spoons and looked at her. They couldn't have looked more amazed if Hugh had announced she had a third breast.

May pulled out her chair. 'It's a long story, and not at all like you make it sound, Hugh.'

'Perhaps you'd like to tell us about it, darling?' said her mother, her eyes twinkling with hope.

'I'd rather eat my breakfast.'

May got through Christmas with flying colours. With Delia Smith in one hand, and a glass of sherry in the other, she was a boon to her mother in the kitchen. She got out the vacuum during every lull in the activity and was the life and soul of the drinks party.

'Hasn't May come out of herself,' she heard on of her mother's WI friends say on Boxing Day. 'It must be that nice man.'

'Oh they're just friends,' her mother replied loyally. 'He's far too old for her.'

'Nonsense! He's only in his thirties! And May isn't getting any younger. If she wants to have babies, she ought to think about it now.'

'Really, Marjorie, things have changed since our day. Women are having babies into their mid-forties, or even later.'

'Yes,' said Marjorie. 'But not *real* women.'

May, for once not feeling obliged to react to this statement, chuckled and retreated to the kitchen for more sausage rolls.

Having avoided even speaking to Hugh, except to thank him for his present, which was a very nice sweater, and accept the thanks for her present to him, which had been a useful but boring refill for his Filofax, the thought of driving home with him was a little painful.

She could try and get a lift with Ian or Andrew. But they had only brought one car and had Saskia, so there would hardly be room for her and her clean washing. It was Hugh or the train – which wasn't running.

'Bye bye, Mummy darling, thank you for a really wonderful Christmas.' She hugged her mother tightly, realizing that the older she got, the fonder of her mother she became.

'Thank you for being so much help. You practically did everything. I hardly had to lift a finger. Perhaps you're growing up at last.'

May made a face. 'I hope not. Now I mustn't keep Hugh waiting.'

'No. He's delightful, May. You could do a lot worse . . .'

'I'm sure I could, but I intend to do a lot better. Byee!'

Hugh was waiting for her in the car. His own goodbyes and thankyous had been formal but sincere. May knew he'd made an extremely good impression, blast him.

He gave May a quizzical look as she got into the front seat. 'Well? Do you regret asking me for Christmas?'

May returned the look with as much honesty she had courage for. 'Not at all. My parents loved you, the neighbours loved you . . .'

'Saskia loved me. But you didn't?'

'You'd hate it if I did. I'm far too bossy.'

'You're quite right. You are, far too bossy.'

'You're quite bossy yourself!'

'Ah yes, but then, bossiness is much more acceptable in a man.'

Seeing that he was laughing at her, May decided not to comment. She closed her eyes firmly and pretended to sleep for the rest of the journey. She knew that in years to come, she would bitterly regret asking him, when all the neighbours asked her, or more likely, her mother, what had become of her boyfriend. But for now, it seemed worth it.

When she opened her eyes a little later, she was surprised to discover she really had slept. 'We're here!' she said. 'That was quick!'

'Hang on. Don't fling yourself out yet. We've another hundred yards or so.'

'It was awfully kind of you to drive me home, Hugh.'

'It was awfully kind of you to invite me.'

'No, really, I mean it. And I was glad you came.'

Hugh stopped the car. 'There. You can get out now.'

May put her hand on his. She wanted to kiss his cheek, to thank him properly, but he was staring across to the canal with a look of horror on his face. 'Hugh?'

CHAPTER TWENTY-SEVEN

Sally was aware of her feet being weighted down with something. She kicked and heard a rustle. She heaved herself upright and wished there'd been a bedside light left over for her room, the smallest and draughtiest, which no one else could possibly have been asked to sleep in. To be fair, James had offered to sleep in it, but as the bed was shorter than average, so it could fit into the space between the dormers, Sally had insisted it was 'utterly sweet', and that she didn't want to sleep anywhere else.

She patted the object gingerly in case it was a dead rat or something hideous. You couldn't take chances on a farm. It was woolly.

She peered at Harriet's luminous clock. Six o'clock. High time she was up anyway, if she was to get the kitchen sorted after last night. She got out of bed, ran to the light switch, and fled back, before her body noticed how cold the room was. The object was a sock.

Sally could hardly believe it. Someone had given her a Christmas stocking. Not even as a child had Sally believed in Father Christmas, but who else would give her a stocking? There was only James and Aunt Sophie in the house, and Aunt Sophie would not have used a sock with a hole in it. Which left old F. C. himself – or James.

It was too early in the morning for emotion, but Sally's throat felt tight with the pressure of her warm and swelling heart, burgeoning with hope. She pushed her hair back from her eyes and opened the first parcel.

It was a sample-sized bottle of port. There was a gift-tag round the neck which said, 'Best taken before breakfast'. Delighted, Sally went on to the next bundle, a chocolate orange. The next package rattled, and was a box of drawing pins. Sally recognized it as one of the two she had bought. She giggled. As it was only a sock, there were only two parcels left to unwrap. One was a bundle of Biros held together with binder twine, and the last was a little jewel-box.

Sally's heart began to race, and in spite of the cold, sweat broke out over her forehead. She opened the box with something akin to holy dread, but inside was not the ring, which she half hoped for and half dreaded, but a brooch, a circle of dark red stones – probably garnets – and pearls, set in gold. There was a note. *This isn't a family heirloom, or not really, but if Lucy sees you unwrapping this, she'll have you sent to the Colonies with a one-way ticket. Please wear it if you want to, she won't recognize it.*

Sally took a long, restorative breath and gave a deep, contented sigh. Then she got up. As usual, James was up before her. The kitchen was immaculate, or as immaculate as it could be without a major revamp. James had made tea.

'Happy Christmas. I was going to bring you up a cuppa.'

Sally had decided she was definitely going to put her arms round him give a real hug, if not a proper kiss. But he was holding a mug of scalding tea, and her style was cramped.

'Thank you so much for my stocking,' she said, hugging him with her heart and mind.

'I'm glad you liked it. Stockings have always been my favourite part of Christmas.'

Sally was instantly racked with guilt. 'I should have done you one!'

'Not at all. You've done far more than all my family put together have for all the Christmases I can remember.

'Have I really?'

'Yes. Aunt Sophie is thrilled. She finds Lucy a bit – conventional.'

Sally's euphoria descended a notch. Was it only for Aunt Sophie's sake that he was pleased with her efforts?

'I'm going to take Sophie up some tea, and then I'm going to make pancakes for breakfast,' said James. 'Dave – you know Dave? You met him when you first came.'

Sally nodded. 'The man who likes to see meat on a woman's bones.'

'Well, he's doing the farm for me today, so I'll be able to be useful.'

He was useful. He hefted the turkey in and out of the oven to baste it. He helped her peel extra potatoes and sprouts when his cousin Damien arrived in the middle of tea, obviously convinced he was expected. In fact, if it hadn't been for James, and the little brooch, and the alcoholic haze produced by two glasses of whisky punch, Sally would never have got through.

There were so many people. From the moment that Lucy and Liz arrived with their families, the knocker was never still. No sooner had Sally nipped into the dining-room and found another set of knives and forks and a chair for the latest cousin, when another one arrived, the last being a Cousin Veronica, whom no one had mentioned, and no one seemed pleased to see.

'She's such an old soak,' muttered Lucy. 'She only appears at Christmas because she knows there'll be booze in the house. And she never even buys the children presents, let alone anyone else.'

Not being there in any official capacity, Sally didn't feel she could ask if they were expecting to stay. The way James was doling out drinks, they would all have to.

Sally spent a lot of time in the kitchen, not only to keep an eye on the dinner, but to keep panic at bay. In the kitchen, with her list, she could keep a grasp on reality and out of the way of a whole lot of people whose names she would never remember and who were embarrassed because they didn't know that James had totty in tow and hadn't bought her a present.

It was nine o'clock by the time the party were seated. Frequent additions meant only adults were allowed a knife, fork and spoon each. The children had to choose just one, and no-one had a pudding fork or side knife. A starter would have been logistically impossible. But the table looked beautiful.

Sally and Liz had found two double-damask tablecloths in

the attic which just about covered the barn door. Because it was so much larger than a proper table, there was plenty of room for the huge, shallow bowl of ivy, candles and clementines with which Sally had decorated it. The curtain may have been an hour and a half late going up, but the set was spectacular.

'What lovely brown potatoes,' said a male cousin, who may have been called Damien.

Sally smiled sweetly. They had been browned under the grill in the little pantry, the Rayburn having decided enough was enough and gone on strike.

'Nice soft sprouts,' said one of Lucy's twins.

They were overcooked – Sally had been about to drain them when she saw Clodagh gulping down the giblets which were cooling on the windowsill. By the time she had decided Clodagh wasn't going to die and that gravy granules would do, the sprouts were mushy. But as the child in question seemed genuinely pleased, Sally wondered if Lucy's children were a bit fed up with everything being *al dente*.

Sally squeezed herself into a chair and found herself next to the cousin who had referred to her as 'totty'. He instantly put his hand on her thigh, which, owing to the shortness of her skirt, was plainly visible.

James stood at the end of the table carving, Liz's husband Peter handing plates up and down, Lucy's husband Alexander dishing out the stuffing. It felt like the first time Sally had sat down that day. When everyone was served, Aunt Sophie raised her glass, the only bit of decent crystal left, and proposed a toast. 'I would like to thank James and Susan, the lovely girl who I understand is soon to be his wife, for this magnificent feast. To be together as a family at this special time of year, is I think, one of the things which makes life worth living. And at my age, there are precious few of those left. To James and Susan.'

Sally was past embarrassment, and thankfully, most people seemed to think that Aunt Sophie was totally dotty rather than that Sally was on the make. After all, they probably reasoned, what would a girl like her marry a man like James for?

'Jolly good bird,' said the cousin, when he had abandoned Sally's thigh for that of the turkey. 'Did you cook it?'

'Well, yes . . .'

'I like a woman who can turn out a decent meal. I expect James does too.'

Sally considered spiking him with her high-heeled shoe, which was certainly what May would have done, had May worn such things, but decided against it.

'I like a man who can behave decently,' she said, all wide-eyed innocence as she got up to bring in the pudding while James and Liz gathered the plates.

'You have to heat the brandy in the *spoon*,' said Lucy.

'Pour some more on,' suggested Damien.

'Want to borrow my lighter?' asked Peter.

Sally dropped a match milliseconds before it burnt her fingers, and the pudding ignited, catching fire to the sprig of holly in the top.

'Oh well *done*,' said Aunt Sophie. 'It's so pretty.'

'The woman's a pyromaniac,' muttered Alexander, Lucy's husband.

'Shall I get a fire extinguisher?' demanded Lucy.

'Certainly not,' said James. 'Sally, I think you deserve the first portion. Then, when everyone's served, we'll pull the crackers.'

Inevitably, the lecherous cousin got the red cellophane fish which told your fortune. Inevitably, it told him that he was incredibly attractive to women. Sally picked up the nutcrackers and looked meaningfully at him.

Sally looked at the clock on the mantelpiece as she slumped in an armchair. It was two in the morning. Aunt Sophie had been put to bed by Lucy and all of the children were asleep. Most of the adults were singing to the accompaniment of Alexander's guitar. They had stopped singing madrigals and carols and had gone on to ancient rock and roll. Apparently, while training to be an architect, he had busked so as to afford to run a car. Now, he busked to his relatives at Christmas, to irritate his wife.

Sally dozed off until the sound of people leaving woke her.

Feeling surprisingly refreshed, she joined James in the good-bye ceremonies and, having his assurance that he had told everybody where they were sleeping, encouraged him to go to bed too. He had had his day off. Farm life would start again early on Boxing Day morning.

Then she went into the kitchen and tidied up. Most of the washing up had been done, by whom Sally could only guess. But she did the bits that washers-up usually forget, like wiping down the surfaces and soaking the roasting pans.

Then, tired again but content, she went up the stairs to her own little room. After a day like today, a cardboard box would seem a cosy place to bed down. Now, the thought of her draughty cupboard with its too-short bed and bare floorboards seemed like heaven.

The sound of snoring alerted her before she opened the door. When she did, the sight before her made tears of fatigue and an overwhelming sense of unfairness well up in her eyes. Lying on her bed, on her back, was Cousin Veronica. What was more, she was wearing Sally's nightdress.

For a moment Sally watched as the massive chest rose and fell, gusts of sound ripping their way out. Lucy was supposed to put up Veronica. In fact, Sally now distinctly remembered her saying so. Sally had been grateful, because every room in James's house was taken.

She considered getting a bucket of water and throwing it over the woman, but that would have made the bed untenable. She thought about picking up the bottom sheet and heaving her out on to the floor, but that might easily strain her back, and unless Veronica was so drunk she didn't wake, Sally would have to find her somewhere else to sleep.

It was too much, it was just too much. She had slaved for this selfish, drunken family, and they were so lacking in gratitude, they left her without even a place to sleep. She was on her way downstairs to evict Clodagh from her sofa when she passed James's door. Without giving herself time to think she opened it.

'James! Your cousin's asleep in my bed.' Her shoes clonked against the floor as she kicked them off. Her dress came off over her head. 'And every other room's occupied.' Her slip and vest joined her dress on the floor. 'What's more, she's wearing my nightie.' Her tights and pants came off in one swift glissando and her bra a moment later. 'So you can either go down and sleep on the sofa, or bloody well shove up!'

James had quick reactions when necessary. He threw back the duvet and welcomed her in.

'Oh Sally,' he muttered as his arms enveloped her. 'If you knew how I've longed for this.'

Sally had spent a lot of time thinking about making love to James, but she had not been thinking about it as she toiled up the stairs to bed. Sleep had been what she craved, and if offered a million dollars for spending one night with Robert Redford she would have said, 'Sorry, I'm just too tired.'

But her body had more stamina than she thought. Instantly they touched, she became aroused. James was already there, and in that narrow bed they rolled and stroked and kneaded with a vigour they neither of them would have thought possible. It was a miracle neither of them fell out of bed. It was a wild and joyous coupling which left them both breathless and sweating.

'God, that was wonderful!' he said into her hair.

Still shocked at what her body had been through in the last ten minutes, Sally agreed with him. Never had sex been so fast and furious, nor so utterly enjoyable. 'Yes it was. Absolutely wonderful. I don't know where you got the energy, James.'

They lay in silence for a few minutes. Sally waited for James to fall asleep. But he didn't, his body was keeping him awake.

'Darling –'

Such a common, over-used word, how could it sound so beautiful coming from him? 'Mmm?'

'We didn't do anything, you know, about contraception. We mustn't risk it again.' As his fingers had already made small acorns of her nipples, Sally didn't take his statement very seriously.

'No, really,' James's hands now cupped each of Sally's

breasts and his breath was getting short. 'It's terribly irresponsible.'

Sally, knowing that if he stopped what he was doing now, she would die of frustration, decided to put him out of his misery. 'It's all right. I'm on the pill.'

'Are you?'

'Mmm. I went on it when I knew I was coming here.'

'Sally?'

'Well, you couldn't tell Aunt Sophie she couldn't come for Christmas because your totty had the curse, now could you? And quite frankly if I had had it, I couldn't have coped.'

Sally could feel the laughter rumble through James's chest. 'Oh Sally, I think I love you.'

They got up early the next morning, too uncomfortable in the single bed to sleep properly. Almost without discussion, they decided to leave the sleeping house and go out into the crisp darkness of Boxing Day morning with Clodagh. In an hour, their house-guests would wake up, want hot water, tea, breakfast, and the moment would have passed.

James had retrieved Sally's things from her room and Sally had put on nearly all the clothes she had brought with her. With James's coat and hat and scarf she was wonderfully warm. James said he didn't feel the cold and kept his arm tightly round her as they followed Clodagh's sedate footsteps.

Sally knew she would be dead on her feet for the rest of the day, and they were all due at Lucy's for Boxing Day lunch. But she would have walked back to London if James had been walking with her.

They reached the village, two miles from the farm, and saw the sleeping houses. Sally imagined the children asleep in their beds, lying higgledy-piggledy, having gone to bed without brushing their teeth, their arms round their toys, cars and dolls and computer games, all cuddled close to plump and careless limbs. Some houses had left their Christmas tree lights on, and in an hour or so the engine of Christmas would start again. Meals, relations, washing up and women worrying. But now, Christmas was a perfect dream, undisturbed.

Sally held James's joking words close to her heart. She knew it wasn't done to take what a man said in bed, after lovemaking, seriously, but the fact that he had used the word love was more than she'd ever dreamed of. Lucy would be so furious.

They hardly spoke at all until they were nearly home. Clodagh was already by the back door waiting to be let in when James said, 'Sally? You know what I said . . .'

At that precise moment, right on cue, Cousin Veronica opened the door. 'Oh, there you are James. I was wondering what you had to do to get breakfast around here.'

James, rather to Sally's surprise, said shortly, 'I'll show you where the frying pan is.'

Boxing Day dragged on. Sally was aching to be alone with James, but Aunt Sophie wasn't leaving until after tea, and until then, had to be looked after. Sally was going to her mother's for a couple of days on the twenty-eighth, so they would only have one day together, and Sally couldn't wait for it to start.

When finally Aunt Sophie was packed into Lucy's car, and the last cousin had bumped down the drive, James rushed to do the milking. Rather than face the clearing up, Sally decided to take Clodagh for a walk. When James came in, they could snuggle up on the sofa, alone but for a roaring fire and a bottle of whisky, but until he could join her she would look up at the stars and admire the silhouettes of trees outlined against a navy-blue sky.

She stayed out much longer than she'd intended, and the house was in complete darkness. Lights on in the farm buildings told her James was still with his cows.

'I'll just pop up and do my teeth and make-up,' Sally told Clodagh, giving her a large slice of turkey, 'And then go and get him out. He must have finished by now.'

As she turned to go up the stairs she noticed a note on the kitchen table.

Your mother rang. Can you ring her back? Something about an interview for 'Hill Life' (what's that?) which you've got to go to as soon as your agent can set it up. I'll drive you back to London when you're ready. Yours, James.

Oh God, why is it, after all these millennia, that your timing is so lousy? Why do you give me a chance with the most wonderful man in the whole world, and then a moment later, give me the chance of a part in one of the most successful afternoon soaps in the business?

She rang her mother. Apparently Sally's agent had been trying to get in touch with her for days and eventually got hold of her mother. The girl groomed for stardom had got pregnant and had had to pull out of the year-long contract. The part was tailor-made for Sally and she had to get to London as soon as possible.

'Darling, it's so wonderful! Such a lucky break! Fame at last, I'm so *pleased* for you. And James has promised to drive you up tonight. He does sound a sweetie.'

Half an hour later when James came in, Sally was sitting at the kitchen table.

'Hello Sally! Wonderful news! Congratulations! Well done! Are your bags ready to bring down? You really deserve this break after working so hard over Christmas.'

Sally eyed him. What was so wonderful about news which was going to take her away from him, she wondered. Didn't he love her? Was all that togetherness and fantastic sex just a bank-holiday romance?

'James – this interview . . .'

'I'm so pleased for you.'

'So you really want me to go, tonight, so I can get to it?'

'Of course! I hate to think of you spending the rest of your life as a cleaning lady.'

Sally closed her eyes. That was telling her. That was putting her very firmly in her place. 'I see.'

'And Sally . . .'

Hope flickered for a moment. 'Yes?'

'Peter – you know? Liz's husband?'

'I know who Peter is, James.'

'Well, he's very kindly offered to drive you up. The thing is . . .'

'One of the cows is sick. You don't need to tell me.'

James ruffled Sally's hair. 'You're so understanding.'

'Yes I am, aren't I. I'll go and pack.'

'OK then, Sally?' Peter turned on to the motorway and speeded up.

'Fine. It's so sweet of you to take me.'

'It's wonderful this part you've been offered, isn't it?'

Sally couldn't pretend any longer. 'Actually, if this part had been offered to me three months ago, I would have been thrilled. But it's come far too late.'

'Oh, why?'

'Because I don't want to be an actress any more.'

'Oh? And is James anything to do with this?'

'Yes. But he obviously doesn't feel the same about me as I do about him. He thinks I'm an actress-cum-cleaning lady who happened to spend Christmas with him.'

Peter cast her a quick look. 'He doesn't, you know. But look at it from his point of view – what has he got to offer you? A tumbledown farmhouse, no money, not even a reasonable standard of comfort.'

'I don't want comfort.' Fatigue and disappointment were conspiring to make Sally cry. 'I want James!'

Peter patted her hand. 'Don't you worry, Sally, he wants you too. I've never seen a man so obviously infatuated. Just hang in there, kid.'

CHAPTER TWENTY-EIGHT

May looked in the direction Hugh was looking. And saw what he saw. A boat was lying across the canal, untied. And as they looked they realized it was *The Rose Revived*. But it wasn't just that it had broken free of its mooring. The white shutters, which had been left closed, were open. One of them was hanging askew, pulled off its hinges. Most of the windows had been broken. And everything was splashed with paint.

'Oh, God.' May's bones turned to jelly and she felt as if someone had kicked her in the stomach, leaving her unable to move or even breathe.

'Stay here,' commanded Hugh. 'I'll go and have a look.'

But before he'd reached the canal, May had reconnected with her backbone and was at his side. Together they stared at the boat, a horrible parody of itself. The broken windows were like grotesquely squinting eyes. The paint looked like make-up applied by a drunken hand, the colours harsh, distorted by the dusk and the orange streetlight.

'Oh, God,' said May again.

Hugh looked quickly at her. 'We'll never get her from this side, we'll have to cross to the towpath. I'm surprised any boats could get past. Perhaps there's not much moving at this time of year.'

May spoke blankly, as if from a long way away. 'No, it would be quite easy. The cut's quite deep here. Anything which came along could just nudge her aside.' She swallowed and took a deep breath. 'I'll go along to that bridge. I can climb up to the road and get across to the towpath side.'

'I'll bring the car round.'

By the time Hugh joined her, she was reaching towards the bow of the boat, trying to catch the rope which trailed in the water, still hanging from its pin. Thank heaven for small mercies, May breathed. Hearing Hugh she turned. 'Hold on to me, will you? I can nearly reach it.'

Hugh caught her waist, and she leaned out the extra inch necessary and caught the rope. The boat came to her like an animal and she heard herself murmur to it as it nudged gently against the side. May looped the rope through a gap in the metal piling which lined that section of towpath. Hugh, who had hold of the stern-line followed her example. A moment later they were both in the cabin.

It was difficult to see, but they were aware of glass crunching under their feet, of the wind whistling through the gaps in the windows. The books had been pulled from the bookcases, and the coal-hod which fed the stove had been emptied on to the carpet. The pictures had been smashed, but had not been prised from the bulkheads. May realized that if the furniture hadn't all been built-in, there would have been more damage.

'I'd better get a broom,' she said.

'May,' Hugh's voice was level, designed to discourage hysterics. 'It's dark. If we clear up before the police get here, we'll destroy all the evidence.'

May didn't have hysterics. She was far too angry. 'Oh come on, Hugh! You know as well as I do they'll never catch who did this, even if there are fingerprints. It's vandalism, mindless vandalism, and it goes on all the time. And I bet you anything you like it's Slimeball and his mates. And I also bet there's no evidence which will stick it to him.'

Hugh considered the validity of her argument. 'Fine. But this'll take a lot of clearing up. Come back with me and we'll sort it out in the morning. It won't seem nearly so bad in daylight.'

May looked at him in bewilderment. 'Have you gone mad? I could no more leave my boat like this, than I could leave a sick dog in a ditch.'

Hugh sighed deeply, obviously of the opinion that it was May who had gone mad. 'Very well. What do you want me to do?'

May thought carefully. 'Light the stove. I'll connect the battery. Let's get some *light* in here.'

May paused in the galley on her way to the engine-room. Here the destruction seemed half-hearted. The plates and mugs which were on display had all been thrown into the sink or on to the floor. But no one had lifted the curtain in front of the shelves where May kept most of her china. Her bedroom and the bathroom were more or less untouched, though the bathroom window was broken.

'They probably couldn't get past Sally's black sacks,' she murmured. Having one floor that wasn't crunchy underfoot was a great relief.

The engine-room door was extremely stubborn. You had to throw your shoulder at it in exactly the right place to get it open. Once in, she felt her way to the crocodile clips, glad that Jethro had made her tag them with tape, insisting that she learn to identify them in the dark. She straightened up and switched on the small fluorescent light and saw that everything was as it should be.

'Thank God I never got round to fixing the door,' she muttered. 'They probably thought it was locked, and didn't bother to break in.'

It meant her tools, which would have been enormously expensive to replace, were untouched. Having managed to find a torch, and feeling a lot more cheerful, she joined Hugh in the saloon.

He had taken off his overcoat and was crouching in front of the stove. May switched on the lights, but nothing happened.

'Bastards, they've smashed the bulbs. Are you managing with the stove?'

Hugh nodded. 'Once I'd found your kindling. They'd just chucked it in a heap behind the stove.'

A part of May she thought she'd never see again smiled. 'That's where I keep it.'

Hugh straightened up. Even in the dark, she knew he was smiling too. After that things improved. The lighted candles were cheering, and although they could now see the full extent of the damage, at least they now knew what they had to deal with. There was broken glass everywhere. Quickly they put the books back in the bookcases. The glass was the next job.

'Got any newspapers? A dustpan and brush? Gloves?'

'Not gloves, I'm afraid. But I can do the rest.' The newspapers were undisturbed, tucked between the steps and the bulkhead, as was the dustpan and brush. 'Here.'

'They were quite desultory for vandals,' said May later, from the kitchen. 'Which makes me certain they were sent by Slimeball. People doing it for themselves would have done a better job in the kitchen.'

'You're probably right,' said Hugh. 'Have you got any black plastic sacks?'

Again May smiled. 'Thanks to Sally, yes, I have.' She found them and he started filling them with packages of broken glass. May slit others open with a kitchen knife and put them over the empty windows, banging them in place with a staple gun.

'I don't know whether to be pleased or sorry,' May went on. 'I mean, if Slimeball hadn't sent them, the boat might not have been vandalized. But if he hadn't, and it was vandalized, it might have been worse.'

Hugh stopped sweeping to unravel this convoluted logic. Failing, he ignored it, but said. 'Well, one way or another, I'm going to put that man out of business.'

'You won't be able to pin this on him, really, Hugh. And I would hate you to get . . .'

'Don't worry, May. I won't go round and duff him up, much as I might want to. The law will be much more effective. And permanent.'

May suddenly felt much warmer.

Every time a sack was filled, Hugh tied it up and put it in the well-deck. In a surprisingly short time the saloon was reasonably clear. With the curtains re-hung, again with the aid of the staple gun, a sort of stage-set normality was restored.

'You sort out your bedroom and the bathroom, I'll deal with the galley,' said Hugh.

'There's a bit of broken glass in the bathroom, but the bedroom's fine.'

'Are you sure?' Hugh seemed surprised. 'It was a terrible mess when I had a look earlier.'

'It was a terrible mess before I went away.'

Hugh's expression combined horror, disgust, disbelief and, somewhere among these, amusement. But he didn't comment.

'I think perhaps they thought someone had got there before them and lost heart,' May suggested.

Hugh cleared his throat. 'Have you got any way of boiling a kettle?'

'Of course. I'll put the gas on. I'm sorry, you must be starving.'

'Well . . .'

May smiled brightly. 'There's some tomato soup left over from the boat trip.'

Hugh's features warmed into a grin. 'I've drunk more tomato soup since I met you than in the whole of the rest of my life. I'm getting to like it.'

May grinned back. 'That's good. It's a family-size tin.'

'You turn the gas on, tell me where I can find a can-opener, and I'll heat it up.'

May, who had noticed the opener lying in the gap between the sink and the stove, handed it to him.

'Don't tell me,' he said, looking pained. 'That's where you keep it.'

May shrugged. 'Sometimes.'

'I don't suppose you've got anything to go with the soup?'

The poor man was obviously starving. And why not, it was at least six hours since lunch. But May had deliberately eaten up all perishables before going away. Then her face lit up.

'I've just remembered! There's a whole box of goodies in the boot of your car which Mum sent me home with. We don't have to have soup at all, if you don't want.'

Hugh shook his head. 'I told you, I like it. But I'll get the box.'

It contained foil packages of cold turkey, cold ham and wedges of cheese. There were also bottles of wine, a bottle of sherry, half a fruitcake, mince-pies, oatcakes, shortbread, as well as a box of cheese biscuits and a loaf of home-made bread.

'Mum doesn't think I eat properly,' May explained. 'She says she wants the leftovers out of the house, but it's just an excuse to get me stocked up. She barely manages not to send up food parcels with Dad every week.'

'Don't knock it. What's in here?' he opened a package. 'Smoked salmon. How wonderful.'

'There'll be a lemon somewhere. Let's take our soup and the box into the saloon, where it's a bit warmer and the light's better, and have a picnic.'

Hugh had brought in the bottle of whisky which May's father had given him for a present. They drank it out of mugs, with smoked salmon sandwiches and the soup. May was slightly drunk when Hugh got to his feet.

'I need blankets. Or better still, a sleeping bag.'

May got up too. 'You're right. It is cold in here with no glass in the windows. I'll dig some out.'

'That's not why I want them.'

'Oh?'

He looked down at her, choosing his words. 'May, I don't suppose there's any point in my asking you again to come back with me to spend the night in my flat?'

May shook her head, instantly sober. 'No. I can't leave the boat all unsecured, with no windows. It's out of the question.'

Hugh nodded. 'I thought you'd say that and I can't force you. So I'll have to stay with you.'

'There's really no need –'

He interrupted her. 'Listen, May. If you're anxious about leaving an unsecured boat, and I don't blame you, I'm anxious about leaving you.'

'You don't need to be. I'm used to being on my own, and they won't come back, surely?'

'I shouldn't think so. But I'm not willing to take a chance.'

'But Hugh . . .'

'I can't make you come, you can't stop me from staying, but I need to tell some people. Where's the phone?'

It wasn't where she'd left it, on charge. She shrugged. 'In the cut, I expect.'

'Why didn't you take it away with you?'

'Why should I? I could use Mum's phone.'

'But what about the people who want to phone you? Unless they know your mother's number, they can't contact you.'

May shrugged. She still hadn't quite grasped that mobile meant portable. 'Well, where's your mobile then.'

Hugh scowled. 'Being repaired.'

May licked her finger and awarded herself a point.

The corner of Hugh's mouth unwillingly acknowledged it. 'I saw a phonebox as I drove over. Now, be a good girl and find me something to sleep under. I'm tired. And you must be exhausted.'

When he was gone the depression which activity and food had kept at bay descended like an avalanche. She fought it valiantly. It would cost a lot of money to replace the glass in the windows, but at least she'd banked the Christmas earnings, rather than stuffing them in a mug as she had been known to do.

Mike would have to wait for his next lump. Which, perversely, would please him. It would give him more leverage to get her off the mooring. And although Sally and Harriet would be sure to lend May their share of the firm's money to make the boat habitable, should she let them? It was forcing them to postpone their own plans for her. May felt she was being pushed backwards down a mountain: just as she got a little way up, life made certain she was put down again, a bit lower than she was before.

She found Harriet's bedding, undisturbed in the locker under the side-bed, and arranged it for Hugh. She added the sleeping bags which Sally used, to keep off the icy draughts which whistled through the plastic sheets. She knew by now that if he'd threatened to go home she would have chained herself to his ankle rather than let him, in spite of her earlier protests. He had been marvellous, a real friend. And she couldn't ask a real friend, and such a wide one, to sleep on that plank.

'Hugh,' she began, as he came through the door. 'I don't think you're going to be very comfortable on the side-bed.

It's frightfully narrow. Harriet can only manage because she's thin and doesn't toss and turn. So I've decided I'll sleep here, and you sleep in my bed. It's quite comfortable there, and the windows aren't broken.'

Hugh's expression became inscrutable. 'The only way I'll sleep in your bed, May, is if you're in it too.'

It took a moment for his meaning to penetrate, it was so totally unexpected. 'Um . . .'

'Offer still open, is it? No? Then good night!'

In bed, warming up at last, but unable to sleep, May wondered how serious Hugh had been about wanting to share her bed. He'd talked about it in such a totally unsexual way. She couldn't really believe he saw her as a woman at all. But he had kissed her, and she had kissed him. And, in the honesty which affects everybody at three o'clock in the morning, she realized that the thought of sleeping with him was anything but repulsive. May turned, so she took up the entire double bunk. He was probably awake too, lying on the side-bed, his shoulders angled, so he wouldn't hang over the edge. Perhaps they both would have slept better together.

Hugh had managed to turn himself back into a lawyer by the time May emerged from her room at seven the next morning. He was washed and shaved and wearing a shirt and suit, neither of which looked as if they'd come out of his suitcase except via an iron.

'There's tea in the pot,' he said. 'And toast. Want some? Your mother's bread is delicious.'

May smiled. 'Yes it is, isn't it? Did you sleep OK?'

He unfolded a chair for her. 'Did you?'

She sat down. 'Not really. I was too jizzed up.'

He grunted, and took another bite of wholemeal toast. 'What are you going to do this morning?'

'Take the boat back to the mooring and organize repairs. I must have windows in before the others come back.' Seeing Hugh's immaculate cuff as he reached for the butter, she added. 'But I can do that on my own. I've taken up far too much of your time already. You've been a saint.'

As usual, he ignored her attempts to be polite. 'I've got to go to the States in a couple of days.'

The news was surprisingly upsetting. She felt a desire to cry she hadn't felt last night, when she'd found her boat in ruins. She coughed and took a gulp of tea. 'Oh. Have you?' she said casually. 'For long?'

'A few weeks. It depends, really. The point is, I won't be around to keep an eye on you.'

May put down her mug. 'Hugh, I couldn't have managed without you last night. I'd have gone to pieces. But I don't need a babysitter. I'm perfectly capable of looking after myself, really I am.'

'I'm not going to argue with you about that now. But what I'm concerned with are my needs. I need to know you're safe, or I can't do my job properly. And a lot of people are depending on me to do that.'

Half touched, half irritated, May tried to placate him. 'I'll be perfectly safe at the mooring. Everyone will be coming home today or tomorrow. And Mike will take extra precautions.' He might also sprout wings and fly, but she needn't tell Hugh that.

He looked at his watch. 'I haven't got to be anywhere until eleven. I'll help you take the boat to Mike's.'

Mike was in his office, waiting for her. He already knew what had happened. He had heard from a passing boat. He managed to appear quite sorry about it and smiled politely at Hugh, who had come with her. But he was uncompromising. 'You'll have to sell now, May. I mean, the repairs'll take quite a lot, and you still owe me a couple of grand. But I'll tell you what I'll do. I won't charge you mooring fees while you're having the repairs done, on the condition that you put the boat on the market.' He straightened up in his chair. 'You gave it a good go, but now's the time to give in. I mean, I could get a couple of guard dogs, but you can't be sure those blokes won't come back, can you? There's no shame in throwing in the towel, not now.'

May got to her feet, feeling frighteningly calm, the calm which goes before the storm of weeping and despair she knew was in wait for her. 'No thank you, Mike. I'll keep on paying you back as fast as I can. And I won't sell. This boat is mine, and it's staying that way.'

Mike looked despairingly at Hugh, who was sitting in

silence in the corner. 'Tell her, will you? Tell her to quit while she's ahead, while she's still got a boat to sell?'

Hugh shook his head. 'This is nothing to do with me. It's May's boat. It's up to her what she does with it.'

Mike shook his head and pursed his lips, as if psyching himself up to say something unpleasant. 'OK. I'll be honest. I've got a buyer for *The Rose*, and he'll pay in cash. And what's more, he'll pay three times what you're *not* paying for the mooring. And he'll pay it every week. I'm very sorry, May, but business is business.'

'You're throwing me off my mooring?'

Mike seemed affronted. 'I'm giving you an opportunity to get rid of your debts and walk away with a tidy amount of change. I'm doing you a *favour*.'

'With favours like that, who needs vandals?' May demanded coolly. 'But that's fine. You want me out, I'll get out. Even if you are breaking the law.'

Mike rose now. 'There's no need to be like that about it. You still owe me a lot of money.'

'I know. And I promise I'll pay you back, every penny. You snake!' She stalked out of the tiny office.

'Even if you don't, I'm still better off without you here!' Mike shouted after her.

May ignored him and carried on down the pontoon and on to *Shadowfax*. She had *The Rose Revived*'s engine going before Hugh had caught up with her.

'Where will you go?' He had leapt on to the boat and was standing on the roof, looking down at her, his voice raised against the noise of the engine.

'I haven't the faintest idea,' she shouted back. 'Haven't you got an appointment to go to?'

'I'll be late.' He came down off the roof and swung himself down on to the counter. 'Can you hang on just a damned minute? And turn off the engine. I can't talk with that racket going on.'

'Keep your mouth shut then. I'm not selling my boat, not for Mike, not for you, not for anyone.'

Hugh ducked down into the engine-room and a moment later the engine noise died away.

May felt suddenly dizzy with rage.

'May,' said Hugh steadily. 'If you hit me with that tiller-bar you'll be on a murder charge without a solicitor who understands you. Now just calm down, shut up and listen.'

As suddenly as it had come, the rage evaporated, leaving May as limp and gutless as a deflated balloon. She'd been fighting to keep strong since last night, and now suddenly she was too tired to fight any more. 'OK. I'm down, I'm up and I'm listening. Speak.'

Hugh sat on the hatch facing her as she leaned against the tiller. Without her belligerence she looked very young and very small. 'You remember I told you about a friend who had canal frontage to his warehouse?'

May shrugged. She couldn't remember anything, but it didn't mean he hadn't told her.

'I want you to go there. There's proper security. You'll be safe. But I need you to wait here till I can get to a phone and arrange it. Will you do that?'

She nodded.

'Promise? You won't take off down the cut?'

She shook her head. 'But you've got to be somewhere at eleven.'

'It's all right. It's only social. I'll cancel.'

'You mean, you wouldn't miss it if it were business?' She teased him because it helped her pretend to feel normal, not to provoke him.

He seemed to understand. 'Good God, no! How do you think I got to be at the top of my profession?'

She tried a small smile. 'By being a right-wing reactionary?'

As a dig, it was half-hearted, but it convinced him she would survive. He smiled back, more wholeheartedly. 'Got it in one. Now, wait here. I might be a while, but I'll be back as soon as I can.'

May cleared up and was just polishing her chimney-bands when she heard the friendly chug of an engine coming up the canal. It was the *Curlew* back from her Christmas visiting. She ran down to their space and caught their ropes.

Like Mike, they had heard what had happened before they

arrived, and weren't a bit surprised to hear that Mike had thrown her off the mooring. They plied her with home-made wine and sympathy and Jethro instantly offered to do the repairs for nothing. 'Pay me when you can.'

May shook her head. 'I'd love you to do them, but I won't let you until I can pay you.'

After some argument a deal was struck and May went back to her own boat. She had just discovered the mobile phone in the cutlery drawer when Hugh arrived. She started guiltily as now she remembered putting it there, but Hugh didn't notice. He seemed unusually boyish and excited. He'd changed out of his suit and was wearing red sailing trousers and a navy-blue guernsey.

'Right, it's sorted. I've got you a mooring. Have you got a canal guide?'

'I think I saw it last night. I'll look.' May grinned, infected by his good humour. 'If I didn't know better, Hugh, I'd say you were a yachtie.'

CHAPTER TWENTY-NINE

'You realize this line means "disused",' said May. 'We'll probably find we can't get the boat in. The arm will either be filled in, or so full or rubbish it might as well be.'

They were poring over the canal guide, and Hugh had just located his friend's property, a warehouse on an arm of the canal. There was even a wharf marked, although May doubted very much that it would still be there.

'Don't be negative. Let's go and find out.'

May didn't take much persuading. Apart from the fact that she badly needed somewhere to moor permanently, she was quite desperate to get as far away from Bryanston Moorings as possible. Even without a powerful motive, the lure of unexplored territory would have been irresistible.

'OK, but I'll just give Sally a ring or leave a message with her mother.'

'So you found the phone?'

May went slightly pink. 'And I'll tell Jethro and Debra on *Curlew* so they know where I am, and in case they want to come too.'

'You surely don't want guests at a time like this!' Hugh obviously didn't. But then Hugh didn't understand canal life.

'Not guests, no. They'll come on the *Curlew*, leaks permitting. It might be handy to have some help when we get there.'

In the end it was a flotilla of three which set off from the mooring. *The Rose Revived* was in the lead, *Curlew*, with Jethro, Debra, Juno and Spike, followed by *Titan*, Ivan's lifeboat which had a powerful engine.

Shadowfax was not of the party. Christmas had upset Jed's sleeping pattern and he was awake, but his boat's engine was more set in its ways than he was, and would take a lot of starting. But he gladly accepted a lift on *The Rose*. Jed, like the others, was eager to explore a new canal arm.

Fleetingly, May worried about how Hugh and Jed would get on. But Jed was such an easygoing soul he wouldn't notice any looks of disapproval which Hugh might shoot in his direction. And although he was the most experienced boat-handler among them, he never gave advice unless it was asked for. He was quite happy to smoke his vegan roll-ups, lend a hand if necessary, but otherwise let others get on with things their way.

In the end, it was useful to have so much extra muscle, for although the disused arm of the canal hadn't been filled in, it was pretty shallow in places. Eventually, with the aid of *Titan*, a lot of shouting, pulling on ropes and pushing with poles *The Rose Revived* was bullied into place. May breathed a sigh of relief. There had been talk at one time of someone actually stripping off and getting into the canal in order to remove the worst of the junk. She wouldn't have allowed anyone else to do this for her, and was grateful not to have to make the supreme sacrifice. It was December, after all.

May ducked down into the engine-room and switched off. For a moment the silence enveloped her, blocking out the sound of distant traffic, voices, and the thump of tackety-boots overhead. The peace was deeper than just a cessation of noise, it represented safety. Somewhat reluctantly, she emerged from the fume-filled warmth of the engine-room.

'I'll get a plank,' called Jed, from the bank. 'So you can get off.'

Hugh jumped down on to the counter beside her. His hair was ruffled and there was a smear of grease on his cheek. She was pleased to see the trip had made its mark on him.

'I've got to go, May,' he said. 'But you'll be all right here. The only access from the road is stiff with security guards.'

'But Debra has made soup and sandwiches for everyone on *Curlew*!' She heard herself sounding like a wife with tea ready to dish up, when her husband tells her he's off down the local for a quick one. She tried to smile.

Hugh shook his head. 'I must get off. I'm borrowing

Jethro's bike to get back to my car. By the time I've brought it back, it'll be getting really late.'

Reality filtered through, reminding her Hugh was going to America, not just to his flat. 'Will I see you before you go away?'

He shook his head. 'I doubt it. I've got a lot of loose ends to tie up.' He hesitated. 'Shall I send you a postcard?'

May had had time to get herself under control. After all, she was becoming used to feeling devastated. She'd experienced the sensation several times since yesterday morning. But the thought of receiving a 'lovely weather, wish you were here' postcard, suddenly sickened her. Besides, she didn't want him to know how much she cared.

'Oh no. It's a frightful bore sending people postcards.'

Hugh's expression seized into immobility. 'Yes it is, isn't it? Well I won't bother then.'

'No, don't.'

'Right.'

'Thank you – thank you so much. You have been – wonderful.'

'Have I, May? Well I'm glad I could be of help. I've got to get off now.'

May moved towards him so as to kiss him goodbye. She wasn't a very demonstrative person, but it seemed odd to have gone through so much together only to part without any physical contact.

He couldn't back away without falling into the canal, but he managed to avoid her attempted kiss. He put his hand on her shoulder and gave it a squeeze. 'Keep out of trouble. If you can.'

Cut to the quick, she said breezily, 'No problem. Goodbye Hugh.'

She went inside quickly, not intending to watch him go. But the moment she was in the saloon, she changed her mind and rushed out again. But it was too late. Hugh had gone.

That night there was a small party on the *Curlew*, which, like the lifeboat, was tied up on the towpath of the main canal. But although a fair amount of home-made wine circulated along with the lentil stew and wedges of brown quiche,

May could not get into the party spirit. This was her life, these were her friends, but their company alone was no longer enough.

'I'm tired,' she told herself, and everyone else. 'I need an early night.'

She walked the short distance to where *The Rose* was moored. Jed had nailed sheets of hardboard over the broken windows while they travelled along, and May now felt perfectly safe. It wasn't fear which knotted her stomach and made her shake with misery – somehow, when she'd been concentrating on something more important and was off her guard, she'd managed to fall in love. With Hugh, of all unlikely people. If she hadn't been so frantic, she would never have let it happen. She was far too down to earth and sensible.

She climbed into her bunk, cross with herself and livid with Hugh. 'It's only because he rescued me. When he's not here, I'll get over him in no time.' She clutched her hot water bottle tightly to her, unconvinced and miserable. 'I don't need a man messing up my life.'

She was still miserable the following morning, a feeling enhanced by the fact that the water pump whined pathetically when she turned on the tap, and no water came out.

'Oh *bugger!*'

She had meant to fill up before Christmas but hadn't, and now she was stuck, unable to move without the aid of a tug, God knows how many miles from the nearest water-point.

Her tongue cleaved to the roof of her mouth. If she didn't have a cup of tea soon, she would die of thirst before she had a chance to die of lovesickness. Briefly, she toyed with the notion of emptying her hot water bottle into the kettle, but decided that tea which tasted of rubber would be worse than no tea at all. There was only one thing for it. She went into her bedroom, fished out the three-gallon Buckby can stuck under her bunk for safety and went to look for a tap. Civilization has made us soft, she chided herself. The old boatmen never had water tanks and taps. They managed with the water in the cut.

'But I'm not an old boatman,' May said aloud and crossed the plank on to the bank.

To her surprise, the huge warehouse door was open. Encouraged, she went in. There was bound to be running water in a place this size. But there was very little of anything. The building was virtually empty, and was undergoing some sort of transformation. She went further in, and was about to call out when she heard a noise like a bucket being kicked across a large space. There followed a stream of invective which, judging by its originality, was the last trickling tributary from a vast river of stress and frustration: all the standard swear-words had been used, this blasphemer was dredging in the mud of his imagination for new ones.

Half amused, half uncertain, May followed the sound, and was just about to enter the room when she heard a broom – she was sure it was something wooden – being chucked against something metal, probably a radiator. She put down her Buckby can and crossed the threshold, ready to dodge if necessary.

'Fucking contractors,' said the man when he saw May, grateful for an audience at last. 'They demand a fucking fortune for a simple job and then fuck off before they've done it!'

'What were they supposed to do?'

'Convert a few flats. That's all. Is it too much to ask? They had plans, they had materials, they had money to pay the men, but did they finish the job? Did they hell. They fuck off to another job leaving me with three Americans due in a month and nowhere for them to go.'

'Oh, dear.'

This response was not what he was after. 'It's more than "Oh, dear", dear, it's a fucking catastrophe! I stand to lose an absolute bundle. I'll never find anyone to finish the job in time now. You'd think, wouldn't you, in a recession, with millions unemployed, you'd be able to find a builder to do some work for you at short notice?'

'You certainly would,' she nodded – sympathetically, she hoped.

The man's anger abated sufficiently for May no longer to

feel personally responsible for the failure of the contractors. 'But no,' he went on, still loud, but less choleric. 'They can none of them do a thing for a month, or two months, or until the summer.'

'How much needs to be done?'

The man seemed to take her in at last. 'Sorry, who are you?'

'I'm May Sargent. I'm a friend of Hugh Buckfast.'

The anxiety on the man's face departed for long enough to acknowledge he did have a friend of that name, who had a friend called May he had been told about recently. 'Oh yes, of course. You're the girl who needed somewhere for her boat. Hi. I'm Rupert Williams.'

'Could I see what needs doing?' A mad idea had come into May's mind and before she could stop it, it had come out again, via her mouth. 'I think I may be able to help.'

'Really? How?'

The mad idea seemed to have a voice of its own and was saying amazing things. 'Well, without seeing what's needed, I can't promise anything. But I'm sure I – er – we could help.' The voice had big ideas, but May let it flow. It had a nice ring to it, and this Rupert person was looking less stressed already.

'How?'

'I happen to know several' – the voice was prone to exaggeration – 'good carpenters and a plumber.' She thought of Jethro and his family, living on *Curlew*, saved from sinking by quick-setting cement. 'And I could get hold of more excellent contractors who are currently between jobs.' Ah, that well-known euphemism for unemployment. 'I run a company which could help you out. Co-ordinate. Get the flats ready for' – the voice had a memory lapse – 'whenever it was you said.'

Rupert regarded May in her dungarees, Doc Martens and baggy sweater. She hadn't washed or brushed her teeth, and her hair was sticking up at the back like a bird's nest. But the slick young man with the pony tail and the mobile phone had let him down. He might as well go with the urchin in need of a bath. As a friend of Hugh's, she would at least be honest.

'OK. If you think you can do it, you've got the job.'

May and the voice combined long enough for them both to feel flattered.

Rupert put an end to that delusion. 'You can hardly do any worse than the cowboys I've had so far.'

'Oh, is there a tap?' May, her head buzzing with plans, deadlines and quite unreasonable reassurances, just remembered why she'd gone into the warehouse in the first place.

'Oh yeah. In there. Help yourself.' Rupert was still talking business. 'If you manage to get the three flats done, before the end of January, within budget, I'll give you a bonus and the contract for the rest of the conversions.'

'Right, fine. I'm sure we won't let you down.' She smiled, to add conviction.

Rupert Williams was already wondering why on earth he'd agreed to let this small and scruffy person near his precious flats. But Hugh obviously thought a lot of her, and he was a fussy devil when it came to women. He smiled back, yet to be convinced.

May staggered to the boat, water sloshing about in her can. She felt extremely lightheaded. It seemed she'd taken on for herself a job which, if she accomplished it, would earn Cleaning Undertaken enough money to pay all her debts, pay the others an equal sum, and leave them enough capital to buy a van and an industrial vacuum cleaner.

She would also have provided work for Jed, Jethro and at least three other itinerant craftsmen she knew. They all lived on boats and, though skilled, led a Giro-to-mouth existence. She had taken a terrific gamble – if only she could bring it off, she could keep her boat and tell Mike to go hang.

'I'll just brush my teeth,' she said aloud, to clear her head. 'Then I might be able to think straight.' She heaved the can of water along the plank and on to the counter. 'I may be wrong, but somehow I don't think this would qualify as keeping out of trouble.'

The thought that she was somehow defying Hugh, who had gone away and left her, was oddly satisfying.

Harriet and Sally arrived by taxi at nine p.m. the following evening. They had no difficulty finding the boat since the whole area was lit by arc lights, and from a warehouse alongside the wharf where the boat was moored there came the scream of power tools being used powerfully.

They exchanged glances, dumped their bags in the well-deck of *The Rose Revived* and went to find May.

'Hi!' May was kneeling on the warehouse floor peering at a set of plans. 'How are you? Can either of you read these things?'

Harriet and Sally tried to shake off the feeling that they'd stepped on to the set of one of those films where people say, *Let's do the show right here!* Harriet joined May on the floor.

'Other way up,' she said.

May regarded both her friends and emerged from her trance. She leapt to her feet and flung an arm round each of them, just managing not to crack their skulls together.

'It's so lovely to see you. I can't tell you all that's happened since Christmas. How are you both? Sally, are you engaged yet?'

A shadow passed across Sally's face. 'No.'

May moved quickly on. 'And what about you, Harry?'

Harriet shook her head. 'No, I'm not engaged, nor likely to be. But you must tell us what on earth's been happening. Why have you moved? What happened to *The Rose*? Everything!'

'It's been hell, but I think it's going to be all right.' She had a pen hanging from a cord around her neck, and picked up a clipboard from a nearby windowsill. 'Do you mind following me upstairs while we talk? I need to check how many hours Jethro's done.'

Sally and Harriet exchanged anxious glances. May seemed to have metamorphosed into someone frighteningly efficient. Before May had helped keep them all vaguely organized, but that was only three of them. This whole building seemed to be throbbing with men sawing, drilling and hammering and all there because of May. Was the May they knew and loved lost to them for ever?

'. . . and so I said we could do it,' May concluded her explanation to her two bemused friends. 'It just seemed like

303

fate. There was I, utterly desperate, nowhere to moor, up to my eyes in debt and broke, and there was he, money coming out of his ears, desperate to get his flats finished. I just had to offer to do it. Luckily I know craftsmen who need work. There's a father-and-son team who between them plumb, do electrics and decorate. They're coming up by boat. They should be here tomorrow. Jed can do anything with wood – marquetry, cabinetmaking, floorboards, roof timbers.'

'So what are we doing?' asked Sally.

'Well, I'm co-ordinating everybody, seeing they've got the materials they need, trying to manage the budget, hold things, stuff like that. And when the time comes, I'll help with the decorating. Jed works at night, so if he needs a labourer, I'll do it. It wouldn't be fair to ask anyone else.'

'So what can I do?' repeated Sally, hiding her doubts behind enthusiasm.

'We need to borrow a truck,' May replied, 'but we don't know where to borrow it from. We need you to persuade someone to lend us one. Jed or Jethro will drive it.'

In spite of its heartbreaking denouement, Christmas had been an empowering time for Sally. 'OK, May, leave it to me. And don't let anyone else do the lighting. I'm an expert.'

'I'll be in charge of colour schemes, décor, things like that,' said Harriet. 'If I can have a free hand.'

'Absolutely,' said May.

'And if you want some really outlandish floral arrangements, I can do those too,' said Sally. She might as well make the most of her experience with fir-tree branches. Anyway, being kept busy would take her mind off her nearly broken heart.

Later, when the saloon of *The Rose Revived* was once again filled with bedding and bodies, the directors of Cleaning Undertaken had a board meeting.

'It would be marvellous if we could bring this off,' said Harriet.

'Mmm. We worked so hard before, and barely kept our heads above water,' said Sally. 'It would be lovely to actually make a profit.'

May, who was very tired, fought back a yawn. 'It's more

than just marvellous, or lovely. It's essential. It's my last chance of keeping *The Rose*. The cash Rupert gave me up-front is keeping Mike at bay for now, but if we don't pull it off, I'll have to sell her.'

There was a moment's silence while Sally and Harriet took this in. 'We will do it,' said Sally firmly. 'We're a team, after all. And it's not just us any more. It's Jed and Jethro and Debra. Not to mention the men you say are arriving tomorrow. I've got a good feeling about this, really.'

On the drive up with Peter, Sally had made a decision not to tell the others about the part in the soap opera that was hers more or less for the asking. They would want to know why she wasn't going to the interview and her reasons might provoke a lot of argument. Sally was going to take Peter's advice and 'hang in there'. If he was right and James did love her, he would, sick cows, diffidence and time permitting, come to London to find her.

And when he did, learning that she hadn't even gone to the interview because she didn't want to be an actress might give him the incentive he needed to propose. Up to now, she'd done all the chasing. Now, if he wanted her, he would have to come out and say so.

As if at an unspoken signal, all three of them yawned hugely. 'Time for bed, I think,' said May. 'We've got work to do in the morning.'

CHAPTER THIRTY

As Harriet closed her eyes she wondered what she would have been doing if she hadn't met May when she first came to London – probably living in a bedsit and working in a chip shop.

Harriet had experienced more chaos since she'd met May than in the whole of her life. And this latest project made the rest of their time together seem like sweet sanity. But however mad, however unlikely, however *undo-able* this latest scheme was, she was determined that it would work, for May's sake, as much as for her own.

Sally felt much the same. And though her heart yearned for an unmodernized Cotswold farmhouse, her pride and loyalty to May meant she would do anything and everything to help bring it off. The flats would be ready – in time, within the budget, whatever it took, whatever else had to go by the board.

In spite of May's insistence that she would still clean, Harriet took over May's regular clients as well as the role of meal-maker. Jed ate with Debra and Jethro on *Curlew*, but if it hadn't been for Harriet, May wouldn't have bothered to eat at all. Harriet couldn't insist she went to bed at a reasonable time, but she could thrust sandwiches and mugs of soup into her hands.

She was doing just this, while May and Jed were in the passage designated on the plans as 'Kitchen'. Hearing what it was destined to be made Harriet sceptical.

'The galley on *The Rose* is far larger than this. You could hardly fit in a microwave, let alone a cooker,' she said disparagingly. 'Isn't there room for a kitchen somewhere else?'

May had been up most of the night working with Jed as

his apprentice and tea-maker. They'd finished off the shower-room, mostly installed by the previous contractors, by boxing in all the pipework and building an airing cupboard. But in the kitchen nothing had been done. She was aching with tiredness.

'I know. I expect it was why the other contractors ran off. Once you've got a cooker and a fridge in here, there's no room for anything else, like a person.'

Jed, who was nearly ready for bed, looked around. 'It's about the size of a butty cabin.' He regarded Harriet. 'Whole families – perhaps six or seven children – were brought up in spaces no bigger than this.'

May suddenly emerged from her pall of tiredness and started flapping her hands and jumping up and down. Small squeaks emerged from her gaping mouth. 'That's it! That's it! We'll treat it as a boatman's cabin!'

Jed started to grin. 'Brilliant! That's bloody brilliant!'

Harriet was unable to share their euphoria. 'I'm sorry, but how does that make it any bigger?'

'It doesn't. But have you seen a traditional boatman's cabin?' demanded May.

'No.'

'Well, it's incredibly cleverly fitted out. They have a cupboard door which pulls down to form a table. Fitted cupboards everywhere. Not an inch of space wasted,' she went on, still as enthusiastic.

'We could use this' – Jed's boots made marks in the sawdust – 'as the bedspace. Only we'll make it the eating area. You could get four people round it at a pinch.'

'And let's face it,' said May, 'these are executive pads. The people who rent them'll take people out if they want to entertain.'

Jed ignored this interjection. 'We'll put the microwave up above, where a cupboard would have been. But with fitted cupboards above the table and below, we'll get a reasonable amount of storage space.'

Well into his stride, his hands held parallel, he gestured where and how each modern unit could be built in, to maximize the space, just as necessity had forced the boat people to do.

'And we can fit the cooker and fridge over here,' said Harriet, getting the hang of things.

'And put the washer-drier in the bathroom,' said May. 'I don't know why more people don't do that. It's where you take your dirty clothes off, mostly.'

'And we've got a lot more headroom than on a boat,' said Jed.

'With the microwave over the table,' said May, getting carried away, 'and with a remote control, you get the door to fly open and the meal to eject itself on to the waiting plate.'

'Nah,' said Jed seriously. 'If you didn't have your plate in the right place, it would never work.'

Harriet, though impressed, tempered her enthusiasm. 'You've got some wonderful ideas,' she said. 'But don't tell Rupert too much about them or he'll try and fit another two flats into the corridor.'

'And if we build-in so much, we'll run out of timber,' said May, coming down from her high. 'We've got three kitchens to do, don't forget. And I don't want to eat into any more of the money for decoration and soft furnishings. Sally's lighting budget has already been pinched from.'

Of course Rupert would give her more money if she asked him, he was thrilled with the progress so far. But it would cut into the promised bonus, and May's pride was at stake. She had to bring in the conversions under, or at least on, the original budget.

Jed, to whom the notion of buying timber was extremely novel, looked bemused. 'You don't buy it, you just get it out of a skip or something.'

May had a vision of herself cycling round London clambering in and out of skips looking for matching lengths of tongue-and-groove. 'It's a lovely idea, but there's the time element as well.'

'We'll reclaim it then. There's a hell of a lot of stuff being taken out of that place in Ashworth Street. And I know none of the reclamation firms are on to it yet, because I asked. All it takes is someone to go and talk the builders into letting us have it cheap.'

May and Harriet exchanged glances. 'Sally's department. Definitely.'

'I don't know what to *say*,' Sally moaned for the hundredth time. 'I can't just waltz in there and ask for it. It's not like borrowing things. You're not intending to give it back.'

'It's quite simple. You put on your shortest skirt, your highest heels and your prettiest smile,' said May. 'Ask to see the foreman and offer him cash for the floorboards. He won't mind. He's working for someone else anyway, it's no skin off his nose.'

Sally looked uncertain.

'Say your boss is giving you a hard time. If you don't go soon, it'll be true.'

'But . . .'

May's patience was gone. 'Oh Sally! You're an actress, aren't you? Fucking well act!'

Quite what Sally did, no one ever discovered. But three loads of reclaimed floorboards were not only delivered to the warehouse, but were carried up the many flights of stairs to the flat by a youth dripping with perspiration and testosterone.

May, feeling guilty, handed him a fiver for his trouble.

The kitchens worked wonderfully well. Not only was every cubic centimetre used, but the boards, waxed and polished by Sally and Harriet to a golden shine, managed to unite the age and history of the building, with the new use of the space.

Rupert was delighted. 'You're very innovative, May.'

'Not at all. It's not what you know, it's who you know.'

'But something's not quite as you'd like it?' He had correctly interpreted her twitching from foot to foot.

'No. I was talking to Sally about the lighting . . .'

'I thought her speciality was twisting men round her little finger.'

May regarded him disapprovingly. 'Sally may be very attractive, but it doesn't mean all she's fit for is smiling sweetly at the right time. She's in charge of lighting.'

'Oh. Sorry,' said Rupert meekly.

'Anyway, she and I were discussing the lack of natural light in the apartments.'

'There's not much I can do about that,' said Rupert, a touch defensively. 'A warehouse is a warehouse. There is an atrium on the top floor.'

'Yes, but the rest of the building won't benefit from that at all. You'll have to consider something else.'

'Am I right in thinking that you have the "something else" in mind?'

'Yes. Balconies.'

Rupert shook his head. 'I do have to keep the outside of the building as it is. I can't have wrought-iron balustrades, or any of that nonsense.'

May gave him a look which told him she was disappointed in him. 'I know that! Sally's idea, and I must say, I think it's jolly good, is that you open the wooden doors – you know, the ones which were used for tipping the grain into the boats?'

Rupert nodded.

'Well, if you open those inwards, and glaze them, you would have like a little balcony. The outside of the building would look more or less the same, but some of the flats would have much more light.'

'Mmm . . .'

'Because you've got those doors both sides of the building.'

'Yes . . .'

'And you could charge more for those flats.'

Rupert regarded May, who looked as much like an urchin as she did the first time he saw her. 'All right. But you're to promise me you won't use recycled glass.'

May was hurt. 'Of course not! Regulation toughened, reinforced, double-glazed, whatever the architect says we must use.'

Rupert nodded.

'And you'll talk to him about it?' May asked. 'I find him – difficult to deal with, somehow.'

May had found the architect difficult to deal with the first time she saw his name on a bit of paper and realized he was the man whose first editions she'd ruined when she worked for Slimeball. He had never known her name, but the fear that he might somehow make the connection made her fight shy of approaching him.

'OK. I'll give him a ring,' Rupert sounded resigned. 'Oh, and I forgot to tell you, Jed said some boat or other has arrived with an electrician and a plasterer.'

'Oh goody. I'll go and see.' She clattered off, her boots loud on the bare wooden floor. She clattered back. 'And can you get on to the lift people? They really should be working by now.'

'You're supposed to be the co-ordinator.'

'I am. Now I'm co-ordinating you. Besides, when I've sorted Bob and Alf on the *Albion*, I've got to chase up the sea-grass matting. If we're going to get these flats ready on time, we've all got to pull our weight.'

Harriet had been persuaded to paint a wonderful mural, a *trompe-l'œil* of a nineteenth-century canal scene. It was as if the huge warehouse doors were open, with the canal full of boats and the surrounding warehouses all in use. She had been working on it for days, and had finally stayed up all night to finish it. It graced the foyer of the building with stunning effect.

'It's wonderful, Harriet,' said May. 'If you don't make a go of painting pictures, you could do this sort of thing instead.'

Harriet, tired, paint-smeared, but satisfied, nodded. 'I would have liked a bit longer at it. But I suppose I could. It does look nice, doesn't it?'

'Rupert will be thrilled. I must remember to warn him it's there.'

'You mean he didn't ask you for it?' Harriet was horrified.

May shrugged. 'He would have said yes if I had. And this way it'll be a lovely surprise for him. I do appreciate how hard you've worked, Harry.'

Harriet put an arm round May and squeezed her. 'It makes up for all the time I spend with Leo, learning art, when I should be cleaning.'

'Silly!' said May. 'Let's give Rupert a ring and tell him to come and have a look.'

Rupert, who was beginning to find it easier to go along with May than to argue, was highly delighted.

'I would have said yes, if you'd asked me, May. So why didn't you ask?'

'Why bother, when I knew you'd say yes?'

'Do you bully Hugh like you bully me?'

'No,' replied May, her euphoria suddenly gone.

CHAPTER THIRTY-ONE

Harriet slunk off the boat for her stint at Leo's, feeling like a noise-sensitive rat leaving a well-provisioned ship preparing for sea – only one such as she would want to go.

Seeing Leo was never an unmixed pleasure. Her feelings for him coupled with his acid perceptiveness made him uncomfortable company, but the promise of quiet, broken only by the coffee grinder and the hoover, both sounds which Harriet controlled, seemed like bliss. She was not, she had recently discovered, temperamentally suited to life on a building site, an environment which suited May extraordinarily well.

'Hi,' said Leo, who happened to be in the hall as she let herself in. 'How are you? Have you got Matthew with you?'

Harriet shook her head, surprised he should have remembered her timetable. 'He's due the day after tomorrow. But quite where we'll put him, I don't know. The boat is a madhouse at the moment.'

'Oh? Why's that?'

Harriet explained, in graphic detail.

'You can have him here, if you like.'

The moment she had seen him, Harriet had been aware of something odd about Leo. He was far too talkative for nine o'clock in the morning. This generous gesture confirmed her suspicions.

'I'm sorry, I'm not with you.'

Leo put his hand on Harriet's shoulder. 'Come into the kitchen. I need to talk to you.'

His solicitude increased her anxiety. He sat her down and set about the business of making coffee.

'I didn't know you could do that,' said Harriet, watching him press the plunger on the cafetière.

He smiled, and poured coffee into the only mug without a chip. 'Sugar?'

'No, thank you.'

He continued to stir his own mug for an agonizingly long time. 'When I said Matthew could come and stay here, I really meant you both could. I'm going away.'

Harriet's heart sank, like a coin in deep water, slowly but inexorably.

'Oh?'

Leo nodded. 'For several reasons. The most important being my work.'

'Oh.'

'Financially, I'm suddenly much better off.'

'Did you win the lottery?'

He shook his head. 'Better than that. My ex-wife has remarried, bringing my outgoings down enormously. And I've decided to sell a couple of paintings.'

Harriet had only a hazy idea how much his paintings would fetch, but by the way he was talking, it was a lot.

'I lent them to an American exhibition years ago,' he went on. 'But although the gallery wanted to buy them, I didn't feel I would ever do anything as good again, so I refused to sell.' His eyes lingered over her in a way which in anybody else would be loving. 'I don't feel like that now. Which means I've got a bit of money at last. And a friend has offered to lend me his house in Spain. It's actually more a cave than a house. But I can live there very cheaply, and paint, with no distractions. Build up enough paintings for another exhibition.'

Harriet took a sip of coffee to ease her dry mouth. 'I see.'

'There are a huge number of distractions here, Harriet.'

'Of course.'

'Not least being that I'm not sure how much longer I can watch you flit about my flat with that hoover and not take you to bed.'

Her heart lurched to the surface. He was going away, that was why he wouldn't seduce her. Surely it wouldn't take much to change his mind? 'Well, why don't you? I mean, I wouldn't object – particularly.'

314

Leo smiled. 'Maybe not, but I'm not totally amoral, and there's also your work to consider.'

'Leo, I don't have work in that sense. I'm just a . . .'

'You have incredible talent. And now you're not chewed up about your son any more, it might really start to develop. *If* you have time and space to pursue it. Which is why I want you to live here, while I'm away, and paint every waking moment.'

'I couldn't possibly afford it.'

'You don't have to pay the mortgage. I can rent it to you, cheaply. Besides, your grandfather told me he's going to give you an allowance. Quite a substantial one.'

This was another shock. 'But *why*? And why tell you and not me?'

'The second is a matter of his pride. He might have found himself having to use words like "sorry" and "wrong". But the money is what he would have settled on your mother, if she hadn't run away to get married. He invested it, obviously extremely successfully.'

'But I still don't see why. I mean, they're reasonably well off, but what with Matthew's school fees and everything, they're not rolling in it.'

'I think he's trying to claw back some of the family closeness he's let slip. He knows he's lost two generations. This is his way of clinging on to the third.'

'I see.'

'It'll be enough for your rent and basic facilities for a couple of years, at least. You'll have to earn enough for your food and materials. Or you could keep up the art classes. You're good enough to teach them all except Elizabeth.' He drained his cup and looked reproachfully at the cafetière. Harriet took the hint, got up and put the kettle on.

When she had poured them both more coffee and sat down again, he delved into his pocket. 'By the way, I ought to give you this.' He produced a small, engraved card and put it into her hand.

'What is it? Who's Paul J. Mark?'

Leo winced and then remembered that Harriet had lived most of her life in an artistic desert.

'He's the most influential gallery owner in London. He's prepared to offer you an exhibition next autumn.'

Harriet was horrified. 'But how can he? He hasn't seen my work! You didn't show him?'

Leo shook his head. 'I wouldn't show him that crap. I merely assured him, and my word does count for something, that you were going to be one of the foremost young artists in the country. And if he wanted you to give him an exhibition he'd better commit himself sooner rather than later.'

Harriet put down her teaspoon. 'But – I'm sorry to be so stupid, but if my work is crap now, it's not going to be a lot better by next autumn. I'll have to work for years and years.'

Leo shook his head. 'I think you'll find that your work will take off. Now you've got Matthew settled and you're free from your grandparents' charity, you should begin to reach your potential.'

Harriet sighed. 'I just pray to God that you're right.'

'I am right,' Leo stated. 'The reason your work has been so tight up to now, is that you've had other, more important things on your mind.'

Part of Harriet was burning with happiness – she had talent, Leo was certain – but another, baser part ached for him. Admittedly, in a different way from the way he ached for her, but if she was prepared to take lust if she couldn't have love, why should he complain? And if she didn't take it now, she may never have the chance.

'Leo.' She tried hard to sound decisive and matter of fact. 'You said that you wanted me. You probably know how I feel about you.' She paused. By now he should have swept her into his arms and carried her to the bedroom, but he was still looking at her in that quizzical, maddening way. 'Is there any reason why – I mean – we're both adults . . .' She baulked at asking outright if he'd go to bed with her, but surely he'd caught her drift by now.

He'd caught it, but chose not to take advantage of it. 'I am very fond of you, Harriet. Possibly fonder than I ever have been of anyone. Too fond, in fact, to take advantage of you. Too fond to put you in a position where anyone could say you slept your way to the top.'

'But no one would know . . .'

'If anyone even hinted at it, you'd blush like a Turner sunset, you know you would. My reputation isn't all it might be. I don't want yours sullied.'

It was a quaint, old-fashioned word, and Harriet realized that, under the anarchic artist, there was a lot of quaint, old-fashioned chivalry about Leo. If she wanted him, she'd have to fight harder.

'But I might never make it as an artist, then I won't even have . . .' her voice tailed away and she finished her sentence in her head: . . . one, sweet memory of true passion.

He put his hand on hers in way which was horribly avuncular. Harriet wondered for a moment if he'd lied about wanting her, and had only said it to make her feel better about her own feelings.

'You will. I'll come to your private view, and when the critics acknowledge your talent, I may well claim you. But no one is going to say you got where you're headed through sleeping with me. Got that?'

Harriet's throat was choked with emotion. She nodded.

'Good. The bath's filthy. Can you do something about it?'

Coincidentally, while Harriet was taking out her frustration on Leo's skirting boards, Sally was venting hers up a ladder, painting a cornice. Until she looked out of the window and saw James talking to May on the quayside.

Her first instinct was to get to him as fast as she could, but she suppressed it. She had made all the running in the relationship so far. It was up to him to show a little keenness now.

May brought James to where Sally was working. 'Hi, Sally, look who I found wandering about like an odd sock. Don't go away without seeing me, James. I've got a job you're just the man for.'

Feeling very alone and nervous at the top of her ladder, Sally looked at James. He seemed bigger and more handsome than ever. In fact, she wondered how she had doubted his good looks when she first met him. Now, his shaggy vastness seemed the epitome of male beauty.

317

'Hello.' He sounded shy. 'I didn't think you'd be here. I thought you'd be in Yorkshire or somewhere, being an actress.'

'No.'

'Why not? Didn't you get the job?'

'I didn't go for it.'

'But why? I thought it was yours for the asking?'

'It was, but I decided I didn't want it.'

'Why?'

'I decided I didn't want to be an actress any more, that's why.'

'Oh? Well what do you want to be? A painter and decorator?' He indicated her drying brush, the half-painted cornice.

Sally shook her head. 'No. I want to be a farmer.'

A slow but irrepressible smile crept across from the corners of James's mouth until the breadth of his grin could have advertised toothpaste. 'That takes years of experience. Some say you have to be born to it. I don't suppose you'd settle for being a farmer's wife, by way of a compromise?'

Sally opened her eyes very wide and regarded him with studied innocence. 'That very much depends on who the farmer is . . .'

The only farmer in the room lost patience. He strode across to the ladder and picked Sally off it, and hugged the breath out of her. 'Oh Sally,' he murmured into her neck. 'I've missed you so much. Clodagh's been pining. The farm seems so empty, and without you, there seems to be no point in anything any more.'

'Oh James . . .'

'I came up to London to see if I could find out your address, and to ask my solicitor how soon I could sell the farm.'

'You mustn't sell the farm! It's your life!'

'Not without you in it, it's not. I thought I could sell it and find another way to earn a living, something which would let you be in London, if that's where you need to be.'

'But what about Clodagh? It would have been cruel!'

'She would have got used to it. And if it had given me a

better chance of getting you to marry me, it would have been worth it.'

'Oh sweetheart! How could you be so silly? I'd never ask you to make all those sacrifices for me. I'm mad about you.'

'Are you? Mad enough to give up a glamorous lifestyle to freeze to death in a farmhouse?'

Sally giggled. 'It will be dreadfully difficult, dragging myself away from this luxurious penthouse flat . . .'

James put an end to her sarcasm in a way which led her to fling her arms round his neck and close her eyes.

May came upon them some time later. Sally was hugely dishevelled and boss-eyed with happiness. James, equally rumpled, just looked ecstatic.

'Harriet's come back and made a cake. But you can't have any unless you're engaged.'

'Darling?' said James. 'Are we?'

'I should bloody well hope so,' said Sally and slithered off his lap on to the floor.

It was a month after Sally's engagement, and Harriet's defection from boat-life to Leo's flat, that Rupert Williams came back into the kitchen of the third flat.

'I still can't work out how you managed to fit so much stuff in, and leave enough space to eat in.'

'It's based on a butty cabin, I told you.'

May would have been quite happy to tell him again, but Rupert didn't feel that was necessary. 'No, no. I do understand. And you say the other flats could have kitchens like these?'

May nodded.

'And so we could fit in an extra bathroom, as well as the en-suite?'

'If you like. But we would need more timber. I haven't got Sally to seduce floorboards out of people now.'

'Did she ever let on how she got that lot?'

May shook her head. 'Nope. They just arrived. Enough for three kitchens, delivered.'

Rupert sighed understandingly. Some women were worth

breaking a sweat for. 'So she's given up acting and has gone to live in the country?'

May nodded.

'Shame. She had terrific legs.'

At one time May would have objected to this sexist statement. But the last month had made her too tired for futile arguments. You had to live in the world as it was, not as you'd like it to be.

'And Harriet? She's going to paint full time?'

'She'll still do the interior decorations, or at least, she'll choose colour schemes and things. But she needs to paint as much as she can, for her exhibition.'

'But you'll be able to do the other flats without them? You don't want to go off and do something creative?'

May smiled and shook her head. 'No. Besides, this is creative. I love taking an empty, disused space and see it turn into somewhere people could live.'

'And what about your workforce? Are they still wrapped round your little finger?'

'Not at all,' said May sternly. 'But they're keen to do as much work as they can, while they can.'

'So everyone's happy.'

May nodded. Indeed in a way, she was happy. All she had told Rupert about finding the work creative was true. But she missed the companionship of the other girls. Work-wise, she was a success. But for the first time in her life she felt lonely.

Rupert seemed to sense her discontent. He put a hand on her shoulder. 'You've done a wonderful job organizing everything and everyone. I do appreciate it.'

May was pleased. She hadn't known that Rupert realized what a strain that could be, keeping everyone busy and happy and feeling valued. Being everybody's best friend and surrogate mother was draining. 'Thanks.'

'Hugh would be proud of you.'

'Have you heard from him?'

Rupert nodded slowly. 'He's going to be in the States for a while. Things are going well there and he didn't think there was any particular point in coming home just yet.'

320

'Oh.' May was too tired to keep the wistfulness out of her voice, or the droop out of her neck.

'Let me take you out for a meal? I'm sure now Harriet's gone you don't eat properly.'

She hesitated. Rupert was very kind and it would be nice to be spoilt for a change. The craftsmen were all kind, easygoing men. They often gave her a friendly pat on the back and bought her a pint, but she had no one to hold her at the end of a long day, no one to make her a cup of tea and tell her she'd done a good job.

Given the right encouragement, Rupert might very well do that and more. But unless the comfort and the hugs came from the right person they didn't work. 'I don't think so, thank you. I feel too tired and dirty.'

'Nonsense, you've got to eat. And the hot water's on. You can have a really long shower in one of these bathrooms.'

May turned away, lest he see the blush which had crept up her cheeks. What with one thing and another, *The Rose Revived*'s water tanks were still empty, and she had been availing herself of Rupert's hot water and newly tiled showers for some time now. A small array of Body Shop products moved from flat to flat as they were completed.

'Thank you,' she said meekly. 'You're very sweet, Rupert.' She reached up and kissed his cheek.

'It's a pity you're spoken for,' he said.

'I'm not spoken for! Whatever gave you that idea?'

'Oh never mind. Go and wash your hair. And put on a dress.'

'I never wear dresses,' she said firmly. 'You can have clean jeans, if I can find them.'

And with that, Rupert had to be content.

CHAPTER THIRTY-TWO

Immediately their train drew in, May spotted Sally waiting on the platform, although it had been nearly four months since she'd seen her.

Sally was wearing cut-off jeans and a cropped T-shirt which matched the busy-lizzies which swung from the station rafters, and trainers. She was dancing up and down with excitement, and even from behind a dusty train window, looked ecstatically happy.

'She looks wonderful!' May said over her shoulder to Harriet, who was gathering bags from the overhead luggage rack.

'I told you she did,' said Harriet. 'Can you take this?'

May took the clutch of bags which Harriet put into her hand wondering what it was about Sally that had changed. It was much more than her clothes.

'Sally!' First out of the train, May dropped the bags and fell into Sally's arms. Sally still smelt marvellous and was still wearing make-up, though much less of it. But her lean, racehorse figure had filled out and turned glamour into real beauty. She had lost that haunted, eager-to-please look which had characterized her as an out-of-work actress and replaced it with one of health, happiness and enormous confidence. She returned May's hug.

'Come on, we must get the rest of the bags off, or the train will go. Sorry!' she called to the guard with a dazzling smile. 'They're my bridesmaids,' she confided. 'So sorry to keep the train waiting.'

The guard, who was as susceptible as most men, thought the few seconds' delay well worth such an enchanting smile.

'The car's this way,' said Sally, having hugged Harriet and picked up most of the baggage.

'I can't believe you're driving,' said May.

Sally grinned. 'I passed my test ages ago, but never had the opportunity to drive. James took me out for lots of practice runs, and now I'm always out and about. I can't tell you what a gesture of commitment it is going on to a man's insurance policy.'

'Surely marriage is a fair amount of commitment,' said Harriet.

'Believe me, a man can marry you twenty times over, but not let you threaten his no-claims bonus. Do you mind sharing the back seat with one of the cases? There isn't room for all of them in the back?'

'But surely, a car this length –' said May coming up behind. 'Oh my God!'

'That's Clodagh,' Sally said. 'And except for James, and you two of course, she's practically my best friend. I never leave her behind if I can help it.'

Chastened, May got into the back seat and looked over into the luggage area, deeply impressed. Clodagh took up most of the space, though there was a little room for baggage to one side. Her huge grey head and dark eyes raised to look at May in return.

'No wonder you were frightened when she reared up from the sofa in James's flat.'

Sally laughed. 'She's a sweetheart when you get to know her. Everyone strapped in?'

Sally started the engine and swooped out of the station car park with great aplomb. 'We'll go to the farm now, and later I'll take you over to the holiday cottage. It's one of Lucy's – she's James's sister. She's older than him, but younger than Liz, who's doing the dresses. She's coming round tonight to check the hems and things. I could have put you up at the house, but it's so full of relations and I couldn't have stayed with you.'

'What's all this about dresses, Sal?' said May. 'I'm not a bridesmaid. I've got a smart trouser suit my mother lent me. Navy blue with white spots. Very weddingish.'

Sally looked in the driving mirror. 'Harriet, you were supposed to tell her.'

'I know. But the moment never seemed right,' said Harriet. 'May – Sally wants you to be a bridesmaid. You don't mind, do you?'

May sighed. Over the past four months she had become so accustomed to being whatever anyone needed her to be – mediator, foreman, carpenter's apprentice or just jollier-along. Why should she object to being Sally's bridesmaid? She decided it was the dressing-up part.

'The dress won't fit anyone else,' said Sally. 'In fact, it might not fit you. We had to guess your measurements.'

'Well, if the dresses are too awful,' May conceded without grace, 'you'll have to make do with Harriet on her own.'

'They're lovely, not pink or purple,' Sally swung the Volvo into the farm gate and yelled at Harriet, who had jumped out to open it, 'If you just unloop the binder twine? And give it a good slam when we're through.'

Having run the gauntlet of the farm dogs, which were much less threatening now they had Sally feeding them, they threaded their way through to the kitchen.

'This is beautiful!' said May. 'Like something out of a magazine.'

'Good, isn't it? It's the room I did first. Most of the things, like the dresser and the table were here. They just needed dolling up a bit.'

She looked with pride at how the sunshine-yellow paint harmonized the old with the new, creating a room which was efficient and yet comfortable. 'We more or less live in here. It's the warmest room in the house, which is very important in winter, and it's where everything gets done, so I wanted it to be nice. I stripped that dresser myself, and waxed it.'

'I should never have let you leave, Sally, if I'd known you were such a dab hand with the wet-and-dry,' said May.

Sally grinned. 'It would have been all right, but we had a couple of poorly lambs to bottle feed at the time, so I kept having to stop, take off my gloves, wash my hands and make up a couple of bottles. In the end I was so confused I was washing my hands before picking up my sand-paper.'

'What about your nails?' asked Harriet.

Sally made a characteristic gesture. 'Sometimes they survive, sometimes they don't.'

'You sound awfully farmy and professional, Sal,' went on May. 'Do you really get up at the crack of dawn to feed the chickens and stuff?'

Sally's grin implied she sometimes found other things to do at the crack of dawn. 'Well, not always. But I do love my poultry. And I'm doing a part-time course on farming.' She unhooked some mugs from the dresser. 'I liked acting when it went well, but farming's more . . .' she searched for the word. 'More *life-enhancing*, if you know what I mean.'

'Mmm,' said May. 'What does your mother have to say about it?'

Sally laughed, pouring tea. 'Well of course she absolutely *adores* James. She's disappointed that I've given up the business, of course. But she knows in her heart I would never have made it, not really. I didn't burn for it, like she did. And farming makes me so much happier.'

Her happiness was evident in every word and gesture, but May wondered how much of it was due to the farm and how much to James. Perhaps some women do need a man to help them grow into themselves. James had certainly done wonders for Sally's confidence. A sigh caught her unawares. She hoped the other two hadn't noticed.

'Did I tell you the old dears from Victoria Mansions are coming?' Sally said. 'You know, Captain and Mrs Walker? Their son is bringing them. I told them they were responsible for James and me getting together and they were so thrilled to be invited. They gave me a gorgeous little china-cow creamer.'

'I hope they're happy with the permanent cleaner I found them,' said May. 'They were about the only clients I felt bad about abandoning when we gave up cleaning and started working for Rupert full time.'

'According to them she's a treasure.'

'Where is James?' asked Harriet. 'Have we frightened him away?'

'Golly, no. He'll be in in a minute. It's his stag night

325

tonight. His brothers-in-law are taking him out. Did I tell you about the wedding?'

'What more do we need to know,' asked May drily, 'now you've told us who the bridesmaids are?'

Sally narrowed her eyes at May. 'There's going to be an exhibition of Appalachian clog dancing. Dave's arranged it, as he's one of the cloggers. He's James's right-hand man. James is terribly honoured, they're always booked up for months in advance.'

'And what is Appalachian clog dancing when it's at home?' asked Harriet.

'It's American, a sort of combination of Irish step dancing and clogging, with a bit of square dancing thrown in. It's really great fun!'

'Mmmm,' said May.

'And afterwards, there's going to be a barn dance.'

'How rustic. One might almost say, bucolic,' May was hiding a smile. 'You haven't invited Piers, have you?'

'No,' said Sally, appreciating the joke. 'He wouldn't enjoy it. But you will, I promise. There are lots of lusty young men in the team and they're all looking forward to dancing with smart London ladies.'

'Well they're in for a disappointment. I'm neither smart, nor a lady,' said May.

'Is Leo coming, Harriet?'

She shook her head. 'No. He's too entrenched in his painting and the Spanish way of life. It's working really well for him, being out there.' Harriet flashed a quick smile, to tell her friends that she was absolutely fine about this, not even remotely brokenhearted.

May, who saw through this bluff with ease, changed the subject. 'Anyone else we know going to be there?'

'Well – um – Matthew!' said Sally, rather quickly. 'Matthew's coming over from school.'

'Oh good. I haven't seen him for ages. Where's he sleeping?'

'He's staying here,' said Sally. 'Apparently he didn't fancy the holiday cottage when it was full of wedding dresses.'

'You didn't force him into being a page then, in knicker-bockers? Or a kilt?' said May.

'No. He's going to be an usher. He'll be fine,' said Matthew's mother. 'When I suggested being a page, he put his foot down.'

'I'm not surprised,' said May. 'So who's giving you away?'

'Liz's husband, Peter. He's been so sweet to me, and I didn't fancy dragging Daddy back from Saudi to do it. It would be so awful for Mummy.'

'I'm looking forward to meeting your mother,' said Harriet.

Sally smiled. 'She's coming tomorrow.'

'Is she bringing anyone with her?' asked Harriet.

'You mean her boyfriend? No, thank goodness. According to Mummy, "He's lovely company, darling, but not the sort of man you want to introduce to your daughter's new family." She's convinced I'm marrying into the landed gentry. Just wait until she sees the place!'

'You can still act then, Sally,' said May.

'As well as I ever could. Oh look, here's James!'

Watching Sally and James greet each other after a parting of only a few hours, May swallowed a lump of sentiment heavily laced with envy.

'So that's the point of getting married.' she whispered to Harriet. 'You can show your feelings to the world.' Harriet glanced quickly at her, and nodded. They had both become practised at concealing theirs.

After he had put his future wife down, James hugged and kissed both the girls with almost as much enthusiasm. His happiness radiated from him like sunshine.

'It's super of you to agree to be bridesmaids,' he said to them. 'I know you weren't keen.'

'If it makes you happy it'll be worth it,' said May, and found she meant it.

'So that's the dress,' said Harriet huskily.

'Yes,' breathed Sally, equally awed. 'It took me ages to work out what I wanted to wear. I wanted to be glamorous, but countrified. I didn't want to be too sophisticated and London.'

May regarded the dress more critically as Sally held it on the hanger. It was straw-coloured taffeta with elbow-length sleeves, the waist pulled in by a dark-green velvet basque which laced up the back and front. Above the basque was a fairly low-cut boat neck, with a frill of lace just inside it. The full, slightly puffed-up skirts were lifted a little with dark-green velvet bows, revealing a plain satin underskirt. A taffeta bow completed the back.

'My mother wanted me to have a train, but I didn't think it was suitable for a country wedding,' went on Sally.

'I think it's beautiful,' said Harriet. 'I like the touch of dark green. It makes it different, yet still weddingy.'

'And the basque makes my waist look tiny,' Sally finished.

'Your waist *is* tiny,' said May.

'Not as tiny as it was. I've put on a stone since I've been down here, but James says the more of me to love, the better.'

'Show us the bridesmaids' dresses then,' said May before Sally became distracted by the thought of James and her body connected.

Sally led them into the third bedroom of the holiday cottage. There, hanging under polythene, were simplified versions of Sally's own dress, only instead of taffetta, they were of glazed chintz patterned with sprigs of flowers.

'Me and Liz racked our brains to try and come up with something you could wear afterwards as evening dresses, but we decided that people never actually do.'

'Gosh,' said May.

'Could you bear to try them on? Liz'll be here in a minute. She took such a lot of trouble over them, she wants every detail to be perfect. Funny, she's usually fairly casual about life, but over her sewing, she's a real perfectionist.'

Harriet and May started to undress. 'Even if Liz has sewed every stitch by hand and sat up all night to do so,' said May, 'I'm still maintaining my right to back out if I look a complete prat.'

She didn't look a prat, but she did look completely different.

'My God!' she breathed. 'I hardly recognize myself!'

Her bosom was fuller than either Sally's or Harriet's, and the tight waist and low neck enhanced her cleavage and the creamy expanse of chest and the elegant line of her neck. She felt voluptuous and feminine, and the period of the dress made her feel detached from her everyday personality. She was no longer May, trouble-shooter, gofer and carpenter *manquée*, she was some other, mysterious creature who was almost beautiful.

'I feel like someone in a play,' she said. 'I just don't look like myself.'

'You look fantastic!' shrieked Sally. 'You'll upstage me! You cow!'

May chuckled. 'I couldn't do that if I tried, but at least no one will recognize me in this disguise. My mother won't believe her eyes when she sees the photos.'

'What do we wear on our heads?' asked Harriet, piling up her silky hair in a bundle.

'Roses all the way round, plonked right on top. Here, try.' Sally removed a headdress from a box and placed it on Harriet. 'Good eh?'

May almost snatched her headdress from the box, silently vowing that if it spoilt the effect of her dress, she wouldn't wear it.

The dark silk roses on top of her shiny dark hair completed her costume. 'It's very beautiful . . .' She shot a quick glance at Sally. 'But this dress is dreadfully revealing.'

Harriet regarded her critically. 'I must say, I didn't realize it would show quite so much flesh.'

'Put yours on, Harriet,' suggested Sally. 'I'm sure they didn't look revealing in the drawing.'

Harriet's dress wasn't quite as low cut and her smaller bust appeared only discreetly. But May's definitely erred on the side of profanity.

'Don't worry,' said Sally. 'Liz'll be here soon. She'll sort it out.'

'You have to be the most unruffled bride in creation,' said May. 'Aren't you at all nervous? I mean, the ceremony?' May was quaking at the thought of going up the aisle, even as a bridesmaid.

Sally wrinkled her brow. 'No, not really. I mean – I know I've got James. If the marquee is blown away, or nobody comes, or the organist throws up in the organ, as long as James is all right, I will be too. Does that sound awfully soppy?'

'Yes,' said May crossly.

Sally was just as insouciant the next day, completely laid-back about everything. Indeed, May wished Sally was being more bridal and neurotic, but while Lucy went to the church to make sure her flower arrangements hadn't dropped in the night, Sally let the children loose in her make-up bag. As May frantically tried to remove the lipstick from Augustus and Gina, she didn't know which she was more frightened of, Lucy, or walking up the aisle in Sally's wake.

When May felt Sally should have been trembling under a facepack, or insisting that it was all a mistake and the wedding must be called off, she breezed about in her heated rollers and underwear, nearly laddering her white, lace-topped stockings on the log basket and not caring.

'It's time for the adult bridesmaids to get dressed,' announced Lucy, referring to her clipboard. 'I hope to God the bouquets arrive in time. They ought to have been here by now.'

'Why don't we have baskets of oranges instead of flowers,' May muttered to Harriet as they clambered into their dresses. 'Then at least Lucy would have one less thing to worry about.'

'I think Lucy likes worrying.' Harriet stepped into her dress and pulled it up. 'At least you've got a bosom,' she added, looking wistfully at her own chest.

'Yes, and a whole churchful of people are going to see it.'

Liz arrived, adding her two young children to the general chaos. She had with her a box which she carried upstairs to the bedroom assigned to the bridesmaids.

'I found this in James's attic the other day and thought it might come in useful so I snitched it.'

'What is it? Camouflage netting?'

'More or less.' Liz opened the box and produced two lengths of silk net. 'It was awfully yellowed of course, but after I washed it in biological washing powder and dipped it in some bleach, it came up beautifully. See how softly it falls. Much nicer than nylon net.'

Harriet was shocked. 'You mean you washed antique silk net in biological washing powder and bleach? It could have been ruined!'

'And think what that stuff does to the environment!' said May, more horrified, but for different reasons.

Liz shrugged. 'I promise you both I won't ever do it again. It's not whiter than white, but just the right colour for the dresses. And there's just enough for both.' She shook a length out. 'Sit down, May, and I'll see what I can do to make you decent.'

Under her clever fingers the net became a fichu, concealing most of her bosom without spoiling the line or style of the dress.

'If you breathe on it, it will fall apart, but with luck, it'll survive the service.'

'You are clever, Liz,' said Harriet.

'Now I look like Snow White rather than Nell Gwyn.' May chewed her lip.

'Here's Suzy to do your hair, everyone.' said Lucy, escorting a small, dark woman. 'Bang on schedule. She'll do you two first, and then Sally. Now,' Lucy scanned her clipboard, 'what's next?'

It was while Sally's gleaming locks were being coaxed upwards that May noticed the condition of the bride's hands.

'You can't be a bride with chicken shit under your nails, Sal,' said May firmly. 'Not even I would do that.'

'It won't show when I've got nail varnish on!' Sally insisted as Lucy advanced on her with an orange stick. 'Really, it won't.'

'Living with my brother has turned you into a slut,' said Liz. 'You were such a nice girl when I first met you.'

Eventually, everyone was dressed and re-dressed. The bouquets arrived and were put in the larder to keep cool. Suzy had done everyone's hair and placed hats and head-dresses just so.

'Right,' said Lucy to her clipboard. 'Time to take the bouquets out.'

Harriet obediently produced the bouquets and Lucy, who had done a Constance Spry course, inspected them.

'There's not enough white in them, Sally, but I suppose they'll have to do.'

'The cars are here,' announced Liz, who had spotted them from the bathroom. 'We'd better get away because they're blocking up the lane. No one can get past.'

Lucy consulted her clipboard again. 'Right. The first car takes Liz, me, Augustus and Adam. We pick up Sally's mother on the way. Then it comes back here and picks up the bridesmaids. The Rolls should pick up Sally and Peter at about the same time.' Lucy looked grave. 'I'm going to leave this with you, Harriet.' She handed over the clipboard. 'You're in charge now.'

Harriet solemnly received the clipboard, wondering if she was a worthy recipient. She made lists on the backs of envelopes. This was like a computer spreadsheet. She glanced down and saw her first responsibility was to get the little ones to go to the loo. Just as she was about to do this, Lucy came charging back into the house.

'Go to the lavatory, boys, quick now! Harriet, you will see that the girls go, won't you?'

At last, Lucy and Liz and the little boys had gone, leaving the house strangely peaceful. Then Peter arrived and doled out glasses of sherry and made bad jokes until the car came back. Harriet kissed Sally warmly. 'Good luck, darling, see you in church.'

They all climbed in, treading on each other's feet, and squashing their headdresses.

'All set?' asked Harriet brightly as the car drew away. 'Ready for the big moment?'

'No,' said Gina. 'I need to go to the lavatory. And I think I'm going to be sick.'

CHAPTER THIRTY-THREE

Sally seemed to be floating on a cushion of happiness. Not even Aunt Sophie's antique wedding veil could shade her radiance.

'Right,' said the photographer who appeared from behind a tombstone. 'Let's have one of the bride getting out of the car. No, you don't have to get back in, just let your friend drape the skirt . . . That's right.' Click. 'And now one with your father.'

'I am not her father,' said Peter. 'I'm her brother-in-law!'

'Well, whoever it is, stand by the bride. Good. Now all of the attendants together. Big smile everyone! Say sex! Good!'

'In my day it was cheese,' said Sally's mother. 'We only thought about sex.'

'If he asks Aunt Sophie to say it she'll hit him with her parasol,' said Liz.

A harassed young man in a cassock appeared. 'Are we here, then? We've got four weddings today.'

'And a funeral tomorrow, I dare say,' whispered Sally's mother.

'Yes, yes,' said Lucy. 'All present and correct. Time to go everyone.'

May took her place beside Harriet and the bridal party filtered into the porch, trying not to step on each other's dresses. The organist ceased his improvizations and Purcell's trumpet tune sounded loud and positive from the front of the church.

The scent of flowers mingled with furniture polish and the inimitable odour of ancient churches wafted towards the party as they moved from the porch into the church itself. Lucy's done a brilliant job, thought Harriet, seeing the beauty and quantity of the arrangements, which filled the church with their fragrance. She glanced at May and noticed to her alarm that she had gone deathly pale.

'Are you all right, May?' Harriet breathed to her friend as they slow marched together.

May moved her suddenly dry lips. She'd just seen what she thought for a moment was a ghost. But as the man in morning dress, who had turned at the change of music, was still looking at her, smiling faintly, she realized it was worse than that. For a moment she thought she might actually faint.

'As long as I'm not sick. Just don't let me be sick.'

'Try and smile just a little bit.'

'I can't.'

'Yes you can. Look, Gus is going to step on Sally's dress. Any moment her skirt will come away leaving her in her french knickers and basque.'

With a huge effort of will, May relaxed her facial muscles enough to reassure Harriet she wasn't standing next to a corpse, and the party ground to a halt. But although she looked relatively normal, May watched the ceremony as if through the wrong end of a telescope. She just about remembered to move and stand and do all the right things, and though she opened and closed her mouth, no sound emerged during the hymns. The service was both as long as a lifetime and over in the blink of an eye. May's entire past seemed to have passed before her several times when suddenly, Widor's 'Toccata' was filling the church with its golden sound.

'Smile, you're being photographed.' Harriet was beside her.

May bared her teeth. 'Did you know Sally had invited Hugh?'

'Um – yes. I forgot to tell you. Is it a big deal?' Harriet wondered how she managed to sound so casual, when she knew in her heart exactly how big a deal it was.

'Of course not. I just didn't know Sally knew him, that's all.'

Harriet's conscience came up and bit her. Hugh had kept in touch with Harriet while he was in the States, and knowing they were missing each other, she had asked Sally to invite him. She was about to begin a farrago of lies by way of explanation, when she was saved by the photographer.

'Er – could we have the bridesmaids looking this way, please?' said the photographer. 'We've quite a lot to get through before you can get to the shampoo. And smile? Please?'

'At least he managed not to mention sex,' said Harriet as, half an hour later, they climbed into the bridal car. 'Though his innuendos were fairly disgusting. My feet are killing me. Isn't Sally being marvellous? She's so nice to people, making everyone feel they're her favourite guest.'

May woke up. 'Oh – yes – marvellous.'

The reception was being held at the farm. In order to have room for the Appalachian clog dancing and the barn dance afterwards, a vast marquee had been put up in the garden. It was so big it extended beyond the flower beds, making the herbaceous border seem like a huge, exotic floral arrangement.

Aunt Sophie, whose patronage was not an unmixed blessing, had insisted on there being a formal line-up, including the grown-up bridesmaids. When May realized she would have to shake hands with Hugh, she started to shake all over again.

Just pretend you're wearing your normal clothes, she told herself. Then you'll be fine. He's just a person. Receiving another anxious glance from Harriet, May thought she'd have a stab at some small talk.

'Where is James taking Sally for her honeymoon?'

'Somewhere hot. He says he's fed up making love with a duvet round his neck.'

'But it's summer!'

'It's the Cotswolds,' Harriet said matter-of-factly. 'It may be hot now, but in two days it could be snowing. Here come the first guests.'

'Oh golly, What do I do?'

'Don't worry. No one will know who you are. Just kiss everyone on the cheek, unless they hold out their hands.'

May remembered her last attempt to kiss Hugh and resolved to hold out her hand first.

Hugh was among the last cluster of guests. He pushed aside her hand and kissed May on both cheeks. But he hardly smiled, and didn't speak. It seemed to May that he was warmer, more passionate, with Harriet.

It's your own fault, she told herself. You rejected his postcards and so rejected him. There was a time when he wanted you, but you sent out the wrong messages. It's sad, but it's too late now.

'We can go now,' said Harriet. 'Come on. I want to see what Matthew's up to.'

Already the noise level was high. Branches of the family who only saw each other on such occasions screeched and exclaimed at each other. My-how-you've-growns and kisses whizzed through the air like party-poppers, landing willy-nilly on whoever was handy. Long conversations about distant relatives were had by people who eventually discovered they were talking about different owners of the same name. Potted histories abounded, ending with a sting as the winning interlocutor got in the words, 'So what are you doing *now*?'

May hovered about at the edge of a group, half wanting Hugh to come and find her, and half hoping to avoid him. She felt so unlike herself; the dress, the setting, and the sheer unexpectedness of his being there, shook the foundations of her personality. She yearned for her dungarees and her building site, to be somewhere where she knew who she was, what she was doing, and why the hell she was doing it.

'Here, have one of these, dear. You look a bit peaky.' A kindly waitress who looked like a benevolent dinner lady was holding a plate of canapés. 'You'll need to keep your strength up for the dancing.'

Dancing! May had forgotten there was more torture in store for her. She had no sense of time, wobbly ankles, and in times of stress couldn't tell her left from her right. She could manage a conga only if very drunk.

'Actually,' she said, 'I think I need a drink.'

The waitress nodded. 'Bill! Over here! There's folk dying of thirst.'

Sally was right about the clog dancing. In spite of herself,

May found herself smiling and tapping her feet, swept along by the exuberant skill of the dancers.

But when the troupe had refused to perform any more and the band had replaced their lost fluid with several gallons of cider, the barn dance began. May found herself instantly surrounded.

It seemed that the entire male section of the Steel Toe caps, who had performed their Appalachian clog dancing so magnificently, were under the impression that May, like Sally, was an actress.

She tried hard to put them right. A sharp, 'Do I look like an actress?' would usually have sufficed, but dressed as the female lead in *Snow White and the Seven Dwarfs* it was less effective.

An arm the thickness of a young oak and the colour of mahogany lifted her off her feet and transported her to a place in a set of dancers.

'Do you know what to do?' bellowed the young giant who owned the arm.

'No!' she replied.

'I'll show you!'

'Be gentle with me!' she implored. But the man, who was probably a blacksmith judging by his mightiness, didn't hear.

For the next twenty minutes, May found herself swung from arm to arm as if she were the bundle in a game of pass-the-parcel. Although she clawed her dress into place between every do-se-do and figure-of-eight, she still felt most of the men were intent on unwrapping her. But at least, she thought, her feet scrabbling for the floor, Hugh would never find her in this rugby scrum – if indeed he wanted to find her.

When she had been kissed by all the men in her set and she thought her arms would never again fit back in their sockets, the dance came to an end. May saw her chance and grabbed it. Before she could be swept to the bar, she had undone the ties between two sheets of the marquee and let herself out into the fresh air.

The smell of honeysuckle wafted towards her from the hedge across the lane. It was such a pure, floral smell after the odour of sweat and Old Spice, going back would be like putting on dirty underwear after a shower. The quietness welcomed her like a freshly turned pillow greets a tired head. Far above the noise of the wedding, a lark was singing.

Across the lane was a field and beyond it, through the gaps in the hedge, she could see a wood. No one will notice if I slip away, she told herself firmly. I'll just hop over that stile and go and sit in the wood for a while. She hitched up her skirts and clambered over.

She realized her mistake before she'd gone half a dozen paces. The field was low-lying, and after a wet spring was practically a bog. Stubbornly, knowing she should cut her losses and go back to the throng, she leapt on to a tussock, balancing on it precariously while choosing the next. But eventually, she was forced to admit defeat. The tussocks were some way apart, and between them was clear water. She would have to pick up her skirts and paddle to the hedge. She was just steeling herself to do this when she heard someone clearing their throat.

She turned round carefully.

'In trouble again, May?'

She wasn't really surprised. Hugh was always around when she was in trouble, but she was cross. Why didn't he appear when she was looking beautiful and in control?

'I'm fine,' she called, hoping he couldn't see the extent of her predicament from the hedge. 'I'm just getting some fresh air.'

'Hang on. I'll join you.'

Short of taking off her shoes and running in stockinged feet into the mire, she had little choice but to hang on. He was with her in moments, his sturdy black shoes far better suited to pastoral idylls than her satin slippers.

'You seem to be having difficulty,' he said.

'Not at all. I'm just admiring the view.'

'Well you've had a good ten minutes to admire it, and from here, it's not all that spectacular.'

She had spent five months yearning for the sound of his voice, the sight of his handwriting, in fact, any indication that they shared the same planet. Seeing him at the church had nearly made her faint – only the thought of how desperately embarrassing and dreadful it would be for everyone had kept her standing. And now the five months were as if they had never been: they were quarrelling again.

'I like it.' So much had happened – so much achieved, yet still she sounded like a petulant child.

Hugh smiled, and his smile turned her heart over.

'Come on. I think we should go back.' As easily as he threw a rope or caught one, he swept her up in his arms and set off for the lane.

May longed to let her head rest on his chest, longed to hear the thump of his heart beneath his shirt. But she held herself stiffly, away from the temptation of his body, convinced that her weight would pull them both down into the cow-pats at any moment. He felt her slipping, and hoisted her up, so she was higher and closer to him. She felt less likely to fall, but no safer.

'You can put me down now,' she said, when they reached the edge of the field and he showed no sign of doing so.

'I don't think so,' he said, and negotiated the stile, still holding her tight. 'Now I've got you, I'm not inclined to let you go.'

'My shoe's coming off. Oh, there it goes.'

But Hugh didn't stop. 'They were ruined anyway.'

'I might have wanted them as a souvenir.'

'You've got another one.'

May wanted to sound sophisticated, in control, to say something which would make him stop treating her like a piece of baggage and give her the respect she deserved. Until the right words came to her, she would keep her mouth shut. But for May silence, like dignity, was hard to maintain. 'You'll have a heart attack if don't put me down.'

She heard his laugh rumble through his chest. 'Nonsense, there's nothing of you. You must have been working too hard.'

'Yes.' Working hard, and not eating. 'I've paid off all my debts.'

Hugh stopped and looked down at her. In his eyes was an expression extraordinarily like pride. 'I know. Rupert told me.'

They were approaching the farm gate now. The marquee

still throbbed with noise, but that and the heat had sent groups of people out into the garden. 'You must put me down now, someone will see.'

He took no notice. He obviously knew where he was going, because he shouldered open the door of a barn. Once inside, he shifted her so she was over his shoulder. Before she could protest, he had climbed a ladder and let go of her.

'What on earth . . .?' As May slithered down Hugh's body and back to her feet she looked around her.

They were in a hay loft. Sun filtered through an arched window on the gable wall, catching the motes of dust stirred up by their arrival. The light was golden, reflecting off the bales of hay.

A picnic had been laid out on a white cloth on top of a blanket. A selection of canapés covered a couple of plates, looking fresh and appetizing. An unopened bottle of champagne waited in a cooler.

'Hugh, what is this?'

'I've kidnapped you.'

'So I see, but why?'

'Because I didn't think we'd get a chance to talk in that crush.'

'But why do you want to talk? You've managed without it for the past five months.'

'Yes, but not very well. I've missed you, May.'

'Then why didn't you come and see me? Or phone?'

May thought of the moment of expectation every time she had answered the phone, or seen a distant figure, the quick, almost unconscious hope which had flickered and become a tiny prick of disappointment. She suddenly felt very angry.

'I only got back from the States the day before yesterday,' he said quietly. 'You didn't want me to write.'

The anger turned on itself and fuelled her resentment of him. 'So what makes you think I wanted to be kidnapped?'

'I didn't think you wanted it. I hoped to pacify you with the promise of food and champagne. I only want to talk.'

She put her hands on her hips and regarded him. Months of loneliness, frustration and longing telescoped into a blind

340

rage. If she'd had proper shoes on she'd have gone for his shins. Only Hugh would set up a scene like this and want to use it for talking in.

'Talk then. But you'd better have something really interesting to say.' She took a step towards him and pushed at his chest with her hand. 'I'm not staying here for a lecture.' She pushed at him again, liking the feel of his shirt front against her palm.

He caught her wrist and stepped back, an expression of acute pain suddenly crossing his features as he fell back on to a pile of hay.

'What? What's the matter?' May rushed to him, all antagonism forgotten.

'I've stepped on something. I think it's a pitchfork.'

'Let me look. You just lie quietly. Which foot?'

'The right.' He propped himself up on his elbows.

'Have you got a hanky? We'll need a bandage.'

Hugh patted his pockets feebly, while May removed both his shoes, and then his socks. 'I can't find it,' he said.

'Oh, never mind.' May pulled the antique silk net from around her neck and spread it on her knee, prepared to bind it round whichever of Hugh's feet was bleeding. Which, at first glance, was neither.

She gave a tentative prod to the sole of one foot. He winced sharply and pulled it away.

'You must let me look, Hugh,' she said, kind but firm. 'I won't hurt you more than I can help.'

He groaned softly.

The other foot seemed just as sensitive, but just as undamaged. 'I can't see anything wrong. Perhaps you twisted your ankle.' Her fingers probed the bones of his ankle and he groaned again. 'Oh, Hugh, I don't know what's wrong. I'm going to get help.'

'No!' Hugh's arm came out and grabbed her, pulling her towards him. 'I don't need help.'

'Yes you do!' May stuck to her guns, which, lying practically on top of Hugh, took some doing. 'You've been groaning, it must hurt somewhere.'

'It does, but it's not my bloody foot!' First his mouth, and then the rest of his body, gave her some indication as to the source of his pain. May began to ache in sympathy.

The bride and groom were about to leave when Lucy came rushing up looking worried.

'Where's May? She ought to be here.'

'It's all right, Luce,' said James. 'We don't need her.'

'Maybe, but Clodagh's just brought this!' This was a very muddy satin slipper. 'It's May's. It's got her name in it.'

'Oh,' said James. 'Well, I should think she's borrowed some boots and gone for a walk or something.'

Lucy seemed satisfied by this explanation, but Sally was still worried. 'It's all right,' he whispered to her. 'She's in the small barn with Hugh.'

'What? Why?' she whispered back.

'Well,' he breathed, 'he asked me to suggest somewhere they could be alone. They've got a picnic, some sleeping-bags and a duvet. I hope it does the trick.'

Sally conveyed this to Harriet, who was also anxious.

'That's all right then. I just hope May's not so nervous she bites his head off.'

Sally grinned. 'I think Hugh can look after himself. Now, what about you, Harry? Are you going to be all right?'

'Oh, I'll be fine.'

And if a tear did slide down her cheek as she waved at the decorated farm cart pulled by a shire horse which was due to carry James and Sally as far as the next farm, it could easily have been put down to sentimentality. She watched for some time.

'Oh there you are, Mum,' said Matthew airily. 'I've been looking for you.'

'Oh? Why? Oh!'

Coming up behind him, very tanned and rumpled in a cream linen suit, his hair bleached to straw, his eyes as blue as the Mediterranean, was Leo. 'I came to check on my investment.'

Harriet put her head on one side, considering him. 'About time too.'

★

'Oh May, I love you so much,' whispered Hugh.

'Do you?' she breathed, looking into his eyes, her own dreamy. 'I thought I drove you mad.'

'You do. Mad with love and lust.' He kissed her more intently than ever, giving the matter the attention he usually reserved for complicated legal documents.

'Did you really hurt your foot?' May asked when they paused for breath.

'No.'

'Hugh!' May summoned a spurious disapproval. 'And you a lawyer.'

'You're a bad influence on me. If you didn't flaunt your body so shamelessly at me . . . taking away the one thing that made you decent . . .'

'It was a bandage! For your hurt foot! You were groaning!'

'After five months your cleavage is enough to make any red-blooded male groan. It's entirely your fault.'

May flung herself on top of him and purloined his mouth for her own use before he could blame her for anything else.

Eventually, he pushed her away. 'This is ridiculous. We're not doing any talking.'

May raised herself on her elbow, her bosom now completely exposed, her cheeks flushed. 'We only quarrel when we do.'

Hugh half smiled, but there was a serious edge to it. A moment ago they'd been glued together. Now suddenly there was distance. 'I don't want an affair, May.'

Panic flickered through her. 'What do you want?'

He hesitated a moment and brushed his hair out of his eyes. Then, very tenderly, he did the same for May, tucking the lock behind her ear. 'I want for ever.'

'You mean – marriage?'

He nodded.

May swallowed, shook her head. She was teetering on the brink of an emotional avalanche. There was still time to step back. But did she want to?

'I'm sorry,' he said. 'I'm rushing you. I've been thinking about this for months. It must come as a shock to you.'

He lowered his gaze so he was no longer looking at her.

343

She studied his head, the thick, dark hair flecked with grey, saw the half-moon of his eyelashes, his crooked, noble nose. 'I have a very nice flat in St John's Wood. You might like it,' he added.

'Oh.'

'Or we could live on *The Rose*. Whichever, whatever, you like.'

'You'd do that for me?'

'I'd live in an igloo if you were there. And we could have a trial run, take it slowly.'

The steady reassurance in his voice soothed her. 'But we fight all the time. I doubt if we could stay in agreement long enough to choose a date or decide where to live.'

He nodded in agreement. 'I know. But I'd rather fight with you than live in harmony with anyone else. Besides,' he hesitated, 'there are areas in which we get on quite well.'

'Sex isn't everything . . .'

'No, but it's a good start.'

And, there being no time like the present, they started straight away.